RUN OUT THE RAJ

Also by Dennis Castle

THE FOURTH GAMBLER
SENSATION SMITH OF DRURY LANE

Dennis Castle

RUN OUT THE RAJ

CONSTABLE · LONDON

Published in Great Britain 1986
by Constable and Company Ltd
10 Orange Street London WC2H 7EG
Copyright © 1975 Dennis Castle
First published 1975 by Bailey Bros. & Swinfen Ltd
ISBN 0 09 467040 4
Printed in Great Britain by
St Edmundsbury Press
Bury St Edmunds, Suffolk

For

SIR HARRY SECOMBE C.B.E.

on behalf of all troops
and troupers who have
known his kindness.

Salaam, tamasha sahib.

ACKNOWLEDGEMENTS

I am most grateful to authors Graham McInnes (*The Road to Gundagai*, Hamish Hamilton) and Sashti Brata (*My God Died Young*, Hutchinson) from whom I gleaned some additional local colour. I also thank Coles of Melbourne from whose long-forgotten *The Funniest Song Book In The World* I adapted 'The Tram Song'. I deeply appreciated the late Roy Plomley selecting an extract from this book enjoining it with Pickwick Papers and James Thurber as his three favourite books in his broadcast on BBC Radio 4 in December 1984.

I am also indebted to the MCC for permission to quote 'The Laws of Cricket' via their then secretary, S.C. (Billy) Griffith, (Sussex and England), who, at the age of 5, began his schooldays in the next desk to mine. He is still ever willing to help me with my homework.

In her autobiography *With Scarlet Majors* (Hammond, Hammond) and written under her pen-name Deborah Morris, Suzanne Wainwright included a 'Major Fortt'. I ask her forgiveness for kidnapping him for a brief but authentic role in my story, but I did after all know his identity and was flattered that she should remember him in her Indian memories.

My thanks also to my brother, Bruce; Gerald Durrell, F.I.A.L., M.I.Biol; Victor Goldman, F.F.A.R.C.S.; James Williams; Alec Harrison; Richard Tomkins; Tim Jollands; David Frith; Tim d'Arch Smith; Pat Garrow; Garard Green; John W. R. Barrow; and lastly but always top of my list my wife, Marie.

D.C.

I have written the tale of our life
For a sheltered people's mirth,
In jesting guise—but ye are wise,
And ye know what the jest is worth.

KIPLING.

Chapter One

THE TOPHAR CRUSADERS

COLONEL EDDGERLEY-WATKYN-REED, Indian Army and captain of the Tophar Crusaders Cricket Club, frowned round at his committee.

"Those atom bombs the Americans dropped on Japan last week," he said, "have completely upset our fixture list."

"Hear, hear, Mr. Chairman!"

"That's why I've called this meetin' . . . however, first things first . . ." He banged his gavel hollowly on the old refectory table. "I now call on our honorary secretary to read the Minutes of the last meetin' . . ."

As Major Baker-Stewart commenced his clipped, precise phrasing, the colonel savoured the historic occasion—the first meeting of the club since the war against Japan had ended. He had founded the Tophar Crusaders in 1939 directly he had been posted to that Punjab hill-station in charge of the Veterinary Directorate. Wherever he had been stationed in his long uneventful military career he had raised, and captained, Crusaders. But for the war he would have retired to Kenya—and formed the Nairobi Crusaders.

But Tophar was the unexpected fulfilment of a glorious pipe dream—for Colonel Eddgerley-Watkyn-Reed had been born there. He had no youthful memory of it, however, as his cavalry major father and side-saddle mother had been posted away when he was a mere year old. To rectify this oversight he was, at one time, apt to transpose his parents' reminiscences into his own. But this ploy was halted abruptly by military 'Intelligence' who eagerly investigated as to whether or not he had falsified his age

9

on enlistment. When war had broken out in 1939, cavalry was
doomed to mechanisation and the idea of 'old Eddgers' con-
trolling tanks was both repellent to him and a nightmare to his
regiment. So GHQ, Delhi, had tactfully 'kicked him upstairs' to
full colonel out of active service harm's way.

Geographically his birthplace was perched precariously on a
hillside in the shadow of the Himalayas, some 7,500 feet above
a far distant sea level. Long before East India Company's trading
days a tent and hovel village had sprung up around a gaunt
Portuguese monastery but, after two centuries of peaceful meditation through constant bribing of neighbouring Sikh warlords,
the monks had suddenly fled. Whether it was at the first sight of
the British red-coated infantry or the fixed lorgnettes of the
ladies of Leamington and Cheltenham who accompanied the
officers, history does not record.

The British took over Tophar around 1840 and now the
Crusaders Committee sat in the old refectory room of the
monastery, for that sacred edifice had become the Queen's Club
and the adjoining chapel the Grand Theatre. To offset charges
of sacrilege the British had built several pseudo-Gothic churches
whose pointed spires rose like stalagmites against the white of the
Himalayas. While young Victoria was beginning her reign in
London, her exiled subjects employed bewildered Tophar
villagers to construct grey stone bungalows, eventually to be
named 'Balmoral', 'Osborne' and 'Windsor' with poles for
strange sun-up and sun-down flag rituals. Tophar's wavering
goat track, unnamed since time began, was suddenly straightened
to become 'The Mall', lined with glass-fronted shops bearing
very British 'trade' names.

Tophar was given 'town' status, eventually to become one of
those exclusive hill-stations where civil and military departments
came only for the summer. This nomadic trek up the narrow
mountain roads every spring and down again in autumn was
devised by the British to avoid working in the excessive heat of
Delhi and Lahore between April and September. The Indians
themselves thoroughly approved. Every trip brought them lakhs
of rupees each way, giving extra employment for coolies, bullock

carts and, later, when the Queen was a widow, the narrow-gauge railway with high-funnelled engines already obsolete in Britain.

Semi-hill-stations, some mere 3,000 feet up, like Poona, could cater climatically for the British all the year round but this static existence bred social boredom. So, for really hot summer centres on the plains, the alternative hill-station broke the monotony . . . until Hitler's war. Then the authorities decreed that, wherever British civil or military departments had last set down their filing cabinets, families and cricket bags, there they stayed, come sunstroke or frostbite, for the duration. So for six unbroken years Tophar had housed an established population—and, to the cricket-obsessed colonel, his posting there had been the crowning point of his life.

"That ends the Minutes of the 55th Meeting," intoned Major Baker-Stewart. "I beg to move their acceptance, sir."

Baker-Stewart was also the colonel's second-in-command in the Veterinary Directorate. He liked young Stewy of course—a good, if erratic, fast bowler, aggressive with the bat. However, the colonel had turned a blind eye to Baker-Stewart's *affaire* with Hazel Short, Senior-Commander in the Women's Auxiliary Corps, as she was also the Crusaders' scorer. Her husband had been safe as a Singapore prisoner-of-war—until now. The colonel made a mental note to warn Stewy, off the record of course, that his time with Hazel was running out.

Baker-Stewart passed the leather-bound book to the colonel. The other five bush-shirted committee members murmured 'aye' in approval.

"Well read, Stewy!" said Wing-Commander ffoliot, stout, cheery and breathless, who always batted with his bat-handle jabbed in his navel. The colonel was deeply fond of Folly.

Baker-Stewart stroked his pencil-thin moustache as he smiled in acknowledgement. His voice had resounded many times in the adjoining Grand Theatre for he was the most popular leading man in the TATS—Tophar Amateur Theatrical Society.

"Yes," agreed Lieutenant-Colonel Nupp-Jevons, honorary treasurer, "excellent timbre, Stewy."

The colonel smiled. Dear old Nuppy, stoopin' a bit now, although six foot two. Must be pushin' fifty-six. Useful 'tweak' bowler an' rocklike bat . . . but he'd be retirin' soon.

"I will sign as a true record, gentlemen." Colonel Eddgerley-Watkyn-Reed unscrewed a thick fountain pen. "Date, please?"

"August 16th, 1945, Eddgers . . ."

The lightning sketch which was his signature ended with a spluttered full stop. Major Innes-Whiffen, tall as a bean pole, reached over and blotted the page. The colonel also thought Whiffy an ideal fellah. Lacked initiative perhaps, for an officer in his middle-thirties employed in 'Intelligence' but he was, nevertheless, a Singapore Straggler wicket-keeper. Beside him was Major Barkside-Twist . . . well, Twisty was 'cavalry', always reliable chaps, and, as a member of the M.C.C., knew the game thoroughly . . . a staunch Crusader indeed.

Soon, thought the colonel, with the war over, Tophar cricket as he knew it would be no more. Perhaps it was for the best. He, himself, was sixteen stone now, hair and moustache grey—he was even finding it difficult to put on his thick woollen cricket socks let alone keep his six feet one erect. All these Crusaders too, they would be going their respective ways. What splendid fellahs they were—with three exceptions of course. Squadron-Leader Heaviside had sent a note of apology for absence through duty. The colonel was not sorry. He did not like Heaviside, he was a blusterer—and a woman-worrier, too, in spite of having played for the Hertfordshire Gentlemen.

Then the colonel's eyes became troubled as he studied the two youngest committee members, both emergency-commissioned wallahs. Strictly speaking, Flight-Lieutenant Hacker held insufficient rank for Crusader committee representation, but the rules had been bent in his case as he had played for the Hampshire Hogs. He was also the only R.A.F. officer in Tophar with 'wings', but active service was not, in itself, a Crusader qualification.

Captain Basil Mott, B.A., curly-haired, pink, round-faced schoolmaster in his early twenties, came from Weybridge and worried the colonel a great deal. Oh, he did play for the Altruists in England—a good side—but public school though he was, he professed a certain pro-Indian socialism—not a top-drawer attitude in Crusader eyes. He talked too much. Son of a parson, he also had a D.S.O. brother but only in the Navy . . . however, the war had turned over quite a few stones.

The colonel's two minutes' silence was up.

"Before dealin' with the rest of the agenda," he began gruffly, "a welcome back to Major Innes-Whiffen from his well-earned leave."

A ripple of applause caused Whiffy to blush and stare down at his long brown shoes.

"Get any cricket in Naini Tal?" asked Baker-Stewart.

" 'Fraid not, Stewy. Just fishin' and boatin' . . ."

"Well, Whiffy," said the colonel, "when you left Tophar the war was still goin' on. But you've returned to see peace break out. Which brings me to the next item on the agenda . . . 'The future of Tophar Crusaders cricket club now hostilities have ended . . .' "

"So sudden, wasn't it?" said ffoliot. "I mean, we knew the Japs were on the run. Rangoon fell last May . . . but those American atom bombs . . . what's different about 'em from the natural ones?"

"Fiddly business, splittin' atoms," said Nupp-Jevons.

"Made a shockin' mess, apparently," said Innes-Whiffen.

"But it'll get us home quicker," said Hacker. "We'd have been here another eighteen months if they hadn't used 'em . . ."

"Ah, but there *is* an ethical side to consider," said Mott.

"Ethical my arse," said Hacker. "Did they consider ethics when Coventry and London were blitzed . . .?"

"That wasn't the Japs," said Innes-Whiffen, "that was the Nazis, not India Command's pigeon at all. Pity it had to be the Yanks who invented that bomb—and dropped it. I mean, you R.A.F. fellars seem to have missed the bus . . ."

Wing-Commander ffoliot clenched his small fists.

"After Pearl Harbour, Whiffy," he said stiffly, "the Yanks were entitled to drop it . . ."

"We're not here to discuss the ethics of the Americans," said the colonel, "they don't play cricket, more's the pity. But with the war culminatin' so suddenly like this, we're up a gum tree. I'd reckoned on another full season at least while Burma and Malaya were mopped up. Now, if everythin' shifts to Japan, Tophar will be tactically off the map."

"Damned tricky wickets in Japan," said Nupp-Jevons.

"I don't know if I should mention this, Eddgers," said ffoliot, fidgeting his fat hands from his shorts to his plump knees, "but we had a top-secret memo this morning . . ."

"A bit late to worry about careless talk now," laughed Mott. There was a stony silence.

"Clot," murmured Hacker, his only ally.

"No priorities have been lifted yet," snapped the colonel. "However, you can rely on our discretion, Folly, even if some officers lack discipline. I'm not mentionin' any names, Mott. Proceed, Folly."

"Well, I've had orders from Air H.Q. to vacate Tophar, close the offices and move down to Delhi at once . . ."

"Oh, no!" Hacker buried his head in his hands. Just when he had succeeded in getting under that brunette's mosquito net at Gulliver's Hotel he was to be posted away—as her husband had been a fortnight ago.

"I realise it is inconvenient, Hacker," said ffoliot testily, "but Joubert wants us down in Delhi—and that's an order!"

"Well, Folly," said Barkside-Twist, "you can really consider yourselves lucky . . . I mean, you R.A.F. have been up here since 1939, a detachment of twenty-odd men on this Himalayan hill-top without an airstrip, let alone a plane . . ."

Folly looked exceedingly hurt.

"Our job is to deal with airmen's postings," he pouted. "Now let me tell you this—an airstrip *was* considered in Tophar. I found a file on it when I took over in '40. And there was only one place it could have been cut."

There were gasps of horror.

"You mean," spluttered the colonel, "our cricket ground—Glenbourn?"

"Where else in this mountainous district?" said ffoliot. "No other level ground for hundreds of miles."

"Gad," expostulated the colonel, "your predecessor, Wing-Commander Lewton-Snape, actually played for us, ate our salt. Was that quislin' actually connivin' to concrete our ground?"

"He was—but I scotched it," said ffoliot smugly.

"You dear chap!" The colonel was delighted. "By the way, whatever happened to Lewton-Snape?"

"Bowler-hatted for inefficiency," said ffoliot. "Sent a load of valuable equipment to Colombia—should have gone to Colombo."

"Mark you," said Hacker, visualising the effect on his women below if he had been able to circle Tophar in a Bristol, "an airstrip would have saved the War Office thousands of rupees. Every day dozens of us have to make the three-day journey down to Delhi and back for conferences. Think of the rail fares and time an airfield would have saved . . ."

"Twirp," whispered Mott.

"All this talk of airfields is most disturbin', Hacker," said the colonel, easing his sam browne. "Glenbourn is part of Britain, what we fought for . . . ever since the old Queen was a young bride . . . it began as a racecourse . . . a British one . . ."

"Hacker," said Wing-Commander ffoliot, "you've upset Eddgers. Apologise!"

"I have? Oh, sorry, sir."

"Thank you," said the colonel, watching Baker-Stewart minute the apology. "Well, as we are to lose the R.A.F., someone propose a vote of thanks for the great job they've done for the Crusaders."

"I will," said Mott.

"I'd rather," said the colonel stiffly, "it was someone else."

So Nupp-Jevons proposed and Innes-Whiffen seconded. Amid applause this moving moment in the club's history was also minuted.

ffoliot rose to his feet, easing his tight shorts.

"Mr. Chairman, gentlemen, the Royal Air Force will look back on its days with the Tophar Crusaders with affection. I

know I can speak for all my men, including Squadron-Leader
Heaviside whom I detailed this morning to handle our move to
Delhi. In spite of the war we were able to play our part, even
though the R.A.F. have only ever been allowed a representation
of three on this committee . . ."

"It must be borne in mind, Folly," said the colonel patiently,
"that the Army started cricket in Tophar. Kitchener an' Roberts
watched it at Glenbourn long before your flyin' corps was
formed. No hard feelin's, eh, Folly?"

"Of course not, Eddgers! May I, through the chair of course,
interrupt the meeting for drinks on the R.A.F.?"

Amid applause and laughter he drew himself up and bellowed,
"BOY!"

As the rest of the committee were recovering from this entirely
unexpected shout, Akkar Singh, senior bearer at the Queen's
Club, opened the door.

"Bara pegs, eck dum, Akkar Singh," ordered the wing-
commander, "the sub-cheese to go on the R.A.F. chitty."

"Large whiskies for everyone, sahib? All on account.
Atchcha."

The Sikh bearer backed out, his bloodshot eyes narrowed in
his bearded, high-boned face. The ancient monastic door hung
loosely on 18th-century iron hinges. And, as always, when any
committee sat, Akkar Singh removed a small cork, its head
rounded smooth and tarred to match the remaining iron bolts
of the upper hinge band, and applied his ear to the hole. Worn
smooth by generations of Indian ears which, from within, would
only appear as a knot in the oak, this listening post revealed the
scandals of British club members reported for drunkenness,
bouncing cheques or adultery. For nearly a hundred years the
British had firmly believed Indians to be psychic. What the
bazaar knew to-day, GHQ would know to-morrow. Bearers
would tell their officer-masters of their postings and promotions
long before the top-secret notification arrived from Delhi for
decoding.

While an embarrassment, this constant leakage of information
was also regarded with some inverted pride by the exiled British.

India was a land of mystery and magic wavelengths and they
adored writing 'home' about it. But, in reality, the key to this
riddle could be found in wide-meshed shutters, ill-fitting windows
and porous doors—plus the incredible carrying power of the
British whisper. Add, too, a bona fide reliance upon service wives
not repeating, over tea, their husbands' hush-hush postings to
more superior stations and the extraordinary British belief that
an Indian clerk could type out top-secret orders without understanding them, and all India's mystique and uncanny djinnism
could be accounted for.

Akkar Singh had already known for three days that the
R.A.F. were leaving Tophar for his cousin was a clerk in Air
H.Q., Delhi. Now all R.A.F. servants in Tophar had been
warned to make ready with tears, blackmail and theft for the
departure of their masters. They would never see them again,
so officers who foolishly left their packing to their bearers while
they drank themselves insensible at the Queen's Club farewell
party or crept through the shrubbery for a final fling in a lady's
bed would, on opening their baggage in Delhi two days later,
find very few personal belongings left. Many a Harrods shirt
would end its days flapping round the skinny knees of an
'untouchable' latrine sweeper, cricket boots would become a new
fashion among Tophar goatherds and an Adastrian blazer would
lose its glory on the shoulders of a money-lender, huddled by his
hookah outside his bazaar go-down.

Once the committee door was closed, Akkar Singh passed the
drink order to little Wahdi, the club's ragged boy of all work
who, among his many other duties, exercised British dogs while
their owners took tea. While officially employed by the club,
Wahdi worked almost exclusively for Akkar Singh. In return
for his loyalty to the Sikh he received his protection. Wahdi,
despite his squalid, orphan life, was alert and ambitious—and
Akkar Singh could trust him. Such dedication in poverty was
rare in India.

As Akkar Singh took the cork from the hinge again, he heard
the colonel saying: "First the R.A.F. leavin', an' now, I hear,
the Burma Civil Service is recalled to Rangoon. They provided a

good side, all seven of 'em. St. Hayward's School has broken
up for the summer hols, too. I'd like to have beaten those boys
just once. However, bein' only children, those matches don't
count in our official records."

The school had provided four fixtures a year for the Crusaders,
two at Glenbourn and two on their own hard bare hockey pitch
where the short boundary only counted two runs. The boys were
highly skilled at beating the Crusaders, exploiting every rut of
their confined ground while, at Glenbourn, the headmaster
always ensured his pupils' victory by dispensing a very potent
lunch-time sherry to the Crusaders. In war-time such a luxury
was irresistible, however much it impaired the vision.

"Our worry is, gentlemen," said Baker-Stewart, "to find
opponents with this end-of-war exodus from Tophar. There's
the Pageant and the Victory Arts Festival coming off next
month. That involves most of the town. I'm rehearsing *Cavalcade*
of course, but I shall fit in my cricket—if there's any going."

"Good show, Stewy," said the colonel. "I'm in the Festival
Pageant too, but I won't let that interfere either—if we get someone to play against. We ought to have one Victory Celebration
match . . ."

"The Music Society have a full festival programme," Baker-
Stewart went on. "Haydn String Quartet, Bach's Mass, morris
dancing, so there's no chance of the music wallahs giving us a
game. The Propaganda Office has disbanded, the British Radio
Unit is moving out of the old tower back to Calcutta, Army
Signals are off to Singapore. The Y.M.C.A. and the Leave
Camp are empty as, the war being over, all leave has been
cancelled. There's just no one left . . ."

"We could," said Mott, "play Indian sides."

There was a silence—a very long silence.

"*What* did you say?" Nupp-Jevons asked slowly.

"Indian sides." Mott looked from one graven face to another.
"I mean, some of them are pretty good . . ."

"Indian sides?" The colonel gazed round the table, spreading
his hands in despair. "D'you hear the boy? *Indian* sides!"

"Twit," said Hacker under his hand.

"How many more times, Mott," sighed the colonel, shaking his head, "have I to tell you Tophar is a British town? We created it."

"What about St. Hayward's School?" said Mott. "They were mostly Indian boys . . . and they beat us at Glenbourn every time."

"That was different," said Barkside-Twist, "a sprinkling of Indians, here and there among the British, is good for morale. But those kids' games are not in our official records so you're out of order in quoting them, Mott."

"But if we don't play Indian sides," persisted Mott, "we've got no one left *to* play."

"It's no skin off my nose now," said Hacker, "but Mott's right, sir. At least you'll get a game with an Indian side . . ."

"It must be this new Labour Government at home," groaned the colonel. "They've been in power about a month now an' every young officer out here is tryin' to tell us how to handle India . . ."

"Attlee's atterboys," sneered Baker-Stewart.

"Apt, very apt," murmured Nupp-Jevons.

"Mott and I have been out here at least three years," said Hacker indignantly.

"I, Hacker," said the colonial imperiously, "was born here—right here in Tophar—during a Liberal Government, too. Ever since then I've remained completely Liberal . . ."

"True, Hacker," whispered Mott, "I've seen him bowl . . ."

"But playin' Indian sides is right out," the colonel continued firmly. "Clubs of the standard of Bombay or Delhi Gymkhana, where there is plenty o' British backbone in the team, yes, but they can never make the long journey up here for a day's cricket. We did invite the Royal Navy from Delhi but we heard, jus' in time, that they included women . . ."

"Camp followers?" asked Hacker.

"No, WRENS! Gels who actually played for 'em . . ."

"Jack-tar memsahibs," said Nupp-Jevons helpfully.

"So we turned 'em down. Some of those women were not even of commissioned rank. No, we're a pukka British club—

an' we will not play low-grade Indian sides. That's me final word on the subject."

Wahdi tugged Akkar Singh's sleeve, placed the tray of drinks on the floor and scuttled away up the stone staircase. Akkar Singh's ear was still at the hinge but his lower lip trembled with rage. He knew the real motive behind the colonel's adamant decision. He would not play local Indian teams because he did not want them casting possessive eyes at Glenbourn. Yet if ever a place belonged to the Indian it was that old racecourse. Akkar Singh steadied himself, straightened his turban, replaced the cork in the hinge and knocked to bow himself in with the tray.

"Shabash," said the colonel, "what should we do without you? Akkar Singh," he told his committee for the hundredth time, "was with me old regiment, yer know. Thikai?"

"Thikai, sahib." Akkar Singh made the namaste sign, pressing his palms together, withdrew and once more filled the hole with his ear.

The wing-commander had risen.

"Gentlemen of the R.A.F. be upstanding . . ." Hacker's chair scraped back as he stood in solitary surprise. "We give you the toast of the Tophar Crusaders . . ."

"Folly!" cried the colonel urgently. "Hold on a minute, please. We must not forget where we are."

He stood, glass aloft.

"The King-Emperor!"

The wing-commander lowered his head, purple shame suffusing his red-veined cheeks.

"Of course, damn it . . . the King-Emperor!"

With hoarse 'God bless hims' they drank at attention. Then the Army resumed their chairs, hiding their elation. Trust old Eddgers to put the R.A.F. in its place. Had a lot too much to say for themselves in this war.

"My apologies, Eddgers," stammered ffoliot. "Now, on behalf . . ."

"Ah, one more toast yet, Folly." The colonel lifted his glass again. "Must remember protocol. Gentlemen! Our president, Judge Trevelhayes!"

They drank to the judge very solemnly.

"Is he quite recovered from his jeep accident?" asked Barkside-Twist.

"Made a fortune in damages," said Baker-Stewart. "His tricycle's as good as new again. The Yanks settled out of court . . ."

"What happened?" asked Innes-Whiffen. "I was on leave . . ."

"An American jeep," explained Mott, "powered by a technical sergeant tanked up on Indian whisky nudged the judge on his trike at high speed. The poor old chap was left careering madly downhill out of control. With the option of death in a rice field some miles below or smashing through a church gate, the trike sought sanctuary. It came to rest against the steps of the Catholic church where Father O'Malley welcomed the judge as a convert. I gather the judge is writing a complete disclaimer to the Pope . . ."

"I say! Really?" Innes-Whiffen was wide-eyed.

"Mott," thundered the colonel, "don't exaggerate."

"Anyway," said Mott, "he's extracted a dollop of damages from the United States Army."

"Bully for the judge," said Hacker.

"Dollop? Bully?" sighed the colonel. "Really, what are His Majesty's war-time officers comin' to? It must be the effect of that disastrous election back home. Churchill gets us through a war an' then the 'dollop' an' 'bully' types vote his party out."

"Ah, but, sir," said Mott earnestly, "we want a Labour Government now. I'm sorry about Churchill but we need a change."

"We do NOT!" bellowed the colonel to cries of 'hear, hear', "I'll have no socialist propaganda at Crusader meetin's, Mott."

"I second that," said Nupp-Jevons.

"At least," smiled Baker-Stewart, "the judge put that sort of outlook in its proper place when he won the day against the Americans."

"A pity they had to send them to Tophar at all," said Barkside-Twist. "They don't fit in with our traditions. Australians would have been better. Had someone to play against then."

"Ah, that reminds me," said the colonel, fumbling in his breast pocket to drag out a crumpled letter.

"Eh, I'd like to propose the toast, Eddgers," interposed ffoliot.

"Not yet, please, Folly," said the colonel. "There is one more item, under 'Any Other Business'. This letter from Judge Trevelhayes proposes a new member for the Crusaders. A Major J. Grahame of the Royal Army Medical Corps, now stationed at the hospital. He tended the judge after the tricycle disaster an' apparently his surgical skill pleased our president. He feels . . ." he consulted the letter again, "that Major Grahame is the 'right type' for us."

"Who did he play for back home?" asked Innes-Whiffen. "A lot depends on that, sir."

"Grahame is not—er—from home," said the colonel, "he's an Australian . . . from Melbourne . . ."

"But that's marvellous," said Mott, "an Australian cricketer —just what we want . . ."

"We have not interviewed him yet, Mott," warned Baker-Stewart. "There are Australians—and Australians."

"Well, this one *is* a doctor," said Barkside-Twist. "We've never enrolled a medical man before. Could add tone . . ."

"Never heard of an Aussie adding tone," said Hacker.

"There is another pertinent reason why he should be a Crusader," said the colonel. "When Phyllisjoy—that's me daughter, she's married to a Gurkha—they have white officers, Hacker, so stop smirkin'—Crutchley-Haybart, Etonian, a major now—when she—er—gave birth to me grandson, Jocelyn, in Calcutta ten months ago, this Major Grahame attended her. He was in the British Military Hospital there an' actually brought me grandson into the world—pity it had to be an Australian, but there it is—P.J., that's our pet name for Phyllisjoy, wrote about this Doctor Grahame, said he was—er—wizard. An' Julia, me memsahib, she agrees with P.J. that Grahame should be a Crusader now he's been posted to Tophar."

"If your mem says Grahame's fit to be a Crusader," said Nupp-Jevons, "then, by God, Eddgers, there's no question of blackball. Damn good judge of a Crusader, your mem . . ."

"She certainly made the right choice of a husband," smiled ffoliot.

"Oh, I say, really, Folly!" the colonel chuckled benignly. "Well, I reckon me own judgement in weddin' Julia was pretty sound, too."

Amid the deep laughter were murmurs of 'hear, hear'.

"She's India's original sacred cow," muttered Mott to Hacker.

"I know," hissed Hacker, "with udders like a pair of braces . . ."

"What are you two whispering about?" enquired Barkside-Twist.

"Hacker mentioned that W. G. Grace was another doctor," said Mott.

"By jove, *so* he was," said Innes-Whiffen. "To have one in the Crusaders would put us on a par with the M.C.C."

"But this one," said Baker-Stewart cautiously, "is *Australian*."

"You think he might be a fugitive from a chain gang in Botany Bay?" asked Mott.

"Or an aborigine witch doctor with a wallaby loin-cloth?" added Hacker.

"Don't be such idiots," fumed ffoliot, "no such person would have been allowed near our chairman's daughter in Calcutta . . . the fellar is obviously a white man . . . after all, he's a major and, damn it, comes from the State of Victoria. He must be pukka!"

Chapter Two

THE AUSTRALIAN

BEYOND the door Akkar Singh had turned swiftly at the sound of two voices, one hoarse and gruff, the other a tuneless treble, raised in a familiar song. In his mess orderly days the Sikh had heard British officers sing it fervently at church parades and drum-head services, a battle hymn which urged Christian Soldiers Onward. But now the words were different.

> *Onward, tram con-du-uctor . . . when you take a fare,*
> *Punch it in the presence . . . of the passenjare.*
> *Punchin' is the tram rule . . . For tickets anywhere,*
> *So punch them in the pre-he-se-hence . . . Of the passenjare.*
> *Onward goes the tramway line . . . You mustn't smoke down-*
>   *stairs;*
> *If you spit, it's a quid fine . . . Punch the passenjares!*

Akkhar Singh had jammed the cork back in the door in horror. Warned by the colonel to expect a Major Grahame at noon, his precise mind admired the punctuality the striking clock of St. John's church distantly confirmed. But he was affronted by the sight of a lean, craggy officer who now strode up to him, hatless, his hair cropped to a corn-coloured bristle. And, grinning beside him, was little Wahdi.

"Quiet!" Akkar Singh raised long arms aloft in admonition. "The committee is in session . . . how dare you, boy!"

"Me show major sahib the way," explained Wahdi, nervously aware of Akkar Singh's intense displeasure. "He teach me Australian war-song."

"Yes, only a bit o' fun, Pop." The long-faced Australian's eyes were alert, searching, and his wide mouth seemed set in a permanent, quizzical smile. "I had time ter kill upstairs so I taught Sabu me tram song . . . not his fault . . ."

"He is not Sabu, he is Wahdi, the dog boy . . . away to the bar, chokra!"

Wahdi, his face creased with anxiety, scuttled away, his bare feet silent on the stone floor.

"There are Queen's Club rules," said Akkar Singh. "Servants are not allowed . . ."

"Look, Pop. I have to see the Crewsaders' Committee . . . in here?"

And before Akkar Singh could bar the door, the Australian had knocked with a hard, corrugated knuckle, shouting, "Bring out yer dead!"

"Wait, please!" rasped Akkar Singh, scandalised. "I must announce you formally in strict Crusader tradition . . ."

Seething with fury he slid into the room and closed the door.

Major Jack Grahame sighed. Fancy callin' a kid 'dog-boy'. As a doctor continually faced with natural laws, he loathed man-made rules. Born and reared near the rail tracks of Melbourne, he did not like India. There was no good Australian beer about nor sheilas comparable to those he'd picked up as a student back home. While Tophar was a vast improvement on the fetid, beggar-filled streets of Calcutta, he felt India's poverty had no defiance, no resistance . . . to him the land of the sacred cow was a fair cow.

Grahame was no stranger to poverty, having lived in its shadow for the first twenty years of his life. Even at Melbourne University where, in the red-brick block, the future medics kept themselves much apart from the egg-head academics in other fields, he could be no big spender. His Irish mother and Scottish father had lived hand-to-mouth since they first landed in Australia early in 1914. With rosy immigrant dreams, the Scot had found work on Victorian Railways . . . then young Jack, signalled to arrive in 1915, further drained already low funds. So he had grown up, frayed and darned, fusing his father's

native shrewdness with his colleen mother's laughing gusto for
happy living on knotted shoe strings. After his father had
returned unscathed from Gallipoli, for evermore a true Anzac,
the Grahames sent Jack to school on saved pennies. The boy
had spent them well. And, on that final day when, in borrowed
cap and gown, he had become 'M.B., B.S.(Mel.)', they wept, his
mother almost as proud as when her husband had been pro-
moted to become guard on Melbourne's ace express 'The Spirit
of Progress'.

As a hospital junior officer Jack had always preferred dealing
with Melbourne's seamier side rather than the 'society' who
were always talking about 'the old country' and an ultimate
mecca called Kensington. He was happiest among the rowdies
of Fitzroy, stitching up dockers after the bars closed or treating
the prostitutes from Little Lonsdale Street who laughed smokily
on empty stomachs. Hell, he wouldn't mind bein' in 'The Lon'
right now!

Or in those sleezy, paint-peeling terraces off Praed Street, near
London's St. Mary's Hospital, where he had landed up in
August 1939 on his first trip to England. Lured postally by an
enthusiastic Aussie pal, he had arrived to reconnoitre medical
prospects in that 'old country' he'd heard so much about. And
what happened? A bloody war breaks out! Caught up in the
beery jingoism of his new-found mates, he had enlisted in the
Royal Army Medical Corps, signing away his skill to the 'old
country'. So he had seen Dunkirk aflame, sailing into the beach
with the lilliputian armada on a freighter mercifully unhit so
that he could work unceasingly on shattered men to land them,
patched, at Dover. All had seemed worthwhile then . . .
although now, he thought wryly, if he had been in Melbourne
at the outbreak of war he'd have joined the Australian Army
Medical Corps, been sent to North Africa and, after Pearl
Harbour had threatened Australia's own shores with Jap attack,
been recalled home. The flamin' irony of it . . . now he was
stuck in India and had to await British Army demobilisation.
Who'd be a patriot . . .?

He sang another snatch of his tram conductor song, a relic

of his student days. Oh, to 'do' a beer again at Young & Jackson's on the corner of Flinders and Swanston Streets—and stare once more at the nude painting in the bar.

Akkar Singh re-opened the door, still visibly disturbed. He had been hard pressed to explain to the colonel that the proposed new member and not himself had knocked, demanding corpses. Of course this Australian would never become a Crusader. Akkar Singh knew British officers only sang when drunk . . . so he threw every sinister implication he could muster into his announcement: "Major Grahame—from the *hospital*!"

The Australian loped into the room and stood, not at attention as befitted the colonel's rank, but relaxed, loose-limbed, his eyes roving round the committee as if scrutinising an identity parade. As Akkar Singh went out and closed the door, he heard the colonel quaver: "Major—er—Grahame", as his eyes checked the crowns on the shoulders in disbelief.

"Yes, that's me, colonel." To the horror of the senior Crusaders present, the newcomer appeared to be looking for a chair. There was not, of course, one available. Rule 18 stated categorically that Crusader candidates must remain standing before the committee table.

"Ah, first," said the colonel, "our club chief bearer has—er—lodged a complaint . . . his name is Akkar Singh, not—er—'Pop' . . ."

"Although," chuckled Mott, "he does look a bit of a weasel . . ."

"Silence, Mott," snorted the colonel.

Grahame looked at Mott in amused silence. The local court jester, he assessed. Melbourne was full of Motts, too . . .

"Judge Trevelhayes has proposed you as a Crusader, Grahame," said the colonel. "Now, what have you to say about that, eh?"

"I dunno." Graham scratched his head. "He didn't tell me much about it, jus' said he was puttin' me up. I mean, what is a Crewsader?"

There was a loud whistle of indrawn breath.

"The Tophar Crusaders," rumbled the colonel, "is a cricket club."

"Come off it," laughed Grahame. "I hate cricket . . ."

The Crusaders looked at each other in limp amazement.

"It's too bloody slow." Graham gazed amiably from one gaping mouth to another.

Mott broke the Crusader silence.

"But you're an *Australian* . . ."

"Look, sport, I don't call me beddin' roll 'Matilda', nor do I kill me meat with a boomerang . . ."

"But," stuttered the colonel, "you've been proposed by our president . . ."

"I didn't ask him to . . . I thought the Crewsaders was some sorta boozin' club . . ."

"Boozing club!" ffoliot half-choked, and Hacker and Mott sucked in their cheeks to avoid exploding with hysteria.

"Look," said Grahame resignedly, "I'm no sportsman, never had time or dough for it. Oh, I've played cricket—even seen it at Lords, but to me it was as dull as seein' *Lohengrin* hopin' to learn German . . ."

"Not German, please," said Nupp-Jevons, shaking his head. "Taboo lingo in Tophar."

"But you've been 'home'," said Barkside-Twist, "London, I mean . . ."

"Well, 'home' is Melbourne, but, like a true exile, I've seen England . . ."

"How did you find the old country?" asked Innes-Whiffen.

"Got off a boat—an' there it was . . . an old country."

"Look, do you act or play an instrument?" snapped Baker-Stewart.

"No, I don't."

"Then," asked a perplexed Innes-Whiffen, "what on earth will you find to do in Tophar?"

"I'm a flamin' doctor! I've got hospital work to do, scabies, dysentry, V.D. . . ."

"Not here in Tophar," gasped Nupp-Jevons.

"We must not forget me daughter," said the colonel.

"Has she got . . .?" Grahame hesitated, and Mott broke in rapidly :

"You delivered our chairman's grandson into the world, sir, in Calcutta—a Mrs. Crutchley-Haybart . . ."

A light dawned in Grahame's eyes.

"Ah, little P. J. Haycart . . . the Gurkha major's wife. Yes, I remember her . . . well, well, so she's yer daughter, is she, colonel? Small world . . ." He raised his eyebrows to Mott, acknowledging his timely intervention. It had been a close call . . .

"I gather me daughter had a rough time," said the colonel.

"She did," agreed Grahame, "but she had plenty o' guts."

The committee winced and Innes-Whiffen turned pale.

"Takes after her father," amended ffoliot quickly, and the colonel grasped his shoulder in unspoken appreciation.

"Well, yes, I'm—er—proud she could take her—er—gruel," he said, "and, be God, that grandson o' mine is goin' to be a cricketer—a left-arm spinner . . ."

"I'll second the proposal of Major Grahame," said Mott.

"You can't," said the colonel, "you hold insufficient rank . . ."

"But aren't we rather rushing things?" said Baker-Stewart.

"Major Grahame is not actually a cricketer," Barkside-Twist demurred.

The colonel frowned. For the first time in history his committee seemed to be questioning his wisdom—*and* that of his wife and daughter.

"Oh, I'll swing a bat for you if yer short," said Grahame. "I played a bit at 'the shop', too . . ."

" 'The shop'?" queried the colonel anxiously. "We have a 'no admittance rule' in the Crusaders, yer know, to anyone in—er—'trade' . . ."

"No, 'the shop' is Melbourne University . . ."

"Oh, capital!" cried the colonel relieved. "A varsity qualification to boot. Right then, that clinches it . . . gentlemen, please show approval."

Normally a new candidate should have retired before the

vote was taken but the colonel was so irritated that the committee doubted his word that he was purposely railroading them.
After all, it was *his* club. The stern-faced committee raised their
arms and Major J. Grahame, R.A.M.C., was duly enrolled as
a Tophar Crusader.

"Good on ya, sport," said Hacker.

"Fair dinkum, digger," said Mott.

"Stand up when you talk to a major," growled Grahame.

The captain and flight-lieutenant sprang to their feet and the
senior committee men guffawed at their embarrassment.

"Quite right, major," said the colonel, enormously pleased.

"Well, see you kids in Rotten Row, eh?" said Grahame,
winking at Hacker and Mott.

Outside the door Akkar Singh shook his head in bewilderment. This Australian was not a true British sahib, he was no
thorough-bred snob . . . yet they had accepted him. How could
first a judge, then the colonel's wife and daughter in childbirth
vouch for such a ruffian?

Within, Grahame thanked the committee for the honour.

"Can I go now, sir?" he went on. "An American jeep has
gone off the road halfway down the mountainside—an' their
own medical officer was in it—so I've gotta try an' piece
together his remains."

"Oh, not *another* jeep accident," snorted Baker-Stewart.
"How many more times must we tell those Yanks that, other
than the Viceroy's and Governor's cars, no motor vehicles are
allowed on Tophar roads? That was laid down in 1909, sub-
section C . . ."

"Was it, now?" said Grahame. "Well, I gotta get to the scene
o' the disaster. If anyone's alive, see, these Yanks qualify for a
wound stripe or somethin'—anyway I have to write 'em an
official report."

"Of course," said the colonel. "Er, dis-*miss*, Major Grahame."

The Australian nodded affably, started to salute, then remembered he was hatless, so strolled out scratching his ear.

"Queer chap," said ffoliot, "really the Army does find
'em . . ."

"He's *Australian*," insisted Nupp-Jevons, "a rum lot ever since Armstrong, Spofforth and Melba . . ."

"A rough diamond indeed." The colonel smiled nervously.

"Perhaps not our usual material," said Barkside-Twist thoughtfully. "Would have preferred to have discussed him in camera rather than accept him to his face. However, it will be useful to have a doctor on the field of play."

"He's got 'M.B., B.S.(Mel.)' after his name," said the colonel, consulting the judge's letter. "Must stand for somethin'."

"He'll probably make splints out of his billabong," said Mott.

"Stop bein' facetious," said Nupp-Jevons sharply. "At least, he put you in yer place. Yes, Eddgers, I'm sure you've done the right thing."

"Oh, yes!"

Baker-Stewart and Innes-Whiffen concurred a little too readily for the colonel's liking. He still sensed a marked degree of reserve round the committee table.

"There's one thing I didn't tell Grahame," he said, now determined to win over his committee fully with a further recommendation. "The judge wishes him to play Captain Cook in the Tophar Pageant. Now there's real prestige for an Australian, if yer like! However I didn't want to give him all the good news at once . . ."

"I bet he'll love that," said Hacker. "Due to our posting, I'll have to give up the part of Bonnie Prince Charlie . . ."

"They'll never find a better Pretender than you," said Mott.

"Quiet, you two," ordered the colonel. "Now, Folly . . . the toast . . ."

"I give you," croaked the wing-commander, rising, his eyes glazed with pride, "the Tophar Crusaders—coupled with the name of our skipper, dear Eddgers—and Julia . . ."

Glasses clinked and, behind the door, Akkar Singh's eyes glinted as he pondered. The Australian doctor was not drunk or 'puggled', after all—indeed, he was sanity itself. He had actually been mutinous in his behaviour—yet the Crusader committee had been unable to stop him joining. The man hated cricket, yet the colonel had likened him to a diamond. Why, had he not

smiled at Akkar Singh on his way past just now, apologised for
calling him 'Pop' and saying that the committee were 'as nutty
as fruit cakes'? This could only mean, in some Australian
comestible sense, that he thought them to be deceivers. They
must, thought Akkar Singh excitedly, be *afraid* of him. There
could only be one reason—*blackmail*!

What, thought Akkar Singh, was that Australian war song of
Major Grahame's again? . . . *'Punch in the presence of the
passenger'* . . .? Of course, that would be great Anzac strategy.
The British were the passengers both in India and Australia,
riding rough-shod without proper tickets. If you punched them
in their presence they would have to compromise to save their
faces . . . so, treat them with contempt, break their rules . . . and
they will be powerless to stop you.

It has, Akkar Singh decided exultantly, taken an Australian
to show India the way to revolution . . .

Chapter Three

MR. SHRINIVASSEN

THE Head Clerk of Sanitation & Drainage Department stood on his bungalow veranda and shivered in the cool morning air. At thirty, Mr. Shrinivassen was beginning to feel old. His face a finely-carved bronze, his H.Q. pass gave him a height of five feet four inches. The under-average size of most Indian clerks in comparison with the British was a handicap in Tophar winters when snowdrifts sometimes reached above first-floor windows. Shrinivassen despised brother clerks who used lack of stature in deep snow as an excuse for absenteeism, especially when they sent their explanatory notes by their even smaller sons. But Shrinivassen was, of course, a cricketer.

A lapsed Catholic of convert parents, he patiently accepted British rule in India but he felt extremely thwarted over Glenbourn cricket. Many times he had re-lived his last innings, 53 for Madras Harbour against St. Thomas's Mount back in 1939. Now, once again, a summer without cricket for him was nearly passed. And he did not relish another Tophar winter.

Headquarters was designed on airy, capacious lines for light breeze intake only as befitted a summer hill-station. The long-dead Victorian Scottish architect had not envisaged a world war causing the British to winter in Tophar. So, from November onward, H.Q. became a whistling honeycomb of icy draughts. Frost snapped telephone wires and the clerks crept around neolithically in poshteen coats, wool from their ragged mittens clogging their typewriters. Coal had to be imported from Tibet, brought in on the backs of steaming yaks as if already ignited. No fireplaces having been constructed, improvised braziers were installed which occasionally burned through into the offices below. The Indian fire brigade hauled their little hand-engine marked 'V.R.' round the hills in their bare feet, grateful for the warmth of every new blazing building. Fire-watching in winter was just as important in Tophar, which never saw a bomb, as it was in England and Germany at the height of the blitz.

But in summer, every Sunday, Shrinivassen watched the British cricket at Glenbourn. Only once had there been a Saturday match when St. John's Church received special dispensation so that the vicar could be available to bowl. The eagerness with which the Crusaders arranged this concession should have warned St. John's . . . too late they found their vicar bountiful and the Crusaders cut him asunder for a multitude.

Shrinivassen knew the British had difficulties in raising sides in Tophar . . . the church team was a pathetic example. He had seen the timid Music Club fielding with their feet to avoid bruising artistic fingers, watched Grand Theatre actors with their long-drawn, resonant appeals and learning their lines in the outfield. When all else failed, the Burma Civil Service turned out always four short, but augmenting only with white men. Once Shrinivassen had politely offered his services, but to be rejected . . . and Burma had played a man short.

Shrinivassen's pride had been hurt. Glenbourn, he felt, was logically a part of India and he and his fellows had, at least, a birth qualification to play there. But he would have taken no action had not Akkar Singh called at his bungalow that morning. Sitting on his veranda steps, the Sikh told him that the Tophar Crusaders had, at their last meeting, refused to play Indians.

"The colonel said you were 'low grade'," he hissed.

"That is invidious insult," said Shrinivassen quietly as a pioneer's dream swept over him. "You are good fellow, Akkar Singh. Your information has not half fallen in the right quarter. 'Tis time we clerks made our presence felt on the field at Glenbourn."

"Soon we shall drive the British to the sea," said Akkar Singh softly. "Not Gandhi's way with pacifistic methods—but with guns . . ."

"No, no bloodshed will be spilled. I am Christian . . ."

Akkar Singh smiled. He had no intention of mentioning Major Grahame's influence on his scheme. The idea must seem to be his own, yet, like all good generals, he wanted others to implement it. He prodded the clerk's chest with his bony forefinger.

"I have the ears of the British," he said. "The old colonel drinks from my hand. I long for the day when there will be no British to call 'Boy!' to me—an ex-soldier of thirty years' service! Now, through their righteous cricket, we have a chance to ferment feeling. You will challenge them to play?"

"I will call a meeting of my colleagues and sound them out. If I get support, yes, then we will invite the Tophar Crusaders to a cricket match."

"They will refuse of course. But that is what we need . . . once they reject us, then we can press for possession of Glenbourn."

"Perhaps they may agree to play," said Shrinivassen loyally.

"Then play them. But if you lose, the Mall will run with your blood. You must humble them into the dust."

"Akkar Singh, if the British accept, 'tis but a cricket match. We can only do our best in a fading light . . ."

"But you *must* win." Akkar Singh scratched an armpit. "A cricket defeat for the British in Tophar is only the beginning. Independence is near. In London, Winston Churchman has been overthrown. Now Atterlee is the primary minister—they say he is on India's side."

"But he will not be playing in cricket match," reminded Shrinivassen, looking at his watch. "Thank you, Akkar Singh, for so vital information. The British have said that they will not play Indians, only in camera, so to speak. We can only prove their selfishness by issuing a challenge forthwith to force them to reply in the open. I will call a meeting this morning."

Akkar Singh remained squatting on the step impassively. Shrinivassen sighed. From a press-stud purse he passed the Sikh five rupees.

"Salaam." The money was folded into the wide red belt. "One must pay for such top-secret information, bhai."

Akkar Singh strode away up the winding path, his slippers flapping. Shrinivassen crossed himself.

"Bribery and eruption," he muttered as he locked his bungalow and set off for headquarters.

With the Japanese armistice, he saw ominous changes ahead for the clerks. Soon their jobs in headquarters would be gone. Many departments must close now and the dire poverty a war had decreased might return. Some Indian politicians had ranted against helping Britain in the war—till Japan threatened the Assam border—but the clerks had enjoyed a new prosperity since 1939. They were pleased the British had emerged somewhat untidily victorious through American 'atom' bombs—but, had the Japanese marched on Delhi, the Christian Shrinivassen knew most of his colleagues would have welcomed them. They had no choice, for the humble working Indian had but one possible code in life—survival at all costs.

As he toiled up the steep incline he pondered on the current bazaar rumours of Independence and the British leaving India. The name 'Pakistan' had arisen. Was this the second title for two Indias, one Hindu, one Moslem? Mr. Jinnah of the Muslim League demanded it—and yet he wore a monacle like the British upper-crust. Shrinivassen found it all so confusing. Would Hindus and Moslems one day settle their differences at cricket like a sort of School House versus New House as the British seem to have been suggesting for over ninety years?

Shrinivassen found no activity in Sanitation & Drainage that morning. The new peace had seemingly unstopped blocked gullies and perfumed choked sewers. Shrinivassen's chief, Colonel Hall-Gomshall, had sent a message that he was rehearsing the Haydn String Quartet, his second-in-command, Major Brunton-Thwaite, had cholera and the pugilistic Sergeant O'Donnell had dysentry.

But before receiving these messages officially by phone, Shrinivassen already knew he would be alone in the department. A peon from Heddles Bank Ltd. had reported, via bazaar tele-

graph, that the manager's office was arranged with music stands
for the Haydn rehearsal, a United Services Club bearer had
whispered the condition of Major Brunton-Thwaite who, in the
snooker room the previous night, had been sick in baulk.
Sergeant O'Donnell's fight with a Signals sergeant in Gulliver's
Hotel had been reported by a sweeper. The Irishman had fallen
back on the row of chamber pots which constituted the urinal
and one had splintered into him. The effect of dysentry was
roughly the same . . . and the sweeper was pleased he had one
less utensil to empty.

The rest of HQ seemed dead too. The decision to hold a
Tophar Arts Festival had seized every senior officer with a
vitality quite unknown in war-time. Shrinivassen, therefore,
could convene a meeting of clerks, safe in the knowledge none
of them would be missed. This was one day when the less-
dedicated clerks would not drive themselves into frenzies of
worry as to how they could avoid their routine tasks.

From its twin forks, Shrinivassen picked the spindly telephone
marked 'Bell, U.S.A.' and spoke urgently to his fellow head-
clerks. To his chagrin, most of them already knew of the
proposed challenge—obviously that five rupee fee for the
information had been collected by Akkar Singh several times
. . . but, at least, there was vociferous enthusiasm for the project.
Shrinivassen received complete co-operation from all departments including 'Posts & Telegraphs', 'Rice Quota Division',
'Office Equipment (Barbed Thorns Section)'—these had been
issued instead of pins and paper clips which had gone into
munitions—'Medical Directorate' which included 'Barbed Thorns
—Blood Poisoning Section', 'Funerals & Burials (Officers:
Interment, Union Jacks & Rifle Salutes)' and its sub-sections,
'Other Ranks (Marked Graves & Next of Kin)' and 'Deceased
Clerks (Pyres & Ghats)'.

Mr. Telik Swarmi of 'Abandoned Families Department'
vibrated the phone like a cash register in his enthusiasm.

"We must play the British swine," he screamed. "It is a god-
send, this god-given moment. It is the start of our fight for
India's freedom. Let us walk on their sacred Glenbourn, let our

names be blazed across history in a hot-cross bun-fire of glory!
We, the under-fed . . ." he paused, gasping, and Shrinivassen
could visualise his eighteen stone quivering with sweat.

"Be calm, Mr. Swarmi. 'Tis only a cricket game I suggest. I
do not seek to antagonise the British, just beat them between
the wickets. Purely personal ambition, Mr. Swarmi . . ."

"Beat the dogs!" came the ranting voice. "We can, by this
match, nail a wedge in the British coffin. And when they are
finally driven back to Sandhurst and have to clean out their
own latrines without Indian servants, they will moan, so
benighted : 'It all began with that cricket match . . . the revolting
clerks of Tophar ran us out of India . . .' "

"Attend the meeting then, Mr Swarmi," said Shrinivassen
patiently. "Twelve hundred hours in our canteen to-day."

"I will be there," cried Swarmi, "in all my person . . ."

Chapter Four

EXTRAORDINARY GENERAL MEETING

INDIAN clerks were rarely prompt for any official duty. At 0900 hours on a working day few actually entered HQ by the main gate. But within half an hour they would be at their desks, having swayed in through windows from the perilously frail fir tree-tops or leave their fingerprints on secret documents after stowing away in coal barrows. The British reluctantly had to dismiss one unpunctual clerk who had made his daily appearance via the sewers.

But, at the stroke of noon on this momentous day, the clerks' canteen was already filled to overflowing. When Shrinivassen made his dignified entrance he was afforded a deafening reception. Clerks banged their tiffin-carrier lids on the stone floor where they crouched eating the meals limited by their various sects.

On a platform at the far end of the canteen, Swarmi had placed a table and three chairs. Shrinivassen's heart sank as he saw one was already occupied by Mr. Mookerjee, the recognised authority on the British way of life among the HQ clerks. A small man, corpulent and bald, his double-breasted olive green silk jacket was fully buttoned across a blue shirt from which sprouted a red bow tie.

The startling career of Calcutta-born Mookerjee included tram depot administration, Indian drama and water-divining. He regarded himself as an expert on English literature, being a voracious reader of any form of journalism from Thackeray to *Tiger Tim's Weekly*. As Shrinivassen and Swarmi also prided themselves on being of 'most well-read vocabulary' which had,

39

after all, brought them their head-clerkships, Mookerjee was no favourite with them.

English was, to all three, a far more exciting language than Shrinivassen's native Tamil, Swarmi's Hindi or Mookerjee's Bengali. These staid, formal tongues had limiting religious roots. English was however 'flowerised with most loquacious idiom' and was taught in schools as 'the mother tongue of India' more in derision than anger by certain reactionary teachers. Mookerjee boasted he could speak English faster than the British themselves and, with this asset, had risen to be head clerk of the Water Catchment Directorate. But his voice was no murmuring brook . . . in fact, he induced a grating, nail-on-slate effect upon uninitiated listeners.

Swarmi, who appeared to have already taken charge, beckoned Shrinivassen to the chair on his right, then addressed the champing clerks.

"Comrades! I am informing you that we are met here at a meeting I have convened . . ."

The clerks rose as one man and cheered.

"Squat down, squat down!" shouted Swarmi. "I will tell you when to give vent to your emotings . . ."

The clerks resumed their attitude of a clutch of wicketkeepers, a curious conglomeration of eastern and western dress, khamsees, jibbas and dhotis revealing twig-like legs in narrow pantaloons while old army shirts and tight American GI trousers were stretched and shined by ricket-knobbled knees.

"Already you have lost control of meetin', Swarmi," sneered Mookerjee, his voice rasping about the hubbub. "I should be chairman. I am most qualified by dint of experience for quellin' unrest an' mob disorder in Calcutta in corn riots."

" 'Tis only a meeting about a cricket match," said Shrinivassen soothingly.

"Comrades," panted Swarmi, steadying his dhotied bulk against the table under which pools of sweat were already forming at his sandalled feet, "allow me to present our good friend and ally, Mr. Shrinivassen from Sanitation & Drainage, who wishes to promote my idea for a cricket match against the British . . ."

"Your idea?" Shrinivassen looked surprised.

Swarmi made the namaste sign to him and smiled through his perspiration.

"This cricket match has been on the tip of my mind for some time . . ."

" 'Tis copycat tactics you employ, Swarmi," snapped Mookerjee. "Always I have thought of this cricket game. But first, I said unto myself, the war must be won by our brave Indian soldiery. Then, an' only then, are we at liberty to challenge the British to their cricket defeat."

"Stuff this nonsense!" bellowed Swarmi. "I did dream of this match on my charpoy nightly over the years of our perilous war-time . . ."

"May I speak, brothers?" Shrinivassen rose quickly.

"Yes, yes, Mr. Shrinivassen, you speak." Mookerjee put an arm round the Madrassi's shoulder. "I will concede, admit an' accept that you have brought my idea to fruitfulness. Take your stomach off the table, Swarmi, an' resume your seatin' capacity. All ears for brother Shrinivassen!"

The munching clerks regurgitated sufficiently to cheer. Swarmi sat down sulkily, thumbing a nostril as a gesture of contempt.

"I feel, brothers," said Shrinivassen in ringing tones, "that we, the clerks of Tophar, should raise a cricket team . . ."

"We, the under-dogged ones," prompted Mookerjee.

". . . to play the British at Glenbourn," cried Shrinivassen. "The only Indians they would play are maharajahs and nawabs. Why should it not be us?"

"No, no!" shouted the clerks.

"Would those princes play against us?" yelled Swarmi.

"Yes, yes!" cried the confused clerks.

"You are all puggled!" rapped Mookerjee, glaring down the canteen. "You are all affirmatin' when complete negetation is required. The princes would not play us. Such is the sad state of nepotisation by nawabs in India. But that is purely localised matter not under consideration at this meetin'."

"Yes, yes!" howled the clerks, now completely fogged.

"It is the British we wish to play," shouted Swarmi.

"Ah-eee!" they shouted, feeling something was still expected of them.

Mr. Shrinivassen drew himself up.

"I personally am very fine cricketer," he said, smiling, "full of runs and most wily bowler. But before we put our names down on roster-list with parenthesised playing ability, we must first ascertain if the British will agree to play us . . ."

Howls of derision spluttered mouthfuls of food into dhoti laps.

"God stave the King!" shouted Uttar Bun.

"But we are told they have refused," snarled Sashi Bokaneer, "that they consider us 'low grade' . . ."

"Ah," said Mookerjee, "that was only within the confines of their own chamber. A challenge from us, the clerks, will bring such perfidiousness into the wide-open spaces of public scrutiny. They must then reply official . . . an' if they still refuse, they must give a reason . . . an' that we can publish in the newspapers."

The clerks clapped ecstatically. Personal fame was now not far away.

"So I propose sending such a challenge to the Tophar Crusaders," said Shrinivassen. "But first, are you all agreed that we raise a cricket team of our very own? Signify your verdict by raising your hands . . ."

Hands were flung high and the three officials were showered with rice.

"Unnonimous!" exclaimed Shrinivassen proudly.

"It is decided then," cried Swarmi, gripping the table with his pudgy hands, tears coursing down his pock-marked face. "Mother India is proud of you to the core of every manjack . . ."

"The British shall not pass," cried Mookerjee, determined not to lose the initiative. "The cricket confrontation is at hand, the game's afoot an' the palm shall go to the victorious clerks!"

They rose, cheering wildly, embracing and shaking hands.

"Like women you scream!" roared a deep authoritative voice.

The room fell suddenly silent. Torkham Wazir was a Pathan,

a hillman from the north-west. In the Khyber when only fifteen
he had killed his first soldier in skirts from Scotland. Some said
he was a 'powenda'—an Afghan gipsy—on the run, wanted for
murder in the Peshawar bazaar. It was certain Torkham Wazir
was not his real name. But, working for the Railway Repair
Department (Military), he had expert knowledge of rock
formations—and kept his pencils in his bandolier.

"What," he snarled, "is our plan to defeat the British?"

Shrinivassen studied the tall Pathan, his red embroidered,
sleeveless coat, baggy grey shalvar trousers, coned fur hat—and
felt fear as he met those kohl-rimmed eyes, saw the sneering thin
lips under the drooping moustache.

"Plan, Torkham Wazir?" Shrinivassen laughed weakly.
"Cricket is but a game, it cannot be prognosticated. There are
rules and who best observes those rules, triumphs . . ."

"Foolish odds," growled Torkham Wazir. "I have seen the
British at their cricket in Kohat and Peshawar. They gallop like
unbroken fillies, all jolly laughter in white, not caring when one
has humbled another and reduced him to the purdah of the
pavilion. What is this cricket to us if there is no disgrace in
defeat, the loser to be shunned by his father, and banished from
his tribe?"

"Cricket is just a game of skill," said Shrinivassen anxiously.

"So is war," said Torkham Wazir. "Are we such slaves of the
British that we must play the game their way? If we defeat
them, do we let them go away smiling and unscathed with no
wounds to lick? No! If we play the British, they must be made
to feel beaten, cowed. There is nothing more positive than a
battle. The victors walk from the field wiping blood from their
swords, the vanquished lie dead and dying."

A deadly pall of terror hung over the canteen now. Like all
his race, Torkham Wazir was an uncomplicated man. The
Scottish nuns who taught him in that Nowshera Mission school
had found him a diligent pupil, repelling only one facet of their
gentle administration—affection. The sturdy orphan possessed
an inheritance which defied even their heavenly guidance. To
Torkham Wazir all men fell into two categories . . . fools if they

believed him, rogues if they outwitted him. These craven clerks angered him now . . . all chatter and no positive strategy. No one was *planning* the campaign against the British.

"You are gossiping like dhobie women banging washing on the rocks," he sneered, "instead of creeping up the river silently to spear the unsuspecting fish."

Narna Bag, gaunt, narrow-chested, rose to his feet, his white cotton shirt trimming the knees of his blue serge trousers.

"You are talkin' mad insanity, Torkham Wazir," he blustered. "This is game, not warlike fray. I am personally not riskin' my eighty rupees a month, plus winter hard-livin' allowance, to garner hatred of the British through mere cricket. The consequentials are too great. I have family to keep an' maintain in conditions as accustomed."

"I 'hear, hear' that," said Mittra. "The British pay our wages . . ."

"They were not paying mine," retorted Torkham Wazir, "when they sent their airplanes to bomb us in the Khyber. That was unfair war."

"Ah," sneered Mookerjee, "those planes were beyond your tip-toed reach. But when you did capture a Britisher what did you barbarotic barbarians do to him?"

"If he lived at all," Torkham Wazir bared long yellow teeth in a twisted smile, "he could no longer breed . . ."

"You cannot disemball the British by our bowling," shouted Swarmi. "You are devil-man, Torkham Wazir. Sew no more the seeds of discord and discontent among your brothers . . ."

"My *brothers*!" The Pathan spat, and two crouching clerks fell back, legs in air, to avoid being defiled and the expense of a Ganges cleansing trip.

"You Pathans are all piss an' wind in the willows," snorted Mookerjee, who had no fear of Torkham Wazir. "You have inherited your back-moded ancestors' cunnin' craft of concoction. You invent grievances an' feudin's, man, just to suit your blood-thirstin' nature."

"To win anything in this earthly life," came the growled reply, "you must hate strong enough to conquer complete. Death is better than disgrace. I live by my code of 'badel' . . . it means 'revenge'!"

"Rewenge is nothin' to do vith cricket," shouted plump Futti Pant with sudden bravado, now Mookerjee had taken a stand. "If Torkham Vazir vants to shed British blood after the game, that's his cup of tea in which I, personally, shall not imbibe. I am wery peaceful John citizen, not varlike varrior."

The clerks, now confident that they were not participating in a British massacre which would affect their pay packets, began to shout their cricket prowess.

"I am farsh bowlah," yelled Bannerjee. "In Shecunderabad shix wickets fell to my whizzhin' trajectoriesh . . ."

"I am vicket-keepah," shouted Futti Pant. "I played in Poonah and let no byes verth speakin' of at all but three vizard catches I caught, mark you, plus one most exceptional stumpin', in the tvinkle of an eye . . ."

"Like greyhound in the slips, I am," screeched Narna Bag. "Hit boundaries too, willy-nilly . . ."

"I am openin' battin' fellow," said Moti Lal, "always I bat as a beginner . . ."

"I, too, am batter to open with," cried Utter Bun exultantly. "Can stop rot and hat-tricks too. Most experienced chap . . ."

"A barnacle door bat am I," shouted Sharrabuddin, "a piece of resistance . . ."

Kazi Mohammed bellowed that he 'bowled surpassin' good', Mustapha Khan had the best average in the Sind Desert, Ahmed Ram, Sashi Bokaneer, Mittra, Ral Mohan, and many others voiced their ability in unison.

"Brothers," cried the confused Shrinivassen, "we will note down all this brilliance as soon as we hear the British will actually play us. That is a fate not yet accomplished."

"I shall umpire," said Mookerjee determinedly. "I am much venerated in Calcutta as umpire with strictly popular decisions. Remember the British will appoint such an official of their own. He will see the game from the Raj standpoint an' give decisions accordin' to his church an' regiment. Already we are sufficient martyrs flaggin' under the yoke of union-jack boot. I shall stand for Mother India!"

Mookerjee sat down to a tremendous ovation. Motti Lal was openly weeping while Futti Pant jumped excitedly on Uttar Bun's last chaupatti.

"I shall be team manager," shouted Swarmi, who had remained sullenly unmoved by Mookerjee's oration. "I shall control tactics and see to gate money."

He was duly booed and he sat down, glaring round the room. His ruthlessness as a head clerk, his tale-bearing against his own people and kow-towing to the British, now told against him.

"Who shall shcore?" asked Bannerjee. "That ish tashk of excheedin' importanch . . ."

"Mr. Desai can put the numbahs on board," said Futti Pant.

"I am not tall enough," cried Desai, a wizened man with thick-pebble glasses. "Allow me, please, to remain most innocent bystander."

"Puttin' up numbers," snapped Mookerjee, "is but the coolie labour of scorin'. 'Tis the documentation on paper with pencil an' rubber that a scorer's appointment carries such inestimable responsibility. We must have our own accountant to see fair play against the cheatin' British scorer."

"Mr. Desai is from 'Field Cashier's Department'," said Shrinivassen. "No man is more qualified."

The little man wriggled in his dhoti, suddenly afraid.

"Oh, I am unworthy, my brothers," he beseeched them. "Admitted I am mathematic expert in my department but a cricket scorebook is tantalisingly ruled so unaccountably."

"Do not hide your light under a bustle, Desai," rasped Mookerjee. " 'Tis a simple thing we ask of you. You have to see we receive our rightful runship. I shall be umpirin', remember, an' will keep you informed of correct proceedin's. I appoint Desai as scorer . . ."

"I am manager," boomed Swarmi. "*I* appoint Desai . . . you, Mookerjee, are merely menial umpire. You only dip your oar in on pitch of play . . ."

"I am on selection committee, am I not?" Mookerjee's beady eyes sought the approval of the clerks. There was an enthusiastic response.

" 'Tis voted then," he said. "Shrinivassen to be captain an' I also to be official ordinated umpire, by appointment."

"Now," said Shrinivassen proudly, "I will send challenge to the captain of the Tophar Crusaders, Colonel Eddgerley-Watkyn-Reed."

"These stupid English names," chuckled Mr. Dikshit.

"But before I can issue and augment the letter, as captain I must have, for our team, an official name."

"Ah, that is most out-righteously important," agreed Mookerjee. "How shall we designate ourselves?"

"As I am manager, it should be 'Telik Swarmi's All-India Eleven' . . ."

A storm of boos greeted this suggestion and the fat clerk tensed under Mookerjee's withering gaze.

"Treated with the contamination it deserved," he said. "But Swarmi has made one good point, however accidental an' flukey. 'All-India' must be included in the name. Are we not sons of that sore-oppressed land?"

"Yes, yes," agreed the clerks.

"We could be Bengal Tigersh," ventured Bannerjee.

"We are not in Bengal," said Narna Bag, "of that I am convinced."

"Why not 'All-India Clerks Eleven'?" asked Uttar Bun.

Mookerjee stared at him in disbelief.

"Do you solemnly squat there, Uttar Bun, an' suggest we call ourselves a mere babu team of under-privileged clerks? Are you out of your rocker? This game is vital to India—we must have a title befittin' our glory . . ."

"Why not the 'Mahatma's Eleven'?" said Moti Lal.

"Because it would not be true," said Torkham Wazir dangerously. "We cannot play cricket against the British without violence."

"I shall keep vicket in my Ghandi cap," said Futti Pant loyally.

"We must keep the game politically free of politics," implored Shrinivassen.

"But, brother Shrinivassen," said Mookerjee, rising, "we must not blind ourselves with bluff. The British will see in our challenge some political motive. They always do. 'Ah', they will say when they receive our impeccable challenge, 'these clerk johnnies are after somethin', don't yer know. Gad, there's more in this than meets the ego.'" Mookerjee took pride in his impersonation of a British officer and his audience screamed with delight. "But, takin' jokes apart, brothers, they will suspect our motives. An' because they will not believe we want just a friendly game of cricket, we shall have to adjust our strategems to match their vile plots."

"True, too true," said Dikshit. "Our hands are too tied to play fair."

"Soon," cried Mookerjee, "the day will dawn an' break when we shall drive the British from India back to their land of crumpets an' maypole dancin'. Soon they will unnerstand that 'Quit India' which is chalked on walls means *them*, the old administration which has ruled our destination since East India Company Limited days, not these new soldiers who have only come here for war-fightin'. They want to go home anyway an' say so, very rudely, with V finger sign which is shockin' abuse of our friendly hospitality. This cricket match is of great signification for India's future horizon."

"You are all talk and no conversation, Mookerjee!" Swarmi was scathing. "Do you solemn-like suggest we call ourselves 'Quit-India Team'?"

"Of course not!" shouted Mookerjee. "As umpire I have authority invested in me from Lord's of London. I am of the considered verdict that our team should be nominated 'All-India Victory Eleven'."

"If we lose the game," came the cultured voice of Jalim Singh, of 'Posts & Telegraphs', "the word 'victory' will appear idiotic in newspapers . . ."

"We shall not lose," grunted Torkham Wazir contemptuously. "Only a Sikh like you, Jalim Singh, would think of defeat."

"India has never won a Test Match against England yet," came the reply.

Torkham Wazir hated Sikhs. Had they not hanged his ancestors from the white minaret of the Mahabat Johan Mosque, strangling as they looked over the best view of Peshawar? "We cannot lose this game," he said, "if we pick a team of men who can really hate."

"But we cannot call ourselves 'British-Haters Eleven'," cried Mittra. " 'Tis too obvious. They would smell a rat among the pigeons."

"How about 'Civil Disobedience All-India Eleven?" suggested Dikshit.

"Is insanity run amuk in your head?" cried Mookerjee. "Such a title would not, perforce, allow us to obey the rules of cricket."

"But *why* obey rules?" asked Torkham Wazir. "It is by not playing as the British expect that we shall take them by surprise —ambush them from behind . . ."

"If there is any behind-ambushin'," said Futti Pant, "I shall not keep vicket. My skilled handiverk needs rules . . ."

"As umpire," said Mookerjee, "I shall interpretate only existin' rules as per my Bombay cricket handbook . . ."

"Why do we not call ourselves just 'All-India Eleven'?" asked Bokaneer.

"Because that contains implication that we are Test players," said Shrinivassen wearily. "If we are publicated as 'All-India' we should get a ticking-off rocket from the Maharj Jumas of Vizianagram who is captain of India."

"But we *are* wery good cricketahs," insisted Futti Pant. "Our name must inform the verld of our strength."

" 'An All-India Civilian Eleven' then," said Jalim Singh pointedly. "It is, after all, true. We are civilians of All-India . . . Hindus, Moslems . . ."

"And Christians," cried a delighted Shrinivassen. "Yes, Jalim Singh is right as so befits a man like him, educated at Punjab University. We shall play as 'All-India Civilian Eleven'."

"Agreed, agreed!"

"I shall write to Delhi too," said Shrinivassen, "to Major Fortt who is in charge of Army Welfare for whom I did once work. He will supply us with cricket bats and pads and gloves. We must not expect to borrow the Crusaders' gear."

"They would not lend it," said Mookerjee. "No, we must be independent of their contaminated equipment. Write to Major Fortt as you suggest, Mr. Shrinivassen, an' let us stock-pile our materials of war."

"Agreed, agreed!"

"Brothers!" cried Shrinivassen, his eyes burning brightly, "the mission is accomplished. I shall now take action, write to Colonel Eddgerley-Watkin-Reed—and throw down gauntlet!"

Cheer upon cheer rent the air. Mookerjee sat, head down, in deep meditation and Swarmi collapsed over the table, heaving great sobs. Only Torkham Wazir remained unmoved. He was cleaning his nails with a long, triangular-bladed dagger . . .

Chapter Five

THE CHALLENGE

THE Indian community of Tophar had seethed impatiently for two long days but there had been no reply to the clerks' challenge. Colonel Eddgerley-Watkyn-Reed, busy on the Pageant Committee, was not on duty in his Veterinary Directorate. It was not until the third day that he found Shrinivassen's note in his 'In' tray—placed there with trembling hands by his own clerk, Mustapha Khan.

Idly the colonel took the ivory paper knife carved as a cricket bat and methodically slit the envelope. Before unfolding the letter, he carefully sliced off the envelope's back seam and placed the oblong front, address downward, in a bulldog clip for rough notes. A GHQ economy order since 1941, the thick pad now stretched the bulldog's jaw to its gaping limit, for the colonel never used it. All his notes had to be transcribed from his heavily-doodled blotting pad, renewed three times a day.

The knife back in its tray, the colonel perused the letter. From mild interest, his eyes began to narrow. With shaking fingers he plucked at his moustache . . . then dropped the note on his desk as if stung. He sat back, puce in the face and quite appalled.

His hand strayed to his buzzer—then withdrew. His Army training told him, reappraise the situation, do nothin' hasty . . . take another look at the enemy lines. He checked an impulse to scribble 'Seen, thanks, but unable to comply' across the note. For, while this HQ routine method of rejection might apply to requests for treating mules in the Burma campaign or foxhounds for the Delhi hunt, cricket was a different matter. The colonel realised he had no precedent upon which to work, no King's

Regulation, no Indian Army Order or Instruction he could quote. There was simply nothing he could scrawl to kill the project stone dead, mark the box file 'closed' and send it, with its solitary letter, for storage and oblivion in the cellars.

So, as on a 'Tactical Exercise Without Troops', he reviewed the situation. Slowly, with coughs and sighs, he read the letter again.

> *We, the clerks of Military HQ, being of sound mind and Indian birthright, do issue this solemn challenge to the Tophar Crusaders C.C. forthwith, in our own right, as sons of toil in this oppressed land, to play them at cricket at Glenbourn. Our team is the 'All-India Civilian XI' affiliated to the laws of fair play. Please R.S.V.P. in your own convenience.*
>
> > *Signed Respectfully:*
> > > *A. Shrinivassen, Captain, All-India Civilian XI. Sanitation & Drainage Dept.*
>
> > *Witnesses: (signed in the presents of each other):*
> > *A. Mookerjee—Umpire.*
> > *Telik Swarmi Esq.—Manager.*

The colonel remained puce and appalled. His reappraisal of the situation had only served to make him more ulcerous and giddy. The devious mind of the Indian clerk worried him just as much as the leftish theories of emergency-commissioned officers like Mott and Hacker. The colonel had handled Indian clerks for much of his service and suffered acutely from their semi-education, their unconscious puns and tautology, their love of metaphor and alliteration, and their almost childish delight in demonstrating their lucky-dip British knowledge. Clerks were an anathema to him and he abhorred their obtuse logic.

Like many regular soldiers relegated from the field to a desk, the colonel made no attempt to understand clerks. That they each possessed individual personalities and ambitions would have surprised him. All he expected of them was undivided obedience. Speaking to them solely in his own pidgeon Urdu was the only concession he made—and this grammarless hotch-potch, scattered with Persian and Arabic he had picked up on his various postings, always received answers in equally random English.

The colonel, having thus met the clerks half-way, felt no further obligations were necessary. He did not realise how he hurt their pride by never using their names, let alone prefixing the coveted 'Mr.'. More enlightened officers had obtained unswerving loyalty from clerks by enquiries after health, hobbies and children—although no experienced British staff man would ever ask after a clerk's wife. That side of his life remained forever a dark mystery. His dog might be discussed at length—but never the mother of his children.

The colonel avoided direct dealings with clerks now. Baker-Stewart, as his second-in-command, handled them entirely. He looked again at the letter. 'Sanitation & Drainage' . . . he consulted the 'top secret' list in his drawer. Colonel Hall-Gomshall's lot. The colonel lifted his phone to find out, at highest level, about this Shrinivassen fellar.

"Numbah please?" said Private Nancy Evans, Women's Auxiliary Corps, on telephone duty.

"Ah, exchange lao? Bolo Hall-Gomshall sahib, eck dum. Malum?"

"Yes, indeed I unnerstand," snapped the insulted Nancy. "I am English-born in precincts of Cardiff cantonment. I will try numbah although, to-day, there is much non-answerin' in all directions."

The colonel sighed. Another damned half-caste girl . . . the Welsh regiment had a lot to answer for in India.

"Hullo? This is department of Sanitation and Drainage speaking."

A cultured voice . . . but the colonel was not fooled. He knew the Indian inflections.

"Ah, mayray wạstay Hall-Gomshall colonel sahib lao?"

"I am afraid Colonel Hall-Gomshall is away, fiddling Haydn at the bank . . ."

"What?" The colonel's phonetic Urdu was outpaced. "Fiddlin' an' hidin' at the bank . . .?"

"Yes, he is rehearsing with stringed quartet for Festival music. The manager is also a fiddler . . ."

"Ah, thikai. I malum. I know the manager, Enoch Dorling-Wells sahib. He's the 'cello wallah. Well, mustn't interrupt that. Shabash. I'll phone bolo again same budgie tomorrow."

"Who shall I say called, pleased?"

The colonel told him and Shrinivassen's heart began to pound. The message could only mean one thing . . . the captain of the Tophar Crusaders had at last received his letter . . . and was checking up on him.

The colonel was now reduced to a last expedient in this, the first phase of his dilemma . . . he must consult his Number Two. As he pressed the buzzer he frowned. Baker-Stewart was a good soldier, even though next to useless in Veterinary. Didn't know a hoof from a fetlock. Trouble with old Stewie was he always *barked* his orders. The colonel didn't mind him barking in the outer office—suited the department perhaps—but on the cricket field it was very tiresome.

As a fast bowler, Baker-Stewart's appeal to the umpire was never a polite query but an irrefutable command. If the decision went against him he would sway in disbelief and stumble back to his mark like the shell-shocked survivor of some terrible retreat. The colonel had spoken to him about it. Gently, of course. Mustn't criticise a fellar on the field of play. Takes all sorts. He'd never get away with it in the cavalry . . . but Baker-Stewart was a gunner—and Woolwich was, as Eddger's wife always insisted, only in suburbia . . .

The khaki-turbaned chauprassi, the senile attendant employed by all civil and military headquarters in India, appeared at the door. His puttee-bound, match-stick legs tottered under his ragged, brass-buttoned khaki tunic. The colonel waited for his 'Salaam, sahib'. Although he summoned this man at least thirty times a day, protocol must be strictly observed each time.

"Bolo major sahib, come idder, eck dum."

The chauprassi observed Shrinivassen's letter on the desk with almost opaque eyes, nodded and withdrew. The colonel drummed his fingers. Now was also as good a time as any for that urgent pow-wow with Baker-Stewart over Hazel. While her husband had been incarcerated, there'd been no point in discussin' it. But now he must warn Stewy before that husband came up to Tophar and learned the truth—as he undoubtedly would. A bit below the belt of Stewy to bed down with a prisoner of war's wife . . . but gunners had a strange code of conduct, always a screw loose over women . . . must be somethin' phallic about a hot gun barrel . . .

Major Baker-Stewart strode in, saluting with one hand and closing the door with the other, all in one practised, precise movement. He then removed his cap which the colonel always insisted he wore when summoned to his office.

"Ah, sit down, Stewy." Use of the nickname indicated the interview was unofficial. "Er—how's Hazel?"

"In the pink, sir."

"Eh? Oh, yes. Er, well, I suppose her hubby will be returnin' soon . . . I mean the Singapore P.O.W.s have been liberated now . . ."

"Yes, sir. But he's staying on there, trying to restart his business."

"Civilian, is he?" The colonel frowned. "Then Hazel has been out of order, yer know, referrin' to him as a 'prisoner of war'. He's really only an internee . . . what was he in?"

"Er, bedding, sir."

"Was he now?" The colonel looked thoughtful.

"Not really top-drawer, I gather, sir. I feel Hazel married beneath her . . ."

"This beddin' wallah . . . must be well off. Plenty of call for beddin' in Singapore. When's Hazel returnin' to him?"

"Why do you ask, sir?" said Baker-Stewart, colouring with suppressed anger.

"Because, damn it, she's our scorer! As skipper I've a right to know . . ."

"Of course! Beg pardon, sir." Baker-Stewart smiled in relief.

"Well, Gerald, that's the husband, is coming to India as soon as he gets things settled in Singapore. But Hazel, being in the armed forces, can't just go rushing off duty for domestic reasons . . ."

"Ah, well, your private life's yer own, Stewy. But watch it, old chap. Don't want the Crusaders involved in a scandal, d'yer see . . . which reminds me, I have here an extraordinary missive. From a fellar called Shrinivassen, head clerk of Sanitation an' Drainage . . ."

"That's Colonel Hall-Gomshall's mob . . ."

"Yes, dear old 'Butters' . . ."

" 'Butters'?"

"Dropped a sitter at mid-off for the Staff College against 17th Lancers at Quetta in '29. Was never allowed to forget it. Took it hard. Never played again."

"Hadn't got the big match temperament, sir?"

"Oh, we called him 'Butters' for other reasons besides his cricket fiascos. He let so much slip in life . . . his mashie, for example, on the Calcutta course—seven stitches in the caddie's head. Even when he stepped back to salute the Viceroy after receivin' his O.B.E., it fell off his chest. Two wives slipped through his hands—his own, of course, he was no philanderer . . ."

"This letter from the clerks," said Baker-Stewart hastily.

" 'Butters' fell in a Taj Mahal pond on his second honeymoon —got covered with algae. God help the Haydn string quartet— with 'Butters' in the team, they're virtually a man short."

"This missive, sir," insisted Baker-Stewart, "from Sanitation and Drainage . . ."

The colonel shook himself back into the present. His little wander from horrible reality was over . . . it never worked . . . the dreadful letter was still there on his desk.

"Read this, Stewy," he sighed, "it's fearfully worryin' . . ."

Baker-Stewart turned red as he studied the neat typing.

"Good God, it's preposterous! We can't play clerks—it's just not done, sir."

"The whole thing's ridiculous, of course." The colonel began to pace his white-walled office. "We must take some sort o' stand . . . but these clerks obviously feel they've a right to challenge us. That specific reference to Glenbourn is very disturbin' . . ."

"May I make a suggestion, sir?"

"Permission granted."

"Well, we can offset this absurd challenge by informing those clerks the Crusaders are no longer accepting fixtures. The war is over and, because of overseas postings to Japan, we've been denuded of personnel."

"Other than the use of the word 'denuded'—a good idea."

"We can get out of it with dignity, sir. War effort must be attended to first, mopping up in Burma, Malaya . . ."

"Yes . . . yes . . . after all, there's hundreds of elephants to be rounded up in Burma . . ."

"Elephants?" Baker-Stewart looked alarmed. "What elephants?"

"I've got a memo in to-day from Rangoon. Elephants are in short supply. The Japs captured thousands, apparently. An' if the teak industry is to get on its feet again, they'll need those elephants . . ."

"But elephants, surely, just supply ivory . . ."

"They also pile teak, Baker-Stewart, with their tusks . . . use 'em like bats, off the front foot, a sort of mammoth cover-drive . . ."

"But, sir," Baker-Stewart was 'buck-passer' supreme, "elephants in Burma are not our pigeon. That's Veterinary, South-East Asia Command . . . we're *India* Command. Our elephants will be in the Delhi Victory Parade, not butting teak in Burma. That's Mountbatten's command, sir. We only deal with Auchinleck's elephants . . ."

"By jove, yer right, Baker-Stewart!" The colonel was enormously pleased. "Someone in Rangoon has dropped a clanger sendin' us that memo."

He scrawled across the paper: "Not, repeat not, India Command responsibility. Burmese elephants on strength of South-East Asia Command to whom this is now passed for action. Recommend strong action be taken against officer

responsible for this time-wasting error in elephant round-up."
He signed with his usual flourish.

"What we can do with elephants, we can do with clerks," he
said, blotting the memo. "Let's get the agreement of the others.
Call a committee meetin' for tea-time an' turn this challenge
down, nicely but firmly. We've got to be careful, of course.
These clerks are a bolshie lot . . . not that I mean any disrespect
to our Russian allies. But I've had trouble with clerks before
. . . usually religious reasons. Fracas about castin' shadows over
each other's typewriters, refusin' to use the same lavatories, takin'
days off for grandmothers' funerals. They plunge into the
Ganges, yer know, to get purified—an' then spend the next two
months in hospital with pneumonia. But now they're tryin' to
get involved in our cricket . . . well, that's goin' too far. Pity
the R.A.F. have gone. Folly would know what to do. Anyway,
convene the meetin'."

Baker-Stewart telephoned Lieutenant-Colonel Nupp-Jevons,
Major Barkside-Twist, Major Innes-Whiffen and Captain Mott
in strict order of seniority, while his clerk, Mustapha Khan,
gathered up his dhoti and sped down the corridor.

Before Baker-Stewart had completed his first call, every clerk
in HQ knew the Tophar Crusaders were meeting that afternoon
to consider the challenge . . . and heard, too, the more terrifying
aspect that the British might be using elephants in their
attack . . .

Chapter Six

EVASIVE ACTION

"CAN'T be done, Mr. Chairman."

Lieutenant-Colonel Nupp-Jevons was quite definite. His tall frame slumped in the small chair, his grey moustache a ragged hem over his pipe stem. "We must turn this tom-fool challenge down."

"Hear, hear," said Barkside-Twist. "Too embarrassing for words."

"No pleasure in thrashin' a weak side," said Innes-Whiffen.

"My guess is," said Baker-Stewart, "half these clerks have never handled a bat in their lives."

"Well," smiled the colonel, "are we agreed . . .?"

"Frankly, Mr. Chairman," said Mott, "I think we should give these clerks a game . . ."

The committee glared at him. Really this schoolmaster was the limit . . . only in India three years and determined to misrepresent it. They knew he had painstakingly learned Urdu, had foisted himself on Indian students in Calcutta, ingratiating himself with Bengalee, Parsee, Musselman and Sikh alike. He had been posted to Tophar because of these nefarious activities. It was all in his secret personal HQ file—as every clerk knew.

Mott guessed what the committee were thinking. But he felt he represented the new British youth. Weybridge, where he taught, was full of keen students who understood the problems of oppressed peoples. He had been involved in some pretty tortuous fence-sitting because he had spoken up in favour of many Indian break-away movements. Every leave he had spent

59

in holy cities, solemnly integrating himself with India, absorbing the legends of Siva and Vishnu. In Benares he had been particularly intrigued by phallic worship.

"I feel, gentlemen," he said earnestly, breaking the icy silence, "we should play these clerks. After all, this *is* their own country . . ."

"Rot!" said Barkside-Twist testily. "You haven't been out here long enough to get your knees brown and you want to reorganise the country. The average clerk is about as intelligent as a ship's parrot in Drake's navy. It'll take another two hundred years for the Indian to understand that birth control would give 'em more food. They let sacred cows wander the streets, eating anything they like from stalls, holding up traffic. No, India needs us. Why, this new Prime Minister at home . . . what's his name . . . ?"

"Clem Attlee," said Mott proudly.

"Sounds very Indian, I must say," said the colonel.

"Yes, this Clemenceau Atlee," said Barkside-Twist. "He said himself the Indian disliked responsibility. It was in *The Times of India* . . . yes, India needs to be governed by us. Who gave 'em the army?"

"We did," said Nupp-Jevons after some thought.

"Who gave 'em hospitals, irrigation, railways . . . ?"

"And those awful trams," said Innes-Whiffen.

"We gave 'em cricket too," reminded the colonel.

"By God, yes, sir!" Barkside-Twist bowed to his chairman. "If we play these clerks we'll belittle ourselves. They don't *really* want to play us, Mott, just make damn fools of us . . ."

"It is odd, you know," said Baker-Stewart thoughtfully, "how this challenge turns up just when we decided at our last meeting *not* to play Indian sides . . ."

All eyes turned on Mott.

"Been blabbin' round the bazaar, have yer?" asked the colonel.

"Me, sir? No, sir . . . Crusader's honour, sir . . ."

"No need to go as far as that, boy," said the colonel hastily.

"Deuced strange, just the same," said Baker-Stewart.

"I feel cricket is a game that can cement understanding," said Mott.

"I don't want my understanding cemented with a clerk's," snapped Barkside-Twist. "We're not in the same stratum. Outside the office they'd be hellishly uncomfortable in our presence."

"But I know them," insisted Mott, "I've been to their homes . . ."

"You've what?" Baker-Stewart clawed his hair. "Are you out of your mind? You might catch smallpox—or rabies . . ."

"You never want to touch dogs in India, Mott," advised the colonel. "Dreadful death, rabies. Injections in the stomach only way to prevent it. You ought to see that Grahame M.O. fellar . . . his sort of disease."

"This new penicillin works wonders, I'm told," said Barkside-Twist.

"I haven't been bitten by a dog," sighed Mott. "All I'm trying to say is, I understand these people. They crave some excitement in their humdrum lives . . ."

"Bang away on 'em all night, sometimes," said Nupp-Jevons.

"The clerks like to act in a British way," said Mott.

"The less the Indian apes us, the better," said Innes-Whiffen.

"You can get rabies from monkeys as well," advised the colonel.

Barkside-Twist pounded the table.

"Mr. Chairman, we've heard enough from this dangerous radical—this offspring of Marx and Keir Hardie. I move we vote on the item."

"Right!" The colonel nodded approvingly. "All those in favour of turnin' down this impudent challenge?"

Four arms flicked up.

"Against? Ah, the flaccid hand of Mott . . . motion carried!"

Baker-Stewart scribbled the minute.

"The challenge will be refused," said the colonel, relieved it was all over. "Boy!"

Akkar Singh withdrew his ear from the hinge, steadied himself and knocked as he entered.

"Ah, Akkar Singh," smiled the colonel, "athora drinks lao."

"Atchcha, sahib." He closed the door with great deliberation.

"I will word the letter to the clerks tactfully," said the colonel, "pointin' out that the Crusaders no longer have a team left, owin' to so many members bein' posted away to Japan."

But Akkar Singh had not stayed to hear that reasoning. Springing up the stone steps, he knew that Retti Moplah, editor of *The Himalayan Bugle*, was waiting outside the club for the latest bulletin . . . soon that stout, be-spectacled gentleman was back in his 'editorial office', as the gothic lettering above his go-down in the bazaar proclaimed, feverishly typing the most daring news story of his life.

As he believed was the Fleet Street system, Moplah devised the headline first, hammering home the exclamation mark, before actually commencing the report. This afternoon he had held no editorial conference with himself. All was clear-cut. In sadly-unaligned capitals the old Oliver beat out: 'BRITISH KICK LOCAL CLERKS IN TEETH—*Tophar Strikes In Revolt At Glenbourn Cricket Injustice*'!

Chapter Seven

STRIKE ACTION

AT DUSK, always a brief, violet twilight, Tophar suddenly became eerie and foreboding. Busy in their bungalows and clubs with their ritual sundown drinking, the British did not at first notice that the Mall, normally promenaded at this time by the more prosperous Indian families, was now deserted. But the limping, emaciated pariah dogs had at once sniffed out the message and now scavenged in the gutters, quick to sense a freedom from sandalled feet and rickshaw wheels. The brown and grey monkeys left the trees to inspect the phenomenon of empty streets and began annexing attractive areas, quarrelling over the bandstand and territories containing drains and manhole covers.

The dance at the Albert Hotel was poorly attended. All rickshaws had disappeared. None could be found to bring guests from the outlying districts of Wellingtonjat, Kitchener's Mount or Robertswadi. The Goanese band also failed to arrive, so the dozen British couples circled round a portable gramophone as alert as the trade mark dog by the horn in the open lid. Victor Silvester's strict tempo was much blurred by years of gritty eastern wear . . . the dancers had to strain their ears to catch the waltz rhythm of 'Destiny' . . .

But weird music came drifting up from the bazaar. Sinister wailing of reed pipes and sittar droning was punctuated by muffled drum beats. The Albert dancers clustered round Victor Silvester, apprehensive and fidgety. Hazel Short, cheek-to-cheek with Baker-Stewart who had cut his *Cavalcade* rehearsal to be with her, clasped him tighter.

63

"Somethin's goin' on out there, Stewy," she muttered. "Oughtn't I to slip into uniform?"

"It's nothing we can't take care of, Haze," said the major gruffly. "Prefer you in mufti anyway . . ."

"Sexpot!" She snuggled her full lips against his ear.

Basil Mott was dancing with a short, blotchy-faced girl of nineteen, in mauve frills. Muriel Barkside-Twist yearned to be 'flirtatious' like Hazel, but upbringing curbed her desire. Mott was hating her, longing to be down in the bazaar. Whatever was going on, he was certain he could quell it by some rational Indian discussion, man to man, knee to knee, on the floor.

"Daddy says you're an Indian-lover, Basil," said Muriel. "Don't we white girls attract you at all?"

"Of course." He averted his gaze from her pimples. "Your father has got me wrong. I just try to understand the Indian point of view as well as our own . . ."

"Nasty smelly people," she said, watching Hazel and wondering whether she was biting or just licking the major's ear. "They're playin' up to-night in the bazaar for sure. It's a strike for more rice or chaupattis or somethin' . . ."

They realised then that the gramophone had stopped.

"Turn the record over, old man," Baker-Stewart called to Mott.

But Mott had come to a decision.

"Sorry," he exclaimed, "but I must find out what's wrong in Tophar to-night."

"You beast . . . you're goin' . . . leavin' me!" cried Muriel, her mouth drooping into the inverted U shape of her father's when given out on the cricket field. "Really, the manners of these E.C.O.s from home. Honestly, this new Labour Government . . ."

"Mott," thundered Baker-Stewart, "come back . . .!"

But the young captain had disappeared . . . and, with him, every light in the Albert Hotel went out. Screams and shouts of dismay echoed in the sudden, plunging darkness.

Some evil power was at work in Tophar and the British locked all doors. Not a servant could be found. Their end-of-garden go-downs were deserted. Memsahibs shrilled for them in vain. Child-minding ayahs disappeared like witches in the night mist and some British infants were actually pacified by their own mothers for the first time in their lives. One, it was later rumoured, was discovered to be a daughter, not a son after all —which was awkward as the parents had put his name down for Eton.

The *Cavalcade* rehearsal was abandoned when the Grand stage darkened, and later that night 'Lady Jane Marryat' conceived in the blacked-out royal box. At the United Services Club the snooker tournament was cancelled with· Innes-Whiffen on the pink. This was not so much due to light failure, which happened later, but the sudden disappearance of the Indian marker. No replacement could be found, so the game was abandoned. The British never, of course, marked for themselves. And, as the bulbs faded in Heddle's Bank, the sight-reading string quartet suddenly reduced haughty Haydn to berserk Bartok . . .

Families in outlying bungalows tried to telephone neighbours, but strange-voiced gremlins answered them, fiends with hollow cackling laughs who knew no more English than 'Quit India'. The British, remembering the siege of Lucknow, dragged out old muskets and stood ready by shuttered windows. The British police inspector was on leave in Bombay and the station empty of his Indian constables.

The hospital, however, remained secure both with light and telephone communication. This did not puzzle Major Jack Grahame as he came off duty. If any Indian strikers got hurt, he knew they would not want to be operated upon in darkness.

The Americans too, at their Blenheim Castle HQ, had lights —and rye whisky as usual. Orders from Washington insisted they never interfered in British-Indian disputes—little realising that they caused most of them by generously over-paying their servants well beyond the British standard rates.

On the darkened Mall, Colonel Eddgerley-Watkyn-Reed and Lieutenant-Colonel Nupp-Jevons, each flashing a torch, walked apprehensively in slow-march tempo. They wore blue patrols, the hostility in the night air seeming to merit such military formality.

"Like the start of another mutiny, Nuppy . . ."

"Yes, Eddgers. Somethin' like this happened at Oudh in the old Queen's time. Perhaps India is on the march . . ."

"But where could India march to . . . Goa?"

"Are you sure this hasn't got somethin' to do with that damned clerks' cricket challenge, Eddgers?"

"Of course not! They don't know our decision yet. It's top-secret. Besides, cricket couldn't cause unrest . . ."

"There was Larwood and bodyline in Australia . . . Parkin fell foul of Lancashire . . ."

"They were only professionals, Nuppy . . ."

They turned in at the darkened entrance of the Queen's Club, shone their torch beams—and both simultaneously cried out in sheer horror!

Swaying ominously from an iron lamp bracket above the arch hung a limp figure. The head lolled grotesquely from a taut rope, the fingers were stiff and splayed—and they protruded from the sleeves of a mauve Crusader blazer!

"My God," panted the colonel, "a member's garrotted himself . . ."

"Not in the Queen's Club!" cried Nupp-Jevons. "His own bungalow would be the proper place . . ."

Another figure seemed to detach itself from the cavernous blackness of the porch behind the dangling form.

"Friend or flamin' foe?" came Grahame's voice.

"Oh, heavens, now it's the *Australian*," moaned the colonel. "Really, this is a terrible night indeed. You're a doctor, man . . . cut the fellar down . . . after all, he's a club-mate of yours, too . . ."

"It's a bloody effigy," laughed Grahame, "painter's overalls stuffed wi' straw, twigs for hands, Wizard of Oz sort o' caper. A bit early for Guy Fawkes . . ."

As he wrenched the figure free, the head broke off and bounced with dull squelching thumps in front of Nupp-Jevons who screamed and tried to crawl away on his knees.

"A melon," said Grahame, wiping his tunic down, "quite a ripe bugger too."

"This is an outrage!" boomed the colonel, recovering. "A mere dummy . . . whose Crusader blazer is that? We guard our colours most carefully . . ."

Grahame shone his torch on the label within the coat collar.

"Does the name 'Hacker' mean anythin'?" he asked. "Wasn't he that little ferrit-faced R.A.F. pilot . . .?"

"That flyin' imbecile!" stormed the colonel. "Obviously he didn't supervise his own packin' when he left Tophar. Some servant must have stolen it . . ."

"There's a note attached," said Grahame, unpinning a ragged card from the lapel. "It says 'GLEMBOURM IS OURS' " . . .

" '*Glembourm*'!" echoed the colonel. "This must be a clerk's foul work. They never can write the King's English . . . none of 'em knows their 'm's' from their 'n's' . . . this is treachery indeed . . ."

"I need a drink," said Nupp-Jevons brokenly. "Without me specs I thought it was Folly strung up there."

"It wasn't there five minutes ago," said Grahame. "When I passed on me way to the post-box, this porch was empty. So, whoever slung it up there can't be far away."

"You're sure of that?" asked the colonel slowly.

Grahame nodded.

"No one passed us on the Mall, either, did they, Nuppy? Oh, do stop whimperin', there's a good chap. Things are quite bad enough . . ."

"I can only guess the motive for this, colonel," said Grahame, "but if it's jus' bin put up, it's had no time to take effect. If we can get rid o' it, hide it or bury it, no one but us—an' the bugger who slung it here—'ull know it existed. But he won't be able to say a word 'cos, if he does, we've got him over a barrel for stealin' a club blazer . . ."

"By jove, yes!" The colonel had at last caught on. "Whoever did it is expectin' us to raise Cain. But—we won't. No, d'yer see, we'll pretend it never happened, ignore the whole thing . . ."

"I follow, Eddgers," said Nupp-Jevons. "We had a case in the old regiment once. A padre was caught wearin' the adjutant's wife's nightdress. But, as far as Whitehall was concerned, it never happened. Of course she had to burn the nightie . . ."

"That's it!" cried the colonel. "Down to the club boiler room with it an' burn it—now!"

"Burn a club blazer!" gasped Nupp-Jevons.

"It's been defiled," snapped the colonel. "Foller me!"

Flashing his torch, he made his way down the narrow, winding steps inside the porch to the vaults of the old monastery, no longer ice-cold as when the monks slept there but warm and sultry as the control point of the Queen's Club heating system. Grahame gave a fireman's lift to the headless Crusader while Nupp-Jevons stumbled fretfully in the rear, muttering about getting an M.C.C. ruling. In the boiler room the colonel grabbed a hooked iron rod and levered open the black furnace door.

"Just a minute, major," said the colonel as Grahame prepared to dismember the dummy. "Hold that—that *thing* . . . out at arm's length in front of me."

Puzzled, Grahame extended the bundle. Breathing heavily, the colonel placed his fingers in the blazer top-pocket—and ceremoniously ripped off the badge of St. George!

"Bravo," wheezed Nupp-Jevons, rapping a slow tattoo with his pipe on a coke bin lid, "drummed out, by God . . ."

"With ignominy," snorted the colonel, "an' disgrace."

"Poor ole Dreyfus Hacker," said Grahame as he prodded the remains into the roaring flames with a shovel. Then the colonel stepped forward himself—and threw in the badge. His eyes were wet.

"Well," said Grahame, slamming shut the furnace door with his foot, "I've humped a few odd blueys in me time but . . ."

"Yes, you could say the Crusaders' colours are a type of cricket 'blue'," said the colonel. "That's why we must keep them sacred . . ."

"We'll ask Akkar Singh if he's seen anyone nosin' round the club," said Nupp-Jevons.

"No, Nuppy." The colonel was quite firm. "Grahame is right. We must tell no one. Hacker is a black sheep, has let us down —but he *is* an officer—an' one of Folly's too, more's the pity. But it does not do to let club servants know about such misdemeanours. Besides, Akkar Singh himself has his pride. He would feel let down just as we do. No, no one must ever know, not even the committee an', by God, certainly not Mott. Me memsahib, too, she must never be told—'ud break her heart. This dreadful disgrace to our colours is, therefore, our secret— an', from now on, gentlemen, it never happened."

The colonel turned on his heel and walked to the door. The listening Akkar Singh sped noiselessly ahead of him round the twisting stairs back to his bar, his scheme having been ruined by the Australian. Hacker's blazer had cost him four rupees in the bazaar and he would now have to replace that overall in the theatre scenic painting room—all for nothing. The British would even deny that the effigy existed to save even Akkar Singh himself, from embarrassment! While it was frustrating, it was a tactic Akkar Singh understood and reluctantly admired. His enemy had been strengthened by the Australian's wiles, and the Sikh found himself once more respecting the untidy doctor. At least he was making the fight more subtle.

As the officers filed into the now sinister candle-lit bar, the colonel said gently: "Actually, Major Grahame, by Crusader tradition, you should now inform Akkar Singh of your presence so that he may ask me if you can join my table. However, we'll waive protocol to-night, but remember it in future."

Akkar Singh served them with three whiskies in strict order of seniority. Graham sipped his and grimaced . . . "What the hell's this . . . lamp oil?"

"I regret no Scotch whisky or English gin," said Akkar Singh. "Thieves have raided my store. Only Indian drinks . . ." He pointed to a row of bottles behind his bar, all bearing labels of clanless tartans and ebony-faced beefeaters.

"Right now," said Grahame nostalgically, "I'd give anythin' to be in Johnny Naughton's bar with a swig of 'Old Court'."

"I didn't know you were also a legal man," said Nupp-Jevons.

Grahame looked amazed and slowly shook his head.

"Akkar Singh," said the colonel, "you must be the only loyal servant on duty in Tophar. What's goin' on in the town, old friend? All the lights goin' out, only local hooch on tap . . . ?"

"All the Indian nurses at the hospital are on strike, too," said Grahame. "I had to do bed-pan duty meself . . ."

"Why?" cried the colonel. "That's what I want to know—why?"

"Because they'd soil the bed linen if he didn't," said Nupp-Jevons.

"I didn't mean that," said the colonel testily. "I mean—why is there this—er—mutiny in the air?"

"Unrest, sahib," said Akkar Singh hollowly. "Something, I know not what, has angered the Indian community. Some say the babus are rising."

"The monkeys?" queried Grahame.

"No, 'babus' are clerks." The colonel looked anxiously at Akkar Singh. "What are they risin' for?"

"I do not fraternise with babus, sahib," came the reproachful reply as Akkar Singh moved back to his bar, his beard hiding his sneer in the flickering candle-light.

"There, damn it," muttered the colonel, "I nearly offended him. You see how tricky it would have been to have told him about—er—you-know-what. He might have been so upset at the slur on the club colours as to give notice. But if Akkar Singh says there is unrest, then it's true enough. Anyway, Grahame," he raised his glass, "thanks for yer help."

While he already regretted making the Australian a Crusader, he realised now, whether the committee liked it or not, Grahame must remain a member however he behaved. He knew too much . . .

"Have you seen Mott aroun'?" asked Grahame, breaking the silence.

"No, I have not," said the colonel heavily, "an' I cannot conceive anyone in their right mind wantin' to see Mott at a time like this."

"Oh, he's a bit uv a nut, I admit," agreed Grahame, "but I like him. We get on despite his bloody jokes. But I've had a memo from Judge Trevelhayes tellin' me I'm to play Captain Cook in a pageant. What the flamin' hell's that about?"

"It is," said the colonel sharply, "a very great honour indeed. You will represent Australia . . ."

"In that case, I'll go as Ned Kelly, headpiece an' all . . ."

"Who did this Kelly play for?" asked Nupp-Jevons.

"Skip it," sighed Grahame. "No, I went to the Albert dance. Mott was supposed to be there with Spotty Backside . . ."

"Who?" exploded the colonel.

"Spotty Backside . . . Muriel Barkside-Twist . . . Mott calls her that . . ."

"Mott should remember she is the daughter of the Crusaders' first-wicket down," growled the colonel.

"Damned apt though," muttered Nupp-Jevons. "Spotty Backside . . ."

"Mott wasn't at the Albert," said Grahame. "I thought he might've dropped in here. That's why I came. But I guess he's gone sleuthin' down in the bazaar among his Indian pals . . ."

"Mott sleuthin' in the bazaar tonight worries me a lot," said the colonel grimly. "Probably he's rabble-rousin'—maybe he'll get stoned . . ."

"Not surprisin' if he drinks stuff like this," said Grahame.

"They could make a human torch of him," said Nupp-Jevons. "Soak him in kerosene—it's been known . . ."

"Full o' this rot-gut," said Grahame, "he'd fry like a true martyr . . ."

"Don't joke about such things," muttered the colonel. "Mott is a menace. I bet even now he's revealin' top-secret Crusader decisions—even before I've had time to write that explanatory letter to that Shrini-sanitation fellar."

"Hush, Eddgers," warned Nupp-Jevons, "careless talk . . ."

"Oh, you can trust me," said Grahame lightly. "I'm a true Crewsader now, aren't I? Bound up be all sorts o' hippocratic oaths."

"Of course you are!" The colonel was suddenly relieved and

serene again. "Doctors have to be . . . Akkar Singh! Dusra
drinks lao . . ."

When Akkar Singh had served them, the colonel raised his
glass.

"Up the old regiment, eh, Akkar Singh!"

The Sikh bowed as Grahame added: "Up yer ole regiment."

Soon the colonel was discussing his grandson with great
enthusiasm. "I want Jocelyn to be a left-arm spinner, Grahame,"
he confided. "You don't remember, do yer, if he showed signs
of bein' left-handed at birth . . .?"

Akkar Singh crept quietly downstairs to the porch where
Wahdi was squatting. With hard knuckles he sharply clipped
the boy's ear.

"If you are to help us in our fight against the British," he
hissed, "you must learn to spell 'Glenbourn' correctly."

"But," whined the boy, "I could not read your writin' clear."

"Remember," said Akkar Singh, now pinching the ear, "you
say not a word to any man ever about this, not on your death-
bed even. We have not entirely failed, for my plan has already
divided the British and made them keep secrets from each other.
That corrodes any army. Had we succeeded with the effigy we
could take full credit and be acclaimed by the world. But, as we
were prudent and did not boast of the venture before we put it
into practice, its near failure leaves us untouched. That, chokra,
is the true way to attain power."

"I now forget forever that I hanged him up," said Wahdi,
"but who is keepin' secrets from who?"

"Secrets? Only the British keep secrets—we in India merely
guard our tongues," said Akkar Singh. "Remember that
Australian's war song . . . 'Punch in the presence of the passenger',
clever, eh? We must not show the Britisher what destination is
on his ticket until after we have punched it. Then his journey is
in our hands . . . his end is in our sights . . . bang . . . and he
travels no more."

Wahdi nodded and began to croon: *'If you spit, 'tis a rupee
fine,'* as he went on eating round the eye-sockets of the bruised
melon.

Chapter Eight

THE 'BUGLE' SOUNDS

RED with fury, Major Baker-Stewart flung the morning issue of *The Himalayan Bugle* on the colonel's desk.

"How the hell did they find out? Who told this bloody rag our decision not to play those wog clerks?"

The colonel clasped his head.

"Please, Stewy, don't bark, there's a good fellar. Me head, yer know . . ."

"Sorry, sir."

"All that local hooch last night. I feel very frail . . . up seven times in the early hours. Were you up at all?"

Having spent the night with Hazel, Baker-Stewart was taken aback.

"Well, er, I did have a bit of a rumble tummy, sir," he confessed. "But have you seen this newspaper . . .?"

"Only *The Times o' India* . . . rubber shares revivin' now Malaya's free . . ." He read *The Himalayan Bugle* headline. "Well, who *has* kicked the clerks in the teeth?"

"*We* have, sir. It's about our decision not to play the clerks . . ."

"But yer don't kick at cricket . . . C. B. Fry did but that was a Southampton football . . . never understood a chap of his calibre takin' up soccer . . ." He paused, studying the paper, his eyes now widening with realisation and anger. "Good grief! How can they print this? I haven't even written the official letter yet . . ."

"There's been a leakage. I bet Mott's at the bottom of this."

"Mott kickin' clerks in the teeth? But he *likes* the fellars."

73

The colonel read the article aloud. " '*The down-trodden clerks employed at starvation wages by Army Headquarters issued a friendly challenge to the Tophar Crusaders for a cricket match at Glenbourn. But the British have refused our sons of India a chance to play at their beloved Glenbourn . . .*' Damn it, Stewy, it's *our* beloved Glenbourn! . . . '*They have rejected the challenge thus denying the clerks the exercise they need, the open-air sport which, by their true heritage, is their right.*' Nonsense, Glenbourn is British territory . . . '*Last night the Indians of Tophar showed their metal . . .*' That doesn't look right . . . '*by going on strike in sympathy with the energetic, hardworking clerks who have done their uttermost to bring victory and peace to India . . .*' One sight of the enemy an' they'd have all worshipped the Emperor of Japan, Stewy. Pity we can't challenge him at cricket . . . show him a thing or two . . . '*The Tophar Crusaders by despotic attitudes have caused the disruption of the town. Tophar has shown the way—now it could happen again—all over India!*' . . . This is ruddy sedition, Stewy . . .''

Hoping he had put from his mind for ever the episode of the Crusader effigy, he was now choking with anger as he crumpled the yellow newspaper into the wastepaper basket.

"Mott's leaked," he snorted. "Must have. He mingles with clerks . . . he's a clerk-mingler. How else could my—*our* decision have got beyond the walls of the committee room?"

"He left the dance at the Albert very suddenly, sir . . . left me to do the turning over . . ."

"Turnin' over?"

"Records."

"Oh, '*Records*'—that's Brigadier Walshe-Wrenbank's mob . . . good bat, old Wrenny, before that Kenya rhino horned him, middle an' leg. But we know Mott's record . . ."

"No, sir, *gramophone* records. The band went on strike . . ."

"Oh, the phonograph . . . odd screechy things . . . ah, now you speak of it, Grahame told me Mott was sleuthin' down in the bazaar. Said he'd left the Barkside-Twist girl . . ."

"Yes, sir. Stranded a white woman . . . left her to walk home alone in the dark . . . did Grahame mention that?"

"No, but I think Spotty Backside was safe enough . . . oh, beg pardon, 'lady's name' an' all that . . . Grahame said it was her nickname . . ."

"Grahame would," sneered Baker-Stewart. "He has a different code of conduct . . ."

The colonel frowned. Other than Mott, none of his remaining Crusader committee approved of Grahame. Last night he had still been prepared to defend his decision to make him a member but this very morning he had received a letter from his wife, now holidaying in Kashmir, saying Tophar gossip had reached her that Grahame had been seen in local dance halls with an Anglo-Indian girl. '*This*,' Julia had written, '*should not be countenanced from a Crusader. Medical degree or not, Grahame is a bosky type and has caused you to make your first blunder as chairman of the club* . . .' Julia, too, could conveniently 'forget' her part in Grahame's nomination but, if she had changed her mind about Grahame, then so had the colonel. However, now he recalled again, with sudden misery, the Crusader effigy. The Australian was too inextricably bound up in that episode—and the colonel could never tell his committee—or his wife— why . . .

"Mott must have shot his mouth off in the bazaar last night," said Baker-Stewart. "He's a danger to Tophar and all it stands for. I hate these do-gooders who come out from home determined to give India back to the Indians. No thought for others . . ."

"Yes, I agree, Stewy. The sooner Mott sees the white cliffs of Weybridge again the better. Where does he work?"

"Army Education—Colonel Coote-Coote . . ."

"Ah, Cooty. Right, I will act." He lifted the phone. "Hullo, exchange lao? Are you British or Indian?"

Nancy Evans shrilled that she was most white girl.

"Ah, then get me Colonel Coote-Coote, 'Education'."

Harsh cracklings and strange clangings like distant Tibetan prayer gongs finally connected Colonel Coote-Coote.

"Cooty, this is Eddgers."

"What-ho, ole man. How's the memsahib?"

"Kashmir."

"Cashiered?"

"No, *in* Kashmir. With me daughter. Had a baby last Christmas . . ."

"Your mem? Good for Julia . . . you ole rogue . . ."

"Nunno. Me *daughter*. Married to a Gurkha major . . ."

"Boy or girl?"

"Eh?"

"Your daughter's child—male or female?"

"Oh, a grandson. Jocelyn . . . goin' to be a left-arm spinner . . ."

"Well, thanks for the news. My mem's in Gulmarg . . . glands playin' her up again . . ."

"Hold on, Cooty . . . it's about Mott . . ."

"Mott? Has he been foolin' around with your daughter, then?"

"Good heavens, no, Cooty. No, Mott's been talkin' carelessly . . . leakin' in the bazaar . . ."

"But we've nothin' secret here in 'Education', Eddgers. Just illustrated alphabet books for sepoys . . . rehabilitation stuff . . . how to till without ploughs . . ."

"No, it's about our cricket club. The clerks challenged us . . ."

"Oh, I've seen the local rag." Cooty's hearty laughter made the colonel wince. "You've certainly stirred up a hornets' nest there . . ."

"That's Mott's doin' for sure . . . tellin' the press our committee's decision before it was official . . ."

"Just a tick, Eddgers." The colonel heard Coote-Coote call Mott . . . the muffled question and then the loud, expostulated denial.

"Eddgers," said Coote-Coote, "Mott gives me his word as an officer and a gentleman, he didn't leak. Frankly, it's not like you, Eddgers, accusin' an officer without definite evidence. As his C.O., I have every faith in Mott, even though he is in Labour . . ."

"He fraternises with clerks, Cooty, he's on their side, wants to play 'em . . ."

"Cricket is a damned silly game, Eddgers." The colonel stared at the mouthpiece indignantly. "My brother got a 'blue' for it and where did he end up? Army School of Physical Trainin'. Won't get beyond 'major' with that 'shower' . . ."

"I feel Mott should be sent home," said the colonel, aggrieved. "He's goin' native, Cooty; he'll be wearin' a dhoti next, sittin' on the floor an' showin' his navel to snakes . . ."

"He's all I've got, Eddgers. I'd never get a replacement now the war's over. Besides, I'm due for a spot of leave soon—Darjeelin', you know—and so I can't have a new man takin' over. No, sorry, Eddgers, Mott is not for postin'. Good fellar, very loyal and amusin' . . . oh, my! Must dash . . ."

"I tell you, Mott is a very bad influence . . ."

"I'm not, sir . . . this is Mott speaking . . ."

"Eh?"

"This *is* Mott, sir. I'm speaking on the telephone."

"What happened to Cooty?"

"Gone to the latrine, sir. He drank some Indian hooch last night . . ."

"So did we all, thanks to you blatherin' to that newspaper . . ."

"No, sir, I swear I didn't breathe a word. I couldn't find out anything last night. I asked questions in the bazaar but they 'no malumed' everything. Lots of strange music about, of course—if Duke Ellington . . ."

"Don't name-drop, Mott . . . *my* father knew the Duke of Cambridge . . ."

At the exchange Nancy Evans was listening excitedly.

"Well, if it wasn't you, Mott," said the colonel, "who was it?"

"Could it be Akkar Singh, sir? He was on duty during the meeting . . ."

"Good God, man!" The colonel went white. "He's a Sikh . . . me old regiment. Backbone of India, on our side through thick an' thin. Just shows how much you know about India, Mott . . ."

"Well, it's a mystery, sir. Must go now . . ."

"I haven't dismissed you yet . . ."

"Must go, sir. Colonel Coote-Coote is back and now I want to go—bloody badly . . ."

There was a click and the colonel slowly replaced his receiver.

"Can't be Mott, Stewy," he sighed, "unless he's a born liar."

"He played for the Altruists at home, sir," said Baker-Stewart. "He was at Winchester, too . . ."

"Ah, yes, then we must be barkin' up the wrong tree, but to suggest Akkar Singh's been eavesdroppin' . . . that's a bit much . . ."

"Mott did that?" Baker-Stewart was shocked. "Accusing a club servant . . . a Wykehamist?"

"Who, Akkar Singh? Good heavens, no! Ex-mess orderly from Ambala . . ."

The phone chimed delicately. Baker-Stewart lifted the receiver, then put his hand over the mouthpiece.

"It's Judge Trevelhayes, sir . . ."

"Ah, just missed his 'blue' at Cambridge . . ."

"I gather he's ringing about something else, sir."

"Hullo? Yes, judge, Eddgers speakin' . . ."

"I've read that blasted *Bugle* . . ." The voice was high-pitched but crystal clear. "As Crusaders' president I'd better know the facts. Did yer kick the clerks in the teeth?"

"Of course not . . ."

"Well, if they can't produce a toothless clerk, you've got a libel action. Sue the editor . . . if I was still on the bench you'd get heavy damages . . ."

"But the Crusaders can't sue, Trevvy. The article says 'the British' . . . that means everyone . . . even the Viceroy . . ."

"Oh, don't involve Wavell . . . got enough on his plate already . . . ah, I get yer point . . . the libel is against the Raj . . . h'm . . . really means His Majesty's Government suin' . . . I'm not sure this new Labour lot would play ball . . . but we must get this editor walkin' the plank somehow . . ."

"Because of a cricket match, Trevvy?"

"Ah . . . that's it. Get the M.C.C. to sue . . . old Plum Warner . . ."

"Is that your considered opinion?"

"Look, Eddgers, you must do *somethin'*, old friend. Can't have Tophar plunged into darkness by these strike wallahs. Absolutely ruined my Arts meetin' . . . I am Pageant Master, after all . . ."

"I know—you've cast me as Clive . . ."

"Yes, an' I want you to double as W. G. Grace later. I can't get enough people. I'm playin' Neptune, yer know, Britain rulin' the waves—that's about all they can bloody well rule. We can't get horse floats to parade through the town so we're usin' bullock carts. A bit wobbly, so wear rubber shoes. I shall use my trike, of course . . . deck it up with seaweed, a few shells an' it'll look nautical by the time I've finished with it."

"Have you," ventured the colonel, "felt any ill-effects from your jeep accident?"

"Jeep? That was an armoured car . . . no, feel as fit as ever. The Americans settled out of court. Mark yer, I had a good case. I was hit from behind. You've apparently kicked the clerks from the front. By the by, glad you've enrolled Grahame as a Crusader. Patched me up beautifully. Quaint chap . . . all the time he was settin' me arm in plaster he sang a hymn about 'punchin' the passengers' or somethin'. Quite tribal, these Aussies. How's the grandson?"

"Oh, Jocelyn . . .?"

"They do at that age but they steady up. 'Bye."

"I don't like to say this, Stewy," said the colonel as, confused, he put back the receiver, "but I'm sure just missin' that 'blue' turned our president's brain at an early age. He says Grahame advised him to punch the passengers in that jeep—which he now says was an armoured car."

"Perhaps he thinks a jeep is a female Jap," smirked Baker-Stewart.

"I have," said the colonel, closing his eyes, "heard that before. From Mott."

Baker-Stewart looked at the ceiling in irritation.

"What about this official letter to the clerks, sir? I mean, when they hear our reason for not accepting the clerks' chal-

lenge, they will have to retract this treasonable newspaper
article . . ."

"Oh, dear." The colonel's temples were hammering . . . and
again there was a vision of a hanging Crusader. "Yes, I suppose
so . . . but it seems to have gone too far for that . . . any aspirin
handy?"

"I'll send the clerk for some . . ." But when Baker-Stewart
returned he was shaking his head in temper.

"Both our bloody clerks are missing. Gone to a meeting in the
babus' canteen . . ."

"What about?"

Baker-Stewart pointed in the basket to the slowly untwisting
Himalayan Bugle . . .

Chapter Nine

THE MISSION

THE paralysing of Tophar for one frightening night had, as Mookerjee anticipated, been 'most strikin' success'. Essential services for the British had been disrupted . . . attention had been drawn to the cricket challenge in 'most cunnin' manner' . . . Mookerjee, the sole perpetrator of the strike, was 'agitator—first-class'! Now, as he hurried along the Mall, the morning was bright and crisp. The August sun was gradually hotting up although there were still pools beneath the rhododendrons not yet soaked away from the recent short monsoon.

Mookerjee noted with intense satisfaction that dozens of drawn-faced, frightened British memsahibs were queuing at the chemists for nerve tonics, proving yet again the hundred per cent effectiveness of the strike. Normally British women shopped, Mookerjee had observed, solely for fashion. Their servants ordered all the food—ah, if only those stupid khansamas would sometimes insert poison while their British mistresses were out being measured by dharsees. However, personal appearance, Mookerjee conceded as he strutted along, was one pride an Indian could learn from the Raj. Most Indians looked like unmade beds. They possessed no svelt line, no curved hip—and the shorter the Indian the longer his coat.

Mookerjee spent most of his salary on sartorial display. He favoured pastel shades, both in shirting and suit length. To-day he had dressed with extra care. The camber-curled brown bowler was the only one in Tophar, his silk suit, a light shade of tan ruled with a thin orange line, was unique east of Suez, setting off to perfection the lavender shirt and his favourite ready-made red bow which flapped beneath his pointed chin like a butterfly enjoying nectar. 'Calcutta Hollywood' white canvas shoes with brown filigree measured his jaunty steps, paced by a swinging silver-knobbed malacca cane. Mookerjee felt at his best when he acted British. He had been the comedian of many 'jatras'—the farces of Calcutta—and had 'taken off' the British with hysterical success. But now he was on 'most secret errand' which demanded his tragedian skill.

Not even Shrinivassen knew why Mookerjee had, that morning, refused to attend the clerks' meeting. But, like Akkar Singh, Mookerjee knew his homeland. Breathe one word of a proposed plan aloud and it would be relayed from cupped mouth to cupped ear, each recipient swearing eternal silence. With the British such behaviour was considered indecorous gossip, but the Indian regarded it merely as the generous sharing of responsibility for guarding a secret. Such load-spreading, however, had the disadvantage of creating far too many derisive critics should the plot fail . . . so the shrewd Mookerjee took no one into his confidence. Retti Moplah had served the cause well in *The Himalayan Bugle* and now, as he walked, Mookerjee was rehearsing a speech to himself. Throughout the night he had laboured, memorising passages from the Bible—for he was now on a mission—to involve the Church . . .

Mr. Mookerjee loved the ritual of religion—any religion—for, while he was a secret agnostic, a faith was a possession and no worthwhile Indian ever gave up an inheritance. He professed to worship Kali, the Goddess of Destruction, simply because she invariably suited his needs. Kali, one of Shiva's wives, was always depicted with protruding red tongue, necklace of skulls and a bloodstained club and was undoubtedly the one wife who gave her husband most trouble with the neighbours. In old Calcutta days her followers, known as Tantriks, sacrificed young virgins at her altar so that gigantic physical powers could be absorbed from her. To-day only goats were used; as many as two hundred daily were still decapitated in Kali's presence. But Mookerjee now needed the aid of a foreign church. Oh, not the British padres who ruled their congregations like humourless civil servants with solemn sermon, nor the smiling Father O'Malley who drank whisky like holy water and sang hymns like 'Cockles and Mussels' late into the night on his own . . . no, Mookerjee knew a more exciting faith than that . . . he was going to involve the American church. He was not sure which denomination. It could be Mormon with a big wife allowance or some Chicago sect of violence. Mr. Mookerjee was about to find out . . .

Mr. and Mrs. Cyrus Q. Weltzer had recently arrived in Tophar. After taking Christianity to Tibet so courageously through the war years, where they had lived on friendly llamas' buttermilk and read the Bible at high altitudes, they were now awaiting instructions—and funds—from New York to continue their mission. Calling-up papers for Cyrus's military service had remained unsigned in a Manhattan recruiting office. However, as the Japanese war was over, the Weltzers had decided that their own G.I.s needed their message more than the impassive Tibetans—so they were now in India to greet the doughboy ex-prisoners of war with God's word.

Marion Weltzer was at her desk cross-referencing her monthly uplift news-letter for the U.S.A. when Mookerjee was announced by little Krischa, her house-boy.

"An *Indian*?" she said incredulously, as if Sitting Bull was at her door. "Really, I am too busy, Krischa. My letter to the 'American Mission of True Hearts' is overdoo—long overdoo. Does he state his business?"

"He says he comes in Christ," said the boy, obeying to the letter Mookerjee's instructions plus the five-rupee bribe to insist upon an audience.

"Say, have we made a local convert? Oh, yes, then send him in . . . for sure, send him right in."

Thirty-five-year-old Marion Weltzer was tall, big-boned, and possessed the broad-strong face of the open-air. Although her thick black hair was drawn back in a tight bun, her piercing brown eyes gave her otherwise home-girl features a radiant intensity. Full-busted, she wore ankle-length dresses of simple black or brown velvet, presenting a nun-like appearance for one who enjoyed her young husband's virility in bed with such commanding regularity.

Ex-actor Cyrus, ten years her junior, had been swayed into becoming her disciple after hearing her preach in New York. The desire to imbue her spirit became too much for him to endure . . . they had been married before a judge one midnight in a hurried, fidgety ceremony. Cyrus was still bewildered by his wife. Her passion for him seemed even greater than her fervour for God. After a brief prayer of thanksgiving for living through the day, the long, hard night would begin . . . To-day Cyrus was out conferring with the American Army at their Blenheim Castle HQ—and Marion hoped he would not be long.

Mookerjee entered and handed his hat and stick to a surprised Krischa.

"These for me?" he asked.

"No," snapped Mookerjee, annoyed that this British custom was unknown to the boy. "Leave them in the hall."

Krischa balanced them on the ibex antlers by the hat-stand and disappeared outside to crouch below the open window, pretending to water potted plants.

"Mrs. Weltzer," said Mookerjee, extending a small hand, "please forgive me intrudin' upon your meditations. But my people are sore oppressed."

"Sit down, Mr. . . . ?"

"Mookerjee, madam, a humble clerk at British Headquarters from which God is absent . . ."

"You are a believer, sir?"

"In justice, in human rights, yes." Mookerjee wiped an eye. "If your God is a protector of such things, then, yes, I am a believer."

"You wish to be converted? Dear friend, the Bible . . ."

"I have read an' digested it many times . . ." Mookerjee had indeed, using quotations when inciting Calcutta tramway strikers before the war. "But I come to seek your aid, madam, an' draw upon your common-sensual experience. You are an American, a lady o' fillum-star beauty, if I may make so fast-bold . . .

distractive as I have never seen at the Elite Cinema . . . you have defeated rock o' ages . . . a veritable Rani . . ."

"Oh, you're too kind . . ." Marion Weltzer's hand fluttered to her bun. "But what makes you think I am 'rani'?"

" 'Rani' means 'queen'—but, as an American, you do not rule this country like the British, with rod of irony. You would have us free . . ."

"Oh, er, sure," she said doubtfully. "Yes, if you belonged to America, sure, you'd be free, good friend. That is God's will."

" 'Tis such an injustice that brings me to beg at your feet," cried Mookerjee brokenly, kneeling and clasping her hand.

"Ah, er, well, for pity's sakes . . ."

"Forgive me, rani. I need the help of you an' your God."

"Sure, sure . . ." She averted her head a little. The strange musk-like scent of the little man disturbed her. Why was Cyrus always missing when she wanted him?

"Only your doctrinial balm can cure our dilemma," said Mookerjee earnestly.

"Please rise and stay right there in your chair," said Marion uncomfortably. "Let us discuss this as in a temple. What can God do for you?"

" 'Tis with our cricket match against the Tophar Crusaders."

"Crusaders? Aren't they men of God, holy warriors like back in British hist'ry . . .?"

"Ah, if only they were! No, these British soldiers who band together heathenistically under such a stained-glass name. We, the impoverised clerks, wish to play cricket against these Crusaders whom we serve so loyally. But these ill-bred an' buttered-upper-crusts have rejected us. They will not let us play at Glenbourn, which is, mark you, in our own country, as any map of India will aver . . ."

"Hold it a moment, hold it, sir!" Marion shook her head bewilderedly. "Cricket? This is a game, I guess . . ."

"Like your baseball . . ."

"A sinful game, sir. In the States men wager upon it . . ."

"Ah, cricket is never bet upon."

"God be praised for that."

"We in India have played it many generations. An open-air, exercise-givin' game. A ball is bounced an' hit harmlessly to count a score, as many as twenty-two can participate but all mus' wear white, pure white . . . for in London the ground is called Lord's . . ."

"You don't say!" Marion clasped her hands ecstatically. "Now you're making sense, Mr. Mookerjee, good, clean, Christian sense."

"But the British are not, rani. We poor clerks have been refuted, rebuffed an' refused to be allowed to play with them at their Lord's game on the sabbath."

"Monstrous!" cried Marion, rising. "That is flaunting God's word. I guess the British did bring that Mootiny on themselves, after all. They are denying you your heritage, your birthright in a game of holy rite. I sure never knoo cricket had such implications. I am mortified—yes, mortified—to hear the British take such an unchristian stand against you."

"That is why I am here, rani." Mookerjee's precise hands guided her elbows, stage-directing the much taller woman back into her chair so that their eyes were on level terms. He was using the moment of Shuva Drishti from the Brahmin wedding ritual—the Auspiciously-Timed Look—when the priest calls upon the bride and 'groom to gaze meditatingly upon each other, usually the first sight either gets of their future life partner. Mookerjee's fierce brown eyes riveted Marion Weltzer's suddenly apprehensive pupils with mesmeric effect. After a pregnant pause he began his rehearsed speech . . .

"Your country, rani, is so god-fearin' an' understan'in' o' our plight. Abraham Lincoln freed your slaves with his Uncle Tom's Cabinet legislation. But our land has been over-flown by the locust British. Did they not treat Christ like a dog in the manger? Do they give us enough loaves an' fishes? They overturn our tables an' take away from us whatever talents we possess. They command their soldiers to 'halt' an' maim, then make us take up our charpoys an' walk. They blast down our walls o' jerry-built bricks with military trumpets—an' send men with the minds o' little children to lead us . . . it has been so since time immoral!''

Mookerjee then found himself enfolded against Marion Weltzer's bosom.

"Now, now," she crooned. "Don't take on so, honey!"

Strangled against the saintly breast, Mookerjee had a terrible thought that milk might be added to the honey . . . he struggled free, dishevelled and, rare for him, quite unnerved.

"I shall rise up on your behalf, Mr. Mookerjee," she said, her eyes now appearing to see far beyond the bulging roof sacking. "I shall take God's word to the British for your cricket. It's such a simple request for Heaven's sake. You want to play games with the soldiers who stole your land . . . offer the hand of friendship of beaten, helpless victims. I *will* be your Rani. Give me the name of this lynch-mob's leader . . ."

"Colonel Eddgerley-Watkyn-Reed is his unchristian sur-name . . ."

"Such a name! He sounds kinda blue-blood . . . a king's man. Write it down."

Mookerjee scribbled on a pad embossed with the 'True Heart'.

"The colonel is old," he said sadly. Then, seeing her mouth droop, added confidentially: "But he has under his command, many young, virilistic, big-limboed officers, thick akimboed arms an' shoulders, with moustaches upon their full-blooded lips that bristle with ardent ardour . . ."

Marion whimpered softly. Mookerjee knew this sort of mem-sahib, had seen them in Calcutta. Under a guise o' do-goodin', they were randy, sex-starved an' writhin' in the heat, burstin' to sin despite their religious convictions. He had met unfrocked white priests drinkin' themselves boozy in the bazaar arrak shops because they had taken such a woman. He knew ex-nuns em-ployed in the brothels who enjoyed their work so much they embarrassed their customers. This memsahib was just another passion-infected one . . .

"Where shall I find these men—this man?" demanded Marion, trying to control her shaking long legs beneath her voluminous skirt.

"They meet at the Queen's Club. 'Tis a hell-hole o' drinkin' vice for British only . . ."

"I have been there," said Marion, perplexed, "but only for tea."

Where the heck was Cyrus?

"Tell the colonel we peaceful clerks want this cricket match," said Mookerjee, his hands gesturing as if modelling invisible clay. "Give him God's word, great rani, an' put our case to him."

"I will! I will! But first I must find strength for this mission. On your knees, Mr. Mookerjee!"

He jumped and backed away. She swayed towards him, her eyes closed.

"On your knees, Mr. Mookerjee . . . let us pray."

"Oh!" Mr. Mookerjee was partly relieved, yet still desperate. If young Krischa saw him, the news would be all over the bazaar in no time. He sank down on his knees, shaking with unexpected superstition, feeling suddenly like one of Kali's sacrificial, bleating goats.

Beside him, Marion Weltzer sent her strong voice aloft. Despite the worry of his trousers losing shape, Mookerjee was deeply impressed. Strange how the United States seemed particularly venerated in the white man's heaven. It accounted for so much, those fast cars, the movies, the flashy swimmin' pools, glamorous bathin' beauties—an' stylish clothes. Americans certainly knew how to get value for bein' 'one nation under God'.

Marion's loud exhortations drowned the entrance of Cyrus Q. Weltzer. He stood bemused, scratching his fair, short stubbled head as his wife and Mookerjee struggled up from the floor.

"Aw, hullo, honey," he said awkwardly. "Got a visitor, I guess . . ."

"We are praying, Cyrus," she cried, eyeing the biceps under the rolled shirt-sleeves of her all-American boy. "Praying for guidance. This is Mr. Mookerjee . . . from India."

"Pleased to know yer, Mooker," said Cyrus, nodding.

"Mooker*jee*, honey," said Marion. "He has asked for Christian aid against the British . . ."

"Lor, honey," said Cyrus, "we aren't supposed to interfere in limey politics . . ."

"But 'tis not fruity government," said Mookerjee hastily, " 'tis God's work. The British do not dominate God's dominion . . ."

"Indeed they do not," snapped Marion indignantly, "as any American will tell you. No, this is a cricket problem . . ."

"Aw, *infestation*," said Cyrus understandingly. "They make that noise by rubbing their back legs together . . ."

"Cricket is a game, Cyrus," said Marion, "where muscular men run about in white on Sundays. It has truly great religious meaning for the British . . ."

"Why," asked Cyrus, staring from the window, "is Krischa in such a mighty hurry, runnin' off down the driveway like that . . . ?"

"Krischa, your houseboy? He is runnin'? . . . Oh, my word . . ." Mookerjee sprang to the door sending small mats slithering. "Mus' go! Mus' go!"

"Surely not," said Cyrus, knowing the look in Marion's eye and anxious to stall for time after his long uphill walk from the American HQ. "A cup o' coffee in Christ, perhaps . . . ?"

"No, no!" Mookerjee was in a frenzy. Young Krischa was a menace. He grabbed his hat and stick from the ibex and chased down through the potted plants. If he did not catch that boy before he reached the bazaar and ply him with more bakshish his reputation could be ruined—as well as his plan. He could already hear the whispers . . . 'clasped in a white memsahib's arms an' prayin' to her god' . . . oh, this would be a mos' calamitous state o' affair!

"Strange guy," said Cyrus, "like a little cricket himself."

"He has set my feet on a new and righteous path of destiny," said Marion dreamily. "I shall fix it as God wills. Mookerjee, poor heathen, shall have his cricket. He will not be spurned by the British. His sect have made me their rani . . . an Indian queen . . . for that they'll say prayers for me in Noo York. Cyrus, lock the door, honey. We must rest together . . ."

God darn this cricket, he thought.

Chapter Ten

DEWAN GUPTA ARRIVES

DEWAN GUPTA, chief reporter for *Clarion India*, leaned, panting and annoyed, against the Mall railings, looking down on the Victorian turrets of Tophar Army Headquarters perched below on the steep hillside. Having just climbed up the precipitous khudside path from the motor road below, he now discovered he had to descend again to reach HQ's entrance. As a newshound he sported the belted trenchcoat and brown fedora favoured by Mr. Alan Ladd in similar Hollywood roles bewitching Gupta to near idolatry in Delhi cinemas. He was, however, hardly a dead ringer for his hero. The dark, creviced, walnut face and pudgy nose were unlikely to throb a dame's heart, but, when uncovering news, Gupta found he obtained far better results as Alan Ladd than as himself.

Now, in the line of duty, he was beginning to swelter. Surreptitiously he loosened the coat, tilted back the hat. His editor had given him two assignments in this area. The first, at Rizmak, a small township twenty miles below Tophar, concerned a British sergeant's alleged rape of an Indian typist in the local whisky distillery. The case had received no publicity elsewhere but *Clarion India* decreed it must be brought into the open for the world to judge. Gupta had arrived in Rizmak from his Old Delhi office, his notebook already filled with suitable headlines and phrases . . . 'Sex-crazed British sergeant deflowers Indian virgin . . .', 'her moans heard above whine of distillery engines' . . . 'India demands corporal punishment for bestial sergeant . . .'

But the story had proved a damp squib. The wretched girl

90

had only made the rape allegation because the works manager
had caught them in the act. The offending N.C.O. had not only
agreed to marry the girl but admitted it was by no means the
first time he had entered her office window to enjoy the girl. In
any case, the girl was not full Indian but just a damned British
half-caste. How he hated them! These girls, however dark their
skin, never wanted to be Indian. They always pretended to be
white and United Kingdom to the core. So he had despatched
to *Clarion India* a merciless feature against the half-breed
scandal of India, their sex-lustings and hypocrisy, and the need
for their ultimate expulsion when India became free. 'Only pure
Indian blood will flow when our land is liberated', he had
written, an edict which might become a prophecy.

His second assignment, to cover the Tophar Victory Festival
of Art, was, he had already decided, an insult to his power-house
brain. His editor had shrilled : "The British are at it again in
Tophar . . . now the war is over they are playin' German an'
Italian music an' actin' in their moral Coward plays . . .' Gupta's
job was not to report facts—but condemn attitudes.

Clarion India held no political allegiance to Congress, Com-
munist or any other party—it was simply 'anti-British'. At two
annas a yellow-pulp copy, it had a circulation of several
thousands among the English-speaking clerks of Central India,
drawing its readership from the military headquarters, civil
service offices, factories, business houses, shops and public vehicle
depots. Edited by a lawyer, struck off the rolls for improper
conduct in 1938, *Clarion India* relied for much of its circulation
upon readers' letters, transporting their senders into paroxysms
of joy at seeing their names in print. The articles were vitriolic,
abusive, with headlines devised with true eastern ingenuity.
Dewan Gupta loved to play upon words fulsomely. Among his
latest gems were 'Birth-Control—British Interfere With Indian
Wives' and 'India's Famine Ignored—Rice Thrown at British
Wedding'.

Advertisements, obtained mainly through editorial blackmail,
were almost all medical in *Clarion India*. Hormone stimulation,
preservation of youth and a 'second wind to your sex-life' domin-

ated the columns, while black-edged, boxed notices on the back page promised readers 'peace of mind' from money-lenders at fifteen per cent.

Dewan Gupta had no faith in the Tophar Victory celebrations as a vehicle for his journalese. No Indians would be taking part, so the 'oppression' angle was out. It promised nothing beyond just another knock at British tradition and was made more difficult for Gupta now the war was over. No longer could he rely on his regular standby approach, the harrowing contrast between front-line Indian soldiers dying in the smoke of battle while chairborne British officers 'lolled, callously indifferent, 'mid cigar smoke in G.H.Q.'.

But now Gupta had sniffed out the germ of a far greater story. Bazaar whisperings as he passed through, toiling on his way up to the Mall, had caused him to buy *The Himalayan Bugle*. His professional disdain for Moplah's front-page story had suddenly switched to vicious jealousy . . . here was a better 'scoop' than the Tophar Festival . . . it was, as Alan Ladd would have said from the side of his mouth, 'the berries'. Questions in the go-downs had revealed to Gupta that the arch-villain was a Colonel Eddgerley-Watkyn-Reed . . .

Dewan Gupta straightened his fedora. So the British were intimidating Indian clerks over a cricket match . . . no propaganda was better suited to his purpose. He strode down the slope to Army Headquarters, crumpling the *Bugle* in his pocket.

At the main gate an old chowkidar regarded Gupta balefully. He hated the man's trilby and mackintosh as much as he hated his own army issue of red turban, khaki smock and puttees for his bare legs. He was suspicious of all Indians in western dress.

"Pass," he splashed, toothlessly.

"Thanks, I will," said Gupta going straight by him.

"Pass!" yelled the chowkidar excitedly, his skinny hand clawing Gupta's epauletted shoulder.

"I have passed." No security guard could check Alan Ladd.

"Pass! Show to me your pass!" The ancient was now screeching as he padded excitedly along beside Gupta.

"The war is finished now," countered the reporter. But he stopped. The old man's yells might bring out more guards.

"Pass!" Why, thought the chowkidar, was it always the Indians who were so difficult? The British always showed their passes unasked—even on their way *out*!

With a sigh, Gupta produced a white canvas folder and flipped it open at his photograph. Obliterating his left ear was a rubber-stamped impression: " Clarion India'—Accreditated War Correspondent". Although he could not read, the chow-kidar knew the pass was wrong. The rubber stamp and the photograph, even to reproducing the fedora and half-raised collar of the trench-coat, were correct—but the cover was the wrong colour.

"Red passes only," said HQ's guardian stubbornly.

"But this is new white pass for peace," said Gupta cunningly.

Nonplussed, the chowkidar resorted to the time-honoured Indian custom of solving any impasse . . . he began again.

"Pass," he said.

"Will this," said Gupta, flashing a ten-rupee note, "make my pass red?"

The chowkidar grunted. The war was over. Soon, they said in the bazaar, the British would be gone and his job with them. From inside his wrinkled smock he drew out his own pass.

"Ten more rupees," he lisped, "and you can have mine."

Gupta snatched it eagerly. Just transfer his own photograph, erase the man's thumb-print and insert his own signature and this pass would give him access to every HQ in India. Well satisfied, he gave the man twenty rupees.

"But how will you get in without it?" he asked.

The chowkidar smiled vacantly, but his eyes had a magpie look.

"The British gave me that pass in 1939 . . . but who do I show it to . . . myself?"

As Gupta entered the main door he had to admit a certain grudging admiration for the Raj. They actually won wars by leaving their military installations to be guarded by the lowest-paid, senile custodians to whom even generals must show their passes. Yet this old dotard was beholden to no one to show his own. Gupta could not fathom the British mind. Cricket seemed the only really serious aspect of their way of life.

The Tophar Festival had left HQ seemingly deserted. Gupta wandered along several empty corridors, up hollow-sounding staircases, studying the swinging signboards. HQ used the Regency coaching inn system to identify its various offices. Then one caught his attention. 'Telephone Exchange—Keep Out!'

Gupta knew Alan Ladd would do no such thing. The phone room was the hub of HQ, the centre of this military maze. With Hollywood stealth he eased open the door . . .

Private Nancy Evans, her bush-shirt undone to the waist, the phone mouthpiece rising like a black orchid from her matching lace brassiere, was munching a sandwich. Her headphones, undulating as she ate, prevented her hearing Gupta.

"Smile, please," he shouted.

She swung round on her swivel chair . . . a little camera clicked in Gupta's hand.

"Aah!" she gasped and, turning away, she hastily tried to button herself up, but the mouthpiece became hopelessly caught up in the khaki drill. "How darah you come a-burstin' in heah! 'Tis forbidden to all ranks except telephone engineerahs. And they only when 'Out of Ordah' sign is hung up outside which is often as this is most ancient-fangled instrument . . ."

"Gupta," he announced casually, "*Clarion India*."

"Private Evans," she replied, "havin' tiffin."

She stared at him uncomprehendingly as he slipped the camera back into his deep pocket.

"Is that a camerah? Hey, you took snapshot of me . . . I was all undone! You rottah . . . dirty peepin' John Thomas, you are . . ."

"I've got a beautiful likeness of you, Private Evans," said Gupta, chuckling, "showing your underwear, improperly dressed in the King's woman's uniform . . . on duty, too!"

" 'Tis hot in heah . . . if I turn on fan, I cannot heah phone . . . what you do want my photo for?"

"I am a reporter . . . but that picture will not be used in my paper if you do as I want . . ."

"I am not that sort of girl," she shrilled agitatedly. "I am engaged to British officah who won't half play old Harry an' kill you with his bare fists . . . I will not be raped in the phone room . . . 'tis out of bounds anyway . . ."

"Rape is not my intention," said Alan Ladd with a curt laugh. "Just talk, sister . . . what do you know about this clerks' cricket match?"

"Oh, that . . ." The dawning relief brought a weak smile to her dusky face. She swallowed some tough mutton and cleared her throat. Alan Ladd had to admit she was a good-looker, a bit lean perhaps, but well developed in the right places. If she didn't open her mouth she could pass for Spanish . . . many Anglo-Indian girl had worked that marriage background trick on stupid British soldiers. The buzzer throbbed and she said: "Headquartahs, Tophar . . . Scrap Metal Directorate? . . . I am puttin' you through . . ."

"You must know facts about cricket match," she told Gupta. "You have the *Bugle* there, stickin' from your mac pocket. The clerks challenged us . . ."

"Us? You are a member of Tophar Crusaders?"

"A supportah," she conceded. "I am, aftah all, British . . ."

Gupta's patience broke.

"You are a half-chat," he sneered. "Don't give me that 'British' hokum. You're the result of a sad, messy union between two races completely unsuited for such a blood fusion. My paper is full of such stories . . ."

Nancy half-rose from her chair with a scream of rage, her father's rich Welsh blood boiling above her half-caste mother's frail Muslim contribution.

"You dare to say my mothah an' fathah were messily united," she stormed. "Get out before I phone for military police . . ."

"You do that," warned Gupta, "and my paper will publish this picture, the semi-naked girl the British employ at their switchboard . . ."

Nancy shivered. To be hauled before Senior-Commander

Hazel Short for such an offence would mean disgrace, court-martial and such *scandell*! Her purple nails pulled at her red mouth, smearing the lipstick . . .

"You would not darah publish that . . . oh, buggah, buggah, I see from your face you would, an' enjoy it. Me a defenceless girl, not given to careless talk . . ."

"Look, kid." Alan Ladd was, after all, human. "Just tell me what you know about this cricket match and I'll not reveal my source of information—or publish your picture . . ."

"Promise?"

"On the old scouts' honour . . ."

"I see . . . howevah, I would like six postcards of that snap for my personal album . . . I have my officah friend . . ."

"That is a bargain."

"You are a swine, man, really." She sighed resignedly. " 'Tis, of course, blackmail . . ."

"A ruse by any other name," he said quietly.

So Nancy talked.

"All I know is Tophar Crusadahs' committee turned down the clerks' offah of cricket match, last night. It was not given out official, but the news leaked. Colonel Eddgerley-Watkyn-Reed thought the *Bugle* had been told by Captain Mott . . ."

"Captain Mott." Gupta noted down the name.

"Two 't's'," said Nancy over her shoulder.

"That is my shorthand," said Gupta loftily.

"But I heard Captain Mott deny he was culprit . . ."

"Heard? Ah, over the telephone. Ear-drums can be instruments of intrigue. You must have listened to many military secrets here . . ."

"Oh, damn an' blast you, you tricked me into sayin' that. Well, Captain Mott thought the bearah at the Queen's Club, Akkar Singh, might have ovah-heard . . ." Gupta wrote the details painstakingly.

"Am I goin' too fast for your shorthand?" she asked.

"Of course not," he snapped, glad of the pause.

"The judge rang the colonel about *The Bugle* . . ."

"What judge?"

"Justice Trevelhayes . . . he is retirahed now . . . is also cricket president in Tophar . . . an' Pageant Mastah . . . I am to be Nell Gwyn . . ."

"I remember that judge in Delhi." Gupta frowned. "He was a real hanging type. I recall his most vicious sentences upon my poor brother Indians . . . one of death on an innocent Punjabi wrestler who killed a mere six men in self-defence. So the judge is involved in the cricket, is he?"

"Well, he advised the colonel to sue the editah for damages . . ."

"That," said Gupta, "has my approval. What is cricket position now?"

"The clerks are meetin' in their canteen." She looked at her watch. "At 12 o'clock—ten minutes' time . . ."

"Ah, I'll attend," said Gupta. "There I will learn more."

"Remembah your promise," begged Nancy, "no names, no packet drill . . . no photo in the papah?"

"My word is my bond and I am tied by it," said Gupta, raising his hat. "And you, likewise, Private Evans, you will not tell a soul I have been here?"

"I am no loony," she snapped. " 'Tis out of bounds . . . if anyone knew you'd been in heah, I'd be for high-jump on my earah."

"Where is the canteen?"

"Across the squarah by the officahs' tennis courts, one floorah down . . . don't forget your promise, man."

"A clear conscience fears no accusation."

He opened the door stealthily.

"If anyone sees you leavin' heah," whispered Nancy, "you are telephone engineerah come about my loose socket . . ."

She listened to his footsteps recede up the corridor, then buried her face in her hands, sobbing loudly. A buzz throbbed the switchboard and she checked herself with a sniff as she identified GHQ into the mouthpiece.

"Disciplinary Action Directorate, please," said a sinister voice.

She gasped as she plugged in, sitting in a petrified silence until the call finished and she cleared the line. Then, with a hard swallow of resolution, she inserted another plug.

"British Military Hospital? Majah Grahame, please . . . oh, this is GHQ speakin' . . . yes, yes, of course, I am most urgent case . . ."

She knew she should not call Jack at the hospital . . . personal calls were frowned on . . . priority must be given to emergencies . . . but she just had to talk to him.

Jack Grahame she had met at a local dance a mere four days ago . . . an Australian Army doctah, so *terribelly* fresh an' cheeky an' *such* a quick workah . . . my word, she had an *awfell* time keepin' his hands at bay. But he had taken her to the cinema to see *Life and Death of Colonel Blimp* an' they'd been dancin' . . . always he was suggestin' 'you-know-what', of course . . . but she was still most pure girl.

But like thousands of Anglo-Indian girls she was now deliberating whether she was wise to put him off any longer. With the war over, these lovely British men would soon be leaving . . . who would be left to marry her? She knew the stigma the resident British put on officers marrying half-caste girls . . . but this did not seem to worry these new-type fellows who had landed in India for the war and did not give a damn what the old-time British thought. Jack was like that—a propah devil-may-care, he an' his daft tram song.

"Hullo, who's that?"

"Jack? It's Nancy . . ."

"You mustn't ring me here, babe . . ." Grahame's voice sank to a whisper. "Hospital regs, yer know. You'll get me shot . . . you must pretend to be a mother in labour . . . army issue, o' course . . ."

"I must see you most urgent, Jack. I am in most *terribell troubell* . . ."

"Now you can't blame me for that, can yer? Have you been unfaithful to me?"

"Oh, Jack!" It was a shaky, woebegone laugh. "You are most *awfell* chap. Just sex-mad . . ."

"Steady, someone might be listenin' . . ."

"If they do, Jack, you should report them . . . 'tis a military exchange at the hospital . . . like heah. But, listen, I have most *dreadfell* problem regardin' the cricket match . . ."

His laughter echoed tinnily in her headphones.

"Don't play then, Nancy. You might get a ball in the . . ."

"*I'm* not playin', fool-man that you are. But I have got involved with a most beast of a newspapah man called Gupta . . . 'tis blackmail . . ."

"Is that true? Alright, chick, see yer to-night . . . Regency Café, 'bout six-thirty . . . you can weep on me shoulder . . . only not in uniform, for the love o' Pete . . . wear that blue dress . . ."

"With buttons all way down front . . . I know . . ."

His chuckle gave her a new confidence.

"*Punch me in the presence of the passenjares,*" she carolled.

"I might jus' do that," he laughed. "See yer later. 'Bye."

Now, Mr. Damn Gupta, she thought as she jerked out the plug, I have got British Army on my side . . .

Gupta was in no hurry to reach the clerks' canteen. The meeting must begin before he made his appearance. The audience must be rapt in attentive silence when he made his entrance . . . only then could the full Alan Ladd impact be made. With still five minutes to go he was stopped short by the sight of a swinging sign. It hung tipsily, out of true, borne down by the name 'Colonel Eddgerley-Watkyn-Reed, Veterinary Directorate'.

This, gloated Gupta, was indeed a turn-up for the reporter's notebook. Taking a deep breath, he muttered: "When in motion, to press on is easy"—and kicked open the door.

The colonel looked up from his desk to see a fawn-coated Indian, hands in pockets and his eyebrows lost under a huge hat.

"Salaam," muttered the colonel uneasily.

"Colonel Eddgerley-Watkyn-Reed?" said Gupta, still remaining framed in the door.

"Atchcha."

"Gupta, *Clarion India.*" He twisted his lips as he spoke. "I wanna story from you."

"A story? Well, I'm not really in the mood . . . however, there was this man who thought a jeep was a female . . ."

"I am a reporter." Gupta had moved in now and sat on the edge of the colonel's desk, revealing the black clocks on his yellow socks. "Now, colonel, give me the low-down on this clerks' cricket challenge."

"Oh, you're the newspapers, are yer? Ah, well, yer've come to the wrong office . . . malum? You must go through proper channels . . ."

"Knowledge is the wing whereby we fly to heaven." Gupta could turn from Alan Ladd to philosopher at will. "Truth is the rock large enough for all to stand upon."

"I've no intention of standin' on any rocks," snapped the colonel. "Take yer backside off me desk an' jaldi jao, badmush!"

"Is that, colonel," Gupta hoped he infused a death knell tone, "your last word?"

"To you it is . . . but I shall have a lot to say to whoever let yer in here . . . Baker-Stewart, at the double, please!"

The major, surprised at this sudden direct call to action instead of via the ambling chauprassi, bounded in from the adjoining office, adjusting his cap.

"A reporter," thundered the colonel, pointing at the now less-confident Gupta. "Broke into me office . . . trespassin' . . . breach of regulations . . ."

"Right, sir! Here you . . . out!" Baker-Stewart advanced threateningly.

Gupta backed away.

"The hasty angler loses the fish," he cautioned.

"I'll bloody soon fish you . . ."

"He's come about the cricket match, Stewy . . ."

"Then he's about to be hit for six." Baker-Stewart made to grab the Alan Ladd lapels, but Gupta twisted out of reach.

"Lay a hand on me," he warned, "and I'll publish and be damned. Can't you see the headlines in *Clarion India*? 'British major assaults Indian reporter in effort to prevent bein' exposed . . .'"

Baker-Stewart dropped his arms hurriedly.

"You little rat, we've nothing to say . . ."

"Observation is the best teacher," said the relieved Gupta. "You have rejected the poor clerks' request for a game of cricket . . ."

"We have not," expostulated the colonel. "They can play cricket if they want to—outside office hours, of course. It's just that we, the Tophar Crusaders, cannot accommodate them ourselves."

"Never walk one way and look another, colonel," said Gupta. "You feel they are not good enough for you . . ."

"I did not say that! We haven't got enough playin' members left . . . now the war's over, we've lost most of our cricketers . . . been posted to different clubs . . . er, units . . ."

"Baloony, wise guy," said Gupta, "you're denying them their right to play at Glenbourn . . ."

"How dare you!" The colonel went white and stood trembling against his desk.

"Ah, I have struck oil, have I not?" Gupta laughed chestily. "Every man is the architect of his own fortune. Who looks not before him, finds himself behind . . ."

"I'll sue you!" roared the colonel, shaking all over. "Be God, I will . . . !"

"Just as the judge advised you to sue *The Himalayan Bugle* . . ."

"The judge?" gasped the colonel.

"The trick cycle rider who recently collected false damages from our good American friends. I personally covered that story for my papers. Perjury was committed by a British lawman . . ."

"Look," muttered Baker-Stewart, "did the judge himself tell you he advised us to—er—sue the editor of that paper?"

"We journalists never divulge our sources of information . . ."

"I've heard enough," stormed the colonel. "Call the guard, Major Baker-Stewart!"

"I have seen him at the gate," said Gupta contemptuously, "a poor old brother Indian who you would place there alone to face any attack on this fortress. He would not harm me as I would not harm him."

He swaggered into the corridor, then turned and pointed a quivering brown finger.

"Truth is the hidden gem we all should dig for," he pronounced. "And you two officers have dug your own graves. My paper shall publish and all Delhi will know how you snobs snubbed the clerks!"

With a deft movement, the little camera was before his squinting eye. As the shutter clicked, the colonel and major were caught in ju-jitsu postures, crouching menacingly. Then, seeing a brass paperweight in Baker-Stewart's hand, Gupta scuttled down the corridor. The missile reduced the 'Timber Department' sign opposite to splinters.

"A full toss, Stewy," wailed the colonel, "you're off yer length . . ."

"My God," breathed the major, "he's got a photograph of us too . . ."

"We'll look like a couple of Australian slips appealin'," moaned the colonel. "I lost me rag, then, I'll admit . . ."

"How the hell did he know about the judge's damn fool advice?"

"This time," thundered the colonel, "Mott has gone too far . . ."

Chapter Eleven

THE POWER OF THE PRESS

GUPTA heard the tirade of ferocious argument from the canteen long before he reached the door. He adjusted his fedora, re-belted his trenchcoat. A first impression of dominating efficiency was vital, making for complete capitulation of his victims—as he had already proved with the colonel, the major and the half-chat girl.

Gupta had covered many anti-British stories but never before from within a military HQ. This was his greatest chance yet. As much as he hated the Raj, he hoped his name would soon be coming off the London printing presses which he visualised as undulating behind glass windows all along a tram-lined Fleet Street.

Within the canteen Shrinivassen was trying to address the howling mob. Already Torkham Wazir and, later, Jalim Singh had walked out in disgust at the clerks' failure to force the British to play the match.

"Brothers!" cried Shrinivassen, "I repeat, the Crusaders have not officially refused to play. 'Tis all hearsaying that you are taking for granted. We can pass no judgement or opinion till Colonel Eddgerley-Watkyn-Reed has answered our challenge officially."

"Burn his effigy as a steak!" shouted Narna Bag.

"Swines they are," sobbed Swarmi, all managerial dreams now dust. "They are avoiding humility with cowardice."

"Vhere is Mookerjee?" cried Futti Pant. "Ve vant his wersion of this wery windictive British attitude in turnin' our challenge down."

"They have not done so, official," insisted Shrinivassen. "That newspaper distorted the degree of disruption . . ."

"It is in print that we have been kicked in teeth," snarled Bokaneer, "that is in black and white, an indelible fact."

"We must not make hasty decision," exclaimed Shrinivassen. "The British, for all their frail failings, have honour staked in their hearts . . ."

He was drowned by shouts of "Double-dealin' Catholic" . . . "Warbonded Slave of Imperialism" . . . "Catspaw in Milk of Raj" . . .

"Mookerjee! Mookerjee!" they chanted, banging their tiffin carriers.

"I have just seen Mookerjee," cried Kazi Mohammed, who had just arrived. "He was chasin' a Hindu boy in the bazaar . . . offerin' him rupees." He laughed loudly. "Mookerjee has no time for cricket with his loins so disturbed . . ."

" 'Tis a foul lie!" shouted Futti Pant. "Mookerjee has not got the homopathetic wice. He is wery voman-conscious, a reg'lah ladies' manhandlah . . ."

But Swarmi's big face had split into a dreadful smile.

"This is news indeed, Kazi Mohammed . . . so much for the reliable Mookerjee. We cannot wait till he has finished his pleasures. As manager I shall start the meeting. The agenda-item next before us is what to do now the British have kicked us in teeth . . ."

As he spoke he became aware of the trench-coated figure beside him. The cries from the floor faded, the anger subsided and there was a silence in the canteen. Dewan Gupta pushed back his fedora with thumb and forefinger, smiled at the frowning Swarmi and agitated Shrinivassen.

"Gentlemen," he said, "to cool a passion, take a long walk."

Several hypnotised clerks at once made for the door.

"No, no, that was mere figure of speech." The trenchcoat was loosened, a cigarette lit from a shoe-struck match. "I guess you all wonder who I am. Well, first and foremost, I am your friend. I know your problem with the dacoit British and their robbery of your cricket rights at Glenbourn. Who am I, you ask, who comes as wiseacre and philosopher? I answer with humble pride. I am Dewan Gupta . . . my newspaper . . . *Clarion India*!"

"A reporter from Old Delhi!" cried Swarmi. "Our cause is now world-wide!"

Tumult broke out, cheer followed cheer. Gupta smiled modestly, his hands dug deep in his pockets. Then he withdrew a hand—and was obeyed by an instant hush.

"I come here, not only as a celebrated scribe whose pen is dipped to right wrongs, but as an ambassador of justice. *Clarion India* awaits my copy on your sad case. The presses have been held, the front page is blank till you decide what you are going to do to the British . . ."

A hoarse roar went up.

"I am Shrinivassen," said the harassed Madrassi. "I feel you are blowing up balloon-wise this hot air business out of all proportion . . ."

"You do?" rasped Gupta, irritated that a man still remained unconquered by his personality. "Well, I have just seen Colonel Eddgerley-Watkyn-Reed . . ."

The awed gasp gratified Gupta.

"Yes, I have confronted your mortal enemy, face to face, in his office," cried the intrepid Alan Ladd. "Both he and his major attacked me but, as you see, I am unscathed . . . and I left them both very frightened guys."

Shrinivassen clutched his head in despair as the clerks rose in tumult. Gupta savoured the applause, then quelled it with his hand.

"No lock will hold against the keys of truth. The British see in your simple request to play them at cricket a plot to annex Glenbourn from them . . ."

"Glenbourn *is* ours!" roared Bokaneer.

"There is no darkness as deep as the British cave-man mind," said Gupta. "We are workers, humble and poorly-paid workers, for our beloved India." He knuckled some fedora-dripped sweat from his eye and Swarmi gave a great cry of despair, hunching his head in his fat arms. "I shall use my newspaper as the bees do a flower, to find the sweetness of life. I shall find out why the British refused your cricket challenge . . . the *real* reason, not their trumped-up excuse that they have insufficient players . . ."

"They have said *that*?" asked Shrinivassen. "Ah, that does put a different complexion on face value of *Bugle* story . . ."

"I shall now take statements from you individually," said Gupta, taking Mookerjee's vacant chair.

"Me first!" screamed Futti Pant. "My name in the news-papahs will comfort my fathah in Poonah. He is confined to his charpoy again by his leg . . ."

"Patience is a monument," said Gupta, opening his notebook. "Perseverance overcomes all obstacles. So line up in orderly Indian file and tell me your stories of British persecution. Your names will be in *Clarion India*, the day after tomorrow, on sale at bookshops, two annas. If you have tears, prepare to shed them now . . ."

Gupta sat till four that afternoon, interviewing each clerk, noting down his venom against the British. Shrinivassen be-seeched him to moderate the wild accusations, but Gupta was in charge. After each interview he ordered the clerk back to his office.

"You must not prejudice your cause by absenteeism," he warned them. "Be blameless in your strict observance of the rules the British have made to enslave you. Uncertainty walks on both sides of us."

Sustained by cups of tea supplied by the now devoted Swarmi, Gupta filled his notebook with copious data. But Shrinivassen would not return to his office. He hovered like a mother hen, which Gupta found irksome. He had won over all the other clerks. Swarmi, now a mountainous jelly of loyalty, extolled him, but Shrinivassen, a professed Christian with British sympathies, had not capitulated. Kept on about cricket, which Gupta only understood superficially, and would not enter in the true spirit of British-bashing . . .

Gupta yawned and looked up. Only one frail little clerk remained, twisting his dhoti round his thin legs in misery.

"Name?"

"R. K. Desai." The little man's thick glasses accentuated the fright in his eyes. "I work in Field Cashier Department. I have been appointed scorer for this non-existent cricket match."

"Disappointment dogs us all. Tell me your story, Desai."

Desai was a Jain who held all life sacred. He never lit candles lest a moth be devoured. Wearing a scarf over his mouth for fear of swallowing insects, he had made the Jain pilgrimage to Mount Abu in the Aravali Hills as a Svetambara—a wearer of white—rather than the more advanced Digambaras, meaning 'sky clad' and therefore naked. Desai was a shy man. And now, faced with this ruthless inquisitor, he was obliged by his beliefs to tell the truth.

"It is Captain Mott who works in Army Education which adjoins my office . . ." he began.

"Mott?" Gupta's eyes rolled up to the clerk crouching by the table. "The self-same Mott who is blamed for fifth column activity by the British?"

"Yes, that is the gentleman, sir. But he is well-meaning, he likes us, has been to my humble home . . ."

Gupta's pencil snapped as he rose threateningly.

"If we had Ku-Klux-Klan in India, Desai, you would be burned to death alive. You must not fraternise with Mott. He has already shown his Achilles tendency by selling British secrets in the bazaar. He can be double-agent, pumping you . . ."

"What can Captain Mott pump from me?" stuttered Desai. "He is my friend and he wants cricket to take place in fraternal happiness. Captain Mott is innocent of these charges, sir. Akkar Singh was the conveyor of the secret British decision . . ."

"He is the bearer at the Queen's Club," interposed Shrinivas-sen. "It is true he relayed the British decision . . . he intended to help us, the good fellow, but his methods, to say the leastways of them, are somewhat conniving and conspiratorial."

'I'll be the judge of that," said Gupta harshly. "Now, Desai, the background of this traitor, Mott . . ."

"I only know what he has told me of his past." Desai was openly weeping now. "He was schooled at Winn-chester and

London and became teacher to British peasant boys at a bridge called Wey. He taught them English . . ."

"So," cried Gupta in triumph, "the children in England are so ignorant that they do not know their own tongue! My paper will print in bold type such a calamitous state of affairs."

"Captain Mott is a socialist," cried Desai, "who believes all men are brothers under the skin. His party is now in power in England. They say all men should have equal opportunity even at Lord's, their cricket recreation centre . . ."

"They call it Lord's," sighed Gupta, "and yet this Mott, a mere captain, expects to deprive the top-dogs of their stranglehold of peerage-power? He should study closer the British here in India with their blue bloody-mindedness . . ."

"I have tried to help him understand India . . ."

"Has he raped your wife?"

"I am not married!" Desai trembled with shock. "Being bachelor, mathematics are my bed, my wife and my progeny . . ."

"So you conceive by figures, little one," said Gupta loftily. "India needs sons, not sums. A big population is propaganda for food and aid from the British. It also helps newspaper circulations. How can we fight battles for India if men such as you remain unmarried and childless?"

"I am not fighting stock," moaned Desai. "Diligence alone is good patrimony."

Gupta flinched. He should have said that.

"Great talkers are not great doers," he cried, banging the table. "Little strokes fell great oaks. If you covert praise you do not deserve it."

"Such wisdomatic words!" Swarmi was lost in admiration.

"I am no cricketer," wailed Desai, now at breaking point. "I am a Jain. I want no violence, nothing must be hurt . . ."

"Go, Desai!" Gupta used his deepest voice. "Ponder on the portent of my words. Cricket is most vital to the British way of life. They allow Australians to play it, West Indians too—even our princes—but when you clerks go, cricket-cap in hand, requesting a game, they spurn you. The public must be told. I am the Press . . . my words will go winging way beyond India.

This Tophar tragedy will echo from Tipperary to Farewell Leicester Square . . ."

Desai scampered away in mortal terror.

"Mr. Gupta," panted Swarmi, "you are not only great writer but a sage of the universe . . ."

" 'Tis all an over-balance of true perspective," said Shrinivassen heatedly. "You are over-enlarging just a small cricket match . . ."

He retreated to the far corner of the canteen, lost in troubled thought.

Gupta was tired of the man. Thrusting his notebook in his pocket, he reset the fedora at the right angle. Throughout the meeting he had been careful not to mention the judge's advice to the colonel to sue Moplah. That, he hoped, the British would implement. But he did not want these oafish clerks warning his journalistic rival. Once back in Delhi, however, he could reveal that choice item in *Clarion India*.

"Where do I find Captain Mott?" he asked.

"You will interview *him*!" Swarmi's eyes rolled under his sweat-filled eyebrows.

"I will rush headstrong into the enemy camp again," said Gupta easily. Mott, an Indian-lover, would present no problem to him.

"He will be at the Queen's Club this evening," said Swarmi, "but Indians are not allowed there . . ."

"The bearer, Akkar Singh, he will be in attendance, will he not?"

"Oh, the deviosity of newspapermen!" cried Swarmi delightedly. "Yes, he is our secret agent . . . he will assist you . . ."

Gupta paused at the door.

"Tell no one my plans," he ordered, "especially Moplah of *The Bugle* . . ."

"I am," whispered Swarmi, "golden treasury of silence."

"Remember," said Gupta, "the British can use this cricket like a drug against you, just as they did opium in the Chinese wars . . . we must be alert with our own elements of surprise."

With a careless wave of the hand, he strode up the slope.

Swarmi clasped his hands, gazing after him, speechless with admiration.

"Was that Dewan Gupta?" rattled the voice of Mookerjee. Swarmi heaved himself round.

"Yes, Mookerjee—and, oh my, what a brain! Full of grey-matter gumption. You think you have word powers but you are child's play in arms to his profound profundities . . . he can move mountains . . ."

"He has certainly moved you, fat one," snapped Mookerjee, "pullin' his will-power over your eyes. I know Gupta by disrepute—he's a vagabond o' verbiage. In Delhi 'tis well known his aim is not truly for India but for self-enrichification. As umpire, I shall see he keeps off our cricket grass."

"I kept saying he was over-emphasising its importance," said Shrinivassen as he joined them. "He is just an aggravating agitator."

"He is genius!" Swarmi swelled with indignation. "While you were boy-chasing in the bazaar, Mookerjee, he was writing our story for newspapers!"

"Boy chasin'?" Mookerjee was withering. "That lad was Krischa, houseboy to American missionary, Weltzer memsahib. I enlisted his aid to make her take up our case. She has agreed to attack the British with her American god . . . the U.S.A. is now on our side!"

Swarmi gulped, suppressing admiration. Shrinivassen shook his head sadly.

"All so exploded up far beyond real motive," he sighed.

"Where is Gupta off to now?" demanded Mookerjee.

"To see Captain Mott and Akkar Singh," said Swarmi sullenly.

"I mus' telephone," said Mookerjee urgently. "If you covert your job as manager, Swarmi, don't let Gupta set foot in the handlin' o' our affairs. His mudlark-slingin' always boomerangs back to the hand that fed it. Moplah is our press representative —not axe-grindin' Gupta!"

Meanwhile, at the main gate, Dewan Gupta was being beseiged by eight old chowkidars all wanting to sell him their passes . . .

Chapter Twelve

AMERICA INTERVENES

COLONEL EDDGERLEY-WATKYN-REED was surrounded by his committee in their exclusive corner of the Queen's Club. No official rule legalised this holding. The alcove had been wordlessly annexed at the outbreak of war and was now as sacred to the Crusaders as Glenbourn itself.

While all other club wall-space was hung with photographs of Grand Theatre productions, the colonel's nook contained the six framed Crusader teams from 1940 to 1945. At a casual glance they all appeared reproductions from the same negative. Eight of the team had remained the same throughout the war and the colonel, centred as captain, arms folded over a tightly-buttoned Crusader blazer, grouped his men by seniority. This patterned the photographs as duplicates of each other—even to Barkside-Twist's inevitable profile, Folly's toothy smile and Heaviside's R.A.F. handlebar moustache.

Only the two cross-legged figures on the grass in front of the senior boots had changed constantly. Three had been later killed in action, two were prisoners of war and one posted away in disgrace for being drunk in charge of a cricket bat. In the current group Mott and Hacker were the 'babes', their broad grins seeming to deride the dignity above them.

Had the many proposed postings of these officers been effected during the war, the faces might have been more varied. But if Delhi dared demand a Tophar cricketer, actor or musician for service elsewhere, the inevitable Indian bush telegraph worked to British advantage. The rumour would reach the hills just in time for the officer in question to change his job. By the time the official order arrived in writing he no longer held the post

111

applicable to the transfer . . . so the memo would be returned marked 'Already posted and no other officer of required rank available'.

Delhi HQ eventually grew tired of this deployment game and went further afield—to Simla, Bangalore, Karachi and Calcutta where no Tophar guile existed. And having no power to commission its own officers, Delhi drew on field regiments, so angry active service officers anxious to have a 'crack at the enemy' found themselves in charge of remote departments hundreds of miles from the front line while mild administrative types were rushed from fan-stirred offices into foxholes and gun emplacements, their fingers in their ears. As the war had dragged on, Delhi discovered that these 'admin wallahs' on active service caused great satisfaction to the enemy. So, after two years of much confusion, base HQ officers were left alone to continue their cricket and theatricals—the safest role for them if the war was to be won.

The colonel had had a trying day. Now surrounded by Nuppy, Stewy, Twisty, Whiffy and, of course, Mott, he felt a shade more secure from being hounded by clerks. Akkar Singh murmured his 'Salaam, sahib' as he placed drinks on the table.

"Courtney and McBurn sahibs send compliments and wish to join you, colonel . . ."

"Shabash, Akkar Singh . . . permission granted . . . bolo them over."

In accordance with this strict Crusader procedure, the bearer beckoned to the two grizzled majors by the bar. McBurn strode over at once, a precise Scot, short, dapper, with greying hair and moustache.

"Ma respects, sur," he said, raising his glass.

The colonel acknowledged the formality in silence, merely lifting glass and eyebrow together. Good bat, old Mac, a nervous starter but sound in the late middle order. Trouble with him was his love of King's Regulations. Nothing he relished more than a brother officer in trouble over regimental discipline. The colonel remembered McBurn's type at his Officers' Training Unit in India during the First World War . . . the instructor's

toady who magnified other cadets' errors with a hissing intake
of breath, not only designed to emphasise the howler but also
to impress with his own efficiency in spotting it. It was this sort
of behaviour which caused McBurn to be tactfully voted off the
Crusaders' committee. Even the revolutionary Mott was a better
choice—at least he knew more about cricket.

Major Courtney carried a game leg, the result of a Christmas
Eve shooting accident on a Bombay rifle range in 1939. In
peace-time the injury would have retired him on pension, but
the war had allowed him to limp on in uniform. Now lost in a
backwater of the 'Map Disposal Unit', he occasionally dispensed
surveys to training battalions who would later complain that the
Jumna, the Ganges or the Sutlej rivers had changed course by
as much as six miles since some long-dead engineer last plotted
those maps on horseback in 1890. Courtney had been a slashing
off-side batsman with the Bombay Oddfellows and now, in his
early fifties, he resented his locked right knee-cap. Good umpire
though he was, he became angry in drink—which was now his
nightly state.

He lowered himself into a chair, his leg and stick becoming
a hurdle for Akkar Singh, and groped in his lumpy bush-shirt
pocket for one of the many carved pipes he always carried.
To-night he stuffed a likeness of Rasputin with black shag and
lit the monk's unruly crown.

"Sorry to hear aboot this fracas wi' the clerks, Eddgers," said
McBurn gravely. "Most worryin' for ye. Must be somethin' in
Indian Army Orders . . ."

"Shoot the buggers," said Courtney, swilling down a large
neat whisky. "Quai-hai!"

"I say, our glasses are still fully charged, old man," said Nupp-
Jevons. "Really, you do go on apace . . ."

"Leg's playin' up again . . ."

"It does every sundown," said Innes-Whiffen.

"What's that supposed to mean?" growled Courtney. "You
want to drink more yerself—get a bit of weight on, you pious
scout pole! At least you could cast a real shadow then—not just
one over the conversation . . ."

"Order, please!" said the colonel sharply. "I want a pow-wow. I'm not at all happy about this clerks' business. First that strike an' runnin' out of scotch . . ."

"I notice it's back behind the bar now," said Barkside-Twist.

"Yes, strange . . . then that terrible newspaper report . . . an' now, to-day, a reporter from Delhi actually invaded me office . . . took a photer of me an' Stewy . . ."

"*Times of India?*" enquired Nupp-Jevons.

"My foot!" snapped Baker-Stewart. "He was from a rag called *Clarion India* . . . a typical Indian agitator, so I threw him out . . ."

"Only metaphorically," said the colonel hastily. "But this clerks business is gettin' us into very deep water. How did they find out we were goin' to turn 'em down before I'd written the official letter?"

"Spy somewhere," said Courtney. "Has Mott been blackin' his face with burnt cork and sellin' our secrets in the bazaar?"

"Of course not, sir. I didn't utter a word . . ."

"Now, Courty, old man," reproved the colonel, "we've had all this out before. Mott's C.O., dear old Cooty, vouches for him . . ."

"Cooty isn't a cricketer," said Courtney.

"His brother got a blue . . . though admittedly Cambridge," said Barkside-Twist. "We must accept his word."

"Nobody seems to want to accept my word," said Mott wryly.

"Oh, but we do, Mott," said the colonel. "You're a B.A. . . . a man of letters . . ."

"It's a pity his father didn't use one," muttered Courtney.

"Thing is," said Baker-Stewart who was watching the door for Hazel, "how do we get out of this mess?"

"Send all the ruddy clerks on leave," said Courtney. "Give 'em a 'victory' fortnight . . . that 'ud get rid of the illiterate swine . . ."

"They're not illiterate," said Mott stoutly. "Some of 'em are very educated . . . Shakespeare, Milton, Edgar Wallace . . ."

Courtney yelled "Quai-hai!" for Akkar Singh to refill his glass.

"Look, young Mott," he growled, "if we play these clerks, we're givin' ground. I know 'em. This isn't for love of cricket, you know . . ."

"I hate to hear that, Courty," admitted the colonel, "but I'm comin' to the conclusion yer right . . ."

"I know I'm right, Eddgers. These clerks are up to somethin'. Cricket is just an excuse for anti-British propaganda. They're out to make right 'berks' of us . . . I can feel it in my H_2O . . ."

"They're succeedin'," said Innes-Whiffen, "already they've got every Indian in Tophar against us . . ."

"Except Akkar Singh," the colonel reminded him sharply.

"Ah, of course, sir. But these clerks are holdin' meetin's in their canteen like Bastille bastards . . ."

"I say," cried the colonel, "best withdraw that remark, Innes-Whiffen. The French, yer know, they're our allies . . . oh, Petain may not have kept his end up, Laval might have fielded substitute for Hitler, but entente cordiale an' all that . . ."

"I withdraw of course, sir," said Innes-Whiffen promptly. "Shouldn't have lost control. Toujours la politesse . . . damn good folk the French, even if they don't play cricket . . ."

"Spoken like a man!" said the colonel. "Akkar Singh, author a round of drinks. Well said, Whiffey . . ."

"Thank you, Eddgers," said Innes-Whiffen huskily.

"Let that be a lesson to you, Mott," added the colonel.

"Who, me, sir? Oh, yes . . . point taken, sir."

"It's all ruddy fine us sittin' here actin' like gentlemen," snorted Courtney, ringing his empty glass with his pipe stem, "but these blasted wog clerks have got us by the short and curlies . . ."

"We have not yet officially refused," insisted the colonel.

"You mean . . . we might actually play 'em?" Nupp-Jevons was aghast.

"What's the use of prevaricatin'?" said Courtney. "Are you all hopin' for a bloody earthquake, or what?"

"They had one here in the 'thirties," mused the colonel. "Only a minor tremor but I gather it shook up Glenbourn . . . became a bowler's paradise."

He became aware then that his fellow Crusaders were staring in surprise . . . he followed their gaze and saw a tall woman in black sweeping down on their sacrosanct corner.

"Colonel Eddgerley-Watkyn-Reed?" Her voice was challenging, demanding. The Crusaders rose awkwardly, save for Courtney who waved his stick above his head, always his compensatory gesture for being unable to stand in the presence of a lady.

"Yes?" said the colonel faintly. The woman had a foreign twang . . . Oh, no! It couldn't be *another* Australian . . .?

"I come with a message from God . . ."

"Eh . . . oh, have you? . . . Eh, thank yer . . ."

"I am Mrs. Marion Weltzer."

"A Nazi frau," hissed Courtney.

"I belong to AMOTH . . ."

"Is Amos your husband . . .?"

"AMOTH is the American Mission of True Hearts . . . I have a complaint."

"The colonel's actually a vet, me dear," said Courtney.

"May I sit down?"

"If you can . . . I mean . . . certainly, ma'am." The colonel looked round desperately, but Marion had already pulled up a chair and now sat erect as Whistler's mother. Confused, the Crusaders re-seated themselves save for Mott whose chair she had taken. In dragging one from a nearby table, he sprawled over Courtney's leg.

"Aaah!" shouted the major. "Clumsy bast . . . B.A. . . ."

Introductions were forgotten in the consternation.

"Now, ma'am," began the colonel hesitantly, "you wish to consult me. Have you a lame horse?"

"A lame horse?" she looked amazed.

"I am in veterinary, d'yer see? You, I imagine, like a ride . . .?"

"Ah, I get you. You have God's gift for healing dumb animals . . ."

"Only on paper . . ." The colonel coughed in confusion.

Marion leaned forward, her eyes intense. In her quaint old-fashioned way, thought Mott, she's quite a doll.

"Here, in India, colonel," she cried, "you treat poor sick animals with the care that is your duty to your Maker. You mend their broken wings, take thorns from their paws, cosset and sweet-talk them . . . yet you can wound men like Mr. Mookerjee . . ."

There was a faint gargling sound from the Crusaders.

"I have . . . wounded a Mookerjee?" The colonel gaped round at his companions. "I deny it, ma'am. Who is this man who makes accusations of bodily harm?"

"Ah, it is not bodily but spiritual harm, colonel." Marion smiled serenely up into the fan-vaulted ceiling. "Mr. Mookerjee wants his rights to play cricket . . ."

"Mookerjee?" Innes-Whiffen was puzzled. "Must be a Minor Counties type . . ."

"Mr. Mookerjee is a clerk." Marion rhymed it with "work".

"Oh, a clerk, as in 'bark'," said the colonel.

"I see what this means," snapped Baker-Stewart. "It's another phase in the clerks' plot against us."

Akkar Singh, hovering behind a pillar, smiled to himself. Mookerjee, while not a good physical specimen, certainly had brains. Involving this American religious memsahib was indeed a stroke of genius.

"Mr. Mookerjee came to see me this morning," she said, "and on his knees asked American aid for his cricket crusade."

"But Americans dinna play cricket," said McBurn.

"And their ruddy football is a pinch on our rugger," said Courtney. "They hate Columbus at Twickenham."

"Mr. Mookerjee sought me because of my work as a sister of God," Marion went on stridently, and heads were now turning from the adjoining tables. "He needed the help of Heaven so that his devoted clerks could play you at a mere cricket game . . ."

"Cricket, madam," said Nupp-Jevons, "is *never* mere."

"I sure know that. It is a game of virgin whiteness, played by the Lord's men, common to both your peoples. A game wherein you can be, shoulder-to-shoulder, as brothers sporting in God's pure air. They ask to play and you have rejected them. In the name of God in his Heaven, colonel, why have you denied them?"

"Well, we haven't actually . . . nothin' official . . . only, it's jus', well, not done . . ."

"We don't *all* feel that way," began Mott.

"Speak through the chair, Mott," snapped the colonel, "an' I don't grant you permission to speak anyway . . ."

"So you won't play with these sons of God?" cried Marion.

"Shockin' way of expressin' it," said Courtney, "but, no, we won't, madam. They're as cunnin' as monkeys . . ."

"You see," said Nupp-Jevons soothingly, "Kipling said: 'East is east an' West is west, an' never the twain shall meet' . . . we are not, madam, compatible with clerks . . . we belong to different stations . . ."

"Where the 'twains' meet." Mott was not able to resist it and the colonel almost struck him.

"The stations of the cross stand for humanity," said Marion. "When you all kneel at your beds to-night . . ."

"Not with my leg, I don't," said Courtney. "I'd knock the jerry over . . ."

"Can you pray?" she went on unmoved, "without a conscience?"

Mott now forgot flippancies in sheer admiration for this calm, handsome woman. The Holy Grail shone from her frank, wide eyes.

"I agree with Mrs. Weltzer," he said, "it is our duty to play this game . . ."

"Judas!" shouted Baker-Stewart.

"Madam," said Barkside-Twist firmly, "this is no concern of the American Mission of True Hearts. We are not members . . ."

"You can say that again, sir," breathed Marion, "you can say that again!"

"Only don't," said Courtney.

"It is a matter between God and yourselves," she cried. "I am but a small voice in the wilderness. The Lord hath said : 'Ye shall hear the small as well as the great, ye shall not be afraid of the face of man for the judgement is God's, and the cause that is too hard for you, bring it unto me and I will hear it.' "

"But GHQ is not His pigeon," said Nupp-Jevons.

" 'Woe to him that buildeth a town with blood,' " cried Marion. " 'Woe to him that covets fields and takes them by violence' . . ."

"Whoa, mare !" roared Courtney. "Who's breakin' the 'thou shalt not covet' commandment, eh? The clerks are covetin' our cricket pitch . . ."

"But is that piece of real estate actually yours?" Marion looked from one embarrassed Crusader to another with a knowing smile. "Glenbourn is in India . . . surely, brothers, that means it belongs to the Indians . . ."

"Oi !" said Courtney. "Your Wells Fargo lot chased your redskins off their huntin' grounds into reservations . . ."

"Good idea for clerks, reservations," said Innes-Whiffen.

" 'Wherefore then'," said Marion hastily, " 'hast thou thought such a thing against the people of God . . .' "

"This is terrible," moaned the colonel, "what with me memsahib in Kashmir . . ."

"Ah, you are moved, colonel !" Marion's arms were raised aloft. " 'Thou hast turned thyself from the fierceness of thine own anger'. Your stony heart is melting . . ."

"Me stony heart is doin' nothin' of the kind, woman," choked the colonel. "I am still very angry indeed. For God's sake go away . . ."

"Colonel, colonel," soothed Marion, "relent, brother, relent. 'But if he neglect the church' remember, 'let him be unto thee as an heathen man and a publican' . . ."

"If I were a publican," said Courtney, "there'd be no room at the inn for you, madam . . ."

" 'For so is the will of God . . .' " she smiled as she shook her unbowed head . . . " 'that with well doing, you may put to silence the ignorance of foolish men' . . ."

"Oh, Mrs. Weltzer!" cried Mott. "You are so right! We must love our neighbours. We must play the clerks . . . even if I have to raise the team myself . . ."

"You can't," barked Baker-Stewart. "Under the articles of association of the Crusaders, only majors and above are so empowered . . . rule 13 . . ."

"Oh, God, hearken unto me . . ." Marion Weltzer, now in a state of trance, slipped from the chair to her knees.

"She's stewed," said Courtney. "Thought so . . . too much communion wine . . ."

"Everybody in the club is lookin' at us," muttered Innes-Whiffen.

But Mrs. Weltzer was now praying, loud and clear.

"Please give these officers guidance, oh, Heavenly Father . . . they stray in the darkness, give them light . . . let the poor clerks have their ball game . . . let there be equality among men upon your earth. Set the British feet in the paths of righteousness and brotherhood . . ."

"Amen," said Mott, now on his knees beside her.

"This is a nightmare," muttered Barkside-Twist.

Marion rose, dusted her skirt and patted Mott's head.

"Thank you, honey," she said huskily. "At least I've made one convert to-night, praise the Lord . . ."

"Oh, but I'm already converted . . . dad's a vicar . . . C of E . . ."

"Mott!" roared the colonel. "Get up off yer knees this instant!"

The Crusaders were aware of the loud laughter from the far tables. Courtney yelled "Quai-hai!" like a drowning man.

"God be with you, gennlemen," said Marion. "Let the clerks play at your cricket field. You conquered their land and bonded them into slavery for your own enrichment of mere worldly wealth. Now is a chance to wipe clean this blemish on your hist'ry . . ."

"What about your negroes?" howled Courtney. "You Yanks are the real slave traders . . ."

Marion was outwardly calm, unmoved, but her unseen knees

trembled. This terrible, irrefutable argument was always catching up with her preaching . . . high time, she decided, for a tangent.

"I shall send a report of this victory to Noo York," she announced. "How we Americans persuaded the British imperialists to play their brother clerks at cricket in the name of God."

"You're . . . you're sendin' a report?" asked the colonel anxiously.

"Yes, via our Delhi Army Headquarters . . . even the word of God has to be censored in war-time . . ."

"Delhi!"

"My God, if the American Forces get hold of this," said Baker-Stewart, "they'll spread it round, make a meal of it . . . they always do . . ."

"The word of God *is* for spreading around," said Marion, now increasingly aware of Mott's devoted gaze. He was young, slight, this boy, but he was obviously her slave. The fight was on again, the restless urge; desire was prickling within her . . .

"Can I see you home, Mrs. Weltzer?" asked Mott dreamily.

"NO!" roared the colonel. "You stay right here, Mott, that's an order, blast yer! You're not goin' out of me sight . . ."

"You're kind, Mr. Mott," said Marion, now recovered into the middle-west country girl whom God had first beckoned. "Call me up some time, honey. We can fix to read our Bibles together . . ."

She strode out of the door without looking back.

"Remember what Crusaders stand for," she called from the staircase . . . "God be with you in your decision."

There was a paralysed silence. The Crusaders looked at her empty chair in disbelief.

"Quai-hai!" thundered Courtney. "Bura pegs all round, for Christ's sake . . ."

"You, Mott," stormed the colonel, "are a complete renegade. First yer fraternise with Indians an' now American evangelists. Don't yer know Edward VIIIth lost the throne of England because of an American woman . . . ?"

"God bless him," sighed Nupp-Jevons, "honorary colonel of me old regiment . . . we miss him terribly . . ."

"And Lord Kitchener himself," said Barkside-Twist, shaking his head sadly . . . "he had a narrow escape from an American showgirl . . . Edwardian courtesan type called Belle Livingstone . . . down in Delhi . . . hid himself away in Wildflower Hall, Simla . . . damn near squeak it was . . . Simla still hasn't got over it."

"I still think Mrs. Weltzer is right," said Mott stubbornly. "What harm can we do, playing the clerks? Might get a few runs off 'em . . ."

"Harm!" bellowed the colonel. "There's enough harm done already . . ."

"The fly in the ointment," said Barkside-Twist, "is obviously this man Mookerjee. Enlisting the aid of the Yanks was downright cunning. Give the U.S.A. a chance of criticising our policies in India and they'll be at it like pariah dogs worrying a dead rat. They've written enough stupid books about the Raj as it is."

"The Yanks ruined Delhi," said McBurn. "When they arrived there, late for a war as usual, they paid clerks far higher wages than us. Yer knoo, they hadna' a single Anglo-Indian typist left in GHQ inside a week . . . all went over to American HQ."

"Rough on our troops," said Baker-Stewart. "The only girls they could get were those already in the pudden club by the Yanks . . ."

"That's all we need," snarled Courtney. "Anglo-Indian-American children . . . they'd have a blood group like a snooker set . . ."

The colonel took his refilled glass from Akkar Singh and looked hopefully into the bearer's impassive face.

"Atchcha," he said. "American memsahib is puggled, eh, Akkar Singh?"

The white turban shook slowly and deliberately.

"Nay, sahib. Much revered in bazaar, that lady. She is like a priestess. They call her Rani. She has a different god but her word is the same. There will be much trouble for my sahibs, I fear."

He walked back to his bar, still shaking his head.

"Yer know," said the colonel bewilderedly, "dear Akkar Singh has rather changed the complexion of things. He's right, d'yer see. We'll only have a lot more trouble. If only we had a second eleven . . ."

"We'd be pushed to raise more than seven men now," said Baker-Stewart grimly.

"Couldn't we extend membership to 'other ranks'?" asked Mott.

"Don't be completely absurd," said the colonel, "our articles state categorically 'officers only' as Crusaders . . ."

"Save a lot of problems," said Barkside-Twist, "if we all went on leave and left them to it."

"I can't go on leave," said Mott. "Colonel Coote-Coote is off on twenty-eight days now . . . he's left me in sole charge . . ."

"Ma God," said McBurn, "I couldna go on leave with Mott left alone in Tophar . . . we'd lose Glenbourn then, for sure. The clerks would seize it, aye, and he'd let 'em."

"We've nothin' in writin' about Glenbourn, have we?" asked Innes-Whiffen. "No title, no deeds?"

"No," admitted the colonel sadly, "we've just—er—possessed it since the British first came here . . ."

"What about 'squatters' rights'?" asked Mott.

"The Crusaders," snapped the colonel, "never squat!"

"You could," snorted Courtney, "have fooled me . . ."

Chapter Thirteen

BODY-LINE

YOUNG Wahdi gasped in terror. Struggling in the grip of a trench-coated stranger in the dark entrance to the Queen's Club, he was at first fearful that the spirit of Akkar Singh's effigy had returned to haunt the scene of his 'murder'.

"My shoulder . . . you're hurting!" he whimpered.

"Akkar Singh," demanded Gupta.

"Me Wahdi—Akkar Singh is in bar . . ."

"Get him!"

"He no come without money," said the boy, squirming.

"Tell him it is worth ten rupees . . ."

"Eight annas also . . ."

"I said ten rupees . . ."

"Eight annas for me," gasped the boy.

Gupta laughed throatily, doubled it and gave Wahdi a filthy rupee note. The boy fled up the stone steps. To make himself inconspicuous, Alan Ladd leaned against the wall, his fedora making an excellent shadow. He was admiring it when a rick-shaw pulled up. A stout blonde woman in WAC(I) uniform heaved herself out, and the chassis clanged up six inches, just as relieved as the four coolies to be rid of the burden.

"Six rupees, memsahib," whined the leader.

"Nonsense, rickshaw wallah," said Hazel Short, smoothing down her khaki skirt. "The fare is *five* rupees. You loose-wallahs, you! I shall get your licence taken away, pronto, if you try to cheat."

She gave them five rupees and clapped her hands.

"Jao! Jao!" she called. The rickshaw creaked away, the coolies laughing among themselves. The correct fare was obviously four rupees . . . honour, thought Gupta, had been mutually satisfied.

Senior-Commander Short surveyed him in some surprise.

"Waitin' for someone?" she asked curtly.

The fedora was thumbed to the back of the head.

"You could say that, sister, you could say that . . ."

"Sister!" Hazel snorted and strode upstairs, clattering her brown block-heeled brogues. Really, these impudent Indians, especially those out of uniform. She must ask Stewy to do somethin' about these loafers round the club door.

"Salaam, memsahib," said Akkar Singh, backing against the wall as she pounded past. "The major sahib is in the club . . ."

"Oh, good-oh, Akkar Singh!" Fine type, this Sikh servant. "There's a fellar outside, hangin' about . . . a civilian. Up to no good, I'd say."

"I am in process of removing him, memsahib."

"Oh, good man!"

Strange, he thought, she is so fat that her Indian General Service ribbon lies flat on her bust like a stamp on a parcel.

"Your husband will be coming to Tophar soon," he said.

"Er, yes . . . I expect so." Suppose he means well, but drat the man . . .

"Prisoners-of-war sail from Singapore next week . . . will arrive in Madras," he said slowly. "He may be on the boat . . ."

"How the hell . . .?" But Akkar Singh had disappeared down the steps. Hazel was too breathless to continue the climb for a moment. Gerald had written to say he was staying in Singapore to get the bedding business going again . . . what had made him change his plans? A rumour perhaps? These Indians knew everything. She gathered up her tight skirt and sorrowfully lumbered on to tell Baker-Stewart that her days as the Crusaders' scorer and her nights in his bed were numbered.

Dewan Gupta heaved himself off the wall as the Sikh surveyed him.

"Akkar Singh?"

"So?"

"Dewan Gupta, *Clarion India* . . ."

"So?"

Gupta frowned. He expected a keener reaction . . .

"I want your story of the clerks' cricket challenge."

"You have been at HQ all afternoon," said Akkar Singh, "you talked to the clerks instead of Mookerjee . . ."

Gupta laughed good-naturedly.

"They needed my guidance . . . they have no idea of propaganda promotion . . . Swarmi said I was a better speaker than Mookerjee . . ."

"Now you want me to talk for your newspaper?"

"In the shell of a nut . . . yes."

"We," said Akkar Singh, "punch holes in passengers like you!"

The next moment Gupta was on his back. The Sikh had moved like a panther, the long brown fingers clutching the trenchcoat lapels. Unarmed combat was a Sikh speciality. As Gupta's bottom hit the Mall concrete there was a terrible wail of pain.

Gupta saw just the broken toe-nails within the leather sandal straps before his neck was kicked. As he tried to roll away he was gathered up like rumpled bedding and dashed to the ground again. Gupta writhed where he lay, experiencing that dread moment of truth in hand-to-hand combat when the doomed man realises his opponent is unassailable. Akkar Singh's hand chopped down . . . Gupta's knees folded conveniently and he was once more held up above the Sikh's head. The fedora fell limply and, with its loss, Gupta's last vestige of courage collapsed.

"Help! Murder! Thugees!" he screamed.

On the club balcony above, the colonel and his Crusaders, reinforced by Hazel, had hurriedly left their drinks to stare over the ledge, aghast at the shrieks below.

"What's going on down there?" barked Baker-Stewart.

"Murder, assassin . . . !" Gupta's head rolled helplessly on his neck as Akkar Singh whirled him round like a hammer-thrower warming up.

"For God's sake, what is it, Akkar Singh?" yelled the colonel.

"Newspaper reporter from Delhi," the bearer shouted, "trying to upset my sahibs by waylaying them for cricket story!"

"Oh, well done, Akkar Singh!" cried Hazel.

"It's the fellar who broke into me office," gasped the colonel, "took our photers . . . good grief . . .!"

"Go, my sahibs," roared Akkar Singh. "Go, do not look." He juggled the screaming Gupta still faster. "I must use my knife on this disloyal son of India!"

"No, no, for God's sake," shouted Barkside-Twist. "My dear Akkar Singh . . . not murder, there's a good chap . . ."

"Yes, yes," yelled Courtney exultantly. "Kill him for his own good . . ."

"Mercy! Mercy!" howled Gupta.

"Akkar Singh!" roared the colonel. "Put him down . . . that's an order . . . remember the old regiment . . . *put—him—down!*"

Gupta was hurled against a shuttered shop. The dull crunch in his left side was not a broken bone—his camera was now in fragments. Gupta, hot coals burning in every joint, lay inert, panting and sobbing.

Akkar Singh wiped his hands on his long sleeves, then raised smouldering eyes to the balcony.

"You are compassionate, my sahibs," he intoned. "You can find kindness in your hearts for this infidel."

"Is he hurt?" called Mott anxiously. "He went one hell of a purler."

"Can an evil mind be hurt?" asked Akkar Singh.

"I'll sue you in the courts," yelled Gupta. "My hat and coat are ruined, my camera is broken, so is my body . . ."

"Thank God that camera is smashed," breathed Baker-Stewart.

Akkar Singh knelt beside the huddled Gupta, his long fingers round Gupta's windpipe but not yet exerting any pressure. Now out of earshot of the British balcony, he whispered hoarsely: "All Tophar is closed to you to-night, Gupta. Do not even seek hospital aid . . ."

"No, I'll—" he felt the long fingers tightening—"I'll not go to hospital . . ."

"If you do, the orderlies there are my blood brothers . . . you will not see day break."

"It was," gasped Gupta, "the Jain Desai who accused you of being a double-agent . . ."

"If you believe him, Gupta," the Sikh bared his teeth, "and repeat his false words, you are dead. Even in Delhi you will not be safe from my knife-throwing cousins there . . ."

"I am forever mum," pleaded Gupta, and the fingers on his neck relaxed. "I shall not tell the British . . ."

"If you did," smiled Akkar Singh, "they would not believe you."

Then he rose and, to accommodate the straining British ears on the balcony, proclaimed loudly: "You are not wanted here, disturbing the sahibs. Our Indian justice would be 'death to the agitator' but the British, while they are here, are merciful—so go back to Delhi where you belong—now!"

Akkar Singh strode back up the staircase.

"I say!" cried Hazel breathlessly. "What *loyalty*!"

The Crusaders hurriedly left the balcony to greet their protector who now stood by his bar, his chest heaving.

"So sorry, my masters . . . my temper was roused. This newspaperman would condemn you . . ."

"Tush!" smiled the colonel. "My dear fellar, yer action was a bit strong but, bless my soul, such an expression of loyalty can't pass unacknowledged. Me thanks, old friend."

He shook Akkar Singh's hand while the committee patted the hard, boned back.

"My word," said Nupp-Jevons. "I'm deeply moved . . . not since the old King died . . ."

"Hope there'll be na repercussions," said McBurn. "I mean, assault is a verra serious crime . . ."

"We should've let him kill the sod," said Courtney. "Justifiable homicide if ever I saw . . . oh, sorry, Hazel, forgot you were here . . ."

Akkar Singh wiped an eye with a glass-cloth. He was now anxious to phone Mookerjee to ensure Gupta's departure without further contact with the British. So he made the namaste sign.

"You will forgive me, sahibs. May I rest for an hour?"

"Of course!" The colonel was full of concern. "Take the night off. The other bearer can serve us—just this once . . ."

"Nay, sahibs, just an hour." He was not risking his tips slipping away in the belt of his understudy. "I will rest and pray awhile . . . then I shall be back at your service."

He swept through the curtains behind his bar amid murmurs of approval from the Crusaders.

"What a man!" said Hazel. "Makes you proud to be British."

Then she remembered his message on the staircase and drew Baker-Stewart aside. "Don't know how he knew," she whispered, "but Gerald may sail for Madras from Singapore next week."

Baker-Stewart looked troubled.

"Odd how they always seem to ferrit out these things . . . still, dashed decent of him to tip us off like that."

Mott had slipped quietly down the stairs into the street.

"I am gravely wounded," sobbed Gupta, levering himself up against the shop front. "Are you a medical officer?"

"No, I'm 'Education', actually."

"Useless," moaned Gupta. "I am already educated . . ."

Mott kneeled beside him.

"Anything broken?"

"Only my confidence in the British. They allow a berserk Sikh to manhandle a loyal subject . . . in fact they condone it. Then they send an education officer instead of a medical one to diagnose my hurts . . . my papers shall publish these facts . . ."

"There's been a misunderstanding," said Mott earnestly. "Let me get a rickshaw and take you to hospital?"

"Nunno," gasped Gupta. "I wish for a neutral bed."

"Where are you living?"

"I have not booked in anywhere yet."

"Look, my flat's near here . . . I'll get a doctor . . ."

"Not an Indian doctor . . . please . . . not in Tophar!"

"Why ever not?"

"Are you, captain, involved in this cricket match?"

"Er, yes, slow left-arm bowler—but I bat right-handed . . . Mott's the name . . ."

The half-closed eyes opened slowly.

"Mott?" came the whisper. "You are Mott? The champion of the clerks . . . the one the babus call 'friend' . . .?"

"Oh, do they?" Mott experienced a surge of warmth. "I try to understand India, you know . . ."

"I am a friend of Desai . . ."

"Ah, the Field Cashier clerk . . . I often pop in to see him . . ." Mott frowned. He felt insincere, for his visits to Desai were not always completely social. Mott's army pay was in a parlous state of stoppages—but the little clerk was always able to warn him in time to take out a bank over-draft before some new debt from a previous posting caught up with him. But he also admired Desai in his strange almost hermit world. And now, in dire trouble, here was a friend of that blameless little Jain.

"Let me help you for Desai's sake," said Mott. "India, after all, is my second home . . ."

"Then take me to it now," said Gupta. "My back feels spineless."

He moved gingerly and grunted in pain.

"We'll get a rickshaw," said Mott. "I can't carry you."

"If you were strong commando you could—but being only 'Education Officer' . . ."

A tinkling bell heralded the approach of a wavering lamp up the dark Mall.

"Rickshaw hai!" called Mott.

"I am not plyin' for hire," shouted Judge Trevelhayes, perched on his tricycle.

"Oh, sorry, judge . . ."

"Who's that on the ground . . . old Courtney sloshed again?"

"No, sir, a newspaper reporter from Delhi . . . he's been hurt . . . it's the cricket match, you know . . ."

"Shouldn't try to play in the dark."

"Is that a doctor?" asked Gupta.

"No," said Mott soothingly, "it's a high court judge."

"Typical of you British," moaned Gupta. "I need medical not legal aid. I suppose if I wanted my portrait painted, you would send a window-cleaner . . ."

"Is he drunk?" The little judge slid from his saddle, peering down at the crumpled form.

"Oh-ah!" Gupta shrank back as the light caught the high forehead under the straw panama hat and the long white side-burns which bracketed the gimlet eyes. "Oh . . . it's the hanging judge!"

"Ah, he knows me nickname . . . looks like a clear case of assault. Who did this to him?"

"Can't sneak, sir . . ."

"Come, come, Mott, you're under oath. I'll get yer for contempt . . ."

"Akkar Singh, sir," said Mott resignedly. "This man interviewed Colonel Eddgers this afternoon—for *Clarion India* I think it was . . ."

"Oh, did he? Eddgers rang me this afternoon too. Said a reporter called Gupta had told him he knew all about me advice to sue that *Bugle* editor . . . are you Gupta?"

The bundle nodded slowly in the tricycle light.

"There," said the judge triumphantly, "I've made him talk. Yer know, Mott, old Eddgers must be goin' soft in the head . . . he actually thought *I'd* been indiscreet . . . been blabbin' . . ."

"I know exactly how you feel, sir."

"Now, Gupta," said the judge, "in yer own words . . . how did you find out?"

"A newspaperman never divulges the sources of his information . . ."

"Out of me way, Mott!" bellowed the judge, mounting his tricycle. "I'm goin' to run him down . . . shred him with me spokes . . ."

"Nunno," pleaded Gupta, "it was the army girl . . . at the telephone exchange . . . she is eavesdropper . . ."

"Ah!" The judge braked hard. "You're a witness to that statement, Mott. A WACK telephone girl, eh? Serious charge, this—sabotage . . . must keep women out of cricket. I'll take this up with WACK HQ. Who's the warderess in charge?"

"Senior-Commander Hazel Short, sir."

"Ah, that fleshy soul from Singapore . . . Stewy's sleepin' bag . . . right, another case solved. And, Mott . . ."

"Sir?"

"Get this fellar off the Mall . . . can't have newspaper litter blowin' about durin' the Arts Festival. Would give you a lift but I'm goin' to a pageant meetin' at Heddle's Bank. By the way, Mott, I've got you down to play Guy Fawkes . . ."

"Oh, no, sir. I must decline . . ."

"Good part for you . . . type-castin' for a Rusky socialist like you . . . think it over . . . it's a straight part . . . no squibs to be stuck in yer ears or any o' that nonsense . . . right, '*Punch in the presence of the passenjares*'."

The singing judge rose from his saddle, trod down hard on the pedals—then swerved violently to narrowly scrape past an oncoming rickshaw.

"Road hogs!" he shouted as he corkscrewed into the night.

"Tiro, rickshaw," called Mott to the scattered coolies. They climbed to their feet muttering vengefully, and brought their vehicle beside Gupta. Mott set the battered hat on the lolling head and slipped an arm round the trenchcoat.

"Ups-a-daisy," he said.

"Is Daisy sahib hurt?" asked the rickshaw leader.

Alan Ladd groaned with outraged pride.

Chapter Fourteen

THE EDITOR

AFTER phoning Mookerjee to take appropriate action against Gupta, Akkar Singh hurried through the dark, columned corridors of the Queen's Club where once monks had chanted their solemn way to midnight prayer. Beyond rickety wooden stairs he crossed through the scenic studio where, during the day, tall English ladies, in short cotton overalls, painted sets for the adjoining Grand Theatre. Akkar Singh knew the room well. On his suggestion, the Tophar Amateurs had bought coal braziers to keep the scenery dry in winter. They had congratulated him on such foresight – which also proved personally profitable to him for, at night, he rented out the warm room as sleeping quarters to rickshaw coolies—a fact quite unknown to the British. Little Wahdi also slept there and kept a tally on the rickshaw coolies for Akkar Singh.

He avoided a Cookham backcloth of a rather oriental shrubbery for *Hay Fever* and a flimsy three-ply dug-out for *Journey's End*. A ship's side for *Cavalcade* listed heavily on *A Rose Without a Thorn* vista of Hampton Court, mellowed, weathered and lichen-covered with twentieth-century age, although, at the period of the play, the palace had just been built.

Akkar Singh shouldered himself into a long overcoat and let himself out on to the Mall. He waited, hidden in shadow, until Judge Trevelhayes had wobbled past on his three veering wheels, then crossed the road to glide down a dark alley into the bazaar.

Mr. Retti Moplah, editor of the *Himalayan Bugle*, was yawning on his charpoy when the knocking came. His day began

133

at 6 a.m. as printer. At 10 he turned into distribution agent to the shops and news-stands, becoming reporter and space-seller from noon till sundown when he returned to his office— as editor.

"Who is it?" he called. Plagued by money-lenders, Mr. Moplah was not anxious to open his door at night.

"Moplah? Open up . . . or I shall force myself in regardless of shutter damage."

The editor sighed and struggled his stout body from the charpoy. Akkar Singh again . . . he spelled 'trouble' in 72 point Bodoni Bold. Clasping a blanket round his middle, he slid back the bolt. Akkar Singh grazed past him furtively.

"Shut up," he said.

"I have not yet spoken . . ."

"The door . . . close it."

Moplah complied, rattling the bolt but not actually sliding it home. All editors needed an escape route sometimes . . .

"I have news for your paper," said Akkar Singh, sitting on Moplah's pillow, his face saturnine in the oil lamplight.

"Oh . . . well, get off my charpoy then. Must prepare office."

With great effort, Moplah moved the wooden bed to a dusty corner and dragged out his huge roll-top desk from the shadows. Oiled with ghee, the casters moved easily. Moplah sat before it, now complete with green eyeshade.

"I am now night editor," he announced.

"Why do you move your desk about?"

"I have to be near telephone. That being screwed to the wall, desk has to be adjacent to it by day and charpoy by night, as in Fleet Street. It is our way of life in the Street of Ink. Now, what is your news item?"

"Dewan Gupta of *Clarion India* was attacked on the Mall just now. The assault was watched by British officers who made no attempt to rescue him . . ."

"Who was the attacker?"

"Unknown. Escaped in the night . . ."

"The chokra, Wahdi, said it was you, Akkar Singh . . ."

"He will be beaten for this," snarled the Sikh.

"Nunno, the boy did not betray you . . . in fact he spoke with such pride of your escapade."

"He must learn prudence. Not all his enthusiasms are wise."

"I paid him five rupees for the story . . . is that not prudent —or wise of the youth?"

"No, for I shall confiscate it—he can spoil our plans by greed."

Moplah sighed.

"Gupta was here to get cricket story from Captain Mott," Akkar Singh went on. "Mookerjee phoned me to stop Gupta at all costs."

"Most astute of Mookerjee. Gupta was poaching my news, tom-tiddling on my ground. But trespassers will be persecuted . . ."

"Yes, I stopped Gupta reaching the British. But if that Mott is allowed free tongue he will also ruin all our subversive plots. He thinks he is on our side, that the game is just cricket—but we know better. I am trying to help you—and India. That is worth twenty rupees."

Moplah shivered in his blanket.

"Fifteen I'll pay . . . Wadhi has the balance . . . now, your report . . ."

"Gupta has broken spirit and no heart left . . . I have got rid of your rival."

"Is he dead?" gasped Moplah.

"On the verge upon. By ambushing him myself the British now have complete proof I am on their side. It is good for morals they think that . . ."

"I know, I know. You are our most gallant agent-provocateur . . . a veritable Scarlet Pimplenelly . . ."

"But something else happened to-night. The American Weltzer memsahib came and prayed for the clerks on her knees in front of the cricket officers in the Queen's Club. Mookerjee had enlisted her aid . . ."

"Oh, this is 'scoop' indeed!" Moplah's eyes were shining. "Gupta did not see . . . ?"

"No, this story is for your newspaper alone . . . she told the British that their god felt they should play the clerks . . ."

"She did? This, I am telling you, solves a jig-saw which has been puzzling me. Mookerjee was seen chasing young Krischa in the bazaar. Is he not the American missionary's houseboy who tells us of her sex-ecstasy cries, morning, noon and night?"

"That is the boy. Mookerjee had to dumb his tongue with bukshish . . ."

"He was telling me that Mookerjee knelt and prayed with her in his best suit . . . ah, a most wily front to put up."

"Mookerjee is clever man," admitted the Sikh. "He knows how to strike the crocodile British in their softest part—their cricket belly. And next to cricket, the British are very God-struck, even using the old temple for their theatre. The American woman quoted their 'Granth' . . ."

" 'Gita' to me, but 'Bible' it is in English. Always I am amazed that the British revere such a quaint catalogue, because they are not mentioned in it once. The American memsahib did quote it to them then?"

"Many times! Almost as good at it she was as Mookerjee." Akkar Singh chuckled deeply. "The officers were not knowing where to look. They lost face in the crowded club and were made laughter-stocks."

"This I must write," said Moplah eagerly. "It will bring American circulation to my paper. Their patron saint is Uncle Sam . . ."

"The American woman is pleased that Mookerjee titled her 'rani'," said Akkar Singh.

"Mookerjee has gone too far there," said Moplah firmly. "Rani, indeed! That is news I will blue-pencil and spike most firmly. The only white queens we will allow in India is on chess-boards."

"My time is up," said Akkar Singh, thrusting out his hand.

With a sigh Moplah bent over an earthenware chatti and counted out some greasy notes.

"You needn't look all-knowing like that, Akkar Singh," he said coldly. "I shall not hide my money in this chatti again—so it is no good you breaking in when I am on my paper round. This is only very petty cash. My fortune is banked in a safe steel safe in an Ambala bank."

As he folded the notes into his red kummerbund, Akkar Singh looked at Moplah contemptuously. He went to draw back the bolt, only for the door to creak open voluntarily.

"You did not close it," he said slowly.

"You do not lock the stable door till after the horse has bolted," said Moplah. "It is one cliché of common-sense for which the British must be admired."

"Moplah," said Akkar Singh from the dark alley, "you must learn to trust people."

Wiping his forehead with his torn bedsheet, Moplah shot the bolt firmly in place, reset his rakish eyeshade and sat at his desk. The night editor had a 'scoop'. He must, as befitted his position, play the part to perfection, even without an audience. The Marion Weltzer story was straightforward, but the attack on Gupta required very delicate handling. Moplah hated *Clarion India* and its bigger circulation. But, cheating scoundrel through he was, Gupta was a fellow journalist. How to show allegiance to Indian journalism and yet register disapproval of Gupta's filching methods—that was Moplah's problem. Inspiration was not long in dawning.

Painstakingly he typed his headline, his eyes bright with anticipation :

'TOPHAR CRICKET SCANDAL !'
'Unknown Indian Cub Reporter Attacked on Mall !'

"And cricket balls to you, Gupta," muttered the night editor.

Chapter Fifteen

THE UNWELCOME GUEST

JACK GRAHAME rose from beside Mott's bed and pulled the sheet up over Gupta. Inadvertently he covered his head and the reporter screamed a terrified denial that he was beyond recall.

"The poor sod's a bit bruised, Motty," said Grahame. "Mostly he's in a state o' shock. I've patched up one cut in the neck . . ."

"It was his toe-nail," wailed Gupta. "Nothing is blunt about a Sikh. I am mortally hurt . . ."

"He certainly looks terrible," said Mott.

"Not bein' a plastic surgeon, I can't help him there," said Grahame. "He's not seriously hurt, nothin' busted, but he ought to go to hospital . . . I can get him a bed in the Indian wing . . ."

"No," said Gupta, "not hospital. I have my own medical adviser in Delhi . . ."

"Well, I can't force you," said Grahame. "Bein' a civilian, you can make up yer own mind. I'll say this for you, though . . . yer tough . . . got a hide like an ox . . ."

"I am," said Gupta, offended, "a vegetarian."

"Yes, he was wearing canvas shoes," said Mott, "not leather . . . cattle must be sacred to him . . ."

"I'm sorry I showed him my braces," said Grahame, putting on his tunic.

Gupta sighed and turned his face to the wall.

"This punch-up has properly mucked up my sex life," said Grahame. "When you phoned, Motty, I was jus' about to have me wicked way with Nancy . . . Why did Akkar Singh rough him up?"

"Damn good of you to turn out at all, Jack. It's this cricket match, you see . . ."

"Cricket match?" Grahame's face darkened.

"Yes, this chap's a reporter . . . up from Delhi to get the gen . . ."

"Is that monkeyshiner there named Gupta?"

"Yes, d'you know him?"

"This is the bastard who blackmailed Nancy!" Grahame ripped back the sheet and Gupta blinked up at him anxiously from the pillow. "Oi, Gunga Din . . . that WACK girl at HQ telephone exchange . . . you took a photer of her with her bush-shirt all undone . . ."

"I say," gasped Mott, "he didn't . . . ?"

"She was hot . . . no fan working', I mean, Mott . . . poor kid wanted a breeze round her bra . . . an' that exchange is supposed to be private. But this keyhole correspondent busts in, takes her picture, then blackmails her into repeatin' conversations she'd heard about this bloody cricket . . ."

"Oh, hell—she's your piece of frippet, is she? Well, you won't have to worry about that photograph . . ."

He pointed to the flattened camera and the twisted, ripped film which now tangled with Gupta's yellow socks and suspenders on the floor.

"That's a relief anyway," said Grahame, covering Gupta once more.

"Well, you aren't going to be pleased about the latest development, Jack. We met the judge and he threatened to mince Gupta with his tricycle if he didn't confess. So, quite wisely, he talked . . . and the judge is reporting your phone girl to Hazel . . ."

"Aw, hell! Still, in that case, I've done the right thing. After Nancy'd finished sobbin' her heart out all over me Defence ribbon I persuaded her to shoot Ma Short the whole sordid story . . ."

"Make a clean breast of it," grinned Mott.

"Yes, you tit-mouse, yes . . . fling herself on the ole cow's mercy . . . explain how she can't help overhearin' on that stone-age switchboard—an' hope she gets off with a severe 'rep'."

"She might. Hazel may be glad to hush it up as it concerns Crusaders' cricket . . ."

"Cricket!" Grahame snorted disdainfully. "Yer as mad as a two-bob watch on that pansy game. I prefer real sport, a few pints o' beer, The Inkspots' record of 'Bless You For Bein' An Angel' and a willin', wrigglin' woman . . ." He began to sing: " '*Onward, tram conductor, when you take a fare . . .*' "

" '*Punch it in the presence of the passenjare,*' " enjoined Mott, more tunefully. "My vicar father would have a stroke if he heard that. Where the hell did you learn it?"

"I performed it as a student . . . hospital revue in Melbourne with the elevatin' title of *Pulses and Ulcers . . .*"

"We did *Titus Andronicus* at King's," said Mott. "I was Titus . . ."

"Who else," sighed Graham. "Anyway, I was so flamin' nervous I got pissed first. You try singin' '*If you spit, it's a quid fine*' under the influence. I was a riot . . . got three encores . . . then I fell over. You think you were 'Titus' . . ."

"Certainly it's caught on in Tophar. I've even heard the judge sing it—and Spotty Backside—that's very daring for her."

"The nurses at the hospital serenade me with it, although singin' a hymn on the way to the operatin' theatre upsets a few patients. But I like the tune . . . makes me homesick . . ."

"Tunes don't back me homesick—but cricket does. I think of Oatlands Park, near home, but . . . 'Thou shalt not sigh, nor hold thy stumps to heaven . . .' "

"What berk said that?"

"Titus Andronicus . . . not quite in a cricket context, of course . . . in fact he was far more bloody than your medical revue . . ."

"You, Mott, would fit cricket into a cannibal weddin' feast. Look what it's done to me Nancy. I've a good mind to bash Gupta some more."

"No, Jack, he's been bashed enough already. Larwood and Voce couldn't have made a better job of it."

The sheet was quivering.

"It was all done in the course of duty to my newspaper," cried

Gupta brokenly. "But I shall not quote the girl. That I swear on my grandmother's grave."

"I'm sorry to hear she's passed on." Mott kept a straight face. "It's the first we've heard of it."

"Yeah, otherwise we'd've had a whip round for a wreath," chuckled Grahame. "Well, what the hell are we goin' to do with yer, Gupta, that is the question? I can't make out a report."

"But I need an official doctor's report to claim damages," cried Gupta.

"You've got all the damages yer goin' to get," said Grahame, sitting on the edge of the bed. "You'll be okay . . . jus' bruisin' an' shock. But I advise you to see yer own witch doctor an' get X-rayed to be on the safe side. But, remember, you never saw me. Outside the military hospital I'm only supposed to treat licentious soldiers, not civilian pimps. Gimme another scotch, Motty."

"I, too, am in need of sustenance," muttered Gupta.

"He's already drank all my Indian brandy," said Mott.

"That," said Grahame, taking the tumbler, "accounts for his state o' shock."

Mott helped Gupta to sit up. Now reduced to his grubby string vest and grey underpants, he felt far from Alan Ladd, but he tried desperately to recover the image.

"Cigarette," he croaked.

But, instead of passing one from his own lips to the stricken hero, Mott ruined Alan Ladd's scene by proffering his case. Gupta sank back, exhaling smoke, his mind gradually becoming mazed.

"Rest is what he needs," said Grahame, "a good night's kip."

"Where?" asked Mott anxiously.

"Wherever he's stayin' . . ."

"I am homeless," wailed Gupta. "I intended to sleep in the station waiting-room to-night and travel down by the dawn train. I have a deadline . . ."

"You damn nearly met it to-night," said Grahame.

"It's after eleven," fretted Mott. "Where can we take him now? Have you got any friends in Tophar, Mr. Gupta?"

"India is full of the friends of Dewan Gupta . . . but I cannot pin-point my finger on one in Tophar . . ."

"Ask a silly question," said Grahame . . . "Ah, wait a mo', I've an idea. Where's the phone, Motty?"

"In the hall . . ."

Grahame hurried out. Mott sipped his whisky and stared into space. What a wonderful woman Marion Weltzer was . . . such strength of purpose, such dedication. Now there was a real lady of character and poise . . . not like Jack's half-chat phone girl . . .

Grahame returned grinning.

"Well, no one can say I didn't try."

"Who did you ask?"

"Well, I thought the editor of *The Himalayan Bugle* might give shelter to a fellar journalist . . ."

Gupta sat bolt upright in bed.

"You didn't phone Moplah!" he gasped.

"I did, an' frankly he doesn't like yer, Gupta, not one little bit. Says you've broken the rules, infiltratin' on his preserves . . ."

"He is but small time," said Gupta defensively.

"Well, he won't play . . . told me most politely he'd put me up for the night, the Viceroy or Gandhi—but not Dewan Gupta. You stink, apparently."

Dropping his cigarette nervelessly to the floor for Mott to retrieve and stub out, Gupta sank back in despair. For Moplah to be gloating over Alan Ladd's plight was too galling for words.

"That editor also warned me all hotels in Tophar are barred to yer, Gupta," Grahame went on ruthlessly. "To coin a phrase, yer blackballed . . ."

"He mustn't stay here," said Mott desperately. "I'm already up to my neck in disaster. If the colonel finds out, I'm a dead duck . . ."

"Well, you can't turn him out into the cold, cold night in his condition. The vultures would get him, for sure. He's a very unpopular man, Motty. The Tophar Mafia are seekin' retribution, probably with poison darts . . . his little tin hide ain't worth a bob. Where's all yer love for yer brother Indian gone, Mott sahib?"

"That's unfair, Jack."

"Why not regard this as a good Samaritan act? An' if the colonel cashiers an' drums you out for it, write to the newspapers . . ."

"Are you out of your tiny mind? It's the newspapers I'm afraid of!"

"Alright, don't get shirty. What time does yer bearer get here?"

"Half-seven."

"Get Gupta outa here by seven. Don't let anyone see him in that ropy mac an' fedora. Put a turban on his nut, wind a sheet round him . . . then, if anyone sees him, he's a sweeper come to clean yer dunny . . ."

Gupta rose from the pillow in fury.

"You will not disguise me as an 'untouchable'!" he panted. "I am Dewan Gupta, *Clarion India*. I'll leave as I came, a reporter seeking truth and justice . . ."

He sank back with a sob of pain. Grahame tilted more whisky between the mauve lips. Gupta became drowsy again . . . the voices began to fade.

"He won't go as a sweeper," said Mott, "that's for certain. They criticise our class distinctions but, oh boy, Indians are the world champions . . ."

Grahame sat pondering.

"You say he's been at GHQ all the afternoon?"

"Yes, he saw Colonel Eddgers. Obviously that was when he also met your Nancy with the laughing bra . . ."

"Okay, then, Motty, yer've nothin' to worry about, lettin' him stay here. You're in the clear as far as HQ is concerned. Gupta must be bona fide . . . he was allowed in . . ."

"Bona fide? Allowed in?"

"To HQ! Oh, don't be a dope all yer life. Now I'm *not* allowed in HQ. Bein' new here, I'm an untouchable dogsbody. I have to get colonels to identify me an' sign chits at the gate before I can hand over me medical bumph to the Hospital Directorate. I'm screened like a syphilitic immigrant. But if Gupta got into HQ, then he must be a V.I.P.—or some high-up brass-hat must've vouched for him."

Swiftly he went to the chair beside the bed, rummaging in the pale blue suit which had been revealed when the trenchcoat had been eased from the bruised back. In a side pocket was a notebook and a red HQ pass.

"My flamin' oath," said Grahame, staring at the photograph, "that beatin' up seems to have rejuvenated him—he's even had his beard ripped off!"

Mott's eyes widened with anger.

"That pass belongs to Groppi Jat, the main-gate chowkidar . . . I know him well . . ."

"I bet you do . . . an' his pet goat . . ."

"The chowkidars are all terribly loyal to us . . . he must have been bashed on the head to part with this . . ."

"We'll ask Omar Khayyam here." Grahame shook the gently undulating Gupta. "Oi, wakey-wakey! Time for brainwashin' . . ."

Gupta muttered in Hindi, opened his eyes—to see the red pass dangled before them.

"How did yer get this?" demanded Grahame. "It's not transferable by law—it says so, on the front."

"A reporter never reveals his sources . . ." but Gupta was grabbed by his string vest and jerked upright.

"Have you killed the main-gate chowkidar?"

"Goodness gracious, no!" Gupta was once again fully awake —and once again afraid.

"Right, Motty, we'll ring the military police," said Grahame. "You'll be in the 'nick' to-night, Gupta, an' all poor Captain Mott's troubles'll be over."

"Will they?" said Mott. "The military police are all I need . . ."

Gupta's lower lip trembled. This bed was warm, snug, his body ached and sleep was so near. And he remembered seeing the British military police in action in Delhi . . . hearing their ruthless, hearty 'Come on, me lucky lads, nice an' quiet or we'll have to git rough agen . . .' as they hurled drunken British soldiers, bleeding, into army trucks. Gupta shuddered.

"I paid the chowkidar twenty rupees for the pass," he

admitted, "but he *did* offer it . . . there was no cajolery on my part . . ."

"Great heavens," cried Mott, "we must inform Security at once."

"Security are all in bed," chuckled Grahame. "The war is over. HQ holds no more secrets—if it was ever able to keep any from India in the first place. No, let it lie, Motty. Sleep on, Gupta, you slimy scribe. But to-morrow, take the first camel out. If you don't, I'll show this pass to the authorities—and you'll get about ten years' hard in Lucknow Gaol . . ."

"Alright, alright," muttered Gupta. "To-morrow I will go . . . early at cock rise . . . only let me sleep now, I beg you . . ."

Grahame winked at Mott as Gupta began to breathe heavily. Then, quietly, they moved into the adjoining lounge.

"Better let me have that pass," said Mott.

"Not on yer nelly," said Grahame, "I know you, mate. You'll only give it back to the chowkidar . . . probably tell him to 'play the game' an' give him a hundred lines in Sanskrit. No, I'll handle this."

"What'll you do, then?"

"Never you mind." He flipped over the closely-written pages. "Cor, stone me, look at this . . . 'British persecution of Tophar clerks' . . . phew, acres of acid comment . . . 'Futti Pant'? Sounds like me old two-stroke Douglas . . . hullo, I see here the name 'Mott' . . ."

"Oh, my God, not again! Why do they pick on me? I'm *for* 'em . . ."

"This book," said Grahame grimly, "is not goin' back to Delhi."

Mott took it, gasped in anguish at the names he recognised . . . Desai, Kazi Mohammed, Shrinivassen . . . Gupta's shorthand was impossible to decipher in detail but 'Glenbourn', 'British intolerance', 'clerks denied cricket' and 'quit India' all added up to another terrible anti-British blitzkrieg.

"We can't just pinch this," Mott began bewilderedly, but Grahame snatched the book away.

"It was," he said, "lost by Gupta in his fight with Akkar Singh."

A match was set to it in a brass ashtray.

"That'll settle Othello's hash," said the Australian. "He black-mailed Nancy—an' we Grahames don't like our women threatened . . ."

"Well, she did listen-in on the blower," said Mott, raising the sash window and shaking the black ashes into the night. "Christ, that's hot!" He picked up the ashtray again gingerly with his handkerchief. "You know, Jack, you ought to watch out for that girl. The Indian Army doesn't take kindly to half-castes —you could get struck off the medical register or some-thing."

"Look, Motty, I'm a doctor, not a soldier. I have to prescribe for meself. Conversationally, Nancy is corny, I'll admit, but she's gotta body you dream about. Now level with me, Titus Mott, B.A., with all yer attitudes, India for the Indians, Glen-bourn for the British, cricket for the workers an' all things trite an' dutiful—who would you prefer on yer nightly mattress— Nancy or Spotty Backside?"

"No comment. Spotty Bee has been thrust upon me."

"You could help her get rid o' those spots, yer know, Motty . . . nothin' like a bit o' reg'lar rumpo . . ."

"Oh, shut up!" Mott did not want his ethereal thoughts of Marion Weltzer profaned by Grahame's psychology.

"By the way," the Australian finished his whisky, jammed on his shabby carmine sidecap, "we were only foolin', yer know, when we threatened Gupta with the military police."

"We were?"

"Since the leave camp closed, the C.M.P.s have gone back to Delhi. There ain't a john left in the place."

"How d'you know?"

Grahame patted Mott's tousled head.

"There's been a marked fallin' off in the hospital's out-patient casualty figures . . ."

His footsteps died away in the night and Mott closed the door. In the lounge he adjusted cushions on the settee. Not to sleep, of course. His vigil would be long if he was to see Gupta safely off the premises . . . so he began to think of Marion Weltzer . . .

When he awoke, daylight had filled the room and his young bearer, Roti Khan, was shaking him.

"Ah, captain sahib has over-drank again," he sniggered. Employed by such an understanding master, Roti Khan enjoyed a carte-blanche unique among personal servants in India. Mott was an Indian bearer's dream. He was solicitous about their families, took a personal interest in their well-being—and did not count his change.

Mott dashed into the bedroom. Gupta, the light-blue suit, trenchcoat and fedora had gone . . . but the bed had been made.

"I help your guest go at six o'clock," said Roti Khan blandly.

"Six? You were ruddy early all of a sudden." Mott rubbed his eyes. "Did my—er—guest have anything to eat?"

"Nay, sahib, no chota hazri—Mr. Mookerjee told me not to give him food . . ."

"Mookerjee!" expostulated Mott. "I might have known that name would crop up. I must meet him—get things sorted out. Take me to him . . ."

"Take you to Mookerjee!" cried Roti Khan in well-simulated terror. "That, captain sahib, would be more than my life was worth!"

"Look," Mott had a sudden great thought, "do you happen to know if Mookerjee is a Mason . . .?"

"Mr. Mookerjee," said Roti Khan coldly, "is *not* in 'trade' . . ."

Chapter Sixteen

BEDTIME STORY FOR JOCELYN

IN THE mooring ghat at Srinagar, the houseboat rested motionless now. The last ripples from the early evening traffic on the Jhelum were stilled and the British promenade along the Bund under the chinar trees was over for the day. Mist was rising above the tall poplars and silver birches of Kashmir as the sun finally sank like a huge red, baleful balloon beyond the distant snow-capped mountains.

Julia Eddgerley-Watkyn-Reed nursed her grandson tenderly. Jocelyn was a big child, their first male heir. Daughter Phyllisjoy, their only child, had admittedly played for St. Paul's second team in England as an erratic change bowler but, in their hearts, Julia and Eddgers knew she only played to please them, that there was no inherited, ingrained love of the game. P.J. tried hard to be a true product of her military upbringing. Dutifully she had married Major Crutchley-Haybart—who had played for the Eton Ramblers—but, since her stay with them in Kashmir, Julia had heard P.J. refer, rather too often, and too earnestly, to Major Jack Grahame. All the signs, thought Julia, her mouth a thin red line, that the Australian had aroused her interest far more than her conventional husband. P.J. harped on how tender Grahame had been after Jocelyn's birth and was always singing a hymn about trams he'd taught her. She was in danger of goin' primitive and Julia must put a stop to it.

So she had altered her original enthusiastic acceptance of Grahame as a true Crusader, and the gossip from Tophar, filtering back that the doctor was nothing more than an adventurer, attracted by half-caste girls, was used as the covering excuse to Eddgers. She could not dare tell him her suspicions of the infatuated P.J. 'Ud break the old chap's heart. But that such a libertine as Doctor Grahame had actually touched P.J. naked . . . Julia shuddered in horror.

P.J. and her husband, on leave from his Gurkha battalion at Bakloh, were across at the Quince-Brocklows' half-timbered Tudor houseboat, *Chelsea Reach*, for sundown drinks. Had Jocelyn been a girl, Julia would have been with them, leaving the child, as she had always left P.J. in India, in the care of a wizened ayah. Julia would have enjoyed the trip in a shikara— a canopied water taxi—through the floating pink lotus, watching the passing white sails, hearing the wet slap of paddles . . . even to smile indulgently sometimes at the names painted on the sides of passing gondalas . . . *Love Me To-night*, *Kiss-and-Make-up*, *Jack & Jill Tumbledown* . . . Really, these boatmen were very quaint—how did they think up such names?

But Julia was on duty. In his last letter Eddgers had told her to get Jocelyn to 'use his left arm as there is a shortage of good spinners who can bowl a "Chinaman" '. This information had caused the letter to be delayed while the military censor sought advice from his superiors—but Julia understood the message perfectly. Cricket was part of her life's ritual. Now, with a dedication and devotion to her cause worthy of Madame Chiang Kai-shek herself, Julia would see Jocelyn perfected this oriental delivery so rare in British cricket.

The baby dropped the glass marble again. Julia, pushing back a lank wisp of white hair, retrieved it from the rush mat.

"Get your fingers right round it, Jocelyn." She forced the ball back into the tiny, convulsive hand. "Grip it . . . I know there's no seam, but first things first. Now, steady . . . ooh, clever boy! Now that one *did* come out of the back of your hand . . ."

She set the child down in the antique wooden cradle, rented with the houseboat. Jocelyn howled for the soft lace bosom again, but Julia was adamant.

"No good appealin', baby," she cooed, "the light's gone now . . . must draw stumps . . . no more play to-day."

Jocelyn gave up in a whimper of spittle and slept. Julia switched on the radio for the news—although she felt that since the Japanese armistice it had never been quite the same. The news readers seemed more casual, the sense of urgency had gone. She felt no longer part of the world's scene. She listened abstractedly, rocking the cradle—until she heard the voice of Ram Lal Menon.

"In my current affairs talk to-night," he purred, "I want to draw your attention to the callous attitude of the British in Tophar. The army clerks in that tin-roofed town issued a friendly challenge to the local British club for a cricket match. In this hour of victory, friends, what finer celebration could there be? But these upstart guests in our land have turned down the poor clerks . . . will not play them."

"Quite right too," Julia told Jocelyn, "mustn't fraternise or they get ideas above their station."

"Sad, is it not," sighed Ram Lal Menon, "that even in this moment of triumph, the British are unable to relax their stern, unbending insularity to the clerks who have served them so loyally . . ."

"Poppycock," snapped Julia. "Your grand-dad's clerk stole the fountain pen I gave him . . ."

"These humble Tophar clerks who have braved the Himalayan winters in that unsuitable place are denied the cricket they so desire at their own hallowed Glenbourn ground."

"Hallowed!" breathed Julia. "They're all too lazy ever to climb down there."

"Colonel Eddgerley-Watkyn-Reed, captain of the Tophar team, and now approaching retirement in an out-moded veterinary department, will not accept the clerks' offer of a game. This is, I am afraid, the British snub deliberate."

"My heavens," gasped Julia, bracing herself, "he's involvin' your grand-dad now, Jocelyn . . . this must be stopped . . ."

"I know the British," said Ram Lal Menon. "I have lived in their green land of constant monsoon, easy irrigation, fresh bread and daily supplies of corn and rice. I know this challenge by the clerks would be readily accepted by the British in their homeland. Why does England send only their most narrow-minded, ungenerous officials for service in Mother India?"

"Because of the people like you," Julia told the radio.

"Even our American friends are sadly appalled by this dogmatic British attitude and have said so in their Delhi newssheet. Mrs. Weltzer, a missionary from New York, has had to intervene in Tophar on the clerks' behalf . . . this brave lady actually went on her knees before Colonel Eddgerley-Watkyn-Reed . . ."

"Hell's teeth!" cried Julia, "an American woman worshippin' at Eddger's feet. Poor old dear! Must have been half out of his mind with embarrassment. Hates church matters, bless 'im . . . never forget Phyllisjoy's weddin', Jocelyn . . . your grand-dad's sword got caught in her train . . . tripped up a page . . . that awful Newton-Rumbold boy . . ."

"This dependence upon the American church by Indian clerks," said Ram Lal Menon, "is surely a tragic indictment of British administration here? What a blow this is to the Archbishop of Canterbury, senior primate of British Christianity, in his Kent cathedral . . ."

"Nonsense, he doesn't live there, Jocelyn! It's a big, draughty place . . . took yer mother there during her school hols one Canterbury Cricket Week—Lancashire got a terrible hidin', I remember . . ."

"When the clerks appealed to the Army for cricket apparatus, it was denied them. At every step our Indian brothers have been frustrated. From the onset of this generous challenge the British have avoided the issue. Are they afraid of being beaten? Where is their much vaunted spirit of fair play? Or did the British leave it on the beaches of Dunkirk?"

"Oh!" Julia was outraged. "This badmush ought to be boiled in ghee!"

"Do the British realise that this innocuous cricket match is again an example of their arrogant, intolerant behaviour which has anchored India to centuries of despair? I am but a humble interpreter of our times . . ." he sighed, using echo-chamber effect . . . "but cow grease and pig fat in mere cartridges began the 1857 Mutiny . . . this cricket match, too, now stands as an edict in destiny . . ."

"The man is 'puggled'," Julia told Jocelyn. "Never use grease or fat in cricket . . . linseed oil on bats, yes, but, even then, never on the splice . . ."

"To show our impartiality, friends," there was mocking laughter in Menon's voice now, "let India speak with words of Shakespeare of Warwickshire whose ground is at Edgbaston, when he says: 'Take it up straight . . . within this hour bring me word 'tis done, and by good testimony . . . if thou refuse, and wilt encounter my wrath, say so!' Words from the Britishers' own 'Winter's Tale', friends . . . to them I say, let the clerks' 'Midsummer Night's Dream' of cricket come true . . . or 'The Tempest' may follow . . ."

Julia jerked the knob so hard that the radio nearly toppled into the cradle. Jocelyn awoke with a snivelling wail.

"We shall write to grand-dad," she told him sharply. "That dreadful sloganist, Menon, must be silenced. All flummery and mummery! Just a wicked propaganda wallah."

She bent over the child and closed his pink ears with her thin, freckled hands.

"Ram Lal Menon," she incanted, "is a blue-arsed fly!"

While others in the east pierced clay models of their victims with pins, this was Julia's own secret sorcery against any attack on her world. The last nominee for her black art had been Attlee . . . And no one, not even Eddgers, had ever heard her use this spell.

Jocelyn's normal hearing having been resumed, Julia opened her small desk, drew forth notepaper embossed 'The Wickets, Srinagar', unscrewed her silver pen and drove it into the attack.

My dearest Eddgers,

Jocelyn and I have just heard the most impertinent broadcast by Ram Lal Menon about you and this stupid clerks' cricket match. There is only one way to silence these cheap, catawauling critics—only one way to put them firmly in their place—and that is: the BRITISH way . . .

Chapter Seventeen

THE DELHI FILE

UNKNOWN to Tophar, the Delhi Welfare Directorate file on the proposed cricket match had reached alarming proportions. Created originally to supply comforts and amusements for troops on active service, 'Welfare' had also been taken literally by all other GHQ departments to relieve them of any confusing memoranda for which they could find no official heading. So, when in doubt, let 'Welfare' handle it—and now the box file on the clerks' cricket match had split its seams.

General Welding-Brightlock looked disapprovingly at his clerk and the indent for a new file he had put before him.

"Why?"

"Old one broken-burst, sir. See, 'tis already strung with string . . ."

"Subject?"

"Cricket in Tophar, sir."

The general swallowed hard.

"Inform."

The clerk stuttered out a garbled story as the general turned the curling pages with a frowning scrutiny. Reluctantly he signed the indent as he growled : "Brigadier!"

"Will call him most immediate, sir." The clerk took the form and scurried away in relief. A moment later Brigadier Kew-Ballance strolled in to find his general drumming his fingers.

"Kewty, you're a cricketer, aren't you?"

"Yes, sir. Warwickshire Pilgrim, Sussex Martlet, Devon Dumpling, Somerset Straggler . . ."

"A cricketer of no fixed abode, eh? Know anythin' about a cricket match in Tophar?"

"Heard rumours . . . but surely not our pigeon . . ."

"My dear chap, there's a file here the size of Gibraltar. Our clerks seem to have been compilin' it themselves. Just had to indent for a new cover for it . . . don't like wastage, you know. However, peruse the case, will you, Kewty? Give me a breakdown of the facts. There seems to be a stink goin' on in Tophar . . ."

Brigadier Kew-Ballance gathered up the wrecked file and returned to his office. Screwing in his monocle, he smoothed out the first dog-eared page.

A Demi-Official note from a clerk called Shrinivassen to a Major Fortt, Officer-in-Charge ASOC (Army Sports Official Council), requested cricket gear for the Tophar clerks.

'*Highly reprehensible, a mere clerk addressing a D.O. to a major,*' the brigadier noted in the margin, before turning the page.

Major Fortt had passed the request to SED (Staff Establishment Department) with the note: '*Our directorate handles troops only but in any case have no cricket gear. While sympathetic no Indian Army Order provides anything for civilian clerks. Pass to you.*'

An Indian clerk in SED had returned the memo to Major Fortt, remarking inter alia: '*We provide only the bodies of clerks. It is not our province to give them stumps. Pass for action.*'

Major Fortt had then written to Officer-in-Charge ACES (Amenities, Comforts and Entertainments for Services), Jhansi Depot, one Major White:

'*Dear Chalky. Can you provide Tophar clerks with cricket gear? Realise they are not strictly army personnel but the war's over now.*'

To which Major White had replied:

'*Dear Sandbag. Unable to provide Tophar clerks as have no such gear. Tiddley-winks, ludo, snakes-and-ladders, yes, but not cricket. Sorry unable to help. Thanks for news of end of war. Lonely here.*'

The brigadier realised by now that Fortt was a real cricketer, a back-to-the-wall batsman who never gave up. He had then approached CAD (Clerks Amenities Department) for cash for gear. The reply had come three days later : *'Funds for clerks' amenities only available for recreations within canteens. Unless indoor cricket has been introduced by some IAO unknown to us, no cash can be forwarded for outdoor batts or bals. (signed) L. Magha Dun (Chief Clerk, CAD).'*

Major Fortt, apparently undaunted, had taken a fresh guard with a memo to FDS (Fauji Dilkhush Sabha) in Calcutta, the organisation for Indian Troop stage shows.

'To Lt. Col. Boyman-Turner from Major Fortt, A.S.O.C.— Sir, Can you advise how Indian clerks in G.H.Q. employ can obtain cricket gear for off-duty recreation? Realise not your pigeon but can find no department to deal with this vital need. Grateful for advice of your experience.'

Memo from Lt. Col. Boyman-Turner to Major Fortt :

'Dear Bastion. Agreed not my pigeon. Advice—tell them to buy gear in shops. If they wait until someone official coughs up the rupees they will be too old for the game. By actually incurring expenditure GHQ will immediately have to look into such a heinous crime. Hear Noel Coward has been touring India. Don't send his one-man show to my sepoys, for Buddha's sake. They are all steamed-up about some cricket match in Tophar of all god-forsaken places, so Coward's "London Pride" might take a fall. As ever, "Boysie".'

The brigadier now observed that Major Fortt's patience had run out. He had made a desperate, rush-of-blood stroke . . . and written to an Indian businessman, Sir Shahoshah Jampelpet, renowned for his generosity in presenting football cups to British troops, which had brought him personal thanks from Viceregal Lodge.

'Dear Sir Shahoshah Jampelpet. The Indian clerks of HQ Tophar are sadly in need of cricket gear. No funds seem to exist to cover this small request. Would you, sir, in your great beneficence, consider helping your fellow-countrymen in this way . . .?'

Brigadier Kew-Ballance whistled and closed his eyes. Reading the reply was a mere formality.

'*Sir. Sir Shahoshah Jampelpet is gravely disturbed that a mere major should approach him direct. In accordance with his Knightage Status, Sir Shahoshah does not enter into correspondence with officers below the rank of brigadier. He is taking the matter up with your general as he is waxed wrath that you should try to involve him in such trivial concerns. (signed) A. Dutt Wicki (Second Secretary).*'

Appended was the dire complaint from Sir Jampelpet to General Hammersley-Hampton Brook. Beneath it the general had scrawled . . . '*Major Fortt to see, and attend me with explanation . . .*'

Then followed the Indian Army Order posting Major Fortt to ENSA, the entertainment section in Bombay, with a note stating : '*This officer appears to be more suited to running concert parties than Army Sport.*' The copy of the sad note written to Shrinivassen apologising for failure from the now 'Captain' Fortt, made the brigadier sigh. He was sorry Fortt was 'out'—he'd batted courageously.

From Army Public Relations there now appeared several press cuttings. *The Himalayan Bugle* claimed clerks had been kicked in the teeth . . . the brigadier marked several passages in red ink . . . but the American Services news-sheet, *Starred & Striped Eagle*, caused his monocle to fall for the first time.

'*BRITISH BRASS KOWTOW TO CLERKS*'
'*American Girl Missionary Settles British-Indian Blood Feud*'
by Tech. Sergeant Hank Wuppleberg.

'*Meet Marion Weltzer, folks, as good a looker as she's good hearted. You won't find her in G.I. pin-ups, but she should be there, boys, she should be there. Marion and her husband Cyrus tour the world bringing God to heathen, primitive places. They are now in Tophar.*

'*The under-privileged clerks there had a bleat, a genuine bleat. They challenged the army officers to a cricket game—sort of women's baseball with blue-blood undertones. You'd think the democratic British war-lords would play ball, give the starved* clerks a break—but no sir! The Lords of the Manners, with their eyeglasses and plummy tonsils, said: "We don't play clerks, old man, old scout, old trout . . ." '

"This," glowered the brigadier, "is Boston tea-party stuff!"

'So it looked curtains on the project till the clerks, through their advocate, Mr. Mookerjee, a real hot potato of a Christian Indian, appealed to our Marion to intercede on their behalf. The Indians have actually made her a "Rani", folks—a Queen!'

"Yuk," said the brigadier.

'God had once more called her into action. Fearless, with her Bible, she faced the British top-brass of Tophar. "All men are equal," she told 'em. "What right have you to deny the clerks to play games in their own land?" She said that, folks, on her knees in front of them! Result? British generals have a big re-think going on.

'So it takes a fair citizen of the good old United States to point the way of decent behaviour to the British in India. Salute this mercy sister, fellars. You know there's a God in Heaven when He puts an angel like Rani Marion Weltzer on His American soil. Now she has tucked the injustice of British cricket in India under God's belt. Heck, folks . . . my eyes are wet . . .'

"And so are my pants," stormed the brigadier. "Sheer Yank mush . . . oh, my God!"

He had turned the page to read: 'I WAS MANHANDLED WHILE RAJ CRICKETERS LAUGHED' by Dewan Gupta, *Clarion India*'s Special Cricket Correspondent.'

'In Tophar now there is grave, haunting unrest among Indian clerks at HQ. They issued a harmless challenge to play cricket against the British officers. But these controllers of an affluent organisation for mere sport in war-time called Crusaders, have refused, point-blankedly, to play our dear brothers in toil.

'I, Dewan Gupta, your experienced man on the spot, went to Tophar. One kind word may turn aside a torrent of anger. I heard terrible tales of British cricket persecution from the clerks, bewildered by the dicktorial manner in which their challenge had been dismissed.

'When I tried to interview Colonel Eddgerley-Watkyn-Reed, captain of the Crusaders, in his Queens Club drinking den, I was ruthlessly attacked by a Sikh servant in the pay of the British, outside the shop of Bosha Dravid, Shoemaker & Leatherworker, by Appointment, 11 The Mall, Tophar (Tel: 691).

'Inspite my almost superhuman struggle for life, the Sikh's advantage of surprise proved too much. And all the time he was egged on by these Crusaders on the balcony above.

' "Stifle the Press," they urged the Sikh, who, unable to curb me with his bare hands, had drawn a knife. "Silence Dewan Gupta!" they cried, "muzzle his all-powerful pen!" Although grieviously bodily-harmed, I managed to twist the knife from the thugee's hand and affect my escape.

'One of these British officers, a minor captain Mott, fearful of what I had to expose, called an Australian medical Major Grahame to tend my wounds in his sumptuous flat. He was harsh and butcherlike in his surgical treatment of me, enjoying my moaning agonies which I bore in such silence. But he refused to report my hurts to the authorities or hospitalise me in Delhi on his written certificate. Mott did beg for my silence knowing my influence throughout India but these two officers admitted they were "tight" and alcoholickly sang warlike songs round my bed calling me a punched passenger.

'These British cricket addicks are going to extraordinary lengths to prevent the clerks playing them. A WAC Private Nancy Evans confessed to telephone-tapping of Army secrets, Judge Trevelhayes threatened my life on his self-balancing bicycle, my notebook value 2 rupees was stolen—but, as I have a memory like a sieve, everything poured out and I did not need it.

'It is in my contract to die for the truth of my newspaper. But I shall not sue the poor, misguided Sikh. He is in British pay and one day will see the horror of his ways. CLARION INDIA poses the Tophar officers one question: "Why will you not play the clerks?" And I, Dewan Gupta, now stricken on sick bed, am doing my horizontal best to find the answer . . .'

"This is quite appalling," gasped the brigadier. He skipped another *Himalayan Bugle* story headed 'AMERICA ENTERS CRICKET DISPUTE' which referred to Marion Weltzer as 'Auntie Sam'—and came upon a transcript of Ram Lal Menon's broadcast.

The brigadier's hands trembled. He knew Menon well as a follower of the late Subbra Chandra Bose, leader of the Indian Freedom Movement, who had supported the Japanese in Burma. Menon's knowledge of Britain was not mere hearsay or the usual conceptions based on the works of Dornford Yates or Ethel M. Dell. He had actually worked in a Fleet Street news agency before the war, he understood the British of *The Times*, the *Daily Mirror* and the *Daily Worker*. His soft dulcet voice over the radio had put him in Indian jails several times but these sentences had only served to increase his following.

With a shudder the brigadier ignored dozens more cuttings from Agra, Lahore, Colombo—even Cairo. He noted an Army postal censor's report that news of a clerks' cricket match appeared to dominate Indian sepoys' letters home from Italy. Congress-headed notepaper showed politicians were becoming cricket-conscious. A letter in praise of the Tophar Crusaders from a Wing-Commander ffoliot was left unread.

Brigadier Kew-Ballance had seen enough. After a terse précis of the hard facts for his general, he summed up his report . . .

'*Everything in this file is dynamite but Menon's broadcast is by far the most damaging. As usual he paints for the clerks their imagined picture of an opulent Britain. Useless to point out the absurdities of his similes. To his audience of small-fry Indians, all molehills begin as mountains.*

'*Every journalist in the file blows up the case purposely to inflame anti-British feeling, flogging this ridiculous situation for all it is worth. Agitators have taken over and it is too late for us to implement machinery to curb it. Whatever logic you might apply to answering these clerks, they will not be convinced and remain obstinately "violated" of their "rights".*

'*A lot of harm has been done, sir. Tophar HQ have handled this very badly, even to accepting without demur, a strike which cut off communications. This would suggest a guilty conscience somewhere. I suggest the game be played but that decision must come from Tophar itself. Our official intervention would only increase the embarrassment Colonel Eddgerley-Watkyn-Reed's vacillating attitude has already brought upon G.H.Q.*

'*DISCIPLINARY ACTION: I recommend enquiries be made into Major J. Grahame, RAMC, Captain B. Mott, Army Education, and Private N. Evans, WAC (India), all stationed at Tophar. The American missionary woman is outside our jurisdiction but suggest a strong complaint be handed U.S.A. Red Cross on her using the title "Rani" illegally. As for Judge Trevelhayes, may I dare suggest we ask that American jeep to try again?*'

On the following day the general wrote 'Agreed' on this report and passed it to the Adjutant-General's office, via the Military Secretariat, where the term 'bowler', in its non-cricket form, was used in reference to the future of Colonel Eddgerley-Watkyn-Reed.

Finally a copy of a Demi-Official letter from a representative of the A.G. to the colonel was added to the file.

'*Dear Eddgers. The A.G. is most disquieted by your attitude to the Tophar clerks and this cricket match. Intense inflammatory press and radio coverage here in Delhi is lowering Indian staff morale. It is also bad for the British image at this crucial time. You know as well we do how certain elements can capitalise on this seemingly small matter.*

'*So the suggestion is, play this match, be gracious about it— and win. To give the game status, we think the Governor should be invited to attend.*

'*Yours aye, "Pinny" (Col. Pinworth-Bodkin).*'

The Anglo-Indian typist, after heading the letter 'Private & Confidential', phoned her clerk-brother in Tophar who passed on the contents to Mookerjee for three rupees.

Chapter Eighteen

SELECTION COMMITTEE

THE Delhi directive acted on the colonel like a 'red-alert' air-raid warning. He dived for shelter in the refectory room with his Crusader committee.

"The A.G.'s displeased," he told them distractedly, "an' that also means the Viceroy an' the C-in-C. There's a flap on. We've got to accept."

"Play the clerks?" gasped Nupp-Jevons.

"However softly worded, this is an order." The colonel waved the quarto sheet. "We play 'em . . ."

"I've said so all along," said Mott.

"Quiet, Mott," said the colonel, nettled. "Nothin' you have done has helped at all."

"All this terrible press," said Baker-Stewart, "and that praying mantis of a Yank missionary . . ."

"Steady, Stewy," said the colonel, "a lady's name, yer know . . ."

"Sorry, sir."

"They're allies, the Americans . . . although I can't say Mrs. Weltzer is exactly my cup of char . . ."

"She's a wonderful woman, sir," said Mott. "The Indians call her 'rani'—she's a light . . ."

"Good God, not 'suttee' . . .!"

"No, sir, a light in our lives . . . the true love of God . . ."

"Missionaries like her," said Barkside-Twist, "taught Indian clerks sedition in their schools . . . she's a crank . . ."

"Talkin' of cranks," said the colonel, "I must tell you that my mem in Kashmir heard that awful Menon broadcast. Had to

close me grandson's ears when me name came up. Now she has
written in no uncertain terms that we should play the clerks an'
put 'em in their place. An',," he added triumphantly, "she wrote
that *before* I got the A.G.'s directive . . ."

"I say! Really? Most significant!" the committee was impressed.

"The mem," cried the colonel proudly, "knows India. She
was born here in India . . . although, of course," he added
hastily, "she's not *of* the country . . ."

All heads shook furiously.

"Daughter of General Furnival-Heathcote . . . 88 not out
against the Navy at Lord's . . . Julia knows her cricket. Had four
brothers at Marlborough. 'Play the babus', she says, 'give 'em a
hidin' ' . . . I've got a lot of faith in me mem's judgement . . ."

"And the A.G. bears out her opinion," said Barkside-Twist.

"But," said the colonel emphatically, "she does advise me not
to involve the Crusaders."

"*Not* involve the Crusaders?" Innes-Whiffen sat forward.
"But that's the challenge, Eddgers, surely? The club against the
clerks . . .?"

"With the R.A.F. gone," said the colonel, "no Burma Civil
Service, an' other players posted away, we must admit we're no
longer up to full strength. But now me mem has come up with
the answer . . ."

"Who will play the clerks, then?" asked Mott.

"The British Army, sir!"

"The Army?" The committee looked dazed.

"The Army," said the colonel positively. "If these babus want
to play at Glenbourn, then they'll face the Army. The Army
made India an', be God, we'll tackle such a challenge alone—
me mem's way!"

"Bravo! Bravo!" The Crusaders stood, applauding their
captain.

Akkar Singh, ear to hinge, was deeply disturbed. Suddenly
the British seemed to have taken the initiative. He cursed
Eddgerley-Watkyn-Reed memsahib for swaying the Army into
action.

"I think," said Baker-Stewart in admiration, "we should minute a vote of thanks to our chairman and dear Julia for the way they have handled this very delicate matter."

"Hear, hear!"

The colonel smiled, looked at his hands.

"Thank the mem be all means," he said modestly, "but, after all, it was me duty as captain . . ."

"Ah, yes, sir," said Mott, "as captain of the *Crusaders*. But will you be captain of the *Army* side?"

There was a stunned silence. The colonel reddened, Baker-Stewart mouthed incoherently.

"Did I hear Mott correctly?" gasped Innes-Whiffen.

"Captain Mott," Nupp-Jevons was breathing heavily, "are you seriously suggestin' we drop the pilot who has steered us through this fearful upheaval, that we go on to the field under any other leader than our own dear Eddgers?" The lieutenant-colonel was deeply affected.

"No," stammered Mott. "What I mean is, if this is to be an Army side, there's a Major B. H. Lyon in Delhi, the Gloucester skipper . . . not to mention Major D. R. Jardine, now, I believe, in Simla and one of England's greatest Test captains . . ."

"They are only majors!" snapped Nupp-Jevons. "Eddgers is a full colonel. Can't you get that into your thick head, boy?"

"I am in yer hands, gentlemen," said the colonel brokenly, his eyes closed. "If it is the feelin' of the meetin' I hand over the reins . . ."

"No, sir, never!" Baker-Stewart clutched his colonel's hand. "*Now* look what you've done, Mott, you bloody fool . . . upset dear Eddgers . . ."

"It wasn't meant personally . . ."

"We're all behind you, Eddgers," said Innes-Whiffen, "barrin' Mott . . ."

"Apologise!" demanded the committee.

"I apologise," mumbled Mott, "but, with first-class army cricketers available, I don't see . . ."

"Unequivocably!" they demanded.

"I apologise unequivocably, sir," sighed Mott.

"Spoken like a gentleman," said the colonel quietly. "When yer make a grave social blunder like that again, Mott, always face up to it. Well, thank you, gentlemen, I'd like that vote of confidence minuted."

"Really, Mott, that was a ghastly boner," said Barkside-Twist. "You're lucky our Eddgers is such a human chap."

"Oddly enough," said the colonel, smiling again, "Mott has, rather indecorously I admit, touched on a point I already had in mind about the Army team. I don't feel we want to import any officers who are first-class players—they are apt to try an' run things. But in Delhi now there's Sergeant-Major Denis Compton an' Battery Sergeant-Major Joseph Hardstaff, both England players. Now *they* might add some weight to our side."

" 'Other ranks' being used, eh?" Baker-Stewart saw his role of opening bowler jeopardised. "Are you sure this is right?"

"These chaps *are* Army personnel," said the colonel. "An officer may be the backbone of the Army but, to be effective, he must have privates . . ."

"Er, quite, sir."

"Fancy playing alongside Compton and Hardstaff," said an enraptured Mott.

"I would remind yer, Mott," said the colonel coldly, "that, if they play, you may be dropped . . ."

"Oh, no, sir!"

"You don't deserve to play, Mott," said Innes-Whiffen. "You tried to depose Eddgers, you patched up that Gupta reporter so that he could write that gallin' muck about us . . ."

"He could have died on the Mall for all you cared," snapped Mott. "Even though he did eventually rat on me, I just couldn't pass by on the other side."

"The other side of what?" asked Nupp-Jevons.

"The Mall. I was the good Samaritan. Marion . . . that is, Mrs. Weltzer, said so. She has shown me a new way of life . . ."

Baker-Stewart's experienced eyes watched him sardonically.

"You can't keep your mind off her, can you?"

"Stop castigatin' Mott, Baker-Stewart," ordered the colonel as he referred to a note on his blotter. "An' go an' ring a Major

Fortt in ASOC, in Delhi . . . he knows the whereabouts of
Compton an' Hardstaff."

Baker-Stewart fairly leapt from the room and Akkar Singh
only just escaped detection by slipping into a broom cupboard
with no time to replace the cork in the hinge. It boded ill for
the clerks that the British were suddenly alert enough to make
Akkar Singh misjudge his timing so badly. He was called in to
supply drinks, brushing cobwebs from his beard and only withdrew when Baker-Stewart had returned, dejected, from the
Delhi phone call.

"Major Fortt has been transferred to ENSA, sir," he said.
"Been posted in disgrace apparently . . . that clerk Shrinivassen
contacted him about the game . . ."

"There, I knew it!" exploded Innes-Whiffen, "The clerks
want Compton and Hardstaff . . ."

"No, Whiffy," snorted Baker-Stewart. "I spoke to Major
Bayley of Welfare. He told me Sergeant-Major Hardstaff had
gone back to U.K. . . ."

"Oh, blast!" said the colonel. "We hadn't finished with him
yet."

"And Sergeant-Major Compton is . . ." He paused, unable to
continue.

"What is it, Stewy?" asked the colonel anxiously.

"Compton is on tour, sir . . . with a GHQ *soccer* team!"

"Soccer!" The committee rocked in amazement.

"Damn it!" roared the colonel. "What's GHQ up to, detailin'
a Lord's Test cricketer to play soccer!"

"He's Arsenal," said Mott, "left-wing . . ."

"Keep your politics out of it, Mott," said Innes-Whiffen.

"This must finish Compton for ever with the M.C.C.," said
Barkside-Twist.

"Well," said the colonel gloomily, "who else can we get?"

"There is," said Mott, "always Major Grahame . . ."

"NEVER!" The rest of the committee spoke as one man.

"'Fraid the judge an' me mem boobed a bit over him,"
admitted the colonel. "That Australian has proved a great social
disappointment to us in Tophar."

"He's just not pukka," said Innes-Whiffen. "Oughtn't we to ask him to resign?"

"Eh—er, no," said the colonel agitatedly. "After all, he's done nothin' officially wrong . . . it's just his manner—but he must remain a Crusader."

"Why must he?" asked Nupp-Jevons.

"Oh, Nuppy, you of all people!" Inwardly the colonel cursed the naïvety of the lieutenant-colonel who had now so completely forgotten the hanging Crusader incident as to be actually raising queries about Grahame's eligibility for the club. As far as Nuppy was concerned, the incident *had* never happened . . . but the colonel still found this mental black-out ploy extremely hard to achieve for himself. "Oh, never mind now, Nuppy," he went on lamely, "but I know the judge, our president, wouldn't stand for Grahame bein' chucked out. He's in the Pageant, remember . . . wouldn't do for us to cause bad feelin' over that . . ."

"I think Grahame's a grand chap," said Mott, "a bit bohemian, perhaps, but he's a fine doctor . . . and a damn good egg, come up the hard way . . ."

"He's certainly hard-boiled," laughed Baker-Stewart.

"I don't care what sort of egg he is," boomed the colonel, "forget him. He is not on the agenda. What we want now are cricketers."

"Sergeant Wood of Ordnance is a good bowler," said Barkside-Twist. "Had a trial for Surrey once, I believe."

"Yes, and took seven wickets against us," said Innes-Whiffen, "when Burma Civil Service 'borrowed' him. But when he rolls up his sleeves—those awful tattoo marks . . ."

"We'll include Wood," said the colonel, "but he must button down his sleeves when he's introduced to the Governor."

"Ah, His Excellency is coming, then?" said Nupp-Jevons.

"I invited him as the A.G. suggested . . . adds tone to the proceedin's. Won't be any hanky-panky from the clerks if H.E. is there."

Akkar Singh mouthed an oath outside the door. Typical of the Raj, making a Durbar out of a simple cricket match.

"We'll line up in front of the pav," said the colonel, "an' I'll introduce H.E. to the team . . ."

"What about the clerks?" asked Mott.

"Don't want to embarrass 'em," said the colonel, "so H.E. will only meet the Army side."

"Private Sinker of the Signals is a good bat," said Mott. "Got a hundred against us . . ."

"Includin' a private seems stretchin' democracy a bit far," said the colonel. "Clerks despise private soldiers. We'll have to upgrade him for the match."

The motion was carried and Baker-Stewart phoned Colonel Blinkhorn-Marsh of 'Signals'. Within the hour an amazed Sinker was sewing a chevron on his sleeve. "Fancy bein' made a lance-jack," he told his bemused 'muckers', "me, wi' a crime sheet like mine!"

"Sergeants Harrison and Frinton both did well for that Rizmak side against the Music Club," said Barkside-Twist. "Harrison was quite fast . . ."

"Yes," agreed the colonel, "poor old Enoch Dorlin'-Wells couldn't play the 'cello for weeks after that 'bumper'. That's why Harrison was never allowed to play at Glenbourn again. Enoch threatened to resign if he did . . ."

"Frinton is rather a rustic cricketer," said Innes-Whiffen. "Cow-shots a lot . . . no style . . ."

"He got a hundred in that match," said Baker-Stewart, "in about forty minutes . . ."

"Pity he smiled when he hit the vicar for those four successive sixes," grumbled Nupp-Jevons, "awful bad form . . ."

"That was sheer exhilaration," said Mott, "I couldn't blame him. Wish I'd been at the wicket for that rubbish . . ."

"Lob bowlin' should be treated with more dignity," said the colonel. "The vicar bowled 'em for Charterhouse as a boy. However I feel that Frinton an' Harrison are certainly the right material for these clerks."

Baker-Stewart checked the list.

"With Major McBurn, sir, that makes us eleven. That is . . ." he looked at the colonel significantly, "if Mott is to play."

"Well, gentlemen," said the colonel, relishing this moment of power. "What do yer think?"

Mott had whitened under his tan. He gripped the arms of his chair. They couldn't . . . they just couldn't . . .

"What's the alternative, Mr. Chairman?" asked Barkside-Twist, sensitive to his daughter's strange infatuation for Mott. "Is there anyone else? Other than Grahame?"

Mott choked and rose to state his case.

"If you drop me," he said slowly, "the clerks may think I'm being ostracised. They might even make more publicity out of it . . . I mean, I am top of the Crusader batting averages with 26 point 7 recurring . . ."

"That sounds like blackmail!" thundered the colonel.

"But Mott is right, sir," said Barkside-Twist. "The clerks could make capital out of it. We know Mott can't keep his mouth closed. If he plays it may avoid another international incident."

"Thank you, sir," said Mott, sitting.

"Stand up agen!" said the colonel sharply. "I gave you no permission to sit."

Mott jerked to his feet.

"If you play," said the colonel ponderously, "will you give me yer word, as an emergency commissioned officer an' temporary gentleman, you won't go leakin' to the newspapers agen . . . an' keep out of trouble?"

"You have my word, sir."

"Right," said the colonel, "so be it. Add Mott to the list."

"Just one suggestion, sir . . ."

"Mott! You gave me yer word . . ."

"I know, sir, but I was going to suggest we played this game for the Red Cross . . ."

"I hope to God," said the colonel fervently, "the Red Cross won't be needed . . ."

"By jove!" Barkside-Twist half-rose. "You know, sir, that's a deuced good idea . . . make it a charity match . . ."

"With the Governor there, too," said Baker-Stewart, pondering deeply, "holy smoke, nothing could go wrong . . ."

By now the colonel was at one with them.

"Ah, I *see*. Proceeds to go to the Red Cross. Yes, that is actually a splendid idea. A charity match would knock out any vindictiveness, what? Yes, minute that, Mr. Secretary. The match shall be played for Red Cross funds . . . proposed by me, seconded by Mott. All in favour?"

Everyone 'ayed' enthusiastically. Mott looked suitably modest.

The colonel stared at him thoughtfully.

"Tell me, Mott . . . were you goin' to suggest this idea, even if we had not selected you?"

"Oh, yes, sir. If I'd been dropped, it was to be my last hope of reprieve . . ."

The committee laughed good-naturedly.

"At least he's honest," said Nupp-Jevons. "Akkar Singh! Autora drinks lao . . ."

After a suitable pause, Akkar Singh knocked and entered. He had hoped to escape with the news to Moplah, but the Crusaders were thirsty to-day.

"I will write to this clerk, er, Shrinivassen," said the colonel. "Give him formal acceptance of the fixture—on behalf of the British Army. Akkar Singh, will you arrange to have the letter delivered?"

"I will convey it myself, sahib," said the Sikh. "In that way it is sure to arrive safely."

"What an obligin' fellar you are, Akkar Singh," said the colonel.

Chapter Nineteen

SECRET SESSION—GULLIVERS HOTEL

NO SUCH historic meeting could be held in a mere canteen. The All-India Civilian team selectors met in Gullivers Hotel which was advertised as '*Ultra-modern. H & C Watered Bed & Breakfast, Lounge à la Parée, extra chic*'. The Anglo-Indian manager had allocated the clerks a small back bedroom on the top floor and nimbu panni—lime juice—was provided. Swarmi opened the proceedings seated on the bedside table, Shrinivassen occupying the only chair while Mookerjee reclined on the rumpled bed.

"I formally declare the momentous meeting open," said Swarmi, his voice cracking with emotion. "The Press took up our cause, America rose religiously on our side. We have won our fair rights. The radio was, sadly, a failure as Ram Lal Menon did not mention any one of us by name, a most underhanded oversight. However, through persistent perseverance on my part after much dalliance and delay by the British, they have agreed to play us . . ."

"Who is dalliancin' an' delayin' now?" snapped Mookerjee. "Cut the crackle, Swarmi, an' let Shrinivassen elaborate position."

"Well, brothers," smiled the captain, "this is indeed moment of fortune's fruition. First I will read the colonel's epistle of accceptance which Akkar Singh brought me to-day at cost of five rupees." He clared his throat. " '*Colonel Eddgerley-Watkyn-Reed sends his compliments to Mr. Shrinivassen, captain of the clerks' team . . .*' "

"He has ignored and abstained our proper 'All-India' name," said Swarmi contemptuously. "That is insult to begin and start with . . ."

"Hush, please," said Shrinivassen. He was savouring this bliss-ful moment. Many times he had typed such formal cards for his own colonel to the Governor's A.D.C., but never before had one been addressed personally to himself. He was to treasure it for life. ". . . *'and informs him . . .'*," he continued . . .

"Where the 'beg to inform'?" sneered Swarmi. "It should be 'beg'."

"Oh, stop beggin' the question, Swarmi," said Mookerjee. "We only have this room for two hours till commercial trader in tooth-brushes returns to re-occupy. Proceed, Shrinivassen . . ."

" *'. . . that owing to the cessation of hostilities . . .'* "

" 'Cessation'?" laughed Mookerjee. "That is good one—'hostilities' are just about to begin!"

" *'. . . the Crusaders no longer have sufficient members to provide a team. Postings away from Tophar and the Arts Festival have depleted our numbers . . .'* "

"But they are again refusing," wailed Swarmi. "Lily-livers . . ."

"You are past-master o' panic stations, Swarmi," shouted Mookerjee. "We know they are goin' to play, this is just customary British prevaricationism an' hum-buggery."

" *'However,'* " Shrinivassen went on, " *'the British Army itself will accept your challenge. The game will be held at Glenbourn on Sunday, 23 September 1945, at 1130 hours in the presence of H.E. The Governor, in aid of Red Cross funds.'* "

"Ah!" shrieked Swarmi. "Suddenly it is all so pomp and ceremonialised . . . like a Viceroy's gardening party . . ."

"I knew about the Governor's presence bein' invited," said Mookerjee thoughtfully, "but now a charity match they have made it for Red Cross. 'Tis not 'zactly as we planned or desired. But, havin' attracted high-power attention o' Adjutant-General, 'tis all complimentary to us."

"If British want vast audience to witness their defeat," cried Swarmi, "it is in our favour. They shall be ground into the ground . . ."

"Is there any more o' the colonel's jargonese?" asked Mookerjee.

"Yes," said Shrinivassen, "he asks that I inform him of my acceptance of these terms. This I have already done by return of Akkar Singh. And the colonel finishes his letter with 'God Save the King-Emperor'!"

"Trust the British to end by flag-waggin' their figure-head," chuckled Mookerjee. "'Tis good you replied quickly, Shrinivassen, or we might find the Army has left Tophar as well . . ."

"That day will come," boomed Swarmi, "they shall be driven out . . ."

"Oh, stop tub-thumpin' your soap-box high-horse," snapped Mookerjee.

"Now, friends," said Shrinivassen, "I have further good and, as yet, untold news to unfold. Captain Mott telephoned me that he has obtained some cricket gear for us . . ."

"It will be useless," cried Swarmi, "the bats will run splinters into our workaday hands . . ."

"Oh, what conspiratorial nonsense you disgorge, Swarmi!" said Shrinivassen impatiently. "Captain Mott has taken much trouble for us. He has borrowed gear from St. Hayward's School games-master, now the pupils have broken out for holidays. 'Tis gesture of goodwill and Merry Christmas in true British way. I personally am glad and grateful."

"'Twill cost us nothin' to accept that gear," agreed Mookerjee. "But, remember, Mott could be two-faced double-agent, pretendin' to be weak idiot but with method in his madhouse. However, ours is not to reason why, but to do, an' cast the die."

"Then," said Shrinivassen, unrolling a list written on a wallpaper sample, "shall we select our team?"

"I am manager," said Swarmi stubbornly.

"Durin' actual play proceedin's, Swarmi," warned Mookerjee, "you are off field, unseen, unhonoured. I am umpire an' must perforce have say in what men perform about me. But any castin' vote must be Shrinivassen's. He is captain who will implement fairly all my suggested tactics on field."

Shrinivassen read aloud the clerks' individual qualifications and their many cricket triumphs. But actual press-cutting proof had only been obtained from Jalim Singh, who had played for Punjab University, and Sashi Bokaneer, a fast bowler from Lahore. For the rest, it was a question of psychoanalysing the strength of their boasts. As the names were sifted through, Shrinivassen automatically put Torkham Wazir in the team and his co-selectors nodded approvingly.

"He will be no good as cricketer," said Mookerjee, "but 'twill avoid murder to choose him. At least he will embarrass the British . . ."

"Futti Pant is the only wicket-keeper volunteer," said Shrinivassen.

There was a furtive tap on the door.

"Hist," whispered Swarmi. "Could be British spy . . ."

"Or tooth-brush salesman back," said Mookerjee.

Swarmi's eyes rolled anxiously as Shrinivassen opened the door.

"It is I, cricket reporter for *The Himalayan Bugle*," said Moplah, his fingertips touched in the namaste. "I come for press conference . . ."

"Ah, most correct proceedin'," said Mookerjee with delight. "We are now selectin' team. I am tellin' you, man, you are now on hot news!"

"Yes," sighed Moplah, "Akkar Singh has been to my office . . . I am not being able to afford him much longer . . . but he has told me it is the Army we now play. I know everything save your individual team, the names of which I must publish as all will want to buy the paper."

"Sit patiently," said Mookerjee, "while we continue to collate . . ."

Moplah slid to the floor by the wainscot and began to pencil down his story.

'COLONEL CLIMBS DOWN AFTER UPHILL FIGHT'

The Army to-day accepted the challenge from the Tophar clerks for a cricket match at Glenbourn on 23rd Sept. The Crusader Club being now in a state of flucks, losing members since Japan lost the war, the Army have taken up cudgels against the clerks instead. At a meeting at Gullivers Hotel (b & b

6 rupees) I was present when All-India Civilian Committee selected their winning team. They are as follows:——

Moplah filled in the names as Shrinivassen called them. Mookerjee was adamant that Kazi Mohammed be excluded for spreading the rumour about himself and Krischa. At last the team was complete and, in spite of bickering between Mookerjee and Swarmi, the latter had his name included for publication as 'manager'.

"Now I can finish my deathless prose," said Moplah, prodding a row of dots under the team. "Just one punch line is needed . . ." He chewed his pencil reflectively, then wrote with a flourish : '*May the best representative team of India win!*'

"Oh, most capital journalese !" cried Mookerjee over his shoulder. "That is really magnificent impartial observation."

Moplah smiled modestly and accepted a glass of nimbu panni.

"Baker-Stewart sahib is giving me his team tonight," he said, "and has also commissioned me for posters to be bill-posted all over Tophar with both teams named . . ."

"Posters !" gasped Swarmi. "Like fillum stars we'll be . . . !"

"No pictures though," said Moplah hastily, "just names . . ."

"There is no hoardin' in India big enough to take Swarmi's picture," said Mookerjee. "Names must suffice, but accomplishments accompanyin' each identity can be inserted accordin'ly. Nothin' more rallyin' than a good poster . . . the public will fill the ground to our support."

"There is to go on the poster also," said Moplah, "the band . . ."

"The what?" Mookerjee gaped in surprise.

"The honourable secretary phoned me . . . the band of the Punjab Grenadiers is to play during the cricket . . ."

Baker-Stewart had not been exaggerating when he advised the Crusader committee that a band would upset the clerks. They sat numbed.

"They did not seek our collusion on a band," snarled Mookerjee. "The British Army is mad as marching hares on their martial music . . . majors an' minors . . ."

"This is most foul keyboard treachery," cried Swarmi, "abandon the band, I say . . . it is cricket, not concert pitch."

"May I point out with sight of hind," said Moplah, fearful of losing the poster order, "that the Punjab Grenadiers band is comprised of our Indian brothers. Only their bandmaster is British and he but mere sub-standard warrant-officer. By excluding them they will lose extra pay. Surely they will be our allies behind their instruments? They will want us to win and use their wind accordingly."

"This is uncommon-sense indeed, Moplah," cried Mookerjee. "You are a seer, a second Tagore, far superior to that British ambassadory, Stratford Cripps. Moplah is right—the band shall play an' blow out their hearts' contents—on our side!"

"I note," said Moplah, consulting the list, "that Dikshit has not been selected . . ."

"I unnerstand British courtesy," said Shrinivassen firmly. "Dikshit cannot play—the Army scorer is a lady . . ."

Chapter Twenty

THE POSTER

IN THE rear of *The Himalayan Bugle* go-down, Retti Moplah, now compositor, sat with tweezers, setting type. The boxed cricket match announcement for his paper, which was also to be a facsimile of the poster, was proving a bigger job than he anticipated—the clerks wanted so much personal data included. Already he had changed his type-faces several times to meet the demands on his limited resources. His Windsor and Cheltenham Bold had been exhausted on the Indian team, which would have displeased the British. Now, even before setting up the Army eleven, he was forced to use fragments of Antique Old Style, Bodoni Ultra and Baskerville. Lack of capital letters was a problem. The *Bugle*'s ten and twelve point Caslon Old Face was useless for poster work. But Moplah loved a challenge. With an affectionate elbow-wipe, he burnished the nameplate of his flat-bed press so that the words 'Wharfdale Model One' shone with more brass brilliance.

He was driving home another wedge when a knocking outside echoed his hammer.

"Come in," he called. "I am in printing works adjacent."

Jack Grahame stooped into the office beyond, cannoned the desk in the darkness before reaching Moplah at his trays.

"You Moplah?" he asked casually. "I've got the Army team list. Major Baker-Stewart's compliments . . . for what they are worth . . ."

"Ah, major sahib, the presses are waiting white-hot for this item."

Moplah was most impressed. A British major in his go-down.

Not a very smart one, admittedly, but, nevertheless, an officer. Moplah had expected young Wahdi to be sent with the list. To acknowledge the importance of the occasion, he lit a joss-stick in a brass holder to fill the room with its heavy, sweet smell.

"I bid you welcome, major-sahib," he said. "I am indeed honoured that the British should give their messenger such personified status."

"I volunteered," said Grahame, settling carefully in a creaking basket chair. "I wanted to meet you, anyway . . ."

"Me?" Moplah spilled some Abbey Text into his aproned lap in surprise.

"Yes, I phoned you about a bed for Gupta . . ."

"Gracious me—the doctor. Ah, yes, you put me between the devil and two deep blue stools over that. Gupta was a brother journalist in trouble—but he was also public-troublemaker Number One. Mookerjee, who runs the clerks' cricket, was most firmly adamant that all hotels and hostels in Tophar were barred to Gupta."

"I thought you Indians stuck together!" Graham's laughter wafted the cobwebs in the rafters.

"Gupta is a snake," said Moplah witheringly. "No scrupulous principles. He came here to pirate my news. Other newspapers would phone and ask 'Moplah News Service' to provide, ten rupees, world rights, but not Gupta. He came nosy-parkering in Tophar for himself."

"Gupta has now landed me in the dirt in his newspaper . . ."

"*Clarion India*, yes, I read his scurvy article. He maligned you for tending his hurts. Said you acted in butcherly fashion, and accused you of being drunk and disaudible in song . . ."

"We were not. Gupta purposely distorted our chat about Shakespeare's *Titus Andronicus* . . ."

"Gupta is not qualified to distort the Bard of Avignon . . ."

"Well, he certainly drew GHQ's attention to Nancy, Mott an' me. My surgeon-general, who can cremate men at a glance, gave me a severe reprimand. Now I've lost promotion—not that I care about bein' a half-colonel, but it means I'm stuck with the 'crown' for the rest of me service . . ."

"Goodness, but surely your King-Emperor . . ."

"I mean a major's 'crown'—but I needed the money that went with an upgradin'. Mott should have got a similar rollickin' but his colonel's on leave. Mott, bein' left in charge, gave himself an absolute pardon. But Miss Evans had to apologise to Senior-Commander Short, which is like offerin' a meat ball to a tiger . . ."

"Ah, she is Major Baker-Stewart's . . ."

"Forget I mentioned her," said Grahame hastily. "I want your co-operation, Moplah. This Gupta bastard promised on the sanctity of Mott's bed an' his own grandmother's grave that he would not print a word about us . . ."

"Alas," said Moplah, "Gupta knew such a promise had no validity. His grandmother would have no grave. She might be left on towers of silence for the vultures or be burned on a pyre and her body set to float away on the river . . ."

"Yes, I've seen that . . . gulls perch on 'em, use 'em as islands . . ."

"They are naughty birds to do that," said Moplah, "but do not joke about death, sahib—it is a most serious occasion in our life."

"No offence meant . . . but Gupta played us for suckers an' now I'd like some equally charmin' last rites for him."

"I shall publish the truth," exploded Moplah.

"No," howled Grahame, "any more newspaper publicity will get me reduced to the rank o' stretcher bearer. Now, you see this HQ pass?"

Moplah studied the photograph through his large glasses.

"Groppi Jat, the chowkidar," he confirmed.

"We found that on Gupta. He says he bought it for twenty chips . . . but, who knows, maybe he beat him up to get it . . ."

"Oh, we do not beat the old! That is monstrously savage of Gupta. The old in India are venerated for their senility. But how can I help you if my pen is to keep mum?"

"Well, you know the Indian Press world, Moplah. I'm not a vindictive sod as a rule, but if you'd seen Miss Evans after that sow Hazel had finished with her, cryin' her eyes out, fit to bust . . ."

"Bust?" quavered Moplah.

"I want Gupta shown up to the authorities. This stolen pass is evidence enough—only don't mention *me* . . ."

"A true newspaperman never reveals the sources of . . ."

"Spare me that, brother. Gupta said that, then buggered off an' revealed all . . ."

"Most unethical." Moplah fingered the pass in a quandary. "There is, of course, the Press Council . . ."

"Now yer cookin' with gas! Report him for bribery an' corruption . . ."

Moplah faltered. Threatening transgressors with the Press Council was simple—but its composition, its function and even where it met remained a mystery to him. He feared all 'governing bodies', mistrusted any concern or power over his livelihood. Bring Gupta to judgement before the mythical Press Council and these ogres might enquire into *The Himalayan Bugle*. He paid subscriptions to a 'Press Fund' every month when a Mr. Kauji Khan called . . . but Moplah was convinced that this was mere protection money as Khan always carried a pistol.

"I must consider this most carefully, sahib," he said earnestly. "To inform upon a brother writer is a big undertaking. However, I am sympathetic that you have been treated badly by India's guttersniping press for which I am most whole-heartedly ashamed."

"You could, o' course, get him arrested . . ."

"On what charge?"

"Breach o' the Official Secrets Act, theft uv a GHQ pass which would have given him access to British war secret weapons— flame-throwers, death-rays, poison gas, atom bombs, ENSA . . ."

"Gracious—all that—here in Tophar!" Moplah shook some more type in his lap. "All this time we have been living here in cloudy cuckoo land on a veritable hotbed of scorched earth policy!"

"Oh, you're safe enough. However, that pass would've given Gupta access to all command HQs, including Delhi. But you,

Moplah, our man in Tophar, you played fair . . . took no such mean advantage . . ."

The point scored.

"Of course," cried Moplah, outraged, "I acceded graciously to the 'No Pass for the Press' HQ rule. Gupta flaunted it by theft—a most dishonourable discrediting of our penmanship profession."

"Jus' think how Gupta could've scooped yer, time an' agen, on military stories if I hadn't relieved him o' that pass . . ."

"My word, yes. I would have been most bewildered by his constant supply of information. Oh, rest assured, major-sahib, I shall use this pass most guardedly for mutual benefit."

"Right." Grahame rose to go. "Nail Gupta for me . . . okay?"

"Just a minute, sahib." Moplah was scrutinising the Army team list carefully. "There is an omission here staring me in the face."

"What?"

"The Army has no manager or twelfth man."

"Should we have 'em?"

"The clerks have them."

"Well, I s'pose, if you stretch a point, the Army's manager is the Commander-in-Chief, Sir Auchinleck . . . no, no! For krisakes, don't write that down! I'm in deep enough as it is. Won't the presence o' the Governor obviate the manager's post?"

"Ah, of course, he is your virtual controller . . . I will omit 'manager' then . . . but a twelfth man the Army must have."

"Why, for God's sake . . . ?"

"Surely it is an insult to the clerks, major-sahib . . . it reveals a British belief that our bowling cannot hurt even one of them . . ."

Grahame's laugh again rattled the tin roof supports and a cobweb floated down.

"The Army, Moplah, hasn't got any more men . . ."

"There is you, sahib . . ."

"Me? They'd run a mile on hot coals before choosin' me. They've been stiff-armin' me for weeks . . ."

"I wish for you to be 'twelfth man'. It is honour due to you

to compensate for loss of your colonelcy. I will print it bold . . .
it will be good advertisement for your doctoring practice . . ."

"Gawd, no!"

"The clerks will be offended if there is no Army 'twelfth
man' . . ."

"I have a feelin'." sighed Grahame, "that, even if I say 'no',
yer goin' to print it . . ."

"What else can I do?" Moplah spread his hands helplessly.
"The poster would be incomplete. I am an artist, sahib. I cannot have people stop me on the Mall and say: 'Retti Moplah,
you have forgot to include the Army "twelfth man"—you are
guilty of printing error'. It would be bad for my business. I am
sure under your rugby exterior you have kind heart . . . you
will accommodate me . . .?"

"A'right. I'll oblige . . . provided you agree to grind Gupta
to dust."

"Er—yes, of course," Moplah gulped. "My pencil is poised
above this pad of half imperial paper for name, rank and
credentials."

"Wha' for? This is a cricket match, not a medical board . . ."

"Look, all your brother officers have inserted their qualifications."

"*So* they have! The big-headed pommie bastards!" He
checked the list again. "Right, mark me down as Major J.
Grahame . . . no, no 'y' and add an 'e' . . . s'right . . . R.A.M.C.
—I did play for a scratch hospital side in Dover . . ."

"You will need more . . . see how many other clubs each of
your players have? Are you not also a Tophar Crusader?"

"Ye-es, well, in name only . . . under duress—*their* duress. No,
leave out the Crewsaders."

"You will see that Mookerjee, our umpire, has inserted his
Calcutta tramway qualification. Are you not also tram man . . .?"

"Mookerjee's a tram man? What d'ya know? I only sing
about 'em . . ."

"Ah, I have heard Wahdi, the dog boy, rend your song . . .
most droll, yet deeply significant . . . '*If you spit, 'tis a rupee
fine*' . . ."

"A *rupee*? He's ruddy Indianised it! Is nuthin' sacred?"

"You British are strange about spitting," said Moplah, "just as you are about clearing your noses. We throw away in gutter —but you bundle up in handkerchiefs, to carry the germs in your pockets . . ."

"You have a hygienic point there, Moplah, but we must, after all, always keep our British phlegm . . ."

"See," cried Moplah, studying his pencilled lay-out. "Your name adds much classical distinction to my paper. You are only Melbourne RAM in advertisement . . ."

"Hey, add the 'C' . . . I know Tophar's opinion o' me, but I don't want it shouted abroad. That's better . . . say, d'you work this broadsheet all on yer lonesome?"

"Goodness gracious, no. I employ two linotype operators, two compositors and one weak tea boy, but they are so unionised as to leave work at six each night. In the morning I regret they are not so punctiliously punctual. Thus most donkey work burden falls upon me. I write everything. The poster too, I am telling you, is also giving me headache. For it I must use wooden type . . ."

"Suitable for a cricket match . . ."

"Ah, you joke willow-wise. But I have insufficient lettering of capital nature so I shall, perforce, have to cut them in leather as well . . . in runic type."

"Moplah, you're a true craftsman. Proud to know yer."

Grahame rose, thrust out his hand. Moplah goggled . . . surely the major did not expect payment as well?

"Cheers, Moplah." The hand remained outstretched.

With a little whimper of realisation, the editor seized it with both ink-stained hands, pumping up and down in delight.

"I will personally escort you to my door, dear major-sahib," he sniffed, deeply moved. Holding his heavy Victorian oil lamp, he guided his precious visitor through the office into the alley.

"Good-night, major-sahib!" He shouted loudly for his neighbours to hear and hated Gupta even more that he could not call Grahame 'colonel'.

The Australian patted his shoulder and was gone, lost in the shadows beyond the dimly-lit kerosene lamps of the bazaar. Moplah stood, tears glistening on his pock-marked face. That such a decent hand-shaking complimentary chap should only be 'twelfth man' and not even be eager to see his name in print let alone accept free advertising as a doctor . . . oh, the British were ever contradictions of themselves.

He scrambled back into his editorial office, adjusted a sheet of foolscap in the Oliver and typed his story headline : 'MAJOR GRAHAME TO BE ARMY TWELFTH MAN — *Singing Australian Tram Doctor To Make Presence Felt At Glenbourn.*'

As he corrected the errors he found in the Army team list, he caught sight of the red pass on his desk.

"This, Gupta," he muttered, "is insurance against you for life . . ."

In a further burst of gratitude he added 'M.O.' after Grahame's name on the poster.

But, with the war over, Moplah knew that, if the *Bugle* was to survive, its policy must continue to follow Gupta's and harass the Raj. Moplah felt an inner sadness. He had always avoided offending the British on whom he relied heavily for circulation. Grand Theatre productions were extolled in the *Bugle*, the British amateurs given star reviews, and, when a Viceregal garden or dinner party took place, the British were most anxious that Moplah knew they were there, thus ensuring that their uninvited neighbours knew too. But this cricket match had killed that policy.

With this poster, Moplah realised that he had finally set the Indian and British as being of equal status. It was a momentous and daring step. He decided therefore to justify it, subtly, in a *Bugle* editorial to coincide with the date of bill-posting in the town, describing the poster as '*a significant step in India's aware-ness of the breaking wind of change . . .*'

By dawn, two days later, the hoardings down at the railway station, shop windows on the Mall, hotel and club entrances, even church wayside pulpit boards and the broadest tree trunks in Tophar, displayed the large yellow, double-crown posters . . .

184

GRAND CHARITY
in the distinguished presence of
ALL-INDIA CIVILIAN XI
Glenbourn (India) Sunday 23rd
Pitching of wickets :

ALL-INDIA CIVILIAN XI.

A. SHRINIVASSEN Esq. (Captain)
    (Madras Harbour, Sanitation & Drainage)
FUTTI PANT Esq. (Wicket)
    (Poona Early-Closing League, Army Surplus (Lanyards)
    Dept.)
JALIM SINGH Esq.
    (Punjab University, Posts & Telegraphs)
SASHI BOKANEER Esq.
    (Lahore Railways, Army Movements (Rail))
TORKHAM WAZIR Esq.
    (Rail-Sleeper Ballast Dept.)
MOTI LAL Esq.
    (Cow & Goat Protection Dept.)
NARNA BAG Esq.
    (Hospital Directorate (Smallpox))
UTTAR BUN Esq.
    (Office Equipment (Hand Punkas))
S. BANNERJEE Esq.
    (Bengal Cycling Club, Cannibalisation of Vehicles Dept.)
GOPI MUKTA Esq.
    (Crop Rotation, Corn Section)
MR. SHARRABUDDIN Esq.
    (Office Equipment, Hat Stands)
12th Man : MUSTAPHA KHAN Esq.
    (Snake-Bite Directorate)
UMPIRE : A. MOOKERJEE Esq. B.A. (failed)
    (Calcutta Tramways, Water Catchment Directorate, Tophar
    Drama Society, (Director in charge))
Scorer : R. K. Desai Esq.
    (Certificate of Merit (Mathematics), Lahore Postal Course,
    Umballa Phillattellic Society, Field Cashier Dept.)
Manager : TELIK SWARMI Esq.
    (Chairman, Swarmi Litterary Society, Abandoned Families,
    (Army) Dept.)

Airs will be played during
The BAND OF THE
(by kind permission of Lt.Col.
under the direction of
ALL PROCEED
Give Generously.   Read all about it in
Sports Editor :
Printed by Himalayan Bugle Press,

CRICKET MATCH
His Excellency THE GOVERNOR
–v– THE BRITISH ARMY
September 1945, 8 ASJU 2002
11.30 m.a.

ARMY ELEVEN

COLONEL EDDGERLEY-WATKYN-REED (Captain)
    (Cairo Crusaders, Baghdad Crusaders, Kuala Lumpar
    Crusaders, Secunderabad Crusaders, Tophar Crusaders)
LT.-COL. NUPP-JEVONS, O.B.E.
    (Aden Nondescripts, Nairobi Nomads, Gold Coast Gym-
    khana, Katmandu Caterpillars, Quetta Quidnuncs, Tophar
    Crusaders)
MAJOR BARKSIDE-TWIST M.C.C.
    (M.C.C., Householed Cavalry, Rangoon Ramblers, Sudan
    Stoics, Khartoum Cryptics, Omdurman Incogniti, Tophar
    Crusaders)
MAJOR BAKER-STEWART, R.A.
    (Royal Artillery (Corfu), Freetown Freebooters, War Office
    C.C., Tophar Crusaders)
MAJOR INNES-WHIFFEN (wicket)
    (Singapore Strugglers, Hong Kong Pilgrims, Penang Priory,
    Tophar Crusaders)
MAJOR K. McBURN
    (Mandalay Stuarts, Kohat Caledonians, Calcutta Scottish,
    Hooghli Highlanders, Tophar Crusaders)
CAPTAIN B. MOTT, B.A.
    (Altruists, Tophar Crusaders)
Sergeant Wood, H.
    (Surrey C.C.C.)
Sergeant Harrison, F.
    (Higgs Haulage (Ilford) Ltd, C.C.)
Sergeant Frinton, J.
    (Little Fallowfield C.C.)
A/U/Lance/Corporal Sinker A.
    (Gretleigh Colliery C.C.)
12th Man : MAJOR J. GRAHAME, M.O.
    (Melbourne University, RAM C)
Umpire : MAJOR G. COURTNEY
    (Zanzibar Zingari, Bombay Oddfellows, Tophar Crusaders)
Scorer : SENIOR COMMANDER H. SHORT
    (Woman's Auxiliary Corps, India)

the intervals by
PUNJAB GRENADIERS
Joyceton-Crombie, O.B.E.)
Bandmaster S. Higginbottom.
TO THE RED CROSS
THE HIMALAYAN BUGLE – 2 annas.   No Dogs Allowed
Retti Moplah Esq.
R. MOPLAH Prop. Estimates Free

Chapter Twenty-one

THE PAGEANT MASTER

VERY faintly across the valley, shadowed by blue moonlight, Judge Trevelhayes heard St. John's church strike midnight, the chimes broken and wafting in the night air. From Monkey Hill to Tophar, the narrow hillside road was a gentle downhill gyration and he allowed his tricycle to freewheel leisurely as he hummed the tram song.

Tonight his casting for the Tophar Pageant of British History had gone reasonably well. Stout Major Brunton-Thwaite had agreed to play Pepys, and his angular wife, Florence Nightingale. Enoch Dorling-Wells would make a good Sir Robert Peel even if it was stretching a point to dress him in a constable's uniform from *The Pirates of Penzance*. Colonel 'Butters' Hall-Gomshall had set his heart on impersonating Handel. Knowing 'Butters'' reputation for dropping 'sitters', the judge had tactfully suggested he appeared as the musician when old and blind but 'Butters' insisted on playing an unaccompanied version of 'Largo' on his violin. This worried the judge. The uneven sway of a bullock-drawn float must affect 'Handel's' already shaky technique and, worse, might madden the bullocks into horning the float ahead on which Courtney, as Wolfe at Quebec, would be dying. It seemed safer to give Courtney a horizontal role.

With so few young people left in Tophar, the judge was forced to cast the half-chat girl, Nancy Evans, as Nell Gwyn but, at least, the oranges would be the right colour. Muriel Barkside-Twist certainly looked sick enough to play Elizabeth Browning. Behind the bullock-drawn Britannia of Hazel Short, the judge himself would be second in the procession as Neptune

186

on his shell-and-seaweed disguised tricycle. Both would, when they reached the limit of the Mall, double back along the lower road to the theatre to change into their Victoria and Gladstone costumes and rejoin the procession.

Old Eddgers was doubling Clive and W. G. Grace, but the judge had qualms that the colonel's enchantment with cricket might confuse him into appearing on the Plassey float in an MCC cap. Major Grahame's request to play Ned Kelly amused the judge greatly. Innes-Whiffen then would have to be Captain Cook—too tall, of course, but he could sit on a ship's barrel.

"Watch out, you buzfuz!" shouted the judge, braking hard. A snarling monkey had swung across the road, his long toe just missing the judge's nose by a fraction in a leap from branch to branch. Normally the judge was used to the Tophar apes—but this macacus rhesus specimen was cloaked in a yellow poster.

"My God," thought the judge, "the monkeys are playin' at bein' Buddhist monks . . ."

Long before the judge's own ancestors settled on this hilltop, the browns and the greys had disputed for its possession. The browns, the Himalayan monkey known to the judge as macacus assamensis, were barer of bottom than the speckled grey specie but were far more congenial. Impish and clownlike, they lived also in trees above the bazaar. The speckled band with their lighter brown fur tinged with ashy grey laid siege, and the browns stood fast. For centuries the war had gone on . . . and now, the judge observed, a new dispute had arisen between them —the struggle for ownership of cricket posters.

In the town these crown sheets were comparatively safe from theft, except by Futti Pant who was posting them off to Poona in reams. But Moplah's enthusiasm in nailing up cricket match publicity in such a lonely stretch of trees going towards the Himalayas could only be interpreted by the judge as a hint to Tibet to challenge the winners. To Moplah's credit, the posters were sturdy and thick-textured and able to withstand a lot of monkey feuding.

Having straightened his front wheel, the judge had an inspiration. He must cast someone in the pageant to play

Darwin. Or would that ruddy vicar object? After all, he was playing St. George—clap down his visor tight and he might not see Darwin was there at all! That's it—Major Grahame could play Darwin—most appropriate . . .

As he zigzagged round a bend the judge saw the lights of Blenheim Castle. He made a rude gesture at the Headquarters of the American Forces . . . for he remembered Blenheim in the old days as an elephant battery's officers' mess. Now these blasted Yanks lived there, not a Union Jack ever appeared on any of the forty poles which sprouted from the turrets.

"Rickshaw! Rickshaw!" croaked a voice.

The judge blew his cheeks in exasperation. Admittedly it was unlikely any rickshaws would be as far from Tophar at this late hour, but to be constantly mistaken for a coolie-hauled vehicle was irritatin'. He drew up beside a crouching figure on the grass embankment.

"Man or monkey?" he asked.

"Hell, am I glad to see a hooman bein'," said a Bronx voice.

"Ah, a Yankee-doodle-dandy . . ."

"Sure, Cyrus Q. Weltzer, American Mission o' True Hearts."

"Of course. Your memsahib god-bothered the cricketers, didn't she? Don't know what you missionaries are doin' in India. As it is, there are too many temples, not enough factory chimneys. I am Mr. Justice Trevelhayes who survived an attack from one of yer armoured cars . . ."

"Yeah, I heard about that." Cyrus stood and swayed against the judge.

"I say," the handlebar lamp was turned on the American, "you're tiddled, aren't yer? . . . High as a kite . . . whisky by the stench of it . . ."

"Yeah . . . used to be able to hold it—but not now . . . and all those god-damned monkeys . . . don't know how you British train 'em as sandwich board-men . . ."

"We have extraordinary methods of employment in India," chuckled the judge. "However, I have washed me hands of that cricket match. As president of the Tophar Crusaders I had an interest, but, now the Army has taken over, they know what they can do with their stumps. I say, you'd make an awfully good Charles the First . . ."

"Charles the what?" Cyrus belched loudly.

"The First. I'm Pageant Master, yer know, Arts Festival. I want a Charles very badly . . . you'd only be seen with yer head on the block . . ."

"It's right there now, sir."

"Your fearful accent wouldn't matter a jot . . . it's all in mime. Yer wife could be beheaded too, as Mary Queen of Scots."

"It was scotch that did it to-night . . . but anythin' you say . . ."

"Can I give you a lift to Tophar? It's three miles away—and these cricket-conscious monkeys hate Yanks."

"A lift? On that?" Cyrus surveyed the tricycle with bleary anxiety.

"This," said the judge, slapping the saddle, "is a Raleigh— also bein' characterised by Barkside-Twist in me pageant—a fine machine. See that box, behind this saddle? Called a boot for some obscure reason, but you sit on it and put yer feet on the back axle. Bit cramped, of course, but I've even carried women on it. Shakes 'em up but I've never lost a passenger yet."

Gingerly, Cyrus put leg after leg over the box and sank down, his knees eventually book-ending his chin.

"Ow!" he yelled. "The lock—it hurts!"

The judge fumbled under Cyrus's crutch.

"It's a Yale lock, you should feel at home . . . ah, still got the key in it . . . that better?"

"A bit . . ."

"Right," said the judge, mounting into the saddle, "off we go . . . into 'those hoary Indian hills' as Matthew Arnold called 'em—only, in my opinion, he misspelled 'hoary' . . ."

The bell tinkled and the tricycle jerked sideways to the very brink of the five hundred feet drop into Wagrah state below, then teetered and weaved back to the grass embankment. Cyrus sobbed with relief.

"Have to tack a bit to begin with," explained the judge, "especially when I've got a load on . . ."

"That makes two of us," said Cyrus.

"How comes it," asked the judge when the machine was at last coasting easily, "that a man of God like you is now missin', believed drunk?"

"I went to Delhi," wheezed Cyrus from behind the judge's black serge coat-tails. "I had to see the American Red Cross. The British sent 'em a crummy note about my wife's behaviour in the Queen's Club over that cricket. They gave it the horse laugh, o' course."

"All you Americans laugh like horses . . . too many teeth . . ."

"They figured that, as Marion had been God's instrument in arrangin' this cricket, some of the charity funds should come to *them*—but the British in Delhi gave that notion the bum's rush, too."

"Good description of GHQ, Delhi, that . . . a rush of bums . . ."

"I came up by rail this mornin', met Colonel Berrick Sims on the train . . ."

"I know him! His medals look like a pyjama pattern book. I had to negotiate me damages through him . . . wanted me to call him 'Berry' on first acquaintance . . . boozy, ramshackle fellar . . ."

"You can say that again, judge. Invited me to lunch at the United States mess, gave me scotch. I could drink it once—but now I'm out o' practice . . . anyway, I got to singin' hymns . . . then I passed out—cold . . ."

"Hymns affect me that way, too."

"But the colonel was my pal . . . laid me out on his foam-rubber bed . . ."

"Trust that Berry fellar to sleep on foam-rubber—chappies in India have beds of nails . . ."

"I can," said Cyrus, easing himself, "appreciate jest how they feel. Anyways, suddenly Berry wakes me. He's reelin' about an' cursin', real mad at me. Flings me outa bed, callin' me 'draft dodger' an' threatenin' to tar an' white-feather me . . . guess he'd forgotten we were buddies . . ."

"Did you dodge the column?"

"Well, heck, I had Christ's work to do . . ."

"Hadn't soldiers? Certainly the Germans thought so. But how on earth did a young fellar like you become a missionary medicine man?"

"Through Marion o' course. I was an actor, see . . . I went to her meetin's for the free coffee—which I could do with right now—an' then started preachin' for her from our trailer pulpit. Then—well—we got married. No more drink . . . jest travel, travel . . ."

"Any money in this?"

"Well, we're kinda subsidised from Noo York . . . but Marion gets that. She jest gives me hand-outs. That's what went wrong in Delhi yesterday—I ran outa dough . . ."

"Funny life for a young feller, savin' people for God when he can't call his soul his own."

"Oh, it's okay in the States—but out here—why, god-damn it, we've even got involved in British cricket—an' clerks!"

"Ah, you must blame Macaulay for the clerks," said the judge. "He started the system for the old East India Company. Not the Yorkshire cricketer, o' course . . . poor chap died in this war. No, I mean Lord Thomas Babin'ton who went to live in Clapham of all places . . . but why did you interfere in the cricket?"

"I didn't. It was Marion an' a little git called Mookerjee . . . she felt the clerks were gettin' a tough break . . ."

"You Americans always think you can understand all about India in a few weeks," said the judge, waving familiarly to a passing monkey wearing another height-of-fashion poster. "But, like your drinkin' habits, yer quite clueless. In Tudor times the British started tryin' to piece together the huge jig-saw puzzle which is India . . . an' they're still at it . . . but the pieces are like jumpin' beans, they won't stay still. Those clerks, me lad, are usin' you an' yer mem to make prize puddens o' the pair of yer . . ."

Cyrus moaned softly, his forehead pressed against the judge's rolling rump. If only this old punk would stop yakking. From his days as a Greenwich Village actor, Cyrus was used to the hazards of drink. But this was the most God-awful experience of all! A mad judge, a seering pain in his fanny, cricket-crazy monkeys all round him, death in a canyon below if the judge misjudged . . . he'd give every dime Marion allotted him to be back in New York right now, happily stoned. Oh, for an aggressive bar-keep, a knee-bruising fire hydrant, garbage cans on the sidewalk and those huddled faceless figures who flapped ragged sleeves to acknowledge him as a brother lush passing in the night.

The judge was lecturing on the Mutiny when the tricycle finally left the dirt road for the smoother macadam of the Mall.

"And so the flag is never lowered at the Lucknow Residency now," said the judge. "Ah, now where d'yer live?"

"Bungalow called 'Virginia Water'."

"Ah, yes, full of dry rot—no offence to yer wife's preachin', o' course. General Hever-Stockpoole's old place. It's haunted, yer know."

" 'Virginia Water'—haunted?"

"Oh, yes. Way back in the 1840s it happened. Wife came home unexpectedly from sick leave, found her major husband in bed with the children's governess. Terrible tragedy . . . the wife stabbed the governess to death with scissors. She was acquitted o' course—there was a disobedience penalty clause in the governess's employment contract. Anyway, she still haunts the place, lookin' for the major . . . hadn't finished, apparently . . ."

"You're a great help," said Cyrus, shivering.

At the wooden gate, the judge dismounted and straightened Cyrus.

"There," he carolled, "right to yer door. That's a Raleigh for yer."

"For lord's sake, keep yer voice low," whispered Cyrus, rubbing his seat and wincing. "Don't wanna wake Marion . . ."

"Quite understand. Got a brandy? I've lost me puff . . ."

"Only coffee . . . but it's late . . ."

"I'm used to coffee last thing—won't keep me up."

"Promise you'll be quiet . . ."

"As the grave."

As Cyrus weaved up the grit path with the judge holding his elbow, he prayed he could get rid of this old buzzard quickly. Then on the chaise-longue in the sitting-room he could continue the sleep Berry had so rudely interrupted. To awaken Marion would be disastrous . . . he was drunk and, after that agonising trike ride, he just couldn't anyway . . .

"Who's that?" he muttered as a shadow moved on the veranda.

"Krischa, sahib." The boy was wrapped in a brown blanket instead of a yellow poster. "Sahib is back so soon? Oh, and with the judge!" The boy bowed. "Salaam, hanging sahib!"

"Got a great affection for me, the Indian," whispered the judge.

"Coffee for two, boy," said Cyrus, "but quietly. Don't wanna disturb Mrs. Weltzer. Go on in, judge."

"I know me way," said the judge hoarsely. "Sat up here all one night in the 'twenties tryin' to lay the ghost . . ."

As he tip-toed past him, Krischa gripped Cyrus's sleeve.

"Sahib has been with the Amerikarners at Blenheim—in the bazaar their bearers are saying you get drunkised and you sing and dance the whoopie . . ."

"Holy mackerel, you mustn't tell Mrs. Weltzer that!"

"Me very poor boy."

Wearily he pressed a bunch of notes into the small hand. In the passage he steadied himself by strap-hanging on the ibex, then staggered into the sitting-room. The judge was already standing by the bedroom door, his finger to his lips and a fierce, exhilarated look in his eyes.

"I've just heard her," he muttered, "a ghostly wail . . . the spirit of the governess in distress . . ."

Cyrus shook his befuddled head. Then, from beyond the door, he, too, heard it. His eyes widened in amazement.

"There!" said the judge triumphantly. "The dead governess . . ."

But Cyrus had stumbled on into the darkened bedroom. He knew that sound. That cry of Marion in passion and last delirious throes had jarred his pleasures round the world. Radios had to be turned up full blast to hide this wifely defect. On their travels, Tibetian gongs, Zulu drums and Chinese fire-crackers had muffled her biological screams of climax. In the western world, reliance had to be placed upon recordings of Brahms, Sousa and Louis Armstrong. Cyrus had spent his married life booking into hotels overlooking busy steelworks and slaughter yards and, when on rail sleeping cars, timing Marion into tunnels.

As the cry died away, the slow burn of realisation came to Cyrus through the whisky fumes. After fumbling with the light switch, he was able to focus the quivering mosquito net, the thick mesh hiding a fluttering agitation within.

"Go 'way, Krischa," came Marion's voice, syrup-thick and drowsy. "Rani-memsahib wants the light out, boy."

Cyrus took a breath. He hated stark reality. Religion was gloriously vague, you could mould it around to suit situations, but a crisis like this meant decisions, quick-thinking. Like most actors, his mind was non-creative. For all his four married years he had been parroting Marion's themes. He could quote the Bible well, he had a trained memory, but now he was faced with finding words of his own—and he was not sober.

"Marion, baby . . . it's Cyrus . . ."

The shrouded bed heaved suddenly as if an earth tremor had struck that corner of the room. Cyrus caught a muffled, alien cough. Then suddenly Marion's head appeared through the netting, her long hair limp and dishevelled.

"Cyrus! You're back! At this time of night. Nothing comes up from Delhi after mid-day—unless you took a cab and risked that dreadful mountain road in the dark . . ."

But, on the wicker chair beside the bed, Cyrus had seen the khaki drill trousers and bush-shirt bearing the solitary dark blue, red and light blue ribbon of the British 1939–45 medal.

"Quit stallin', Marion . . ." Cyrus remembered some lines from one of his pre-AMOTH gangster roles. "Who's de guy under de shroud wid ya, huh?"

Even in her anguish, she frowned.

"Cyrus . . . you're not . . . drunk, are you?"

"Sure, I am! Loaded, sister!" He wracked his brain for more appropriate dialogue from his drama tours in the sticks. "Wid Colonel Berry . . . had a few shots, yeah . . ."

"Oh, Cyrus! Drinking again. In front of young Krischa, too. Go to the kitchen, honey, and let the boy get you a hot drink. Marion will be with you in a minute . . ."

"No dice," he growled. "You're not makin' a fall guy outa me . . ."

"No, Cyrus!" she screamed as he advanced. But he was more confident now. His role had been wrong . . . she was no gangster's moll, she was the woman caught in adultery . . . he was on far safer ground with the Bible.

" 'Wives shall give to their husbands honour, both great and small,' " he ranted. " 'Wife of Uriah the Hittite . . . who is the David who lies with you? For he is cast into a net by his own feet . . .' "

"Oh, Cyrus . . . go thou and have a hot drink . . ."

"Hypocrite without hope!" He snatched up the bush-shirt. "Whose raiment is this?"

"No, Cyrus, no!" But he ripped the netting from her hands, tore it apart. Marion shrieked as he pulled her forward. She fell to the floor, where she crouched naked, weeping noisily. Cyrus threw the bush-shirt over her.

"Steady," said Captain Mott, "that's the King's uniform, you know . . ."

Cyrus, speechless with surprise, grabbed at the pink body, but Mott wriggled up to the head of the bed, where he sat Buddha-like, a pillow clasped to his stomach.

"It's a fair cop, Mr. Weltzer," he said, resignedly.

"Where's the dead governess?" said the judge from the door. "She certainly made a fair old racket . . ."

"The judge! Oh, no!" groaned Mott. "I'm afraid I can't rise, sir . . ."

"Give me my dressing gown," cried Marion. "Basil's shirt doesn't quite reach—and we've got company."

Cyrus unhooked a red dressing gown from behind the door.

"He, judge," he said, pointing at Mott, "hath defiled my wife."

As he draped Marion, Cyrus scented freedom from her. The war was over, no more need of her protection . . .

"Ah, Mott," said the judge, rubbing his hands, "one wild oat too many, eh? As you sew so shall you rape . . ."

"So you knew all about Basil and me, Cyrus," sobbed Marion, collapsing into a chair, as she tightened the cord round her waist. "You had the judge come along to catch us sinning. Oh, honey, not *divorce*, not here in 'Virginia Water' . . ."

"Divorce?" Mott's eyes widened as he clutched his pillow tighter.

"Yeah, divorce, you son of a bitch," said Cyrus thickly.

"Slanderin' his mother won't help yer case," said the judge.

"Oh, judge," cried Marion, "let me explain my deadly sin to Cyrus. I must not kill his faith . . . Cyrus, I am penitent . . ."

"Lot's wife!" said Cyrus.

"Have there been others?" enquired the judge.

"Remember our work for the church," pleaded Marion.

"All loused up," said Cyrus. "I'm makin' tracks for Delhi tomorrow an' a plane home to fix the divorce. You're jest a harlot, Marion. I've got Krischa as a witness too."

"Oh, no you don't," said Mott sharply. "As a schoolmaster, I forbid a young boy like that to be involved in this filthy business. No, we won't contest the evidence. I admit to cuckolding you, Mr. Weltzer . . ."

"You big bum!"

"The court will ignore that remark," said the judge. "But whatever his physical features, the co-defendant admits adultery. When the divorce is made absolute, will you marry the lady, Private Mott?"

"I'm a captain, judge . . ."

"You won't be when all this comes out."

Mott closed his eyes in horror.

"Yes, judge, I'll marry her . . . it's my bounden duty . . ."

Marion sobbed loudly. The Mission of True Hearts council

had been difficult enough when she had decided to marry an American actor—but New York would never accept a divorce, let alone an English co-respondent.

"Hot drinks is served in the lounge," said Krischa from the door. "Coffee I have brewed for three—and one tea without sugar for the captain sahib—as always."

"So you've been here before, have you?" Cyrus was now genuinely outraged.

"Five times," Mott admitted. "I loved Marion at first sight, you see . . ."

"Cyrus also loved me at first sight," said Marion tensely, "didn't you, honey . . . ?"

"Krischa," said the judge sternly, "go home to the bazaar, jaldi jao. This is no place for a chokra."

"Me come back morning time," said the boy, bowing. "Salaam, memsahib and sahibs. Me also love memsahib first sight."

He strutted away, to break into a run when he reached the gate.

"Oh, the dear little thing," sighed Marion.

"Krischa is only in love with yer money," said the judge, looking straight at Cyrus.

"I'm through with her—don't rile me, judge," he said.

"Our marriage cannot end like this," cried Marion. "I know I am a weak, foolish, fallen woman . . ."

"Oh, I wouldn't say that," said Mott.

"Your comment is inadmissible," said the judge. "The dead governess has confessed."

"No, judge," said Marion knowingly. "My work is *not* dead, even if I did try to govern Cyrus . . ."

"He didn't mean that," said her husband. "He thought you were a ghost . . ."

"I am a ghost," said Marion, deeply, "a ghost of my former self. But, Cyrus, we can profit by my sin of the flesh . . ."

"Five sins of the flesh," amended the judge.

"What's all this 'ghost' business?" asked Mott. "I can assure you Marion is far from dead . . ."

"She's haunted you, lad," said the judge. "And you, Cyracus . . ."

"She'll haunt me no more," said Cyrus from another play. "I'm going back to the theatre . . ."

"Dashed unpredictable life," mused the judge, "more money in God. However, we will now adjourn to my chambers for that coffee while this self-confessed adulterer dresses himself. I'm tired of him sittin' there with that pillow like a Tibetian yapsin."

Marion followed him into the sitting-room, hiccupping painfully. But Cyrus stayed to watch Mott edge off the bed and drop the pillow.

"With that," said Cyrus, whistling appreciatively, "you will make Marion very happy."

"I say," said Mott, delightedly, "thanks."

As he dressed he could hear Marion crying and Cyrus mumbling as cups clinked beyond the closed door. This is it, he thought, out on a limb—two limbs in fact . . . and the crazy judge as a witness. He thought of his vicar father in England, "Dad, meet my wife, a missionary from America . . ." His brother Norman and his wife, Janice, would be sure to say Marion was too old for him. And the Altruists certainly would not take to her . . . Marion was not the sort to help with the teas during a home match . . .

"Callin' Captain Mott," shouted the judge from within.

Mott tied his shoe laces, ran Marion's comb through his hair. In the mirror he looked tired and drawn.

"I expect my tea's getting cold," he said as he opened the door.

"Now," said the judge, seated at Marion's desk. "Let's run through the evidence . . ."

"Make it quick," said Cyrus, the whisky now sour again on his coffee-awakened taste buds. "I wanna go to bed."

"Not you as well," said the judge. "We cannot have collusion. Now . . ." he held up a letter, "I see from this document that a man called Mookerjee suggests that you, Mrs Weltzer, should preach to the British in front of the pavilion at the cricket tiffin interval to-day . . ."

"That's a private letter!" gasped Marion. "You've no right rifling my desk . . ."

"Aw, hell, Marion," growled Cyrus, "our own Red Cross in Delhi told us to keep outa British politics. Don't get snarled up in this cricket no more, for Chrissakes . . ."

"Preach in front of the pavilion?" Mott was aghast. "Oh, Marion, you didn't tell me . . . you'll get me hung if you do . . ."

"The clerks wanted me to," declared Marion. "As their rani, I must make an appeal on behalf of all oppressed Indians. After all, it is the sabbath day . . ."

"That match," said the judge, gazing at his ancient gold hunter match, "is roughly nine hours away. These clerks are very clever, ma'am. They knew yer presence will embarrass the Army. However, even as president of the Tophar Crusaders, I'm bound to admit they deserve all you could give 'em . . ."

"I say, that's a bit hot, Mr. President," said Mott. "We've had to import players . . ."

"Humbug," said the judge. "The Crusaders just don't like gettin' beaten. Any excuse to keep the records intact. That's why I won't be there. However, neither will you be preachin' at Glenbourn, madam, not after this little sexual episode . . ."

"You would tell them about Captain Mott and me?" panted Marion. "You—a judge?"

"No," he said, smiling as he tapped his fingertips together, "but little Krischa will. Right now, the bazaar'll be hummin' with the news . . ."

"Oh, my cripes!" said Mott.

"Your 'cripes' are not evidence," said the judge, sipping his coffee. "Now let's deal with the wronged husband. I gather from our conversation on our way here, Cyracus, you have to rely on yer wife's—er—hand-outs . . . I think that was the phrase you used . . ."

"Hand-outs?" gasped Marion. " 'What need hath a man of money' . . . ?"

"I hath a great need," said Cyrus firmly. "You've done me wrong. I'll tell you somethin'. You gotta pay me off."

"Have you no dignity?" snapped Mott.

"There would, in court, be a pun here about the Mott callin' the Weltzer black," said the judge solemnly. "I would advise you to refrain from such comment, Mott. At the moment you have about as much dignity as a meth drinker at a cockfight. If we are to solve this case before they pitch wickets to-day, let's be relevant. Now, Mrs Weltzer, when you marry Mott, where will you live?"

"In Noo York, judge," said Marion very definitely. "My roots are in purest America. Basil will work with me on my tours, spreading the gospel . . ."

"Basil?" queried the judge. "Is Mott a 'Basil'? Good heavens, Greek for 'kingly'. There's a St. Basil's Cathedral in Moscow— Red Square, I think it is . . . very appropriate."

"Hey, wait a minute, judge." The Altruist all-rounder was indignant. "I don't mind wintering in America, though missing the indoor nets is a bit of a bind, but not in summer. My cricket . . ."

"He's jilting me, judge," wailed Marion, "for this drug, cricket! You're hooked, Basil . . . oh, you were merely being lewd and lustful when I thought I was succumbing to your true love . . ."

"Couldn't we live here," said Mott miserably, "or Australia or the West Indies . . . ?"

"With your darned cricket," flashed Marion. "What a fool I've been. These Indians got me praying for cricket when all the times it's just a form of devil worship."

"I say, steady on," said Mott indignantly.

"Right," said the judge, "we've reached an impasse. The guilty parties cannot agree on a place of residence."

"I'm all tuckered-out," mumbled Cyrus. "Can't this be fixed in the mornin'?"

"In the mornin'," said the judge, "you an' Mrs. Weltzer will leave Tophar together to return to America . . . the rani is unfrocked . . ."

"She's been unfaithful . . ."

"I think you can live with that, Cyracus, many men have. This Mott episode would not have been revealed if I hadn't found you drunk by the roadside playin' with monkeys . . ."

"Monkeys, Cyrus?" cried Marion.

"Yer husband, ma'am, had been ejected from the American Forces' Mess because they had found out he had avoided enlistment in the services—an' that *you*, madam, had protected him . . ."

"You ole basstard . . ." Cyrus was white and shaking.

"Contempt of court doesn't help yer case," said the judge. "I find it not proven. I will exercise my discretion over the co-defendant's admitted adultery . . ."

"Scram, the bloody lot o' yer!" roared Cyrus, rising unsteadily, "I'm goin' to bed—get to hell outa here . . .!"

He blundered out through the door.

"But, Cyrus," implored Marion, "we must pack. Krischa has gone . . . and that Swiss alpen horn is such a difficult souvenir to travel . . ."

From within the bedroom Cyrus made a rude noise.

"I'm boss now, Marion," he shouted. "Hallelujah for the British captain . . ."

Mott's cap came sailing out of the bedroom.

At the gate the first streak of morning light had slit the black sky.

"Another case settled," said the judge, mounting his tricycle.

"I'm terribly grateful, judge," muttered Mott, "although I guess I've had it now . . . the scandal and all that . . ."

"Nonsense, boy. Done Tophar a great service—if you get me meanin'. I'll see you get the credit. On one condition."

"What's that?"

"You play Guy Fawkes in the pageant."

Mott groaned softly.

"It's a small price to pay . . . it's a deal, judge."

"And Grahame will play Darwin."

"You can't have *him* in the pageant—Darwin, I mean . . ."

"Oh, yes, but keep it a secret. If the vicar sees Grahame in his whiskers on the day, tell him to say he's Alfred Tennyson . . ."

The light in 'Virginia Water' went out and the judge sighed.

"Pity I've lost those two Yanks for the pageant. Still, I'll try

Colonel Berry—he'll make a good Cromwell. Come on, Mott, hop aboard. I'll run yer home. You must get some shut-eye before the match."

"Thanks, no," said Mott, "I'll walk. Want to think. You know, Marion was a wonderful woman, in many ways. I often heard my father preach, but he never moved me as she did . . ."

"Been damned unhealthy if he had . . ."

"She was the real church for me—but then, you hate churches, don't you, judge . . .?"

"No, I like churches . . . the trouble is they will put parsons in 'em. Oh, Mott, I know exactly how yer feel. Somethin' irresistible about a religious woman who's born both pretty an' sexy. Mine was a Salvation Army lass . . ."

"No!" Mott grinned in the grey shafts of dawn. "Did you . . . actually . . .?"

"What the hell else d'yer think got me sent to India?" The judge rang his bell, calling as he pedalled off: "My youth was a lovely time o' day, too, yer know . . ."

Chapter Twenty-two

GLENBOURN

THE day dawned into inevitable sunshine. Tophar cricketers' fierce patriotism for England did not mean having to share the old country's uncertain summers. Other than the predictable monsoon period in July, rain never stopped play. A ground mist enshrouded Glenbourn, but the Himalayas stood glinting white against a clear blue sky. By nine o'clock that morning the low haze was moving gradually, lifting shadows and revealing the shelved fields of emerald green mountain rice in the valleys below.

Yesterday, under the direction of the Governor's head mali, loaned from the courtly gardens of the Residency for such an onerous occasion, the outfield had been scythed by coolies—and not a toe had been lost. Now Indian women were groping in the damp mist at their feet, removing loose grass. They appeared to float like dark wraiths, the hems of their saris invisible in the ground vapour. Bangles clinked as they raised the baskets of cuttings to their heads, their eyes expressionless as their backs straightened. Their husbands, laughing over their hookahs under the nearby trees, were enjoying a pleasant change at Glenbourn. For six days a week they were forced to lie under barren red rocks on the mountain roads while their wives chipped stones, their hip-carried children, red-eyed with dust, being grittily breast-fed without unduly delaying the production of railway sleeper ballast.

As ordered by Major Baker-Stewart, Sergeants Wood, Harrison and Frinton and Lance-Corporal Sinker were busy laying the matting wicket. Tophar's grass was of a delicate texture. Polo and horse-racing it had stood for some eighty years, but cricket pitches formed alopecia patches within a few moments which took months to grow again. So the twenty-two yard canvas strip was being truly laid. Wood and Harrison issued orders while Frinton pegged the matting taut and Sinker grumbled that, now he was an N.C.O., he should not be doing coolie's work. High up on the banking behind a bush, Swarmi watched them vigilantly through field glasses . . . just to make sure the British did not put loose stones beneath the canvas to make the ball bounce awkwardly, a ploy invented by oriental cricketers at the turn of the century.

When the mist finally swirled away, Glenbourn was a rich green sheen and the Indian women, saris drawn up over their heads against the whistling British N.C.O.s, walked sedately back to the trees. The strange, soughing breeze recalled to Frinton his river-bound Wiltshire green, Harrison remembered the summer flats near West Mersea and Wood a girl on Tooting Bec Common. To Sinker it was 'joost a bloody draught'.

The verandahed wooden pavilion, its bathing machine design only slightly relieved by ornate carvings round the eaves, stood varnished as new by the Grand Theatre scenic artists. Now its shining surface was spotted with dead moths and bluebottles. Bunting loaned from the pageant committee hung in red, white and blue triangles from the nearby knoll of trees to the pavilion roof. A Union Jack hung limply, overlong for its short pole, beside a rostrum and a circle of music stands. The whole pavilion area was cordoned off, the ropes blancoed a stark white.

The Punjab Grenadiers came straggling through the trees with their instruments, a sagging group in yellow uniforms, red sashes and brown turbans. As if sleep-walking, they passed between the two wooden posts which provided the only gap in the roped section, to sit before their music stands.

Behind them, Bandmaster Samuel Higginbottom stepped imperiously from his regimentally-crested rickshaw. The short, bullet-headed man under his black-peaked cap stood, proud, in his dark blue uniform, the satin-frogged tunic reaching his knees, the red trouser stripes rising like two wrinkling flames from his little black boots.

The only white man in the band, he enjoyed a power well beyond Sir Thomas Beecham at his most irascible. Salford-born Higginbottom's musical ability had been transferred to the Punjab Grenadiers on an exaggerated reference from a relieved Kneller Hall colonel. Higginbottom never gave up trying to elevate the status of bandmaster. Socially inferior to officers, his short temper had little respite in India. To-day marked another occasion when he could demonstrate his successful training of Indian musicians in western music. He had rehearsed this cricket match programme with the hypnotic intensity of Svengali. Now he tested his rostrum gingerly . . . astute use of a fretsaw by an offended Indian carpenter had once dropped him sprawling in front of the Viceroy.

Spectators in light summer frocks and striped blazers were now arriving by rickshaw at the British rope. Parasols and boaters, thermos flasks and portable gramophones—which Higginbottom eyed with bloodshot hatred—were disembarked by the deckchairs, the ladies giving shrill instructions to their rickshaw teams to return 'after tea'. The coolies were accustomed to this vague order. Eating only one meal a day themselves, the British division of the hours by meal-times amused them greatly.

But with little else going on in Tophar on such a day, the coolies settled themselves in the adjoining trees. To-morrow they would be at loggerheads with the clerks again, but now they were partisans, united in this war against the British.

The Indian Civilian team had at last gathered in the trees, carrying cricket accoutrements they had collected from St. Hayward's School. Some clerks, possessing no white trousers, wore painters' overalls over their everyday pair. Others wore skin-tight white linen which spelled disaster when stooping. Many shirts were collarless, others sported their grey winter vests. Only Shrinivassen, Jalim Singh and Bokaneer could have passed fit for Lord's. Futti Pant was wet with sweat, having worn his wicket-keeping pads all the way from the bazaar to ensure recognition.

Once assembled, chattering excitedly and pushing each other, Swarmi cried: "Come, my men—we must take our rightful place in the pavilion."

But once they had followed him into the open, saw the flags and parasols, the clerks scuttled back to the trees, completely overawed.

"Cowardice!" shouted Swarmi, striding on.

"Let him go," said Mookerjee to Shrinivassen. "If we sat within the British sector they would overhear our plans to defeat them. We are best here in solitary confinement o' foliage."

Swarmi reached the pavilion rope, lifted a leg to cross it . . .

"Ah," said Hazel, "put your leg down and help me move this table."

"I am manager," he began, but the table was rammed against his stomach and Hazel backed him helplessly to the scoreboard.

"Atchcha, thikai," said Hazel, rubbing her hands. "Off you go, back to your trees. We'll call your captain when we're ready."

Swarmi staggered away, his face damp under his panama, his shantung suit clinging to his bulk. Coolie work indeed! These awful British memsahibs did not stay at home minding goats and children, but actually gave orders like men. Women at cricket —it was uncivilised!

Shrinivassen was already in trouble over his team selection. Dikshit was mortally offended at being omitted. Moti Lal had brought his brother, 'a bowlster of repute', and Mustapha Khan, the twelfth man, was demanding a place. After all, he had delivered the challenge to the colonel in the first place. "Sickerty-six against Haghai Cannin' Factory!" he screamed. "Yet I am excommunicated from team . . ."

But it was the irrefutable logic of Mookerjee which restored order under the trees. Waving a copy of *The Himalayan Bugle*, he shouted: "We, the therein-named, are the committed ones. The editor's decision is final!"

At a nod from Baker-Stewart, Higginbottom raised his baton and drew from the stony-faced Punjabis the first ragged notes of the overture 'Plymouth Hoe'.

"Damned inappropriate," said Barkside-Twist. "We're not the Navy and we aren't playing bowls."

Reinforced by the stirring music, the Army cricketers chatted to their ladies, noble in their calm before going into action. Colonel Eddgerley-Watkyn-Reed watched the wrangling in the trees with the same worried frown as he had on the Frontier in '34.

"Got the child safe?" he asked Julia hoarsely.

"Of course, Eddgers." Julia had recalled herself from Srinager to be at her husband's side for the match. Phyllisjoy was most happy to let 'mumsie' take Jocelyn with her. Now she could have a few days alone with her husband without being sensitive to rocking the houseboat.

"Terrible match to blood the boy with," said the colonel.

He wandered off in his shaggy purple Crusaders blazer as Jocelyn's pram became surrounded by admirers. Out of the corner of her narrow eyes, Julia saw Major Grahame but she refused either to acknowledge him personally or pass on P.J.'s 'kind regards' to him from Kashmir. Yet she was equally furious that he showed no interest whatsoever in the baby he had delivered, so denying her the chance of a deliberate snub.

The colonel, however, went over to the Australian who was rather sketchily outfitted for the game.

"Who made you our twelfth man?" he demanded.

"The printer, sir."

"Did he? Er, did you make those trousers yerself?"

"They're Mott's battin' trousers, sir. He lent 'em to me . . . rather a tight fit . . ."

"Where is Mott?" demanded the colonel.

"Here, sir." Mott stood to attention in his dove grey Altruists' blazer and knife-edged flannels.

"Ah, thank heavens. I thought you were over in those trees creatin' all that noise among the babus."

"Me, sir? No, sir."

"Transferred your affections to the Americans now, have yer?"

"I have?" Mott blushed in alarm.

"It's all over Tophar . . . that missionary woman gettin' a divorce because of you . . ."

"No, sir, that's not true. You ask Judge Trevelhayes . . . he sort of acted as my legal adviser after the, er, act . . ."

"Do you normally take a lawyer with you when yer go ravishin' . . .?"

"No, sir. But I did offer to make an honest woman of Marion, but she wanted me to live in New York . . . give up cricket . . . I just wouldn't do it, sir."

"You turned her down for cricket?"

"Yes, sir."

The colonel's rheumy eyes were moist as he patted Mott's shoulder.

"I've misjudged you, lad," he said gruffly.

"Got your battin' order yet, Eddgers?" cried Hazel, her green scorebook already damp from moisture under her arm.

"Haven't tossed yet, me dear." The colonel hoped to heaven she wouldn't call him 'Eddgers' in front of the Governor when he arrived. He fingered his lucky silver rupee anxiously and tried a practice spin.

The band had reached the climax of 'Plymouth Hoe', the 'Rule, Britannia' variation, when Shrinivassen appeared diffidently before the British rope and bowed to the colonel. The British watched with anxious eyes. This was the first confrontation.

Shrinivassen put out a tentative hand. The colonel grasped it over the white rope. Julia led the ripple of applause.

"Colonel sahib," said Shrinivassen nervously, "my team is as publicated. I have judiciously kept my eleven to exactly eleven."

"Shabash, atchcha, thikai." The colonel showed complete understanding.

Together the two captains went to inspect the matting, the dignity of the colonel's purple blazer being somewhat emphasised by Shrinivassen's faded black alpaca coat and bicycle clips.

"I hope the blasted British win," screamed a frustrated Mr. Dikshit from the trees.

Having disposed of 'Plymouth Hoe' unapplauded, Higginbottom cursed the band into a *No, No, Nanette* selection. The colonel hummed delightedly.

"Ah," he cried, "Char for doe."

"Two teas?" queried Shrinivassen anxiously.

"It's a tune from a musical tamasha boloed 'Nay, Nay Nanette Miss-sahib'."

Then, flicking his silver rupee high in the air, he commanded: "Tum bolo!"

Caught by surprise, Shrinivassen lapsed disastrously.

" 'Flats'!" he shouted.

The colonel looked astounded.

"I mean 'heads', sahib," gasped Shrinivassen. "In Madras we always tossed with a bat."

"Ah." The colonel parted the grass and stared at the coin. "You're right. Dekko . . . the King-Emperor's head!"

A normally reserved man, the strain of opening the proceedings now told on Shrinivassen. Composure slipped entirely.

"First blood!" he ejaculated. "We have drawn first blood! We shall proceed to bat, colonel sahib. Your king has favoured us . . . if only he would be so kind as to send more rice to starving Bengal . . ."

He rushed back to the trees waving his hands to his delirious team. The colonel ambled to the pavilion shaking his head.

"That fellar's puggled," he sighed. "Talked of drawin' blood already. Right, chaps, we're in the field. Governor here yet?"

"No, sir," said Baker-Stewart, slipping off his Gunners' blazer.

The band were now taking 'I Want To Be Happy' in march tempo. Although unlikely ever to be based on the Charing Cross Road, the Punjab Grenadiers affected the same disdainful look common to orchestral instrumentalists the world over—a sullen determination not to appear to enjoy their job.

A calmer Shrinivassen came to the British rope again, now with the panama-hatted Mookerjee in his trailing white coat.

"Colonel sahib," said the Indian captain apologetically, "this gentleman is Mr. Mookerjee, our umpire of worthiness and impartiality, regardless of caste or creed."

So this was Mookerjee. The Army gathered round the little

man, sizing him up. This fellar had involved the Americans . . .
the colonel took the smirking Mookerjee's outstretched hand as
if it were a live grenade.

"Salaam," he muttered.

"I am delighted to make your old acquaintance, colonel,"
shrilled the umpire. All British heads in the deck chairs turned
abruptly at the jarring voice which also triggered off a few
wrong notes from the band. He now stood between the two
captains, gripping their wrists.

"I want this game played in true spirit o' King Willow," he
cried. "When I say 'out', I expect no quarrelsome behaviour or
fisticuffs. My word is the law of Lord's which booklet o' bye-
laws is in my pocket now reposin' for ready reference in cases
of altercation !"

The British were speechless, the colonel almost apopletic.

Shrinivassen handed a creased list to Hazel.

"Our batting strength and order, memsahib."

She took it between thumb and forefinger, wrinkling her nose
with distaste.

"Where's your scorer ?" she barked.

"In the trees with a book of his own . . ."

"He should be here, beside me."

Mookerjee gleeked round the silent deck chairs.

"Captain Mott ? Is he playin' ?"

"Of course I am," said Mott heatedly.

"Oh, surprised we are," said Mookerjee. "Weltzer memsahib
has left for America without you then ?"

The deck chairs gasped. Muriel Barkside-Twist burst into tears
and buried her face in her father's M.C.C. blazer.

"Yes," snapped Mott, his cheeks flaming, "so she won't be
preaching here to-day, Mookerjee, as you asked her . . ."

"Silence, Mott !" roared the colonel. "We're ready to start."

Shrinivassen had rushed away on Mookerjee's reference to
Mott, 'horrified', as he told Swarmi, 'at such snide bad taste in
the mouth'. But Mookerjee, inwardly seething that Mott knew
about his letter to Mrs. Weltzer, remained apparently oblivious
of the consternation.

"Where is my partner in the justice o' this cricket contest?" he asked blithely.

Courtney limped forward buttoning his white coat.

"I'm ready," he snapped, "but first I've got to stop that ruddy music."

He hoisted himself over to Higginbottom who was now threshing his musicians through 'The Yeomen of England'. The bandmaster brought up his percussion as he inclined his head.

"You 'ave a special request?"

"Yes, I have. Shut up!"

The band, recognising a voice of authority, dropped their instruments abruptly, leaving Higginbottom cleaving silent air.

"Who the 'ell . . .? Ah've instroocions to play at this match . . ."

"I'm a major in this coat, not a ruddy ice-cream wallah. I'm instructin' you, Ramsbottom, to shut up."

The bandmaster reddened.

"The name is Higginbottom . . . sir . . ."

"Does it matter?" said Courtney. "Does it *really* matter what the hell your name is? While there's cricket goin' on out there, you shut up your Band of Hope . . . got it?"

"What about Debussy's 'Children's Suite' . . .?"

"Tell 'em to suck it quietly."

Higginbottom breathed heavily. To be treated like a private in front of his own band . . . *Rams*bottom indeed!

Akkar Singh, on duty dispensing refreshment to his officers, sidled up to the colonel.

"Be kind to the clerks, sahib . . . they are like children . . ."

"Tikai, Akkar Singh . . . don't know what we'd do without yer . . ."

Courtney propelled himself to the wicket beside Mookerjee.

"You have bad leg?"

"No, you blitherin' idiot, I'm a rockin' horse . . ."

Mookerjee frowned. He knew this type, of course, the perpetually angry men of British India with whisky-impregnated livers. He could smell it on the heavy breath now.

"Six balls to an over," he chirped. "Six for lost ball . . ."

"I know the rules," snarled Courtney. "I was at Sandhurst." At the pavilion, the colonel kissed his wife.

"Right, chaps, *now*!" he ordered with a beckoning arm.

To fervent British applause, the Army took the field, the officers pallid with tension—as, defiantly, the band struck up 'The Arcadians'.

Chapter Twenty-three

ACTIVE SERVICE IN THE FIELD

As the Army reached the matting, Nupp-Jevons watched Sergeant Wood roll up his sleeves to reveal the blue dragons and fully-breasted girls his arms had accumulated on His Majesty's Service.

"Gotta beat the buggers to-day, sir," he said cheerfully.

The lieutenant-colonel blinked. He turned to Innes-Whiffen, immaculate in pads, gloves and Crusader cap.

"I've a feelin', Whiffy, this match is a terrible mistake . . . it's a war of nerves."

"It's certainly got on mine. That poster said I was Singapore *Struggler* . . . God knows what the Stragglers will say."

"Think what that printer might have done if you'd played for Bucks . . ."

Behind them, Sinker pulled chewing gum from his mouth in a long strand.

"That's a filthy American habit, corporal," snapped Barkside-Twist.

"Aye, they've got a lot, sir," said Sinker knowingly.

"Especially their missionaries," said Wood.

"Less lip from the pair of you," ordered the major.

They V-signed behind his back.

Mott, still trying to control the stomach butterflies caused by Mookerjee's sneer about Marion, licked a finger, held it up.

"Breeze coming from Tibet," he told Sergeant Harrison, "should swing the ball a bit with the shine on."

"Sod Tibet," said Harrison. "Give me the breeze from Ilford gas-works every time."

Sergeant Frinton looked at the affronted Mott sympathetically. After what had happened to the captain last night, he was powerless to reprimand Harrison. Yet, as Frinton well knew, had not Harrison himself been accused of rape in Rizmak distillery and been forced to marry that Anglo-Indian girl?

McBurn and Baker-Stewart brought up the rear.

"Hear Mott was found abed with that Yank woman," said the Scot rapaciously. "Must be a court-martial of course . . ."

Baker-Stewart shrugged. He could hear Hazel's loud voice from the scorers' table . . . and he was a superstitious man.

"No, Mott's got away with it, Mac. Had the judge take up his case. Eddgers told me Mott wouldn't marry her as she wanted him to give up cricket. That puts him in the clear as regards Crusader membership."

Courtney was already in a fuming temper. He puffed furiously at his Kitchener bowl pipe, giving the general a hot red wig.

"That Mookerjee," he snarled, "doesn't know the rules from my arse . . . !"

"Steady, old man," shouted Barkside-Twist over a sudden burgeoning of Grenadier brass. "We'll have to tell that band to stop . . ."

"I've done that already . . . what's the bloody use . . . ?"

"Sergeant Harrison," commanded the colonel, "bolo the band to taro."

"Thikai, sahib," retorted Harrison mutinously, and the colonel coughed in confusion. He was quite unused to British N.C.O.s.

Harrison resented the order as well as the Urdu. He was the senior among the four N.C.O.s on the field. So he ordered Lance-corporal Sinker to inform Higginbottom to shut his muckin' row. But the bandmaster, flailing away on his rostrum, gave the hesitant corporal one withering look.

"Get some service in afore you speak to me!" he sneered, bringing a fugue-like interpretation of 'I've Gotta Motter' up to fortissimo.

Just as Sinker, having failed ignominiously to carry out his first order as an N.C.O., returned to the wicket to tell the colonel that Higginbottom had 'gone doolally', Hazel took over. With one stentorian, soprano cry of 'Halt, instruments!' the terror of the WACs stopped the band. The music squeaked to silence and the musicians crouched in fear. From the trees came derisive cheers which even the British applause of relief could not drown.

Redder than ever, Higginbottom stamped into the pavilion. He looked at the row of bottles, raised an eyebrow at Akkar Singh who passed him a bottle of Parry's gin. Higginbottom was not supposed to have gin—as Akkar Singh well knew. The Punjab Grenadiers' medical officer had forbidden the bandmaster alcohol ever since he had run amuk in the bandroom emptying his revolver at the tuba. But now he felt justified in taking a small nip.

"For free?" he asked guardedly.

"Bandmaster is temporary V.I.P.," said Akkar Singh gravely.

Higginbottom flipped off the metal cap. Here at least was one wog who recognised his importance. "Bloody women at cricket," he muttered.

Moti Lal and Uttar Bun, opening batsmen for the Indian civilian team, appeared from the trees as if pushed. Both seemed thoroughly impeded by their loosely strapped pads and were arguing fiercely. Neither wanted the honour of taking 'first knock'. On reaching the matting, Uttar Bun lost a toss of 'flats' or 'rounds' and, seeing such reluctance to face him, Baker-Stewart deliberately added five yards to his normal run.

"Stand well back, wicket-keeper," he called in his parade-ground voice. "I shall be bowling 'bumpers' . . ."

"Is 'centre' required, Uttar Bun?" asked Mookerjee over the stumps.

"What . . . whatever you have." Uttar Bun's eyebrows undulated with terror. His cricket boasts in the canteen now seemed the voice of another man as he stood in the middle of Glenbourn facing a British fast bowler. Baker-Stewart, in the distance, was stamping his mark as if killing a scorpion.

"Your bat is all a-wobble," said Mookerjee. "How can I give guard . . .?"

"Guard? What must I guard?" Uttar Bun now resorted to feigned ignorance to delay an inevitable fate.

"You have 'centre'," said Mookerjee. Uttar Bun had not moved his bat, but the umpire felt it prudent to forgo further formality.

From the pavilion end, Baker-Stewart thundered up to the crease. Uttar Bun, blinking in fear, crouched miserably over the limply-held bat. As the stumps clattered back, there was a yell round Glenbourn which the Himalayas fed back in echo.

"Got the bastard!" yelled Harrison.

"Well bowled, Stewy," cried the colonel, "a great break-through . . ."

"Not out!" bawled Mookerjee.

"What's that?" Baker-Stewart's eyes flashed murderously.

"Not out," said Mookerjee, firmly. "I did not call 'play'. The bowler did not give me time. 'Tis rule 18 o' Marybone C.C. London . . . 'play' is to be shouted by official umpire before game is authorised to begin . . ."

"Thikai," said the colonel sadly, silencing the Army protests, "umpire's faisla is final."

Baker-Stewart staggered back to his mark, muttering to himself, and began an even faster run.

"Was that a 'no ball'?" shouted Hazel from the score table, having now indelibly recorded Uttar Bun's dismissal.

Hearing his beloved's voice, Baker-Stewart slowed down.

"Play!" screamed Mookerjee.

"Bowler's name, please," cried Desai with his scorebook in the trees.

"Is plot to put me off!" wailed Uttar Bun, backing to square-leg.

Baker-Stewart, quivering with frustration, stopped at the crease.

"We're starting again, Hazel!" he shouted.

"Why, Stewy?"

"The umpire hadn't shouted 'play' . . ."

"But I just have," said Mookerjee.

"Bowler's name!" came Desai's distant hail.

"Hazel," yelled Baker-Stewart, "for God's sake get the clerks' scorer to sit next to you and tell him who I am."

"He won't sit next to me," shouted Hazel. "He thinks I'm an 'untouchable' or somethin' . . ."

"Not 'er of all people," said Wood to Sinker. "Not old round-'eels 'Azel . . ."

Swarmi dragged the whimpering Desai by his dhoti to the British rope.

"No, no," he was shouting as he was thrust into the chair beside Hazel.

"I am manager," said Swarmi. "This is our scorer, Mr Desai, memsahib, noted for correct notation of balancing sheets . . ."

"He'd better start a fresh page," said Hazel, seeing the betel juice stains on the clerk's scorebook. "Come along, use your loaf, man."

"My loaf?" Desai looked miserably vague.

Swarmi retreated hastily with some confused idea that the British scored by means of bread pellets. Even his envy of Desai, now seated in the British enclosure, was overcome by his desire to escape from the blonde senior-commander.

On the field, Mookerjee wagged a warning finger at the colonel.

"Come, come," he said. "All this procrastinationism is thievin' away time. Play!"

So, for the third time, Baker-Stewart ran up to deliver the first ball of the match. As it reared off the matting, Uttar Bun cried "Aaagh", ducked low and punched the ball with his gloved hand. Innes-Whiffen held the catch and drawled his appeal.

"Out!" said Mookerjee firmly—much to the Army's surprise.

"Out?" screeched Uttar Bun, still kneeling. "How can you say that and be deemed truthful man? My bat was untouched, my stamps still stand erect. My remarkable eyesight enabled me to fend off menacin' missile. Otherwise I would be dead upon this mat."

"Out!" commanded Mookerjee. "By your own admission you tipped the ball to wicket-keeper an' it was a hit, a parallel hit, as Hamlet says in the fillum o' that name. Go, Uttar Bun, your innin's is extinct!"

Narna Bag, who had raced from the trees in great jubilation, pulled Uttar Bun from the crease.

"I am next man in," he cried. "Go 'way an' hatch your duck's egg . . ."

Swarmi and Shrinivassen came and dragged the hysterical Uttar Bun back to the trees. "I will not field," he screamed. "I shall go home."

"This," groaned the colonel, "is an appallin' start."

Baker-Stewart, flushed with this early success, bowled another bouncer. Narna Bag ducked too, but the ball hit the shoulder of his bat to land high in the wicket-keeper's hands. Now the appeal was deafening and the colonel wiped his brow.

"Not out," said Mookerjee promptly. "Narna Bag obstructed my line of vision. Who can say ball did not bounce between batsman an' wicket-keeper?"

"I can," snarled Courtney from square-leg. "Out!"

"The decision is not yours, major," snapped Mookerjee. "I am adjudicator at bowler's end . . ."

"Play on, for Allah's sake," ordered the colonel.

"Yes, play on, Narna Bag," said Mookerjee, "but carefully, please. We are backs to stone walls now . . ."

So Narna Bag hit the next ball high into the pavilion. As the British deck chairs scattered in the stampede for cover, the delighted Indian spectators capered in and out of the trees.

"Six! Oh, my word!" Mookerjee, too, danced a jig, worthy of Ram Ghopal. "Desai! Have you recorded that monumentous hit, man?"

The beaming Narna Bag shook hands with his team-mates who had deserted the sobbing Uttar Bun to hug their hero on the field.

"It'll be lunch before the first over's bowled," said Wood. "Like bloody kids, ain't they?"

At the score table, Desai put down his pencil. His head was swimming. Never before had he been in such close proximity to a white woman. Hazel's perfume was not sandalwood oil to which he was accustomed, that low-cut frock barely contained those melon-sized breasts. His mother had been a purdah woman and Desai had been taught by Jain priests that women were the cause of all sin. Only by reincarnation as men could women ever reach Nirvana. And now fat silken legs beneath the table kept brushing his thin shanks.

"Pardon," he said, standing.

"Granted," she said, staring out at the game.

"I have to absent myself . . ."

"What for?"

"I . . . er . . . toilet." He scurried away, very near tears.

"If this is goin' to happen every time someone hits a six," she muttered, "God knows how I'm goin' to manage . . ."

Baker-Stewart had at last completed the first over, which had taken eleven minutes. He was seething with rage as Narna Bag had edged the last two balls high over slips for boundaries.

"Ten up!" called Hazel briskly.

Young Wahdi, on duty from the Queen's Club, rushed to the board. After a prolonged search among the numbered tins on the grass, the result was '01 − 0 − 1'.

"Telegraph!" shouted Barkside-Twist, whose M.C.C. membership called for exactitude. "Scorer! Your board's wrong!"

With a heavy sigh, Hazel adjusted the figures. Then, seeing Nancy Evans, hand-in-hand with that awful Major Grahame, she called in her voice of authority: "Private Evans, I'm detailin' you for scoreboard duty!"

Nancy, her black brassiere visible through her pink frock, scowled.

"Damn ole cow. She thinks she owns me aftah tickin' me off ovah that newspapah reportah . . ."

"At least," said Grahame, "she didn't make a bigger issue out 'uv it, like my colonel did. Better play ball. I'll help you put the numbers up. But when the Army bat, lovie, I'll be free to tickle yer fancy . . ."

"Devil you are," she giggled. "Don't trifell with me . . ."

"Evans!" shouted Hazel.

"I am off duty, ma'am," said Nancy, swaying to the table.

"I know, me dear," said Hazel with sudden sweetness, "and very pretty you look in yer mufti. But put the numbers up as a personal favour to me. Indians are no good at it. I need an intelligent white girl like you. And, of course, you'll be presented to the Governor when he arrives."

Nancy began sorting the tins feverishly, a seraphic smile on her brown face. As he joined her, Grahame grinned. Senior-Commander Short was, he had to admit, a clever bitch.

Moti Lal was now facing Sergeant Wood, whose one trial for Surrey before the war had resulted in 0-126 on a plumb Guildford wicket. Courtney gave the batsman guard as if sentencing him to be shot from the cannon's mouth. Moti Lal, like Uttar Bun, felt insecure at this bitter moment of truth. Wood knew he had a 'sucker' here . . . he grinned as he delivered a whipping ball from his tattooed arm. Moti Lal was standing in slips when his stumps fell.

"Moti Lal," roared Mookerjee, "that is most disgustin' spectacle of fear . . ."

But the batsman had scurried back, grateful for the obscurity of the trees, where he sank down trembling on a pile of jackets. Shrinivassen, with his considerable technique as a captain, asked : "What is bowler doing, Moti Lal?"

"Is out to kill us," came the tremulous reply.

Blue-turbanned, bearded Jalim Singh strolled elegantly to the crease. No cricketer in the world approaches the wicket with more nobility than a tall, lithe Sikh. Punjab University was a great cricket centre, as Wood now discovered. Two late cuts reached the ropes from mere wrist flicks before third-man Frinton could move.

"By!" said Sinker, as he watched the graven-faced Jalim Singh continue carving himself runs between gully and cover. "He's champion—for a wog."

At 52 for 2, at a despairing signal from his captain, Nupp-Jevons took off his faded Nairobi Nomad sweater. Narna Bag smiled contemptuously as the veteran trundled up and wound his arm over. But, in the anticipation of easy pickings, Narna Bag's bat over-described the arc. The ball sailed up almost vertically . . . there were half a dozen barked suggestions—but the colonel retained his command with a hoarse shout.

"Mine! This pakarna is mine!"

His hands cupped like a vast red tulip, he teetered beneath the falling ball. From his wrists it bounced up to clip his chin smartly . . . he fell back . . . from his knuckles the ball rose again, now going beyond reach . . . but the colonel dived, full length. With a terrible, tortured 'uff', he hit the grass with the ball clenched firmly in his left hand.

"Shabash!" he gasped, his face a dull mauve. "Dekko!"

"Oh, well held, sir!" The Army gathered round their skipper.

"Pity the Governor wasn't here to see that," said Baker-Stewart.

"Three tries the fat one had," grumbled Narna Bag as he retired to the trees for 19, shaking his head in anger.

Sharrabuddin arrived at the wicket as the colonel was being re-stood at mid-off, grateful for Akkar Singh's timely appearance—a peg of whisky was ideal for a pounding heart.

As Mookerjee gave the new batsman guard, he pointed at Nupp-Jevons.

"Beware, Sharrabuddin," he warned, "this ancient bowler is most cunnin' gogglie type. Many a good tune is played by old fiddler . . ."

"Play!" shouted Courtney from square leg.

Sharrabuddin lacked muscular co-ordination. Now hampered with a bat beside his limbs, the decision as to which to move first confused him. As Nupp-Jevons was still burning with fury at Mookerjee's remark, he was off target, and Sharrabuddin remained static watching the ball float by. But finally came a slower—and straight ball. Sharrabuddin moved his right leg back on the stumps.

"How's that?" growled the bowler with satisfaction as the ball tapped the schoolboy pad.

"Not out," said Mookerjee brightly. "Now, now, bowler, there is no need to look daggers drawn at me, as if looks could kill. The batsman was indeed in front o' his wicket for lbw—but the ball was so slow it would not have reached wicket. Not out!"

On the last ball of the over, the thin Sharrabuddin solved his

handicap. He lashed one-handedly at the ball without moving
his feet. The ball flew between slips for four.

"Boundary!" yelled Mookerjee, signalling furiously. "Have
you registered that, Desai?"

"He's not here," shouted Hazel.

"Stop the game," cried Mookerjee dramatically. "Where is
our scorer, our very own scorer, who should be assessing our
runship?"

"He's got trouble with his water works," called Hazel
irritably.

"But Desai is Field Cashier Department," said Mookerjee.
"*I* am Water Catchment Directorate . . ."

Harrison explained in a brief, lurid phrase of his own which
Mookerjee mistakenly attributed to Hazel.

"If I had known she was that sort of outspoken memsahib,"
he cried, outraged, "Dikshit could have played . . ."

Jalim Singh had watched Sharrabuddin's efforts with cynical
disdain. Just another cretin from the maidans, rooted to the
pitch like a banyan tree. The Sikh therefore deliberately and
successfully 'farmed' the strike. Sharrabuddin, after his initial
four, saw no more of the bowling, and the Sikh, with a satanic
gleam in his eye, cracked the ball all round Glenbourn.

A finely-deflected glide off Harrison brought up the Sikh's
fifty. Delirious screams drowned the polite British handclaps and
dozens of dhoti-clad figures rushed on to the field to embrace
the batsman. Only Sharrabuddin did not applaud.

"Jalim Singh is takin' all bowlin' for himself," he complained.
"Is selfish like all Sikhs, as my ancestors have warned me in
mystic dreams. You are umpire, Mookerjee—tell him I wish for
battin' turn."

"Jalim Singh is performing miracles," snapped Mookerjee.
"You are remarkable, Sharrabuddin, only in that you are still
here. Believe me, your wicket is still only very temporary
structure."

On the last ball of Harrison's over, Jalim Singh cantered
down the wicket for the inevitable single from a push to extra-
cover—to find Sharrabuddin standing his ground.

"Return from whence you came, Punjabi," he shouted. "I wish to bat."

Jalim Singh's impeccable poise deserted him.

"Run, mad-crazy one!" he snarled, trying to barge Sharrabuddin from the crease. But he seized Courtney's coat for anchorage.

"Leggo, heathen infidel!" yelled the umpire, struggling.

"I demand a battin' 'go'," shouted Sharrabuddin.

Jalim Singh tried desperately to get back, but Sinker's throw to Innes-Whiffen had been accurate and the bails were off at the deserted end. The Sikh walked erectly back to the trees. He turned but once . . . to shout Sharrabuddin's name and draw his now ungloved hand across his throat.

"The biggest mistake we can make," Courtney told Sharrabuddin, "will be to get *you* out."

As captain of the All-India Civilian XI, Shrinivassen was greeted with sustained applause. On arrival at the wicket he felt duty-bound to shake hands with the colonel again.

"Governor sahib pahaunchna?" enquired the Army captain.

"His Excellency is not yet coming," replied Shrinivassen.

Having captured the strike, Sharrabuddin flashed one-handedly at Baker-Stewart's first ball. The ball took the edge of the bat, flew into slips to crack McBurn on the knee, and drop to the grass.

"Butter fingers!" screamed Mookerjee.

The howl of rage, the agony of the hopping major, brought cheers and mocking laughter from the trees. This was what they had come to watch. Britons in pain were very funny.

Barkside-Twist and Innes-Whiffen held McBurn down, ostensibly to rub his knee, but their grip was firm. The Scot's eyes had misted over, his fingers worked convulsively. At that moment Mookerjee's life was not worth a bawbie.

"Too hot-headed," the colonel told Nupp-Jevons. "This is why old Mac is not on our committee . . ."

"Pity he can't hold his catches like you, Eddgers . . ."

"Ah," the colonel smiled modestly. "Do me best to set an example—'specially with me grandson in the pav."

Nupp-Jevons patted his shoulder, unable to reply.

The batsmen had run three while the Army showed its concern for Major McBurn, and now Shrinivassen steered two fours and a two from his angled bat before over was called.

The colonel looked at his watch in sudden apprehension. One o'clock . . . if the Governor were to arrive during lunch . . . that would be most awkward.

"Eck budgi," he shouted, "tiffin interval."

The Army trooped off gratefully with the clerks 95 for 4, Sharrabuddin not out 7 and Shrinivassen already a bold 10.

"Tell me, Motty," said the colonel, dabbing his glistening brow, "you profess to understand these chaps . . . it can't get any worse, can it . . . ?"

But the Altruist choked—could not speak. Eddgers had called him 'Motty' . . . he was a real Crusader at last!

Chapter Twenty-four

TIFFIN INTERVAL

SEEING the exodus from the field, Higginbottom swayed from the pavilion into the sunlight. Neat gin had heightened his musical appreciation. Focusing his feet, he mounted the rostrum . . . and the 'Ride of the Valkyrie' reverberated into the Himalayas. The Grenadiers were in full cry . . . trombone slides moved in a ruthless flank attack, the drummer clubbed pigskin, clashed cymbals, and the trumpeters' cheeks were extended like taut parchment. Glenbourn trembled with a forte-fortissimo Bayreuth had never known. Aroused birds sailed cawing from the trees, scattering leaves and feathers, while several Muslims bowed towards Mecca. Higginbottom swung himself about wildly on his rostrum, a fanatical light in his eyes . . . this was great music, the real 'stoof' . . .

"It's a bloody German tune," fumed Innes-Whiffen.

"Hope the Governor doesn't hear it," shouted the colonel.

"He's not here yet," mouthed Baker-Stewart, hands over ears.

"But he could hear this din," roared Courtney, "even if he was in China!"

"Eddgers," cried Julia, "the band has made Jocelyn cry."

"That does it! Hazel . . . handcuff that bandmaster!"

The senior-commander pulled Higginbottom's sleeve.

"Too loud and Teutonic," she howled. "Stop!"

Reeling under the insult, Higginbottom dropped his arms. His musicians knew the form now—one yell from the fat memsahib and they ceased playing. So the music cut off abruptly as if Wagner had left the score unfinished . . . and, in the sudden,

225

unanticipated silence, the English continued their bellowed confidences between each other for several more destructive seconds. Mott heard how he had been 'caught in the act', Baker-Stewart gulped at a terse reference to Hazel's husband 'knowing about the Stewy affair', the colonel heard with stupified disbelief the suggestion that he was 'past it now' . . . while Sergeant Wood had to apologise to Nancy for a remark he had made to Sinker about 'layin' the digger doctor's half-chat'.

Hazel, noting the empty gin bottle beside the rostrum, decided the bandmaster was incapable.

"Now, you sepoys," she announced to the band, enunciating slowly and precisely. "You—will—play—quiet—mus-ic . . ."

"They don' unnerstan' English," slurred Higginbottom, struggling to retain command, "but I know their lingo, ma'am, I'll interpret . . ." He swung round on his musicians and roared: "Pianissimo, you black heathens!"

Akkar Singh handed round sherry to the British deck chairs to 'In a Monastery Garden' and the picnic meal of tinned ham and salad, peaches and custard was given a background of 'The Indian Love Lyrics' which Julia sang to Jocelyn in a reedy soprano.

"How's McBurn's knee?" Mott asked Grahame.

"Pretty crook," said the twelfth man. "I suggested I fielded for him after lunch, but he stared at me as if I was tryin' to stop him goin' down with his ship . . ."

"My trousers look as if they've been on the ocean bed already." Mott pointed to Grahame's green-stained knees. "I didn't know you were really a botany boy . . ."

"Ah, it was the heavy dew . . . bin helpin' Nancy with the scoreboard . . . but nature does come into it, Motty. These trousers'll be a lot worse by the time this game's over—I hope . . ."

The Indian team squatted in their trees chewing chaupattis and smoking bidhis. Mookerjee warned them that the road was still long and had no back turnings; Swarmi harangued all the dismissed batsmen save Jalim Singh. Torkham Wazir was daring the Sikh to kill Sharrabuddin who now sat protected within a complete barricade of interlocked bicycles. Desai remained alone by his personal tree, quietly mouthing prayers to himself, his eyes moist and red.

In the pavilion the colonel was very worried.

"If they get 150, it'll be the devil to get . . ."

"Oh, I think we're amongst 'em now, sir," said Mott.

"Amongst 'em?" McBurn hobbled to a chair in fury. "We're reet in the middle o' the whole savage pack . . ."

"Bosh," said Julia. "That Sikh was useful, admittedly, kept bat and pad close together, but the others are rabbits . . . the hutch is wide open. I agree with Mott . . ."

"You do, me dear?" gasped the colonel. "Well, yer never wrong. But we must win. The Viceroy and His Excellency expect it."

Coffee followed the austere meal with port and cigars for the officers. The strains of 'The Princess of Kensington' were punctuated with castanet effects from the hiccupping bandmaster. Beyond the normal Tophar gossip, conversation among the British had one vital theme—conjecture as to the Governor's time of arrival.

The voice of Judy Garland informing Glenbourn that it was 'A Great Day For The Irish' caused the colonel to blink in surprise.

"My daughter," explained Barkside-Twist, "playing her gramophone."

"Shurrup that mechanical moosic," growled Higginbottom, about to order his musicians to attack Offenbach.

"Tiro!" yelled the colonel. "Musicians—ah—at—ease! Down instruments! Bandmaster, give yer men a breather. We wish to relax. Now, Muriel, dear, not an Irish record, please. We may have our Black an' Tan troubles, too, but put on somethin' more appropriate."

"I'll put on the other side," said Muriel, " 'A Pretty Girl Milkin' Her Cow' . . ."

"No, gel," snapped the colonel. "Indians worship cows . . ."

Really, the kids of to-day, their music was impossible. Jocelyn would be brought up on Lehar . . . no, he was probably German

. . . no, on Noel Coward and Ivor Novello . . . now they were really tuneful johnnies if you like.

Vera Lynn began to sing 'Over The Hill' . . .

"Look!" gasped Innes-Whiffen, pointing a wicket-keeper's disjointed forefinger.

All British eyes turned to the trees. A fedora, mushrooming over a belted trench-coat, was slowly approaching the pavilion.

"Dewan Gupta," groaned Mott. "Little Bloody Sir Echo himself. He's all we need . . ."

"Akkar Singh!" commanded the colonel—and the Sikh fell in beside him.

"No, you can't, sir," pleaded Baker-Stewart. "What if the Governor arrived to witness it . . . no more bloodshed . . ."

"Thikai, colonel sahib," said Akkar Singh quietly. "I will not harm a hair of Gupta's head . . . but just let him know I am here . . ."

Gupta's hand-in-pocket meander was a mere bold Alan Ladd front. Within himself he was terrified. His editor, after reviling him for incompetence, had ordered him back to Tophar because the *Himalayan Bugle* had 'scooped' *Clarion India*—Gupta's vitriolic copy from hospital had been too late. The cost of a new camera and note-book had been stopped from Gupta's salary and he had to re-establish himself or be sacked.

He knew he was among mortal enemies . . . on both sides. After his promise to the clerks, not one of their names had appeared in print because he had lost his precious note-book. And Mott, Grahame and the telephone girl were all watching him now. The business of the appropriated HQ pass hung over him like a storm cloud. He had not dared tell his editor that such enterprise had failed. His editor would only have admired him *if* the plan had succeeded. He reached the scoring table, his whole career in the balance.

"May I," he asked Nancy hoarsely, "have the lunch-time score?"

"You've got a damn cheek, man," she flared, "after what you did to me . . ."

"Keep yer voice down, kid," said Grahame, "otherwise

Tophar'll think you were as good to him as you are to me . . ."

"Quiet, you tom-fool man." She pushed him playfully.

"Well, what d'yer want, Gupta?" asked Grahame.

"Merely the state of the match . . ."

"Tell yer newspaper we're both very happy," he said, his arm round Nancy. She closed her eyes . . . he was *impossibell*, this gorgeous man!

Gupta sneered. All this flirtatious dialogue should have come from Alan Ladd, not this damned doctor in whites.

"Look, Gupta," said Grahame, "when I patched you up, you promised not to mention a word about me, her or Mott . . ."

"My editor forced me to reveal the names . . . I was sick in my Delhi bed . . . my job was in jeopardy . . ."

"Ah, he blackmailed you for the truth, eh?"

"Yes, I am biter bit," confessed Gupta abjectly. "Moplah's story in *Himalayan Bugle* was out before mine owing to my injuries. A convoy can only travel as fast as the slowest ship . . ."

Akkar Singh had trodden past the deck chairs in sandalled feet and, balancing a solitary glass of port on a tray, was suddenly beside Gupta.

"With the colonel's compliments," he said quietly.

"For me?" Gupta backed away from the Sikh in terror. "I do not want it . . . I do not drink . . ."

"That's a flamin' lie," said Grahame. "You swigged all Mott's brandy that night . . ."

Gupta's eyes darted from one enemy to another. He was cornered. He had been prepared to meet Grahame and the Evans girl in this desperate mission—but not the Sikh bearer. That port was undoubtedly poisoned.

"You refuse the colonel's drink?" said Akkar Singh.

Gupta nodded wildly.

"If you do not want colonel's port, I do," said Nancy, taking the glass. She tossed it back—and coughed convulsively. For a moment Gupta thought his suspicions correct.

"Who, Gupta, is seeing the horror of his ways now?" quoted Akkar Singh, as he moved back to the pavilion. This unexpected encounter was a good, unplanned sideshow . . . Gupta was still available to play his unwitting part in the scheme to rattle the British cricketers.

"I reckon, Gupta," said Grahame, "that you should go an' find Moplah. He's got in his possession a certain HQ pass . . ."

"Moplah has that?" Gupta swayed, cupped his cheeks in his palms and ran off, distraught, towards the trees.

"I knew that would hit him where it hurts," said Grahame, stroking Nancy's dusky cheek. "Like another port, princess?"

"Just anothah sniftah then, Jack . . . '*punch in the p: sence of the passenjah . . .*'"

She had a husky singing voice which Grahame found sooth-ing. It mattered nothing to him that the deck chairs were whispering and Julia was scowling at him. He was immune from Tophar conventions. As a student, girls had been his main hobby. When he got back to Melbourne out of the Army, well, he'd have to watch his step . . . but now, with this pretty girl rarin' to go, a few ports might help.

Within the trees, Gupta slowed his pace. The trench-coat lining was damp, the fedora dropped beads on his eyebrows. Moplah stood by a bush eating blackberries.

"So you are again trespassing on my preservation, Gupta. You have already had one damn good hiding—do not risk another."

"There is no law against my coming to Tophar. When Gandhi came to Simla last year, every paper in India was represented . . ."

"Simla is not Tophar," said Moplah, adding logically, "nor was Gandhi playing cricket. If you stay here for the story, I shall publish news I have temporarially spiked—a story of an old chowkidar who had his HQ pass wrested from him by a blackguard reporter . . ."

"I did not wrest it . . ."

"Ah!" Moplah was triumphant. "You have given yourself away red-handed by that unwary remark. I did not say it was you. It was trap to catch mackerel . . ."

"It was not. Major Grahame told me you had the pass . . ."

"Oh!" Moplah's face fell. Really, these strange British—how they always ruined all elementals of surprise.

"Look, Moplah," Alan Ladd was willing to climb down prudently, "my editor made me come. And you wrote in your article that the freedom of India's press was at stake when I was attacked . . . you were on my side . . ."

"I am on India's side in the war, but I did not approve of my fellow-countryman Chandra Bose and his pro-Japanese policy. If you want cricket report, you can get it from 'Moplah News Agency', second rights, ten rupees . . . the cricket is my pitch and territory."

"But it is the Army, not Tophar Crusaders, who are playing . . . that makes the match world-wide interest . . . we are brother journalists, we must hang together . . ."

"You hang—I stay alive and kicking." Moplah wagged a warning ink-and-berry stained forefinger under the fedora. "If you pirate this story, I shall publish feature of chowkidar's pass, with copy to Press Council. You will go to gaol, discredited, in chains of your own forging."

"I see it is useless to appeal in professional friendship," said Gupta with a sigh, "but he who never tries cannot win prize . . ."

"A chair unsound soon hits the ground, Gupta."

Clarion India turned, defeated, and slowly trudged up the steep path away from Glenbourn. The new camera by which Gupta had hoped to scoop Moplah with 'action pix' of the match remained in the trench-coat pocket.

Moplah rubbed his hands in a glow of satisfaction and waved joyously to the distant figure of Major Grahame. But his friend was too busy bending over a girl in pink. Obviously she was a patient of his, for he appeared to be rubbing her chest.

Chapter Twenty-five

THE CLERKS ALL OUT

MOOKERJEE approached the pavilion almost treading on the hem of his white coat.

" 'Tis time to recommence, colonel sahib," he piped, doffing his panama. "Our battin' men are refreshed from appetisin' food an' have kep' free from alcoholic beverages."

"Thikai," sighed the colonel, awakening in a deck chair.

"Ah, a little baby," crooned Mookerjee over the pram.

"God, you keep away from him!" boomed the colonel, now bolt upright.

"He is yours?"

"Me grandson."

"He is *white*, too . . . a foreign child!"

Mookerjee knew how to hurt the British. The colonel lay back speechless with rage.

Courtney limped over. Without solids for lunch, he felt much better after the whisky, very much better.

"You consult me before you decide when the game re-starts," he told Mookerjee as he struggled into his coat.

"Allow me to assist in view of your leg . . ."

"I don't put me coat on me leg! Keep away . . . I don't trust yer . . . you'd probably pick me pocket and steal me six stones . . ."

Mookerjee sighed as he watched his fellow umpire light up another pipe, now in the likeness of Gladstone. All that smokin' an' drinkin'—this man would be joinin' his ancestors very soon—which made Mookerjee very sorry for the ancestors.

"And you, Bandmaster Rowbottom," yelled Courtney, "stop that infernal row . . . we're startin' . . ."

Higginbottom cut off 'Tit-Willow' in its prime and staggered blindly into the pavilion. First he'd had to stop his band while the British listened to records of Judy Garland, Bing Crosby dreaming of a white Christmas and Vera Lynn singing 'Yours'. Then, some damned half-chat girl had requested 'Onward Christian Soldiers' so that she could sing about trams . . . now he'd been called 'Rowbottom' and they'd buggered up his *Mikado*. As Akkar Singh passed him a new bottle, the Punjabi bandsmen produced leaf-enfolded food from within the scores of 'West-end Musical Successes' and slid from their chairs to the more natural comfort of the grass.

The crowd had increased round Glenbourn. Word had gone through the bazaar that the bara sahibs were in trouble and, in the trees, was an ever-swelling throng of dark-skinned figures, agog with excitement.

"They're massin'," said McBurn apprehensively, "there's native unrest in yon trees."

The Governor had not made his appearance when the Army took the field again. The officers were heavier of foot than the four N.C.O.s, who, rationed to one bottle of Solan beer each, still retained a spritely light-infantry step. With this situation in mind, the colonel threw the ball to Sinker for the first time.

Sinker had bowled in the East Riding League. Sharrabuddin, he observed, had only one stroke, a one-handed lob. This Sinker immediately exploited and a stomach-high full toss was hit back tamely into his hands, first ball after lunch. Gopi Mukta scratched one run and was then lbw to Sinker, Courtney's finger going up a split second before the appeal.

For one who had wanted to call his side 'The Tigers', Bannerjee's attitude at the wicket was surprisingly mouse-like. Shrinivassen looked pained as he watched his number eight draw away from the first ball from Sinker, head averted, eyes shut, shouting 'ooh!' as it just missed the off stump. He also drew away from the last ball, ending up hiding behind Innes-Whiffen as the wicket-keeper took the ball.

It was, however, after Shrinivassen had scored a single off the fourth ball of Wood's next over, that Bannerjee really complicated the field.

"Oi," said Courtney, ready to give guard. "You were a right-hander down this end. Now you're battin' *left*-handed!"

"I know," said Bannerjee, "but now bowlin' ish from other end . . ."

"This man," said the colonel firmly, "must make up his mind which way round he is goin' to bat . . ."

"He is left-hander," said Mookerjee. "He has his rights as left-hander."

"But when he gets down this end again," said Courtney, "will he change his ruddy mind?"

Bannerjee now looked mutinous.

"I am holdin' bat with both left an' right handsh," he argued. "What more ish it you want?"

"He hasn't a clue," sighed Innes-Whiffen.

"I do have clue," snapped Bannerjee, "an' my clue ish you are all tryin' to confushe me into battin' bewilderment with your Army quick-march, left right, leftsh, double-croshin' me with double-dutsch. I no longer wish to partishipate in such criminal procheedin'sh."

So, in left-handed stance, he backed away to allow Wood's full toss to clip his off stump.

"Am not rishkin' wind an' limb," he shouted as he walked away. "I am for pashive reshistanch. I jusht did not try—sho there!"

An embarrassed Shrinivassen apologised profusely to the colonel.

"We are but a scratched side. Our committee had only un-solicitated testimonials of our players to work upon and we were not able to check, verify and investigate each trumpet-blown claim of cricket skill."

"I malum thoroughly," smiled the colonel. Three wickets down for a mere three runs—a great after-lunch transformation. This would please the Governor . . . when he turned up.

But the arrival at the wicket of Torkham Wazir brought a

sudden atmosphere of evil over Glenbourn. Except for old tennis shoes, his was the costume of his tribe, the long grey flapping shirt, open jurgi waistcoat and gilt basket-style turban wound with lengths of loose white cotton. Without pads on his baggy blue shalvar trousers, he gazed round malevolently from kohl-rimmed eyes.

"Did anyone rub a lamp?" asked Mott.

If Shrinivassen looked uneasy, the colonel was thunderstruck.

"A Pathan!" he breathed. "An' I can't remember a word o' Pushto . . ."

"I see, Torkham Wazir," said Mookerjee, "that you are for ignorin' pads an' gloves. The British bowl fast an' wild, man . . ."

"I, too, am fast and wild," said Torkham Wazir.

Major McBurn repressed a shudder.

"Takes me back," he muttered to Baker-Stewart. "These blighters half-decimated the battalion in '29 . . ."

Mookerjee loathed Torkham Wazir but enjoyed the effect he was having on the British.

"Do you require guard?" he asked.

"I can guard myself."

Torkham Wazir's only sport had been 'bushkrashi' on horseback but he had studied his team batting with the purposeful observation for which his race was famous. Now he crouched correctly as Wood bowled, fast and short, a fraction outside the leg stump. The bat blade flicked like a darting cobra tongue but the ball beat it for pace—and met the Pathan's shin with an ugly, pistol-shot crack.

As one man, all on the field gasped, participating in the excruciating agony. Even Courtney clutched at his own stiff leg before limping impulsively to help the batsman. But the Pathan stood, fierce and indignant.

"Do we not run?" he asked . . . and galloped down the matting.

"Go back, man," moaned Shrinivassen, his eyes watering in telepathic pain. "The ball has mercifully gone for four leg byes. Are you not mortally hurt?"

"Hurt—by the British?" The Pathan bared long pointed teeth. "Never!"

At the sound of the terrifying impact of ball on bone, Baker-Stewart had called, with his famed clarity of diction, "Doctor Grahame! Man hurt!" and a cursing, dishevelled 'twelfth man' had unwound himself from Nancy to dash from behind the pavilion. Grahame possessed no colourful cricket blazer and he despised the British officers' fetish of wearing mufti at every possible off-duty moment. Rather than stain a perfectly good 'civvy' jacket of his own, he preferred to spill beer down the King's uniform—so he appeared on the field in his khaki tunic, belt flapping and brass buttons lustreless. Uncertain of the victim, he turned over the first prone figure he saw.

"Where are you hurt, colonel?"

"I'm not . . . jus' restin' . . . it's that Pathan wallah . . . ball on shin."

Grahame hurried towards Torkham Wazir who eyed the approach of the hated British uniform with smouldering fury.

"Take care, mon," shouted McBurn, "he's a hillman . . ."

"Well, he's certainly not a Morris Cowley," said Mott.

"Remain melancholy, Mott," warned Grahame, "or you may be the next victim . . . kicked in the dingle dongles for bad jokes."

"Stand back, Englisher," said Torkham Wazir menacingly as he dropped his bat.

The Australian obeyed this inappropriate order instantly—for the Pathan was now holding a long thin dagger.

"D'you know," said Innes-Whiffen, tapping his gloves together, "I don't believe I'm really here."

"Hurl the next missile," stormed Torkham Wazir, pointing the blade at Sergeant Wood.

"Put that bloody pig-sticker away first," stuttered the grey-faced bowler.

"Give it to the umpire to hold, old man," said Mott.

"He's not givin' it to me," screeched Courtney. "I'm not bein' paid any danger money to stand in this game. And you can appeal till you're all blue in the face but that fuzzy-wuzzy won't be given out from my end . . ."

Mookerjee, however, stamped over and snatched away the knife.

"Pathan butcher!" he shrilled. "Charity Red-Cross match is not for blood-lettin'. Let Australian doctor see your injury . . ."

But gradually, a strange, surprised look crossed Torkham Wazir's dark face. He put a shaking hand to his brow, heaved convulsively—then slowly keeled over, crumpling to the mat.

"My leg!" he gasped in sudden shock.

Grahame knelt beside him and, taking the knife from Mookerjee, split the ankle band of the shalvar trousers.

"Whew, what a crack! Must get him to hospital for an X-ray . . ."

"No," grunted Torkham Wazir. "I bat on . . ."

"You're crazy, you can't even stand on that . . ."

"I have breath in my body—I fight on . . ."

Gently, Grahame moved the Pathan's knee, testing reaction. "Now," he enquired, "how's that?"

"Out!" cried Mookerjee. "Leg before W! Why did you Army take so long to appeal?"

"Dear Mookerjee," whispered Shrinivassen gratefully, "you are indeed man of tact. This is most astute way of overcoming disaster."

Torkham Wazir slumped again and Grahame laid him flat, folding his own tunic under the lolling head. Having loosened the long white gauze pugree from the Pathan's turban, he began to bind both legs together.

"You are making a mummy of him already?" asked Mookerjee coldly. "While he still breathes . . .?"

"If you had ever been a boy scout, Mookerjee," said Grahame, his long fingers busy, "you'd know I was usin' his one good leg as a splint for the other . . ."

"His leg is broken snapped?" enquired Shrinivassen mournfully.

"Well, I'd say it was certainly fractured . . . anyway, they'll know at the hospital."

"Anything I can do, Jack?" Mott enquired.

"Yes, get some soft material I can bind his legs with. Not rope
. . . but old shirts, say . . ."

"Old shirts?"

"The Crusaders never wear old shirts," said Innes-Whiffen.

"Lend us yer stuffed ones, then," said Grahame impatiently.

Mott trotted off to the pavilion calling, "Any old clothes!"

Barkside-Twist sank on the grass beside his captain.

"Damn nearly a frontier incident, that, Eddgers . . ."

"Who appealed, Twisty? That Pathan was given out . . .
hardly sportin' . . ."

"It was Grahame . . ."

"But he's not even *playin'*! Really, these Australians . . ."

"It's a good job he's here, Eddgers. Best thing to give that
hillman out, knife and all. Otherwise 'retired hurt' on the score-
sheet might make more newspaper trouble for us."

The colonel turned his anguished face to the clear blue sky.

"Not likely to be any rain, either," he sighed.

Mott returned from the pavilion carrying a rather meagre
assortment of bandage material. His request of 'old clothes' had
deeply offended the British deck chairs. Heads had been averted,
so Mott had to improvise with Akkar Singh's glass cloths, a
frayed Altruist tie and a yellowing flannel shirt from the deep
recesses of his own cricket bag, a chiffon scarf which Nancy
pressed on him with strict instructions to tell 'Doctah Jack' she
had sent it—and a pair of silk stockings.

To Mott's amazement, Muriel Barkside-Twist had beckoned
him from behind the pavilion. Putting her hand on his shoulder
for support, she had whispered : "I wouldn't do this for anyone
but you, Basil," and, fumbling feverishly under her skirt, had,
tantalisingly, drawn the stockings down her sturdy legs. "They're
still warm," she said as she draped the stockings over his arm.
Then she kissed him and scampered away, her face a bright pink.

Dazed by her daring, Mott tottered back on to the field with
his miscellaneous collection. "Any rags, bottles or bones!" called
Harrison derisively.

"Call this 'totting'?" replied Mott. "Feel these stockings . . .
they're still warm."

Harrison gaped in amazement. There was jus' no stoppin' this sex-maniac captain.

Mott dumped the assortment on the matting and Grahame immediately reinforced the Pathan's ankles with the Altruist tie. He ripped the shirt up the back and Mott sighed in sadness to see this relic of his English cricket days so ruthlessly dismembered.

"That's Nancy's scarf," he said loyally as Grahame bound Torkham Wazir's knees together.

"Keep his legs straight, Motty . . ." Grahame turned to binding the Pathan's thigh . . . "Whose stockin's are these, for God's sake?"

"Spotty Backside's . . ."

"You took 'em by force, you Weybridge werewolf . . ."

"No, honestly . . . she shed 'em in my presence, quite voluntarily. Frankly, she shook me rigid. I saw right up her suspender belt . . ."

"I know the symptoms. She wants you, Motty. Your American reputation is payin' off . . . get under her mozzy net to-night an' clear up her complexion like a good, randy citizen . . ."

Mott turned away. Grahame was only echoing a thought which had entered his mind behind the pavilion. But fancy bedding down the daughter of an M.C.C. member! Yet, let's face it, she had a good figure . . .

"Eh, Grahame," said the figure of her father suddenly beside them, "don't leave the ground, will you? Colonel's orders. If anything violent happens, we must think of the womenfolk."

"Mott was doin' jus' that," said Grahame. "Right, I'll stay on tap to staunch the blood."

Hazel returned from the green bell-tent marked 'Ladies (British) Only' to see Grahame and the four N.C.O.s carrying Torkham Wazir, stiff and flat, on a bench to the trees.

"What's goin' on, Desai?" she snorted. "Leave you a moment an' somethin' happens."

"Most tragic dismissal of Torkham Wazir." Desai was shaking. "Leg-before-wicket minus pad to Sergeant Wood—for zero runs."

"A duck, eh?" Eagerly she filled in the details.

"There was also four leg byes . . ."

"Dash it, that makes another seven-ball over Mookerjee's given . . . really, as a clerk you'd think he'd be able to count, even if anythin' over ten meant he had to take his boots off."

Desai had only recorded six balls to that over, but said nothing. To draw her attention to it only meant she would lean over again, touching his shoulder with her almost visible breasts as she studied his book.

"Private Evans!" she yelled. "The score is 98-8-nought."

Nancy hung up the plates, her hair sprouting with grass cuttings, a seraphic smile on her face. If Jack hadn't been called away jus' then—oh dearah, he'd been very nearly thereah! That chiffon scarf had been sent out as a reminder not to be long . . .

"Really, Major Grahame does lead her on, so," muttered Hazel, swatting at a persistent wasp with a folded newspaper.

"No, please," said Desai urgently, "never kill God's creatures."

"Rubbish. They sting God's creatures too . . . get *off*!" She smashed again at the wheeling wasp. Desai, who habitually shook his bedding gently every morning to release any inadvertently trapped insect, sighed. No wonder Jain priests averred that women were evil.

The N.C.O.s had returned to the field of play after helping Grahame strap Torkham Wazir into a rickshaw to avoid any body weight on the trussed legs. The Indians were stunned to silence. If the British could do this to their most warlike player, what chance did lesser mortals stand? As Grahame scribbled a note to the hospital, Swarmi approached him quivering with fury.

"You have assaulted and batterised our best player . . . I demand damages . . . I am manager . . ."

"You're jus' the man I want then, Fatso. Go with this Thief o' Baghdad an' give this chitty to the duty doctor at the hospital. An X-ray is wanted—an' there's no bloody phone here at Glenbourn."

"Ah, it is an out-moded place you British choose for your cricket. Why don't you, as doctor, travel with the dying man?"

"Because I'm 'twelfth man' an' the only doctor on the ground.

Anyway, this chap'll live. He shouldn't've batted without pads . . . after all the trouble Captain Mott took to get 'em for you from St. Hayward's School, too. However, treat him gently in that rickshaw. He's in a state o' shock, so give him some hot, sweet tea . . ."

The major left to find Nancy, and Swarmi stared after him shrugging his fleshy shoulders contemptuously.

"Who will volunteer?" he demanded of the team.

"The doctor sahib said you were to go," said Narna Bag, "we shall be bowlin' and fieldin' soon . . ."

"I am manager, cannot leave post," said Swarmi imperiously. "Here you, coolie . . ." He passed Grahame's note to the rickshaw leader. "Hospital jaldi karo. Torkham Wazir zakhum. Duty doctor sahib ko yea khut doo."

"Pundra rupee . . ."

"Fifteen? You thieving badmush!" Swarmi shook his head, gave him the fare, making a note in his managerial notebook of another twenty rupees expenses. The rickshaw jerked away up the incline, Torkham Wazir's head lying inert against the folded hood. The clerks did not watch him go—they preferred to ignore failure.

Back on the field, the Army watched Futti Pant waddle to the wicket. The rotund little man in his Gandhi cap was not wearing the schoolboy pads of his team-mates but a pair designed for a much larger man. The top of the right pad flopped over at the knee, obviously weakened by years of unorthodoxy.

"My verd," he cried as he took guard, "that Pathan von't bat vith no leg-pads no more, I am tellin' you—hey, vat is ideah?"

Barkside-Twist had, with a purposeful thrust, turned back the top of the drooping pad. Marked in red ink was the name 'ffoliot'!

"The wing-commander's pads," cried the major hoarsely. "I knew I recognised them!"

Futti Pant stared down at him indignantly.

"He is my cousin from Ahmednager . . ."

"You are a lying fellow," said Barkside-Twist. "Wing-Commander ffoliot comes from Harrogate."

Shrinivassen hung his head in horror. So much for the fate of the R.A.F. cricket gear when they left Tophar, sold off by their servants instead of being faithfully packed . . .

"Dear old Folly's pads!" stormed the colonel. "Got forty for us once in those . . ."

"Forty-three," amended McBurn precisely, "against the Literary Society. Fancy the wing-commander bein' so lax—do hope he kept the Crusader colours safe . . ."

The colonel's heart missed a beat—the hanging blazer—and the face of this new little Indian batsman was just like a melon.

"I buy these pads in bazaar, secon' han'," said Futti Pant sullenly. "The ving-commandah mus' have pawned them . . ."

"Pawned 'em? Old Folly?" Nupp-Jevons laughed hollowly. "He had private means . . . his old mother owns acres of Norfolk . . ."

"Never mind that now," said Mookerjee, "time is wastin' for no man. Futti Pant is innocent of R.A.F. pad-stealin' treachery. He is honest clerk in *Army* Surplus Department . . ."

"Terrible pads anyvays," said Futti Pant, "von is all broke . . ."

"Play on," said the colonel jadedly. "We'll sort it out later."

The Army's hopes of getting the last two wickets cheaply now received a tantalising set-back. Futti Pant and Shrinivassen edged runs all round the wicket against the fumed heads and leaden feet of the commissioned men, all of whom, save Mott, fielded far too close to the wicket. Futti Pant, realising this, became the artful dodger, much to the hysterical delight of the Indian spectators. Mott's slow spinners gave him particular pleasure. He gambolled down the wicket, swiping and sometimes swatting over-arm, always hitting the ball past the inner ring but never as far as the out-fielders.

Short singles were now more fascination than boundaries. The Indians in the trees chanted, inciting Futti Pant to even greater risks. He waved his bat to them and again war-danced down the mat as Mott came up to bowl. Twice he had stopped in his run and thrown the ball past the advancing Futti Pant, but each time Mookerjee called 'no ball'.

As the four N.C.O.s ranged round the boundary became

incensed by their officers' lethargic display, 'overthrows' became another attraction. The batsmen scampered extra runs from wild throws aided by complete lack of backing-up ability by the officers. Shrinivassen was disquieted. The sahibs were getting rattled. It was, after all, just a friendly game. If only the Governor would come . . . 'God Save The King' always calmed the British . . .

" 'Tis my success in Poonah all ovah again, Shriniwassen!" Futti Pant called between the overs. "I am in vondah form. Have got all soldiah bowlahs at sea, I am tellin' you."

Then the little man hit one from Baker-Stewart, now reduced to a gasping half-pace, straight along the ground to the colonel at mid-off.

"Vun run to the colonel sahib as always," he carolled as he ran.

The outraged colonel had stooped, but anger and inertia retarded him. The ball jogged on between his legs.

"Again, again!" screamed Mookerjee. "The colonel has missed it! Gone through like a croquet hoop, it has . . . run, run!"

"This isn't a cricket match," howled Courtney, "it's a bloody congress meetin'!"

At 138 for 8, the colonel, who had been confident his officers could mop up the tail-enders, was forced much against his will to hand the ball to Sinker again. Such a batsman as Futti Pant would not have lasted five minutes in Yorkshire, and the corporal cunningly gave away two runs, drawing Futti Pant down the wicket with a gentle half-volley. He watched the fat batsman's smile of anticipation—then released the next ball from well behind his shoulders. The oncoming Futti Pant realised too late that it was sailing high over his head. With a cry of alarm, he tried a tremendous over-arm smash with one hand . . . but the ball was already behind his squat figure. He fell on his face as Innes-Whiffen whipped off the bails.

"Fool, Futti Pant!" screamed Mookerjee. "Look where you are, inert on the mattin'. I have no alternative . . . you are out stumped, miles from your unoccupied crease!"

Futti Pant slowly levered himself up, scowling furiously.

" 'Tis svindlin', bowlin' too high," he bleated. "I am but five feet vun in my bare socks. Never had such hoodvinkin' bowlin' like that in Poonah. Not even from vite men . . ."

He could not have offended the Army more deeply.

"How dare he say that," muttered Barkside-Twist. "I remember R. H. Bettington bowling that ball for the M.C.C."

The Indian crowd gave their little bandy hero a thunderous reception for his 31, but shook their fists at the field of play. Their clown was out . . . those bloody British again!

"Ought to report that fellar to the Conference," snorted Nupp-Jevons, whose average had suffered by Futti Pant's tactics.

"Don't know what you're all grousin' about," said Courtney, limping past. "It wasn't out really . . . Whiffey took it in front of the wicket . . . but I'd have given it too, had it been my end . . . me bladder's near burstin'."

"I must pump ship too," said McBurn. "That damned sherry's run straight through me."

Within a minute, only the four N.C.O.s remained on the field.

"We have one player to come," screamed Mookerjee, waving his rule book. "Eleven men to bat . . . that is the law!"

"I made no gesture of declaration—I hope," said a worried Shrinivassen as they hurried to the pavilion together. Higginbottom, in a vague haze, saw the field clearing, and struck up 'In a Persian Market'.

Grahame told Mookerjee where the Army officers were.

"Ah," said the umpire, clicking his tongue in remonstration. "That is what alcohol does for you, doctor. To look on the wine when red is to play jackanapes with the kidneys . . ."

"You have a point there, Chatterjee," said Grahame.

"My name," came the haughty reply, "is Mookerjee."

"It ought to be Chatterjee . . ."

The little umpire was struck dumb with anger.

The colonel apologised to Shrinivassen when he returned with his more comfortable officers. Courtney had snatched another nip, filled a likeness of Lloyd George with tobacco and felt really well again. With a shriek that echoed to the Himalayas, Hazel silenced the band and, as Akkar Singh steered Higginbottom back to his bottle, the Army returned to the attack. The Governor had not yet appeared . . .

Sashi Bokaneer was waiting at the wicket and, around him, the four British N.C.O.s were doubled up with laughter. The batsman had an abdominal protector between his legs, but strapped *outside* his trousers.

" 'E's got 'is bollock box showin' !" howled Sinker, doubled up.

The colonel reeled and held Mott's shoulder for support.

"Tell him, someone, for God's sake . . . there's womenfolk in the pav . . . it's disgustin' . . ."

"What is trouble afoot now?" asked Mookerjee.

"Tell your batsman," barked Baker-Stewart, "to turn his back and put his 'box' on *inside* his trousers . . ."

"But," said Mookerjee, "he is only clerk beside Jalim Singh to possess such a cricket appendage . . . naturally he is proud to reveal it . . ."

"It goes inside," said Innes-Whiffen, tapping his trousers hollowly with his gloves, "as I'm wearin' mine now . . ."

"Steady, Whiffy," said the colonel. "No need to lower the tone . . ."

"The box is not then," said Mookerjee, "worn like a Scottish sporran . . .?"

Mott forced McBurn away.

But Shrinivassen had already taken action. The protesting Bokaneer was turned about to face the Himalayas as the N.C.O.s readjusted his unique acquisition, much to his embarrassment.

"I wonder," said Mott, "if there's an R.A.F. name in that box . . ."

"That we shall not investigate," snapped the colonel.

From the ringside point of view, it would have been better if the British had allowed Bokaneer to keep his box exposed. But now he fidgeted, rubbed his thigh and kept peering down the top of his trousers, grumbling that he was 'bein' rubbed raw like sandpapah !' The British ladies became fascinated as he clutched and fumbled with himself . . . and several deck chairs collapsed through undue restlessness, while Hazel broke two pencils.

But Bokaneer batted better than a number eleven. Though Mookerjee insisted he was primarily "magnificent bowler of collosus stamina", he also possessed a keen eye. The Army reeled again under this unexpected attack as Bokaneer hit at everything. He also shouted as he smote the ball, a deep baying sound caused by the chafing box, and the Army dropped three catches in the echoes. But at last he was caught on the ropes by Harrison for 28, to give Mott his only wicket. The All-India Civilian XI were all out for 179, Shrinivassen being undefeated for 26.

The players trooped off as Higginbottom, now conducting what appeared to him to be double his usual band strength, drew forth 'The Fishermen of England'.

"It's terrible . . . terrible," said the colonel, shaking his head.

"Oh, sir, 180 is gettable," said Baker-Stewart.

"No, not that," rasped the colonel. "Dear old Folly's pads . . . he must miss 'em terribly."

Chapter Twenty-six

THE ARMY BAT

HAZEL checked and re-checked Desai's tragic scorebook. His frequent absences from the table should have caused many blanks but, to her surprise, every available space was filled with cob-web thin handwriting. His lower lip trembled as he saw her scornful scrutiny.

"Has not been easy," he said. "Have you, memsahib, managed to record in narrow space provided : 'Narna Bag Esq., caught Eddgerley-Watkyn-Reed, bowled Nupp-Jevons, 19?' That monumental entry pushed all my other batters down into wrong squares . . ."

"You abbreviate 'em . . . here, see my page . . . 'E-W-Reed'."

"You have foreshortened your own captain?" Desai shook his head. "Memsahib, that is not honourable."

Taken aback, she inked a large '179' over the little man's pencil, initialled it and slid the book back to him.

"At least we're agreed on the total," she said.

The colonel placed his Army batting order on the table, saying, absently, 'Battle order', and Hazel, after studying it, gave a cry of shocked surprise. Desai hoped that a kindly wasp had stung her, but she was reacting to the terrible decision taken by the colonel. In view of the obviously exhausted state of his officers, he was sending two N.C.O.s 'over the top' first.

In the pavilion he prayed that the Governor would arrive soon—the men needed a moral-booster like that. They had, of course, behaved perfectly splendidly, but battle fatigue was showin' through . . . and the officers had, after all, borne the brunt.

"How's Jocelyn?" he asked Julia as he peered in the pram.

"Quietly confident," she replied.

Higginbottom had heralded the Indians on to the field with a *Chu-Chin-Chow* selection as they scampered on to the matting immediately the Army vacated it. They barged and struggled exuberantly for possession of the new ball all through the British-enforced ten-minute interval. Torkham Wazir was hors de combat and Uttar Bun had, as he had threatened, gone home. His efforts to get Moplah to omit his name from the newspaper report had met with a stern rebuke.

"*The Himalayan Bugle* tells truth. You have achieved ignorminious duck, Uttar Bun . . . the world must know."

Twelfth-man Mustapha Khan and Mittra were pressed into service. Futti Pant was delighted at Mittra's inclusion.

"He is my fren' from Poonah," he cried, ready to keep wicket in Folly's pads. "Ve alvays verk as a team, Mittra bein' very out-of-or'nary long-stop . . ."

Mustapha Khan was still angry at his exclusion from the original team and when told that, as a substitute, he could not bowl, he, too, prepared to mount his bicycle. But Mookerjee explained that he would be taking part in an historic victory over the British—and, with this guarantee, he decided to stay.

"I shall catch them all," he said dramatically, "with my eagle eye . . ."

"Save your energies," Mookerjee warned the capering team. "This is vital period wherein we must consolidate strength of our total compiled with such fearful oddities. Now to mow down British wickets . . ."

As he watched them from the pavilion, Baker-Stewart said: "That 180 will take some getting . . . the babus are using a new ball."

"Only fair," said Mott. "We did."

"But that's one hell of a red cherry out there," said Innes-Whiffen. "Looks like a hot coal . . ."

"Probably left over from a fakir's fire-walkin'," said McBurn. " 'Pon ma soul, what a country! Needles in tongues, beds of nails, walkin' through fire barefoot . . . they do daft things in the sight o' their god."

"By playin' this match," growled Courtney, "could we be doin' a dafter thing in the sight of *our* God?"

The vigorous British applause for the opening Army batsmen quickly diminished when it was seen that it was only Sergeant Harrison and Lance-Corporal Sinker. Courtney limped after them, wiping his moustache, lighting W. G. Grace, his cap a holed metal windshield. Well-smoked for many years, the Doctor now looked more at home in Harlem than at Lord's. And four more scotches had made the umpire feel really well again.

Hazel's command stopped the band, snapping off the last of 'The Cobbler's Song'. Higginbottom at once weaved towards the pavilion, but Akkar Singh guided him behind it. Now the officers were batting, it was no place for a mere white-trash non-commissioned bandmaster. Higginbottom was, however, past remonstrating. He took a fresh bottle of gin and, against the slatted wooden back, he sank down in the long grass.

"Gerrof, clumsy bastard," shouted Grahame—and Nancy, beneath him, squeaked in frustration.

"My pardon, major sahib," said Akkar Singh. "Bandmaster is not allowed in the pavilion now it is 'officers' only."

"Stuff him in his big drum, then."

"Would not do, sahib, Governor is coming . . ."

"Bloody women at cricket," mumbled Higginbottom, "no 'preciation o' moosic. To hell with Debussy . . . want Judy Garland, Vera Crosby . . . all my special 'rrangements up t'spout . . ."

"Ah, sloshed, is he?" said Grahame, pulling down Nancy's frock and helping her up. "Come, witch, we mus' find another bower for our nuptuals."

"What about the scorah-board, Jack . . . old Ma Short . . .?"

"One of the N.C.O.s will oblige," said Akkar Singh. "I will tactfully arrange with the colonel . . ."

"Good on yer, Akkar," said Grahame, flipping the Sikh a ten-rupee note. "Now where can I take this lady an' be undisturbed?"

"To the far side of Glenbourn," said the Sikh, pointing. "There are no cricket watchers there, there is moss and rocks . . . you will be unseen, sahib . . ."

"That's me boy," said Grahame. "Come on, sexy . . ."

"Oh, reely, Jack . . ."

Nancy hated the smouldering amusement in the Sikh's eyes. Anglo-Indians had, as far as he was concerned, no status. Back in Amritsar where she had been born, true Indians often spat in her path. But now Jack gave her confidence . . . and he must have lakhs of rupees to spend so freely.

Akkar Singh watched them run off, hand-in-hand, a cold smile on his face. Because he had overheard the colonel say that Grahame was not 'pukka', he regarded the Australian as true ally to the Indian cause, far more valuable than Mott. He was the new British sort, a 'not-give-a-damn' sahib of war-time who never bossed Indians; a revolutionary—yet a doctor qualified with degrees . . . Akkar Singh felt he might well spare Grahame a lingering death when the rebellion came.

On the field of play Bokaneer opened the bowling from Courtney's end. Mookerjee arranged this. Bokaneer, being a 'class' bowler, could look after himself with the foreign umpire. It was the weaker ones who would need Mookerjee's protection.

Gripping the bright new ball, Bokaneer bowled with a skipping action. His first ball, a full toss, was hooked disdainfully by Harrison . . . only for him to scream with pain as his bat shattered into pieces.

"That ball!" he howled, leaping about the matting, his deadened hands under his armpits. "It's bloody made o' concrete!"

"What the hell . . .?" Courtney limped down the wicket to stare at the ball which, even after being hit really hard, was still on the matting only six inches from the batting crease.

"It's a cannon ball, not a cricket bugger," shouted Harrison.

"This must weigh a ton," growled the umpire, balancing the ball on his hand. "It wasn't sewn, it was ruddy smelted . . ."

"The ball smells?" queried Shrinivassen anxiously.

"Too heavy, not regulation . . ."

" 'Each side may demand a new ball', Law 4," quoted Mookerjee from his book. "That one was sold to us in good faith by Lilli White and Son in Butti Bazzar who are sports outfitters an' hardware merchants . . . 'tis now 'dead ball'."

Sinker had returned to the pavilion, explained to the colonel and was now back with a precious new ball belonging to the Tophar Crusaders. Mookerjee studied it under a magnifying glass.

"Yes, this I pass. 'Tis marked 'Wisden' by appointment to the late King George Vth. What is fit for a king to bowl, is fit for us."

"What about my bloody bat?" stormed Harrison. "New in Bombay this year . . ."

So Frinton ran out with his own precious Surridge-Sutcliffe which Harrison took without thanks. Frinton went back to the pavilion with the shattered bat and rejected ball.

"My God," said the colonel as he examined it. "It's a composition ball . . . more suitable for puttin' the shot. What's that, Hazel? Oh, yes, me dear, they're startin' again with a proper ball . . . one of ours, blast it . . ."

Harrison liked the feel of Frinton's bat. He flexed as Bokaneer rushed past Courtney. The lighter ball was square-cut crisply, Narna Bag leaping aside with a strangled cry to allow it free passage to the rope. As Courtney signalled jubilantly with his stick, Bokaneer turned to him.

"You are smokin' pipe, umpirah," he said. " 'Tis not in rules. Smoke got in my eyes as I bowled . . . quite unfairah . . . that four must not count . . ."

"Of all the damned . . . I always smoke me pipe umpirin' . . ."

"Sashi Bokaneer is correct," said Mookerjee, crossing to them.

"You keep outa this, you quislin' . . ."

"You will observe that I do not smoke when umpirin'. In that vice I am guiltless as driven snow. I have no wish to smoke an' get weak chest like your down-trodden Welsh miners . . ."

"I am not Welsh," howled the major, rocking on his stiff leg, "nor have I trodden on miners' chests . . ."

The colonel lumbered on to the field, his blazer flapping.

Although number ten in the Army batting order, the fact that he already wore his pads showed a singular lack of confidence in his team.

"Courtney," he ordered, "put out yer pipe . . . that's an order."

The umpire gulped down the whisky Akkar Singh had made the colonel secrete in the folds of the Crusader colours and mutinously knocked out W. G. Grace on the back of Sinker's bat.

"This is the last time," he said, "I'll see fair play in India."

"Doesn't count then—that first one?" smirked Bokaneer.

"Not in any case," chuckled Mookerjee. "Pipe smoke or not, the major did not call 'play' . . ."

Courtney closed his eyes. He knew that if a wicket had fallen, Mookerjee would not have reminded him of this oversight.

"Oi," called Harrison, "don't I git that four?"

"No," snapped Courtney, "and it's 'oi, *sir*', if you please, sergeant. Right . . . 'play'!"

Harrison gazed at the umpire with practised British Army dumb insolence. Bloody ole bastard—pie-eyed with booze, he was. Harrison allowed his mind to wander . . . officers like Courtney had made him marry Pearl after that Rizmak distillery rape nonsense. It was either that or losing his stripes. And already the union had gone sour on him—what the hell would they say about Pearl in his Ilford home? Bokaneer, sensing the loss of concentration, bowled a slow ball. Harrison, his thoughts still on his dusky bride, took a wild swing . . . but his head was better positioned for aircraft recognition than batting—and his middle stump leaned back.

Wild banshee shouts greeted this All-India success. Dancing began both in the trees and on the field. Harrison returned to the pavilion where his remark that Courtney was 'effin' shikkared' caused him to be put on a charge by Baker-Stewart. But the fielders' jubilation suddenly turned to fierce anger as they pointed to the scoreboard where Frinton had just hung '4-1-4', at Hazel's command.

"Memsahib!" shouted Mookerjee, rushing to the table. "No

four! Obliterate that illegitimate boundary .. you are perjurin' your goodself . . ."

"Have you all gone ravin' mad?" Hazel threw down her pencil in despair and Desai rushed back to his tree again.

"How many times did we start again, Eddgers?" she gasped as the board was altered. "This book's like a ruddy mosaic already . . . and their scorer's done another bunk . . ."

Barkside-Twist, red and yellow M.C.C. cap perched on his greying head, batted now as if he were still at Lord's. Bokaneer's next five balls were met with a disciplined straight bat. But the field-change at the end of the over would have offended Lord's. During the match several close friendships had sprung up between the clerks and now they could not bear to be parted—so the field was, for the most part, patrolled by small discussion groups.

Gopi Mukta bowled the second over and Sinker smote every innocuous long hop for four, scattering the clerks as they hopped away shrieking from his vicious hooks and slashes. When Shrinivassen remonstrated with Moti Lal for deliberately side-stepping a ball hit directly at him, the reply was withering.

"I use typewriter for my meagre wage. No mere lance-corporal is goin' to maim my fingers for life . . ."

Gopi Mukta took his solar topee from the umpire at the end of the over, also in a state of mutiny.

"Am not bowlin' to this low-rank fellow any more, Shrinivassen," he said, hunching his shoulders. "Am takin' myself off—so there!"

Shrinivassen sighed, crossed himself furtively and moved to mid-off. As Barkside-Twist crouched, toe-tapping, to face Bokaneer, he suddenly raised his gloved hand. Bokaneer slithered to a halt and cursed.

"Why stop?" he demanded. " 'Twas to have been my best ball."

"You can't have the sight-screen moved, Twisty," shouted Courtney. "It's the bloody Himalayas . . ."

"There are two Buddhist monks," said Barkside-Twist, "moving about directly behind the bowler's arm."

The field turned. In the distance, at the deserted end of Glenbourn, the white mountains emphasised the saffron robes of two figures edging their way nervously along the boundary rope.

"Move on!" yelled Barkside-Twist, waving his bat. "Jaldi jao! Get right away, please!"

But the monks stood mesmerised.

"Get away from behind the wicket!" roared Courtney, gesticulating with his stick. "You're behind the bowler's arm . . . buzz off and meditate somewhere else . . . we've had enough religion in this game already."

The monks seemed hesitant, undecided, but, with the whole field now screaming at them, they gathered up their robes in a most un-Buddhist style and dashed out of sight behind the rocks.

"Odd, the way they shave their heads," laughed Barkside-Twist as he settled at the crease again. "Wonder they don't catch their deaths . . ."

Within five overs, the fifty was up. Sinker continued his merciless onslaught, both Bokaneer and now Narna Bag being deeply insulted by such savage treatment. Barkside-Twist shook his head sadly at the other end.

"For a Yorkshireman," he said to Courtney, "this N.C.O. has been terribly badly coached—no style at all."

"My God, if ever a batsman was right for this jungly lot, Sinker is," said the Army umpire. "You haven't even scored yet . . ."

"Oompire!" called Sinker. "Some booger's bin an' spat betel juice on t'wicket . . ."

Courtney and Barkside-Twist joined him to stare unbelievingly at a red stain on the matting—exactly on a length.

"More bloody sabotage!" croaked the Army umpire.

"My sorrow," smiled Futti Pant, revealing reddened stumps of teeth. "A stray hiccup as I vas passin' an' voops!—all is ovah the shop . . ."

"A blasted accurate hiccup," snapped Barkside-Twist.

As Courtney stamped in almost uncontrollable rage, Sinker used a grimy khaki handkerchief on the stain while Barkside-Twist rubbed it with grass. The result gave the spot an areola of green which remained as obstinate on the canvas as the impressionist school itself.

"Why worry over betel nut?" asked Mookerjee. " 'Tis good for the digestion an' is, after all, red like your Russian allies . . ."

Courtney was seen to raise his stick and the colonel came hurrying from the pavilion. He viewed the spot thoughtfully.

"That mark's reet in me eyeline," complained Sinker.

"Get yer runs from the other end then," snapped the colonel. "That's an order, corporal. I've got enough worries in the pavilion without traipsin' out here to dekko betel nut."

"Governor arrived then, Eddgers?" asked Barkside-Twist.

"No," muttered the colonel, "but when we unfolded his special coat-of-arms deck chair just now, it had been daubed 'Quit India'!"

"Good God . . .!"

"We can't scrub that out, either. Now I've got to shift every V.I.P. down a chair. That doesn't please the president of the music club . . ."

"Tell Enoch to lump it."

"How can I, Twisty?" sighed the colonel. "He's my bank manager . . ."

Mookerjee shouted 'play' and the game resumed. Shrinivassen put himself on to bowl, determined in all fairness not to exploit the betel juice patch. His highminded action resulted in the ball pitching on to it so accurately as to bowl Sinker with a 'shooter'. The batsman looked at the bowler with the eyes of a mortally-wounded deer.

"Sorry, old fellow," said Shrinivassen dejectedly. "Genuine error of judgement on my part and parcel . . ."

Sinker marched off mutterin' 'cheatin' wog' and received only desultory British applause for his 48. After all, Tophar had come to see the officers bat . . .

Mott walked to the wicket discomfited that Grahame could not be found to return his batting trousers. Pad straps could ruin his best fielding pair. Opera glasses from the deck-chair handbags watched him pulling on gloves and adjusting his Altruist cap. Under the scattered applause was a ravenous buzz of tongues. Muriel Barkside-Twist's nervous fingers inflamed her complexion even more as she prayed for his success. At least that American woman had proved Basil was interested in sex.

Mott dabbed his bat on the crease line and looked at Mookerjee.

"Middle and leg, please."

"Of course." Mookerjee tilted back his panama. "You are, naturally, an authority on legs, Captain Mott . . ."

"You tittle-tattlin' . . ." Courtney brandished his stick again.

"All right, sir," said Mott, as if refusing a blindfold before a firing squad. "Don't lower yourself . . ." He judged his guard for himself on the matting, his face drawn. Mookerjee, he knew, hated him for preventing Marion's oration that day.

"Is ready?" asked Shrinivassen politely. Mott nodded grimly.

His bat glanced the ball crisply off his pads down past two quarrelling fine-legs to the boundary.

"Out!" screamed Mookerjee, thrusting up a quivering finger. "Leg before W he is out! Ho, ho, ho, 'twas writ in the stars . . ."

"It was off his *bat*—not his pad!" howled Courtney. "And, anyway, no one appealed . . ."

"How's that!" screeched Futti Pant.

Glowering, his jaw clamped tight, Mott returned to the pavilion. Only an Altruist could have remained so controlled. Barkside-Twist was holding Courtney by his coat.

"If you fly off the handle like this," he cautioned the berserk umpire, "the C-in-C might have to take action."

"I wish to hell I had me Winchester . . ."

Grahame and Nancy were locked in love behind the rocks. Murmuring and biting each other's neck softly, they writhed contentedly on the moss.

"Such a beautiful time, Jack," she was saying when, beyond his right ear, she saw the two Buddhist monks.

"Oh—er!" she gasped, trying to push down her frock.

Grahame opened his eyes, swung round on his elbow.

"Oh, sod it! I say, brothers, take a powder . . . we're . . . on our honeymoon . . ."

Nancy, despite her fright, was lost in admiration. Such quick thinkin' her Jack had . . . and it meant marriage was in his mind.

The priests looked at each other questioningly.

"Tibet?" ventured the taller one, stepping forward.

"*Where?*" Grahame sat up, managing to make himself respectable under the flaps of his khaki tunic. Mott's flannels were now a deep moss green on the knees.

"Tibet," repeated the curt voice.

"Over there." Grahame pointed vaguely at the Himalayas. "Quite a hike . . . 'bout eighty miles, I'm told . . ."

The priests began whispering together. Nancy, while sharing her Welsh father's fanatical Christianity, also retained much of her half-Indian mother's fear of all holy men. These stern priests were eyeing her with calculating interest . . . they knew she had been sinning . . . 'twas *terribell*!

"Ap kis paltan men naukari kar rahe hain?" asked the taller man.

"What's that?" Grahame stood up, beating leaves and twigs from his tunic.

"He asks what regiment you are servin' in," said Nancy anxiously.

"Tell him to mind his own holy business. Now the war's over all these priests can go back to Burma for all I care . . ."

"Jap var finish?" gasped the tall man.

"A month or so ago, mate. Don't yer high priests tell you anythin'? All is peace agen. No more Japs snipin' in trees, the risin' sun's gone down in honourable surrender, the Yanks've taken over all the geishas . . ."

To the lovers' surprise, the two priests began to laugh and shake hands.

"Major!" The tall man stiffened to attention and saluted. "I am Kapdain von Breck of General-Feldmarshall Rommel's Panzer Army, Africa . . ."

"Ker-riste! Are you off course, sport . . .!"

"Ve vere daken prisoner in Middle-Eas'd. Undil fife veeks ve vere inderned in Dehra Dun Prisoner of Var Kemp. Dis is Oberleutnant Schmidt who escape vid me . . ."

"Escaped P.O.W.s . . . swipe me!"

"Germans!" whispered Nancy, quaking on the ground. "Oh, Jack . . ."

"In fancy dress, too," he laughed. "You chose the wrong time to make a break . . . you're on the run for nuthin'. God bless you, Jerry mental men, let nuthin' you dismay . . ."

"De var is over, you say," said von Breck haughtily. "Ve vish to redurn to Dehra Dun for repadriation to de Farderland."

"If I had me way," said Grahame, "you'd still be escapin' to Tibet. How did you get hold o' those orange nighties?"

"My name is Kapdain von Breck, my number it is . . ."

"A'right, a'right, play it by the rules . . . not allowed to reveal yer sources of information, I s'pose . . ."

"De var is ober, ve are free men . . . de Geneva Conwention . . ."

"Ah, *now* you quote it! Well, never havin' taken any prisoners before, 'specially while on the nest, I'd better hand you over to someone in authority. Quick march, Private Evans—you're the escort. We'll deliver 'em to the colonel. They might be useful to him—Rommel's tactics are about all that can beat these clerks."

"A minute, please. Ve do nod vish to be accompanied by dis woman . . ."

"You don't? Ah, now you've disappointed little Schmidt, captain," said Grahame, watching the younger German keenly assessing Nancy. "But this lady *is* in the Army . . ."

"So?" Von Breck smiled coldly. "She is like Japanese kemp-follower . . .?"

"Oh, no!" Grahame laughed unroariously. "In spite of what you've seen, she's not one o' those."

"Jack, what does he mean . . . camp follower?"

"A sort of Nippon girl-guide, babe, a sort o' Naafi geisha . . ."

"Vhich regimen' does your colonel command?" asked von Breck.

"He's a vet—quite good enough for your purposes. We'll hand you over to the Army cricket team—ever seen cricket before?"

"Ah, so!" Von Breck bowed. "From your vhide drousers ve guess you are snow ski-drooper. Now I see you are pard of de cricked game."

"Oh, don't call it a game," said Grahame, urging them forward. "Like the old League o' Nations, cricket is a symbol o' brotherhood an' trust. You stick yer head in the sand—an' hope they won't bowl at yer arse . . ."

Chapter Twenty-seven

GÖTTERDÄMMERUNG

AFTER Mott's dismissal, Innes-Whiffen had joined Barkside-Twist at the wicket to stop a Shrinivassen hat-trick. This he did by the courtesy of Mustapha Khan who failed to withdraw his hands from his tight pockets in time to catch a tamely-spooned ball. But the same stroke, repeated in Shrinivassen's next over, spiralled the ball gently to mid-on. Narna Bag uttered a shriek of dismay, dropped on his knees, clawed the air—and found the ball in his right hand. After three seconds he realised the glorious truth and rolled, over and over, to the boundary rope where Swarmi revived him with the hot, sweet tea he had denied the now valueless Torkham Wazir.

"Man," panted the catcher, sitting up among his delirious supporters, "that ball was travellin' like lightnin' . . ."

With Nupp-Jevons as partner, Barkside-Twist continued his unproductive duel with Bokaneer's seamers, only to be caught brilliantly by Jalim Singh low down in slips. "The only fellar on the field likely to catch it," sighed Barkside-Twist to his captain in the pavilion.

"Get any runs?" asked the colonel brusquely.

"I amassed six, Eddgers . . ."

"Not good enough," said the colonel. "Three officers out with the score at 56 for 5, which include 2 byes an' 48 by an actin' unpaid lance-corporal. We've gone to seed . . ."

McBurn arrived at the wicket, fiercely exultant.

"Grahame has just brought in two escaped prisoners . . ."

"Japs in Tophar?" said Nupp-Jevons incredulously.

260

"No, Germans . . . fra' Dehru Dun Camp . . . aye, an' dressed as Boodhist monks . . ."

"Heavens, they might have run into those real Buddhists who held old Twisty up when he was battin' . . ."

"That *was* 'em!" McBurn's tone was accusatory. "Auld Twisty was wavin' 'em away . . . helpin' 'em to escape!"

"Stop gloatin' and get on with the game," said Courtney.

McBurn's limited batting skill demanded full concentration at all times but now his mind was overwhelmed by the inefficiency at Dehra Dun. He fluked a desperate two between his legs, groped ineffectively at Shrinivassen's gentle deliveries and, off the last ball of the over, scored another single because Moti Lal and Mustapha Khan both shouted 'yours'.

"Shockin' about those P.O.W.s," McBurn told Courtney as the field made its token change. "Ah mean, one of those Boche actually speaks Urdu . . . aye, learned it at the camp . . . somethin' radically wrong . . ."

"You're battin' like a ruptured duck," said Courtney, pushing him back up the wicket. "To hell with the Huns, keep yer mind on the game . . ."

But the Scot was drugged in his military paradise. He played right back to Bokaneer's first ball and teetered to avoid falling on his stumps as it hit his pad. Even those sitting in the trees appealed. Courtney raised his finger slowly aloft, a look of agony on his face. He felt he would be lynched if he dare refuse this absolutely plumb leg-before-wicket.

" 'Macduff was from his mother's womb, untimely ripped,' " he cried. "You stupid haggis, will yer never forget King's Regs . . . ?"

But McBurn had returned to the pavilion still obsessed with inefficiency at Dehra Dun. The colonel was fretting with anxiety while the two saffron-robed Germans watched him contemptuously.

"Damn Grahame for pickin' 'em up," he growled. "They're Rommel's officers, have to be treated as gentlemen. But impersonatin' Indian priests is hardly cricket . . ."

"The C.O. at Dehra Dun must get a rocket for this," said

McBurn. "Who taught 'em Urdu? Someone's boobed . . . wouldna' like to be in his shoes. What'll yer do wi' 'em, Eddgers? No phone here . . ."

"I've sent Mott for the military police."

"Ah don't think there are any M.P.s in Tophar now . . . aye, if there's not, someone ought to be on the mat for *that*, too . . ."

"Damned inconvenient altogether," said the colonel. "By the way, Mac, what's the bowler doin'?"

"Turnin' a yard, Eddgers . . ."

Higginbottom, having had a full hour's sleep behind the pavilion, now staggered back to his lethargic musicians. He was thirsty again and mounted the pavilion steps. Then paused. Colonel Eddgerley-Watkyn-Reed was raising a glass to two Buddhist monks, saying: "To peace, gentlemen"—and they were replying: "Heil Hitler!"

With a strangled cry, Higginbottom ran back behind the pavilion—the doctor had warned him it could happen again . . .

Joe Frinton, who had come out with the score at 59 for 6, now batted as if he had forgotten the dark faces round him. He was back in time on Fallowfield Green facing old Ted, the postman, and grocer Sam in his braces. With a wide smile he sent the first ball humming towards the Himalayas where it stopped a yard short of the rope. Two runs had been completed while the clerks argued as to who should fetch it. And, when Bannerjee was selected, he merely walked, warning his team that it was the 'lasht' time he'd oblige. Frinton refused Mookerjee's offer to settle for a boundary and ran on, eight being scored from the stroke.

The clerks, other than Jalim Singh, also could not throw far. This Frinton exploited, gathering runs in threes, fives and sevens which could have won the match before tea had not Nupp-Jevons aged with every run. Eventually he collapsed in the middle of the matting, begging the opposition to run him out. This they did and the veteran was assisted to the pavilion for reviving brandy.

With the score at a more hopeful 107 for 7, Baker-Stewart's first action when he reached the pitch was to call Frinton for a mid-wicket conference.

"The colonel's most displeased with you, sergeant . . ."

"What have I done, sir?"

"Making Lieutenant-Colonel Nupp-Jevons run like that . . . he's getting on, you know . . . you ought to have had more sense."

"I was only trying to win the game . . ."

"We don't do it that way, sergeant, not by upsetting experienced officers. However," Baker-Stewart rotated his shoulders, "you now have to face the last over before tea. Know what to do?"

"Yes, sir," said Frinton bewilderedly.

He had 44 to his credit and the first ball from Moti Lal he cut past Jalim Singh. Calling, "Two there, sir," he ran. But Baker-Stewart refused to budge from his crease.

"We never score runs the last over before tea," he snapped.

Frinton, now beside him, gaped in astonishment as Jalim Singh's arm drew back for the throw.

"We always play doggo, last over before any interval," barked Baker-Stewart. "Now, you fool, you've run yourself out . . . where did you learn your cricket, lad?"

"Out, you parrot!" Courtney confirmed Futti Pant's hysterical appeal and, with a sympathetic shrug at the dejected Frinton, took off the bails, announcing: "Bloody tea-time!"

"You prize pillock, Stewy," he said, limping beside the striding Baker-Stewart, "you can't fool me . . . you did that on purpose . . . you never wanted 'other ranks' playin' in the first place . . . an', by God, haven't they shown you up in this game . . . !"

Baker-Stewart coloured and hurried on to the pavilion.

Tea was snatched hastily, the clerks being served with it on the field by their delighted supporters. At 107 for 8, the Army were in a desperate position and the colonel was speaking severely to Baker-Stewart about Frinton's run-out.

"Yes, I know we always sit on the splice the over before tea," he growled, "but this is not exactly a gentlemen's match . . . this is war!"

"Time's up," shouted Courtney, who, after a few reviving

nips, wanted to get on with the game. "Get out there and castrate the sods!"

The looming figure of Colonel Eddgerley-Watkyn-Reed accompanying Baker-Stewart to the wicket in slow-march step brought frenzied applause from the British deck chairs. In the middle of the matting the two batsmen held a brief conference. The crowd chattered excitedly; obviously a major tactical discussion. But all the colonel said was: 'No sign of the Guv'nor yet . . ."

The two Crusaders batted stubbornly, risking nothing save flicks and dabs for the occasional single. Futti Pant, behind the wicket, had long since lost his co-ordination with long-stop Mittra, once apparently so successful in Poona. Now they were at snarling loggerheads, with Mittra, defiant at square-leg, refusing to act as Futti Pant's second line of defence any more. This breach in the enemy lines was noted by the batsmen who conveyed joint appreciation by mere raised eyebrows—and now any ball outside the off or leg stumps was severely left alone. Stationed a few indecisive yards back, Futti Pant, each time he crouched, became semi-trussed in Folly's pads. By the time he could disentangle himself the ball was past him and byes were briskly run.

"Oh, hit it sometimes, colonel sahib," he pleaded. "I am fast tirin' in this heat vave . . ."

Mercilessly, however, the two Veterinary men galloped on. Tension grew in the pavilion. The score passed 150 and the clerks' bowling was becoming wilder and more off-target.

There was one moment of near disaster however. The colonel played a ball down at his feet and stooped, as all Tophar Crusaders did, to throw the ball obligingly back to the bowler without troubling the fielders. Such chivalry towards opponents was approved of by the British . . . but Baker-Stewart yelled in time.

"Don't touch it, sir, don't touch it!"

The colonel looked up in surprise—then saw Mookerjee alert with anticipation.

"Ah, I get it. You'd give me out 'handled the ball' or 'obstruction' eh?"

" 'Tis in laws 29 an' 30," said Mookerjee, smiling.

"Right," said the colonel, stepping back. "Fetch it, wicket-keeper."

"Vhy me alvays?" grumbled the sweating Futti Pant.

By the time he reached it the colonel and Baker-Stewart had crossed for a single. Mookerjee screamed at Futti Pant who kicked the ball away in anger, enabling the batsmen to take another run.

The British, relieved that victory was near, laughed good-humouredly in the pavilion but the frustrated onlookers in the trees now viciously booed and catcalled every snatched run or bye. Swarmi prayed desperately for a Himalayan landslide. The score had reached 175 with the batsmen appearing impregnable and even Mookerjee was looking strained. So Shrinivassen took a bold gamble. He put Jalim Singh on to bowl.

Despite his protests that he was out of practice, the Sikh was an instant success. A swinging full toss rapped Baker-Stewart's rib-cage and he fell back on his stumps with a choking cry.

"Oh, my God," screeched Hazel, rushing on to the field and cradling his head to her breast. "Where have they hit you, Stewy, darlin'?"

"Stewy darlin' is thikai," said the colonel jadedly. "It's only a flesh wound . . . jus' an accident . . ."

"Accident or not," said Mookerjee excitedly, "he is out 'hit-wicket', a mos' careless manner o' dismissal . . ."

"No, no, Courty!" bellowed the colonel. "Put that stick down. Remember we have two German officers present . . . don't want to give 'em the wrong impression."

Mookerjee looked startled.

"You have Germans playing? 'Tis against rules . . . the *British* Army we are supposed to play . . ."

"Mr. Mookerjee," thundered the colonel, "we happened to have apprehended two escaped German officers durin' this match. They are now our guests in the pavilion—so behave yerself!"

Mookerjee was speechless. The British were, without doubt, the most astonishing race in the world. They could capture

Germans in the middle of a cricket match and invite them into
the pavilion—yet they would offer no such hospitality to Indians
who had served in the war on their own side!

"You British," he snarled when he had recovered speech, "are
complete iniggerma variations . . .!"

Hazel assisted the wheezing Baker-Stewart from the wicket
amid sympathetic applause and much nudging between deck
chairs. The score-board now read 175-9-18. The highest score
of the Army innings was Futti Pant's 51 byes. Now Sergeant
Wood left the pavilion jauntily, quite confident of getting the
five runs wanted to win in one mighty blow.

At that moment the Governor arrived.

Chapter Twenty-eight

HIS EXCELLENCY

THE dark-blue double rickshaw used for such semi-state occasions came rocking through the trees, its white hood emblazoning the royal standard. The four red-uniformed sepoys cleared the way with hoarse cries as the British stood up in a flutter of excitement. The colonel came trotting from the pitch, met Sergeant Wood and hissed to him to "About turn an' roll down yer sleeves over that tattoo, man." Barkside-Twist hid the Germans behind a screen in the pavilion while Higginbottom was assisted on to his rostrum by his havildar-major and propped up.

The double rickshaw caused speculation. Had H.E. brought Her Ladyship as well? But, as the shafts were lowered, the Governor's A.D.C., Captain The Honourable Fyffe-MacHouston, stepped down, immaculate in the glengarry, red tunic and kilt of his clan. The colonel greeted him formally with a bow, being unable to salute in cricket apparel, and stood respectfully at his side. The little A.D.C. stared about him as if to command silence—then tapped his silver-knobbed swagger cane on the hood three times. Out stepped His Excellency.

A dapper, smiling man in a light grey linen suit, he waved a matching trilby at the cheering British—then stiffened to attention as the drum rolled for the National Anthem. Higginbottom, his mind now a hot-house of tenuous, trailing thoughts, dragged the tempo so *largissimo* that spectators' efforts to join in tailed off beyond the eighth bar as chord followed chord as if arranged as an exercise for backward children. But Higginbottom was determined to savour every second of this, his big moment of the day.

At which precise bar he fell from the rostrum only the band

267

knew, but there was a sudden cracking, the rail splintered and Higginbottom crumpled at the bare feet of his brass section. Under shouted orders from the havildar-major, the band then galloped the anthem to a finish.

His Excellency smiled again, although apprehensively dabbing his forehead with a lawn handkerchief, and to his A.D.C. he muttered, "Blitz!" The Hon. Fyffe-MacHouston, already engaged to the Governor's daughter, nodded understandingly. If H.E. was enjoying an occasion he would whisper 'Linger' but if he wanted to get away quickly the code word was 'Blitz'. He moved along the line of Army cricketers swiftly, busily levering their hands. Mott was absent, still in search of the military police, but the gap had been filled by Jocelyn in his pram, gurgling under a mauve cover adorned by the St. George Cross of the Tophar Crusaders. Julia bobbed a curtsey and H.E. patted the child.

"Me grandson," panted the colonel in his effort to keep up, "left-arm spinner . . ."

"Not to worry," said H.E., "medical science works wonders these days."

The colonel had forgotten most of his team's names but H.E. covered his confused 'ers' and 'ums' by saying how well he knew everybody, including Sinker who called him 'yer reverence'. But it was only when H.E. reached the last in the line that he paused to actually speak individually to a cricketer. But Major Grahame's stained, green-streaked trousers seemed to fascinate him. "Well fielded, sir," he said. Courtney threw back his shoulders as he shook the great man's hand, emitting a long hiss of pleasure which caused H.E. to back away sharply. "Sorry I missed the lunch party," was all he said.

Hazel, at the end of the line beside Nancy, curtsied so terrifyingly, stretching every seam of her thin frock, that the Governor averted his eyes. Nancy, not realising that such obeisance was expected of her, took fright and ran away. H.E. shrugged and crossed to Desai at the score-table to admire his book. The spectators sighed with admiration . . . H.E. was such an understanding man.

Desai, who had automatically stood on the arrival of the great man, now found himself actually in his presence. In his terror, he clutched the table for support, his limbs almost uncontrollable. He heard the Governor ask his name.

"Desai," he whispered, "scorer for All-India . . ."

"Are you indeed?" came the reply. "We've been looking for you for over a hundred years, Mr. Desai. And is the present score to your liking?"

Desai, dazed, smiled timidly.

"The Army need five to win, sahib," he explained, "and one wicket only is left. The game is in the balance . . ."

"It certainly is. Thank you for scoring, Mr. Desai."

Hazel was blinking, suppressing her rage. H.E. should have asked *her* the state of the game . . .

A wailing siren suddenly shattered the stately calm. Indians came screaming in fear from the trees. A jeep, bulging with steel helmets, rifles and sten guns, ploughed through the undergrowth on to the cricket ground.

"Not on the wicket!" shouted the colonel. "For God's sake keep that motor off the square . . .!"

The jeep screeched to a halt in front of the pavilion. Amid the bristling armament Mott could be seen in his dove-grey Altruist blazer. As the A.D.C., in a swirl of tartan, leaped to his master's side brandishing his swagger stick, the Governor raised his eyebrows. If this was an assassination attempt, they were being rather obvious about it. Then, as the militia jumped clear, he saw the white star on the jeep's side.

"Oh, God," gasped the colonel, "Mott's done it again . . . brought in the Americans . . . to arrest *our* prisoners!"

"You've taken prisoners—at a cricket match?" The Governor sank down, thunderstruck, into a deck chair.

"They're Germans," explained Julia. "They got behind the bowler's arm, yer see . . . don't understand the game, more's the pity . . ."

"Ah, colonel," said Mott, saluting, "there are no British military police in Tophar now, the Indian civil cops have no jurisdiction over P.O.W.s—so I had to get the American Army . . ."

"You damned fool," muttered the colonel, "you're American-mad . . . don't you realise the Governor is here? And you don't salute me in cricket flannels . . ."

"Hullo there, colonel," rasped a cropped-haired, much-ribboned veteran, carrying a steel helmet. "Colonel Berrick Sims, sir, at yer service, Commander, United States Army, Tophar Division . . . you can call me 'Berry' . . .

"Can I?" stuttered the colonel.

"We're the 'get-up-and-go' boys . . ."

"You can pop off now as far as I'm concerned," said the colonel.

"Unnerstand you've found two German escapers in yer ball game . . ."

"Oh, they weren't playin' . . . they don't, d'yer see . . . but they've escaped from Dehra Dun. However, with the war bein' over . . ."

"They're still belligerents, colonel, still god-damned no-good Nazi bastards. We'll take 'em over . . . we can handle 'em . . ."

"They're officers, remember . . ."

"They're krauts, colonel." 'Berry' laughed harshly. "We've got our methods . . . they'll talk, brother, will those punks talk!"

The two Germans came down the pavilion steps, holding their robes high to avoid tripping. They stared hard at the jeep and weapons.

"Ve are unarmed," said Captain von Breck with teutonic calm.

Colonel Sims gaped.

"These de guys . . .?"

"In disguise," agreed the colonel.

"Dressed as monks, eh? How d'yer like that? Gee, don't they look cute sons of bitches! Sergeant . . . frisk 'em . . ."

A chewing sergeant dragged a revolver from a vast holster, covered the Germans and ran his hand up and down the saffron habits.

"They're clean . . ."

"You did not dake our verd," snapped the kaptain. "De Bridish did . . ."

He nudged Oberleutnant Schmidt for support but the younger man's eyes were straying for a last look at Nancy. In all his war he had never seen such a girl . . . so free with her sex favours, she was. And she actually enjoyed it . . . not like those dark Sidi Barani girls . . . they were just sandbags under you . . .

"Climb aboard." The sergeant jostled them with his revolver.

"Vhere are you daking us?" glowered von Breck.

"Headquarters, wiseguy . . . for interrogation. Don't push yer luck . . . git movin' . . ."

The saffron robes took the place of the Altruist blazer in the jeep amid the fawn and glittering steel, caught now by the early evening sun. Soon the first automobile in history to reach Glenbourn began its tearaway journey back up the steep footpath.

"Stop!" yelled McBurn. "Yer haven't signed a receipt for the prisoners . . . damn it, it's a breach of . . ."

"Let 'em go, Mac," ordered the colonel. "Remember the Governor's here."

"God, it was a terrible trip down," said Mott. "It's a wonder we didn't overturn. The driver just braked hard and slithered like a sledge from the Mall to the bottom."

"You, Mott, are a blasted fool," said Barkside-Twist, "involving the Yanks again . . ."

"But there was no one else to call, sir . . ."

"Aye, but they'll take the credit for capturin' our prisoners," growled McBurn.

"They won't," said Grahame cheerfully. "I've just told me old mate, Moplah, editor o' the *Himalayan Trumpet* or whatever it's called, how Private Nancy Evans o' the Women's Army, India, captured 'em with her own single fair hand . . ."

"Oh, jolly good," said Mott, "now Hazel might promote her . . ."

"Mott," said Barkside-Twist, "keep your comments to yourself. You've already turned the Governor's visit into an Al Capone gangster film . . ."

Bewilderedly, His Excellency had watched Rommel's officers escorted away. They seemed to be undergoing very rough justice for merely getting behind the bowler's arm. He was also very tired of Jocelyn so rose from his deck chair and, signalling his equally short-statured A.D.C. (the great man could never appoint an aide taller than himself), he moved among the Army team again.

"Is that Captain Mott?" he asked the colonel.

"Er, yes, sir. Got a blonger, first ball, I'm afraid . . ."

"I'd like to meet him."

"You would? Oh . . . certainly, sir."

Mott bowed over his handclasp with the Governor.

"Sorry about your duck," said the great man.

Mott flushed with pleasure.

"I actually hit it . . ." but, behind H.E., the colonel shook his head violently.

"When I saw you in that jeep," said the Governor, "I thought the Americans had arrested *you*, Captain Mott."

The team laughed merrily. H.E. was a 'card' and no mistake.

"And I wouldn't have been surprised—after what I've heard."

Mott looked at his boots and McBurn quivered in excited anticipation. Mott was right on the carpet now.

"Quite a Robin Hood with the Maid Marion," smiled H.E.

The Army rippled with laughter.

"Or should it be Will Scarlet?"

A great guffaw now and Mott giggled feebly. It beat him how Indians always arrogated that governors were dull-witted throw-outs from Whitehall. This old codger was right on the ball.

"Never mind, Mott," said H.E., "the war's over now and you've learned what a hot-gospeller is." He skilfully sidestepped Jocelyn in Julia's arms. "Must be off, colonel. Good luck for the match. Exciting position, five to win, one wicket to fall. A pity I can't stop to see the finish."

He and his A.D.C. were in the rickshaw and away within seconds of the band striking up 'For He's A Jolly Good Fellow', conducted by Hazel whose idea it was. The red uniforms curled away up the treacherous slope amid strenuous handclapping and ardent cheers until the rickshaw disappeared within the tall trees.

The colonel sighed with deep pleasure. Jocelyn had met the Governor. He picked up his bat again, called Sergeant Wood and together they descended the pavilion steps.

"Five wanted, sergeant . . . we'll get 'em in ones . . ."

Then his eyes bulged. Glenbourn cricket pitch was empty.

"Get that Indian side back on the field!" he roared to Harrison.

"They've packed up, sir . . ."

"Packed up? But they can't. Our last man hasn't been in yet . . ."

But the field remained deserted. Stumps and matting had gone, leaving an oblong yellowed strip in the green. And the sound of shrieking delight from the trees was hair-raising.

"What the blazes . . .?" began Barkside-Twist as he watched the clerks strapping pads on bicycles and tying up the roll of matting while their supporters capered round them deliriously, slapping them on the back.

Mookerjee, now in his black alpaca jacket, approached the pavilion. He did not pause at the rope now—he came between the two posts and strutted up the pavilion steps of the British sector—a man in possession. The colonel stood at the top, his eyes like stones.

"I demand an explanation . . ."

"We have won, colonel," smiled Mookerjee, "by default."

"By *default*?" echoed the colonel faintly.

"Yes, your last man was more than the specified two minutes allowed for the striker to reach the wicket." He waved his rule book folded back at the vital page. "See, 'tis law 45, clause b . . . *'The umpire shall decide whether the delay of the individual amounts to a refusal of the battin' side to play'*. I decided."

"You should've consulted me, you worm," yelled Courtney.

"You were not on field but attached to a bottle here," said Mookerjee sneeringly. "Note the rule says 'umpire' in most singular form. I was only umpire left doin' his duty. The decision was therefore mine—an' the victory is ours!"

"But the Governor . . ." began the colonel.

"There is no cricket law that says capitalistic governor can stop cricket like that. You did not consult us clerks for special case to be made, did you? No! So, by the laws of Lord's, we have won an' beat the British Army. Our Ashes shall be Glenbourn . . ."

Shrinivassen pulled Mookerjee away before he overplayed his victory role and the British murdered him. The Indian captain looked drawn and harassed as he shook the colonel's hand.

"No malice-afterthought, sir," he begged. "I was but a prawn in this game."

"Thikai, thikai," muttered the colonel. "Julia . . . get that child away from here."

Shrinivassen and Mookerjee hurried away, the little umpire turning just once to bow ironically to the limp flag. The Army stood stunned. Hazel was crying noisily and Desai was actually smiling.

"Memsahib is abject in cricket defeat," he said quietly as he closed his scorebook. "Perhaps when your real husband is back, you will once more be happy, normal womans . . ."

She fisted her cheeks in despair and Baker-Stewart, in spite of his throbbing, bruised chest, led her gently away, while Courtney was trying to lever himself up from a crate of empties.

"The swine," he choked, "it was all a bloody plot from start to finish . . ."

He threshed with his stick and tried to hobble after Mookerjee. His brother officers knew the signs . . . they lifted him bodily into a rickshaw and strapped him in. The coolies waited patiently for fifteen rupees which honorary treasurer Nupp-Jevons paid them with great reluctance. Akkar Singh dropped a bottle of whisky on the twitching lap and Courtney was whirled away shouting 'Fascist pigs!'

After the long, arduous climb to the Mall, Courtney was still writhing furiously. And the sight of Gupta in fedora and trench-coat made him strive even more to burst his bonds.

"Will you make a statement," smiled the reporter, "on the British debacle . . .?"

The major obliged but not even *Clarion India* could print it. The half-strangled cries died in the distance and Gupta smiled.

His dismissal from Glenbourn had borne fruit. First he had seen Torkham Wazir taken to hospital terribly mutilated by the British who would not lend him pads. This was a far better story than a mere tame cricket match . . .

But that had not been his biggest 'scoop' of the day. Never before had he covered such a story as was now recorded in his little Japanese camera. Otherwise his editor would never believe that H.E. the Governor and his scotch-skirted A.D.C. had helped to push a stranded American jeep up from Glenbourn because his royal rickshaw could not pass. And included in the photographs had been two Buddhist monks helping the American soldiers, in fact, doing most of the work. The Governor had made one statement, but it was involuntary as a technical sergeant had stepped back on his foot.

And Dewan Gupta himself had lent his herculean Alan Ladd strength to get that jeep back to the Mall. Any further delay might have brought Moplah hurrying to the spot. Yes, Gupta had the real 'scoop'—Moplah could keep his puny cricket story —even if the clerks *had* won.

"We learn even by our failures," Gupta told himself, "a truth ascertained is a life-pension gained . . ."

He hurried away down the Mall to the lower bazaar to hire a car back to Delhi.

Silence reigned in the Glenbourn pavilion. Long since faded were the mountain-echoing cheers as the triumphant All-India Civilian team were mobbed by their fans up the spiralling path.

"Where the hell's that bandmaster?" asked the colonel, looking up from his much-labelled cricket bag.

"Havin' a bo-peep, sir," said Wood. "He's Mozart . . ."

"The *Figaro* wallah?"

"No, sir, Mozart and Liszt . . ."

"I'm not," slurred the bandmaster, saluting as he lurched up the steps. "I deman' me right to mee' t'Goov'nor . . ."

"He's gone," said Mott.

Samuel Higginbottom burst into tears and Frinton laid him to rest behind the pavilion again.

On the veranda the colonel watched his team pack their bags.

Then, when the last strap was pulled, the last buckle holed, he drew himself up to his full height.

"Havildar-major!"

"Sahib!" cried the bandmaster's dignified deputy.

"The King-Emperor!"

Grabbing Higginbottom's sweaty, cork-handled baton from the grass, the bulky, turbanned figure stood tense—then pointed at the drummer.

The roll was soft as distant thunder at first, then swelled resoundingly as the solemn notes once more filled the trees of Glenbourn.

The British stood ram-rod stiff—but silent. The Anthem was now in correct tempo but who could sing 'send him victorious'?

The flag swayed once in a sudden chill breeze—then was still.

The colonel dropped his hand slowly from his statuesque salute of the colours as the bandsmen began to pack their instruments. He was looking perplexed as a startling thought gradually turned his misery to fury.

"Mott!" he shouted. "It's all *your* fault . . . *your* idea . . ."

"What is, sir?"

"Durin' the match," stormed the colonel, "no one went round with the hat for the Red Cross . . . !"

Chapter Twenty-nine

CLOSE OF PLAY

THE celebrations had begun in the bazaar. Amid bells, pipes, sittar plucking, drums and cymbals, Mookerjee's parrot voice could be heard, a thin, vibrant scream of triumph.

The Indian team were as bewildered by their victory as the British were in defeat. The clerks felt their win lacked the real taste of sweet success. The last Army wicket should have fallen and the colonel jeered and jostled to the pavilion. In spite of Mookerjee's assurance that they had won by the rules, the British had not been made to grovel—even though Desai had mentioned that the fat senior-commander memsahib had been reduced to tears. But when he revealed that he had actually talked with the Governor, his fellow clerks immediately sent him to Coventry in disgrace for fraternising with the enemy.

But the clerks had won and Moplah was there to record it in *The Himalayan Bugle*—posterity for all concerned. The editor sought out Mookerjee across the alley where all shops and go-downs were open to the victors.

"I must have statement from you on victory," he said, "for I am foxed on rule by which the clerks annihilated the British Army."

" 'Tis a British rule from Lord's," explained Mookerjee. "If a batter is more than two minutes reachin' the wicket, his stumps is forfeit, he is OUT! The British have been entrapped by their own law. Jus' like the rule that says no Indian can join the Queen's Club, yet they can give drinks to Germans an' send them off in motor jeeps while we have to resort to bikes an' our own shanks' puny."

Moplah copied the rule from Mookerjee's handbook. It would look well in Baskerville italics. And, for the first time in his life, he had two front-page stories. After 'CLERKS PENS PROVE MIGHTIER THAN ARMY SWORDS AT GLENBOURN' he also devised 'INDIAN GIRL CAPTURES ESCAPED NAZIS SINGLE-HANDED — *"Judo most effective,"* says *Private Nancy . . .'*

In the Queen's Club the port mortem had, as Grahame said before he left to meet Nancy, developed into an autopsy. The colonel was no longer interested in the time-limit rule discussion or Mookerjee's chicanery. By his handshake with Shrinivassen he had acknowledged the clerks were the technical winners—he had conceded defeat. What did rile him was, when checking the scorebook for his own 'not out' score, he found that Hazel had credited the clerks with four leg byes from the same ball which had dismissed Torkham Wazir leg before wicket.

"Without that four," shouted Mott, "the match is a tie— we've got 'em . . ."

"You try," snapped McBurn, "you jus' try persuadin' those head-hunters, noo, that the game is a tie. They're whoopin' it up in the bazaar—they'd never listen to ya'. Our disgrace'll be all over Delhi tomorrow. Don't know where to put ma face . . ."

"You ought to have spotted those four leg byes, Hazel," coughed Baker-Stewart, rubbing his aching chest.

"I tell you I was in the 'Ladies'," she shouted furiously. "Desai cheated me. He implied two balls had been bowled to the Pathan . . . oh, go to hell, Stewy . . . I must have an early night . . ."

"I'll see you home," he said, struggling from his chair.

"No, stay here," she commanded. "There was a message for me back at the bungalow. I'm meetin' Gerald in Delhi to-morrow . . ."

She waddled out, moist-eyed and rather drunk. The party was over.

"Now we've lost Britannia for the pageant," said Barkside-Twist. "As a scorer, a very loyal woman. Not her fault she gave 'em four runs too many. Shouldn't have picked on her, Stewy. Now she's gone, hating you . . ."

"I'm in the dog-house with the mem too," sighed the colonel. "She says I should have stayed at the wicket an' made the winnin' hit while *she* welcomed H.E. But, much as I admire the mem, it would not have been correct protocol . . ."

He tried to sound casual but he could not reveal to his brother Crusaders the true depth of his mortification. His personal disgrace at losing to the clerks was nothing to Julia's terrible, vicious reaction. He never imagined his mem knew such a shockin' phrase, let alone fling it in *his* face—Julia had called him a 'blue-arsed fly'. . .

"And then, Mott," he went on, still assessing his own particular miseries, "you forget to make a collection for the Red Cross . . . we'll have to make a donation if we're to keep faith . . . mustn't be less than a hundred rupees . . . then you call in those outer-space Americans . . ."

"I had no option, sir. There *was* only the Americans . . ."

"I think," said the colonel heavily, "you've done an' said enough, Mott. Where is all that gear belongin' to St. Hayward's School . . .?"

"Oh, Christ!"

"Exactly. Down in the bazaar with poor dear Folly's pads." The colonel passed a tremulous hand over his brow. "We shall have to make good that gear personally. Can't expect the Tophar Crusaders' account to pay. Not their fixture, after all . . ."

"Hear, hear!" Slightly mollified, the Crusaders put their cheque books on the table.

"My God," sighed Innes-Whiffen, "this hurts."

"I think it was seein' Folly's pads that hurt me most," said the colonel. "That Indian clerk wearin' 'em was an omen, yer know. I don't think we shall ever play at Glenbourn agen . . ."

Akkar Singh approached, clutching a handful of bills.

"Colonel, sahib . . .?"

"Ah, loyal Akkar Singh!" The colonel pressed the bearer's gnarled brown knuckles. "You stuck by us like a brother. Credit to India, you are, my good chap."

"Hear, hear!" Glasses met and rang. Akkar Singh bowed gravely.

"While you are writing cheques, my sahibs," he said, "I have here some bills for lunches and drinks I supplied. There are, too, some rickshaw costs. One, Swarmi, now downstairs, manager for the clerks' team, wishes me to present this account for expenses he has incurred." He looked disdainfully at the creased bill. "For Gullivers Hotel, rickshaw to hospital, entertaining the press, food for the manager himself, some bicycle repairs . . ."

"I have some accounts too," grunted Nupp-Jevons. "Sergeant Harrison's broken bat, new ball supplied to the clerks, drinks for German officers, Courty's rickshaw . . . as treasurer of the Tophar Crusaders I do not feel we can honestly meet these from club funds . . ."

"No, quite right, Nuppy," said the colonel emphatically. "The Crusaders must not be involved. The clerks only beat a scratch Army side—the Crusaders' record at Glenbourn still remains intact!"

"Hear, hear, sir!"

Despite the cost, some honour had been preserved.

"You are wanted on telephone, sahib."

Little Wahdi stood staring at Colonel Eddgerley-Watkyn-Reed. He had never dared address him before—but now times had suddenly changed and, as Mookerjee later said, the dog-boy was having his day. With a distracted 'thikai', the colonel pushed past him to the phone on the bar.

He gave his name—and listened. Faintly the Crusaders could hear a terse, authoritative voice and they watched the colonel's amazing changes of reaction. Earnest at first, he became anxious, then downright apprehensive. The Crusaders saw their captain shrinking before their eyes, his hands trembling as he gripped the phone. Quickly, Mott swung a chair under his quivering bulk. He sank down with a low groan, obviously receiving some terrible judgement.

"Yes, sir . . . of course, sir . . . if that's the C-in-C's order . . . to-morrow, sir . . . well, it *is* short notice, of course . . . I see . . . an' you couldn't get a reply all day? Wasn't there a duty

officer at our HQ today? . . . oh dear . . . most reprehensible
. . . there should be one, of course, sir . . . not my pigeon,
naturally, but . . . no, sir, 'Duty Roster Section', actually . . . but
we had this important cricket match . . . the A.G. made us play
actually . . . we were against it but it was an order . . . no, sir,
we lost on a technicality . . . yes, sir, I'm afraid we *did* lose . . .
yes, I will implement the C-in-C's order, eck dum . . . yes, an'
me own personal arrangements . . . 'bye."

Akkar Singh took the phone from the shaking hand and the
colonel remained crouched in the chair.

"That was the Military Secretary," he gasped, "been tryin'
to get us all day apparently. Could get no reply from HQ . . .
him of all people to ring! Who was supposed to be duty
officer?"

Baker-Stewart turned brick red.

"I was, sir," he mumbled, "but we've never needed one
before. I mean, we always shut up shop on Sundays, right
through the war . . ."

"It doesn't matter now," cried the colonel, "the C-in-C is
closin' Tophar Headquarters down—not jus' for the winter as
in the old days—but *for ever!*"

There were gasps of amazement.

"I bet Mountbatten's behind this," fumed Nupp-Jevons.

"We start packin' to-morrow," sighed the colonel, "an' must
be ready to open up all departments in New Delhi by the end
of the week . . . so, down the hill go the British, families an'
all . . ."

"All of us," croaked Mott, "to Delhi?"

"All of *you*," said the colonel broken, "except me. They're
sendin' *me* home . . . on pension . . . under a Labour Government, too . . ."

"*Punch in the presence of the passenjare*," chirped Wahdi.

"Hi, you cheeky monkey," shouted Mott, "where did you
learn that . . . ?"

" 'Tis our battle music," said Wahdi, grinning. "We have
punched the presence . . . at Glembourm . . ."

"Forgive the youth," rumbled Akkar Singh, patting Wahdi's

matted head rather heavily. "He is carried away by clerks' victory . . ."

Wahdi gazed up at the Sikh with awe and admiration—Puck acknowledging Oberon that the 'Dream' had come true. Then Wahdi dashed off to girdle the bazaar with the stupendous news that the British were leaving Tophar for ever!

"He was singing Grahame's tram conductor song," said Mott, puzzled.

"I thought he was a doctor," said Nupp-Jevons.

"That boy said 'Glembourm'," said the Colonel slowly. "An' was also quotin' Grahame's tom-fool song . . . yer know, it all began with Grahame . . ."

"I will," said Akkar Singh, suddenly businesslike and brisk, "immediately write out your bar bills to close all accounts."

"All these expenses," quavered the colonel. "An' me now on pension . . . had no time to consolidate . . . wanted to go to Kenya . . ."

"Never mind, sir," said Mott, "at least you'll be seeing England again soon."

Colonel Eddgerley-Watkyn-Reed sat with bowed head.

"England again?" he muttered. He looked round slowly at each of his loyal Crusaders in turn while seeming to fight a rising tide of emotion within himself. "Julia . . . the mem . . . she's been home a few times with P.J. for her schoolin' . . . but yer might as well know the truth . . . I've been east all me life . . . commissioned here durin' the Kaiser's war . . . I've never been to England. What's it like, Mott? I mean . . . will a fellar like me fit in . . . now?"

WITHIN ten minutes all Tophar bazaar knew the British were leaving . . . were retreating in disgrace, were routed or had even surrendered on the Mall with a white flag pleading for mercy. The local Indians did not accept the validity of an Army Order nor its stated 'commonsense policy of strategic economy' of now placing a peace-reduced General Headquarters all under the one Lutyens roof in New Delhi. As for the recent installation of

air-conditioning to facilitate HQ workers there in all tem-
peratures—that reasoning was also ignored. No, Tophar, with
a logic which would have made a stage Irishman proud, took
the full credit. They had themselves run out the Raj from the
town 'most single-handed'—and so created their own legend as
the first free men of India.

In the darkness they descended again to Glenbourn to re-
name it "Mookerjee's Field'. A Victory bonfire was needed, so
they fired the cricket pavilion. As it blazed they chanted 'Jai
Hind' and 'Punch the Passenjare' . . . throwing the Union Jack
which the British had forgotten to lower, pole and all, into the
flames. Branches ripped from nearby trees, British deck chairs
and the bandmaster's rostrum were all heaved on the fire amid
a shower of sparks and ecstatic cheering.

The British themselves, now opening old, creaking cabin-
trunks, saw the flames from their bungalow windows—the
funeral pyre of Glenbourn. Sighing, they sat down and wrote
out hopeful new labels to guide their possessions to Kenya and
Rhodesia . . .

Only Mr. Shrinivassen was not among the winning team
being feted by the idolising crowd down at Glenbourn. He stood
on the Mall above, gazing over the fence. From below, through
the smoke haze, there drifted up the soft scent of burning pine.
His nostrils twitched appreciatively. Like incense it was—offered
up to the Gods of Liberty. How would they treat all-India now?

Above him, in the trees, two monkeys snarled as they
wrenched for possession of a cricket cap bearing the badge of
St. George.